"Where's your daug
Beck asked.

His tone alone would have alarmed her, but there was more than a sense of urgency in his expression.

"Aubrey's with her nanny. Why?"

"Because I was just trying to put myself in the killer's place. If he came here to scare you off and it didn't work, then what will he do next?"

His stare was a warning.

Faith's heart dropped to her knees.

Beck took a step toward her. "He might try to use your daughter to get to you."

"Oh, God." Faith grabbed her phone and prayed that it wasn't too late to keep her baby safe.

Dear Reader,

We hope you enjoy the Western stories *Branded by the Sheriff* and *Expecting Trouble*, written by *USA TODAY* bestselling Harlequin Intrigue author Delores Fossen.

Harlequin Intrigue books deal in serious romantic suspense, keeping you on the edge of your seat as resourceful, true-to-life women and strong, fearless men fight for survival.

And don't miss an excerpt of *Most Eligible Spy* by Harlequin Intrigue author Dana Marton at the back of this volume. Look for *Most Eligible Spy*, available September 2013.

Happy reading,

The Harlequin Intrigue Editors

BRANDED BY THE SHERIFF
&
EXPECTING TROUBLE

DELORES FOSSEN

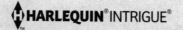

ISBN-13: 978-0-373-68919-4

BRANDED BY THE SHERIFF
& EXPECTING TROUBLE

Copyright © 2013 by Harlequin Books S.A.

The publisher acknowledges the copyright holder of the individual works as follows:

BRANDED BY THE SHERIFF
Copyright © 2009 by Delores Fossen

EXPECTING TROUBLE
Copyright © 2009 by Delores Fossen

Recycling programs for this product may not exist in your area.

Printed in U.S.A.

www.Harlequin.com

CONTENTS

ABOUT THE AUTHOR

Imagine a family tree that includes Texas cowboys, Choctaw and Cherokee Indians, a Louisiana pirate and a Scottish rebel who battled side by side with William Wallace. With ancestors like that, it's easy to understand why *USA TODAY* bestselling author and former air force captain Delores Fossen feels as if she were genetically predisposed to writing romances. Along the way to fulfilling her DNA destiny, Delores married an air force top gun who just happens to be of Viking descent. With all those romantic bases covered, she doesn't have to look too far for inspiration.

BRANDED BY THE SHERIFF

To Debbie Gafford,
thanks for always being there for me.

Chapter One

LaMesa Springs, Texas

A killer was in the house.

Sheriff Beck Tanner drew his weapon and eased out of his SUV. He hadn't planned on a showdown tonight, but he was ready for it.

Beck stopped at the edge of the yard that was more dirt than grass. He listened for a moment.

The light in the back of the small Craftsman-style house indicated someone was there, but he didn't want that someone sneaking out and ambushing him. After all, Darin Matthews had already claimed two victims, his own mother and sister. Since this was Darin's family home, Beck figured sooner or later the man would come back.

Apparently he had.

Around him, the January wind whipped through the bare tree branches. That was the only sound Beck could hear. The house was at the end of the sparsely populated County Line Road, barely in the city limits and a full half mile away from any neighboring house.

There was a hint of smoke in the air, and thanks to a hunter's moon, Beck spotted the source: the rough stone chimney anchored against the left side of the house. Wispy gray coils of smoke rose into the air, the wind scattering them almost as quickly as they appeared.

He inched closer to the house and kept his gun ready.

His boots crunched on the icy gravel of the driveway. No garage. No car. Just a light stabbing through the darkness. Since the place was supposed to be vacant, he'd noticed the light during a routine patrol of the neighborhood. Beck had also glanced inside the filmy bedroom window and spotted discarded clothes on the bed.

The bedroom wasn't the source of the light though. It was coming from the adjacent bathroom and gave him just enough illumination to see.

Staying in the shadows, Beck hurried through the yard and went to the back of the house. He tried to keep his footsteps light on the wooden porch, but each rickety board creaked under his weight. He knew the knob would open because the lock was broken. He'd discovered that two months earlier when he checked out the place after the murder of the home's owner.

Beck eased open the door just a fraction and heard the water running in the bathroom. "A killer in the shower," he said to himself. All in all, not a bad place for an arrest.

He made his way through the kitchen and into the living room. All the furniture was draped in white sheets, giving the place an eerie feel.

Beck had that same eerie feeling in the pit of his stomach.

He'd been sheriff of LaMesa Springs for eight years, since he'd turned twenty-four, and he'd been the deputy for the two years before that. But because his town wasn't a hotbed for serious crime, this would be the first time he'd have to take down a killer.

The thought had no sooner formed in his head when the water in the bathroom stopped. He had to make his move now.

Beck gripped his pistol, keeping it aimed.

He nudged the ajar bathroom door with the toe of his boot, and sticky, warm steam and dull, milky light spilled over him.

Since the bathroom was small, he could take in the room in one glance. Outdated avocado tile—some cracked and chipped. A claw-footed tub encased by an opaque shower curtain. There was one frosted glass window to his right that was too small to use to escape.

Beck latched on to the curtain and gave it a hard jerk to the left. The metal hooks rattled, and the sheet of yellowed vinyl slithered around the circular bar that supported it.

"Sheriff Beck Tanner," he identified himself.

But his name died on his lips when he saw the person standing in the tub. It certainly wasn't Darin Matthews.

It was a wet, naked woman.

A scream bubbled up from her throat. Beck cursed. He didn't know which one of them was more surprised.

Well, she wasn't armed. That was the first thing he noticed after the "naked" part. There wasn't a gun anywhere in sight. Just her.

Suddenly, that seemed more than enough.

Water slid off her face, her entire body, and her midnight-black hair clung to her neck and shoulders. Because he considered himself a gentleman, Beck tried not to notice her small, firm breasts and the triangular patch of hair at the juncture of her thighs.

But because he was a man, and because she was there right in front of him, he noticed despite his efforts to stop himself.

"Beckett Tanner," she spat out like profanity. She swept her left hand over various parts to cover herself while she groped for the white towel dangling over the nearby sink. "What the devil are you doing here?"

Did he know her? Because she obviously knew him.

Beck examined her face and picked through all that wet hair and water to see her features.

Oh, hell.

She was obviously older than the last time he'd seen her, which was...when? Just a little more than ten years ago when she was eighteen. Since then, her body and face had filled out, but those copper brown eyes were the same.

The last time he'd seen those eyes, she'd been silently hurtling insults at him. She was still doing that now.

"Faith Matthews," Beck grumbled. "What the devil are *you* doing here?"

She draped the towel in front of her and stepped from the tub. "I own the place."

Yeah. She did. Thanks to her mother's and sister's murders. Since her mother had legally disowned Faith's brother, the house had passed to Faith by default.

"The D.A. said you wanted to keep moving back quiet," Beck commented. "But he also said you wouldn't arrive in town until early next month."

Beck figured he'd need every minute of that month, too, so he could prepare his family for Faith's return.

It was going to hit his sister-in-law particularly hard. That, in turn, meant it'd hit him hard.

What someone did to his family, they did to him.

And Faith Matthews had done a real number on the Tanners.

"I obviously came early." As if in a fierce battle with the terry cloth, she wound the towel around her.

"I didn't see your car," he pointed out.

She huffed. "Because I took a taxi from the Austin airport, all right? My car arrives tomorrow. Now that I've explained why I'm in my own home and how I got here, please tell me why you're trespassing."

She sounded like a lawyer. And was. Or rather a lawyer who was about to become the county's new assistant district attorney.

Beck had tried to convince the D.A. to turn down her job application, but the D.A. said she was the best qualified applicant and had hired her. That was the reason she was moving back. She wasn't moving back alone, either. She had a kid. A toddler named Aubrey, he'd heard. Not that motherhood would change his opinion of her. That opinion would always be low. And because LaMesa Springs was the county seat, that meant Faith would be living right under his nose, again. Worse, he'd have to work with her to get cases prosecuted.

Yeah, he needed that month to come to terms with that.

"I'm *trespassing* because I thought your brother was here," he explained. "The clerk at the convenience store on Sadler Street said he saw someone matching Darin's description night before last. The Rangers are still analyzing the surveillance video, and when they're done, I figure it'll be a match. So I came here because I wanted to arrest a killer."

"An *alleged* killer," she corrected. "Darin is innocent." The towel slipped, and he caught a glimpse of her right breast again. Her rose-colored nipple, too. She quickly righted the towel and mumbled something under her breath. "Before I got in the shower, I checked the doors and windows and made sure they were all locked. How'd you get in?"

"The back lock's broken. I noticed it when I came out here with the Texas Rangers. They assisted me with the investigation after your mother was killed."

Her intense stare conveyed her displeasure with his presence. "And you just happened to be in the neighborhood again tonight?"

Beck made sure his scowl conveyed some displeasure, too. "As I already said, I want to arrest a killer. I figure Darin will eventually come here. You did. So I've been driving by each night on my way home from work to see if he'll turn up."

She huffed and walked past him. Not a good idea. The doorway was small, and they brushed against each other, her butt against his thigh.

He ignored the pull he felt deep within his belly.

Yes, Faith was attractive, always had been, but she'd come within a hair of destroying his family. No amount of attraction would override that.

Besides, Faith had been his brother's one-night stand. She'd slept with a married man, and that encounter had nearly ruined his brother's marriage.

That alone made her his enemy.

Faith snatched up her clothes from the bed. "Well,

now that you know Darin's not here, you can leave the same way you came in."

"I will. First though, I need to ask some questions." In the back of his mind, he wondered if that was a good idea. She was only a few feet away…and naked under the towel. But Beck decided it was best to put his discomfort aside and worry less about her body and more about getting a killer off the streets.

"When's the last time you saw your brother?" he asked, without waiting to see if she'd agree to the impromptu interrogation.

With a death grip on the towel, she stared at him. Frowned. The frown deepened with each passing second. "Go stand over there," she said, pointing to the pair of front windows that were divided by a bare scarred oak dresser. "And turn your back. I want to get dressed, and I'd rather not do that with you gawking at me."

It was true. He had indeed gawked, and he wasn't proud of it. But then he wasn't proud of the way she'd stirred him up.

"Strange, I hadn't figured you for being modest," he mumbled, strolling toward the windows. He could see his SUV parked out front. It was something to keep his focus on, especially since he didn't want to angle his eyes in any direction in case he caught a glimpse of her naked reflection in the glass.

"Strange?" she repeated as if this insult had actually gotten to her. "I'd say it's equally *strange* that Beckett Tanner would still be making assumptions."

"What does that mean?" he fired back.

Her response was a figure-it-out-yourself grunt. "To answer your original question, I haven't seen Darin in nearly a year." Her words were clipped and angry. "That's in the statement I gave the Texas Rangers two months ago. I'm sure you read it."

Heck, he'd memorized it.

The part about her brother. Her sister's ex. Her estranged relationship with all members of her family. When the Rangers had asked her if Aubrey's father, Faith's own ex, could have some part in this, she'd adamantly denied it, claiming the man had never even seen Aubrey.

All of that had been in her statement, but over the years he'd learned that a written response wasn't nearly as good as the real thing.

"You haven't seen your brother in a long time, yet you don't think he's guilty?"

Silence.

Beck wished he'd waited to ask that particular question because he would have liked to have seen her reaction, but there wasn't any way he was going to turn around while she was dressing.

"Darin wouldn't hurt me," she finally said.

He rolled his eyes. "I'll bet your mother and sister thought the same thing."

"I don't think he killed them." Her opinion wasn't news to him. She had said the same in her interview with the Texas Rangers. "My sister's ex-boyfriend killed them."

Nolan Wheeler. Beck knew him because the man used to live in LaMesa Springs. He was as low-life as they came, and Beck along with the Texas Rangers had been looking for Nolan, who'd seemingly disappeared after giving his statement to the police in Austin.

Well, at least Faith hadn't changed her story over the past two months. But then Beck hadn't changed his theory. "Nolan Wheeler has alibis for the murders."

"Thin alibis," Faith supplied. "Friends of questionable integrity who'll vouch for him."

"That's more than your brother has. According to what I read about Darin, he's mentally unstable, has been in and out of psychiatric hospitals for years, and he resented your mom and sister. On occasion, he threatened to kill them. He carried through on those threats, though I'll admit he might have had Nolan Wheeler's help."

"Now you think my brother had an accomplice?" Faith asked.

He was betting she had a snarky expression to go along with that snarky question. "It's possible. Darin isn't that organized."

Or that bright. The man was too scatterbrained and perhaps too mentally ill to have conceived a plan to murder two women without witnesses or physical evidence to link him to the crimes. And there was plenty of potential for physical evidence since both victims had been first shot with tranquilizer darts and then strangled. Darin didn't impress him as the sort of man who could carry out multistep murders or remember to wear latex gloves when strangling his victims.

Beck heard an odd sound and risked looking in her direction. She was dressed, thank goodness, in black pants and a taupe sweater. Simple but classy.

The sound had come from her kneeling to open a suitcase. She pulled out a pair of flat black shoes and slipped them on. Faith also took out a plush armadillo before standing, and she clutched onto it when she faced him head-on. She was about five-six. A good eight inches shorter than he was, and with the flats, Beck felt as if he towered over her.

"My brother has problems," she said as if being extra mindful of her word choice. "I don't need to tell you that we didn't have a stellar upbringing, and it affected Darin in a negative way."

It was the old bad blood between them that made him want to remind her that her family was responsible for the poor choices they'd made over the years.

Including what happened that December night ten years ago.

Even now, all these years later, Beck could still see Faith coming out of the Sound End motel with his drunk brother and shoving him into her car. She, however, had been as sober as a judge. Beck should know since, as a deputy at that time, he'd been the one to give her a Breathalyzer. She'd denied having sex with his brother, but there'd been a lot of evidence to the contrary, including his own brother's statement.

"You got something to say to me?" Faith challenged.

Not now. It could wait.

Instead, he glanced at the stuffed baby armadillo. It had a tag from a gift shop in the Austin airport and sported a pink bow around its neck. "I heard you had a baby." Because he was feeling ornery, he glanced at her bare ring finger.

"Yes." Those copper eyes drilled into him. "She's sixteen months old. And, no, I'm not married." The corner of her mouth lifted. Not a smile of humor though.

"I guess that just confirms your opinion that I have questionable morals."

He lifted a shoulder and let it stand as his response about that. "You think it's wise to bring a child to LaMesa Springs with a killer at large?"

She mimicked him by lifting her own shoulder, and she let the seconds drag on several moments before she continued. "I have a security company rep coming out first thing in the morning to install some equipment. Once he's finished, I'll call the nanny and have her bring my daughter. We'll stay at the hotel until I have some other repairs and updates done to the house." She glanced around the austere room before her gaze came back to his. "I intend to make this place a home for her."

That's what Beck was afraid she was going to say. This wasn't just about her new job. It was Faith Matthews's homecoming. Something he'd dreaded for ten years. "Even with all the bad memories, you still want to be here?"

Her mouth quivered. "Ah. Is this the part where you tell me I should think of living elsewhere? That I'm not welcome here in *your* town?"

He took a moment with his word selection as well. "You being here will make it hard for my family."

She had the decency to look uncomfortable about that. "I wish I could change that." And she sounded sincere. "But I can't go back and undo history. I can only move forward, and being assistant D.A. is a dream job for me. I won't walk away from that just because the Tanners don't want me here."

He could tell from the resolve in her eyes that he wasn't going to change her mind. Not that he thought he could anyway. At least he'd gotten his point across that there was still a lot of water under the bridge that his brother and she had built ten years ago in that motel.

But there was another point he had to make. "Even with security measures, it might not be safe for you or your daughter. The man who killed your mother and sister is still out there."

Oh, she was about to disagree. He could almost hear the argument they were about to have. Maybe that wasn't a bad thing. A little air clearing. Except the old stench was so thick between them that it'd take more than an argument to clear it.

She opened her mouth. At the exact moment that Beck caught movement out of the corner of his eye.

Outside the window.

Front yard.

Going on gut instinct, Beck dove at Faith and tackled her onto the bed. He lifted his head and saw the shadowy figure. And worse, it looked as if their *visitor* had a gun pointed right at Faith and him.

Chapter Two

Faith managed a muffled gasp, but she couldn't ask Beck what the heck was going on. The tackle onto the bed knocked the breath from her.

She fought for air and failed. Beck had her pinned down. He was literally lying on her back, and his solid weight pushed her chest right into the hard mattress.

"Someone's out there," Beck warned. "I think he had a gun."

Just like that, she stopped struggling and considered who might be out there. None of the scenarios that came to mind were good. It was too late and too cold for a neighbor to drop by. Besides, she didn't have any nearby neighbors, especially anyone who'd want to pay her a friendly visit. Plus, there was Beck's reaction. He obviously thought this might turn dangerous.

She didn't have to wait long for that to be confirmed.

A sound blasted through the room. Shattering glass. A split-second later, something thudded onto the floor.

"A rock," Beck let her know.

A rock. Not exactly lethal in itself, but the person who'd thrown it could be a threat. And he might have a weapon.

Who had done this?

Better yet, why was Beckett Tanner sheltering her? He had put himself in between her and potential danger, and once she could breathe, Faith figured that maneuver would make more sense than it did now.

Because there was no chance he'd put himself in real harm's way to protect her.

"Get under the bed," Beck ordered. "And stay there."

He rolled off her, still keeping his body between her and the window. Starved for air, Faith dragged in an urgent breath and scrambled to the back side of the mattress so she could drop to the floor. She crawled beneath the bed amid dust bunnies and a few dead roaches.

Staying here tonight, alone, had obviously not been a good idea.

Worse, Faith didn't know why she'd decided at the last minute to stay. Her plan had been to check in to the hotel, to wait for the renovations to be complete and for the new furniture to arrive. But after stepping inside, she thought it was best to exorcise a few demons before trying to make the place "normal." So she'd sent the cab driver on his way, made a fire to warm up the place and got ready for bed.

Now someone had hurled a rock through her window.

There was another crashing sound. Another spray of glass. Another thud. Her stomach tightened into an acidy knot.

Beck got off the bed as well. Dropping onto the floor and staying low, he scurried to what was left of the window and peeked out.

"Can you see who's out there?" she asked.

He didn't answer her, but he did take a sliver-thin cell phone from his jeans pocket and called for backup. For some reason that made Faith's heart pound even harder. If this was a situation that Beck Tanner believed he couldn't handle alone, then it was *bad*.

She thought of Aubrey and was glad her little girl wasn't here to witness this act of vandalism, or whatever it was. Faith also thought of their future, how this would affect it. *If* it would affect it, she corrected. And then she thought of her brother. Was he the one out there in the darkness tossing those rocks? It was a possibility—a remote one—but Beck wouldn't believe it to be so remote.

Her brother, Darin, was Beck's number one murder suspect. She'd read every report she could get her hands on and every newspaper article written about the murders.

She didn't suspect Darin, though. She figured her sister's ex, Nolan Wheeler, was behind those killings. Nolan had a multipage arrest record, and her sister had even taken out a temporary restraining order against him.

For all the good it'd done.

Even with that restraining order, her sister, Sherry, had been murdered near her apartment on the outskirts of Austin. Their mother's death had happened twenty-four hours later in the back parking lot of the seedy liquor store where she worked in a nearby town. The murder had occurred after business hours, within minutes of her mother locking up the shop and going to her car. And even though Faith wasn't close to either of them and hadn't been for years, she'd mourned their loss and the brutal way their lives had ended.

Still staying low, Beck leaned over and studied one

of the rocks. It was smooth, about the size and color of a baked potato, and Faith could see that it had something written on it.

"What does it say?" she asked when Beck didn't read it aloud.

His hesitation seemed to last for hours. "It says, 'Leave or I'll have to kill you, too.'"

Mercy. So it was a threat. Someone didn't want her moving back to town. She watched Beck pick up the second rock.

Beck cursed under his breath. "It's from your brother."

Faith shook her head. "How do you know?"

"Because it says, 'I love you, but I can't stop myself from killing you. Get out,'" Beck grumbled. "I don't know how many people you know who both love you and want you dead. Darin certainly fits the bill. Of course, maybe he just wrote the message and had Wheeler toss it in here for him."

She swallowed hard, and the lump in her throat caused her to ache. God. This couldn't be happening.

Faith forced herself to think this through. Instead of Nolan being Darin's accomplice, Nolan himself could be doing this to set up her brother. Still, that didn't make it less of a threat.

"Listen for anyone coming in through the back door," Beck instructed.

There went her breath again. If Beck had been able to break in, then a determined killer or vandal would have no trouble doing the same.

Because she had to do something other than cower and wait for the worst, Faith crawled to the end of the bed where she'd placed her suitcase. After a few run-ins with Nolan Wheeler, she'd bought a handgun. But she didn't have it with her. However, she did have pepper spray.

She retrieved the slender can from her suitcase and inched out a little so she could see what was going on. Beck was still crouched at the window, and he had his weapon ready and aimed into the darkness.

With that part of the house covered, she shifted her attention to the bedroom door. From her angle, she could see the kitchen, and if the rock thrower took advantage of that broken lock, he'd have to come through the kitchen to get to them. Thankfully, the moonlight piercing through the back windows allowed her to see that the room was empty.

"You don't listen very well," Beck snarled. "I told you to stay put."

She ignored his bark. Faith wouldn't make herself an open target, but she wanted to be in a position to defend herself.

"Do you see anyone out there?" she barked back.

She clamped her teeth over her bottom lip to stop the trembling. Not from fear. She was more angry than afraid. But with the gaping holes in the window, the winter wind was pushing its way through the room, and she was cold.

"No. But if I were a betting man, I'd say your brother's come back to eliminate his one and only remaining sibling—you."

"Maybe the person outside is after you?"

He glanced back at her. So brief. A split-second

look. Yet he conveyed a lot of hard skepticism with that glimpse.

"You're the sheriff," she reminded him. "You must have made enemies. Besides, my mother and sister have been dead for over two months. If that's Darin or their real killer out there, why would he wait this long to come after me? It's common knowledge that I was living in Oklahoma City and practicing law there for the past few years. Why not just come after me there?"

"A killer doesn't always make sense."

True. But there were usually patterns. Her mother and sister's killer had attacked them when they were alone. He hadn't been bold or stupid enough to try to shoot them with a police officer nearby. Of course, maybe the killer didn't realize that the car out front belonged to Beck, since it was his personal vehicle and not a cruiser. Therefore he wouldn't have known that Beck was there. She certainly hadn't been aware of it when she had been in that shower. Talk about the ultimate shock when she'd seen him standing there.

Her, stark naked.

Him, combing those smoky blue eyes all over her body.

"Dreamy eyes," the girls in school had called him. Dreamy eyes to go with a dreamy body, that toast-brown hair and quarterback's build.

Faith hadn't been immune to Beck's sizzling hot looks, either. She'd looked. But the looking stopped after the night he'd given her a Breathalyzer test at the motel.

A lot of things had stopped that night.

And there was no going back to that place. Even if

those dreamy looks still made her feel all warm and willing.

"I hope you're having second and third thoughts about bringing your daughter here," Beck commented. He still had his attention fastened to the front of the house.

She was. But what was the alternative? If this was Darin or her sister's slimy ex, then where could she take Aubrey so she'd be safe?

Nowhere.

That was a sobering and frightening thought.

But Beck was right about one thing. She needed to rethink this. Not the job. She wasn't going to run away from the job. However, she could do something about making this a safe place for Aubrey. And the first thing she'd do was to catch the person who'd thrown those rocks through her window.

She could start by having the handwriting analyzed. Footprints, too. Heck, she wanted to question the taxi driver to see if he'd told anyone that he'd dropped her off at the house. Someone had certainly learned quickly enough that she was there.

"I think the guy's gotten away by now," Faith let Beck know.

He didn't answer because his phone rang. Beck glanced at the screen and answered with a terse, "Where are you right now?" He paused, no doubt waiting for the answer. "Someone in front of the house threw rocks through the window. Check the area and let me know what you find."

Good. It was backup. If Nolan Wheeler or whoever was still out there, then maybe he'd be caught. Maybe this would all be over within the next few minutes. Then she could deal with this adrenaline roaring through her veins and get on with her life.

Faith waited there with her fingers clutched so tightly around the pepper spray that her hand began to cramp. The minutes crawled by, and they were punctuated by silence and the occasional surly glance from Beck.

He still hated her.

She could see it in his face. He still blamed her for that night with his brother. Part of her wanted to shout the truth of what'd happened, but he wouldn't believe her. Her own mother hadn't. And over the years she'd convinced herself that it didn't matter. That incident had given her a chip on her shoulder, and she'd used that chip and her anger to succeed. Coming back here, getting the job as the assistant district attorney, that was her proof that she'd risen above the albatross of her family's DNA.

"It's me," someone called out, causing her heart to race again.

But Beck obviously wasn't alarmed. He got to his feet and watched the man approach the window.

"I see some tracks," the man announced. "But if any-body's still out here, then he's freezing his butt off and probably hiding in the bushes across the road."

The man poked his face against the hole in the window, and she got a good look at him. It was Corey Winston. He'd been a year behind her in high school and somewhat of a smart mouth. These days, he was Beck's deputy. She'd learned that during her job interview with the district attorney.

Corey's insolent gaze met hers. "Faith Matthews."

He used a similar tone to the one Beck had used when he first saw her. "What are you doing back in LaMesa Springs?"

"She's going to be the new assistant district attorney," Beck provided.

That earned her a raised eyebrow from Corey. "Now I've heard everything. You, the A.D.A.? Well, you're not off to a good start. You breeze into town, your first night back, and you're already stirring up trouble, huh?"

The *huh* was probably added to make it sound a little less insulting. But it only riled her more. She'd let jerks like Corey, and Beck, run her out of town ten years earlier, but they wouldn't succeed this time.

She would continue full speed ahead, and if that included arresting her own brother, she'd do it and carry out her lawful duties. Of course, because of a personal conflict, the D.A. himself would have to prosecute the case, but she would fully cooperate. It helped that she had been estranged from her mother and sister. That wouldn't help with Darin. It would hurt. But duty had to come first here.

Beck reholstered his gun and glanced around at the glass on the floor. "Secure the scene," he told Corey. "Cast at least one of the footprints, and I'll send it to the lab in Austin. We might get lucky."

"You think it's worth it?" Corey challenged. But his defiance went down a notch when Beck stared at him. "It just seems like a lot of trouble to go through considering this was probably done by those Kendrick kids. You know those boys have too much time on their hands and nobody at home to see what they're up to."

"There's a killer on the loose," Beck reminded him.

That reminder, however, didn't stop Corey from scowling at Faith before he turned from the window and got to work. He grumbled something indistinguishable under his breath.

Beck looked at her then. He wasn't exactly sporting a scowl like Corey, but it was close. "I need you to come with me to my office so I can take a statement."

It was standard operating procedure. Something that needed to be done, just in case it had been the killer outside that window. Besides, she didn't want to be alone in the house. Not tonight. Maybe not ever. She would truly have to rethink making this place a home for Aubrey.

Faith grabbed her purse and got ready to go.

"I don't believe it was the Kendrick kids who threw those rocks," Beck said to her.

That stopped her in her tracks. "You think it was Darin?" she challenged.

"If not Darin, then let's play around with your assumption, that your mom and sister's killer was Sherry's ex, Nolan Wheeler." He hitched his thumb toward the broken glass. "If Nolan was outside that window tonight, he could want to do you harm."

She shook her head. "Stating the obvious here, but if that's true, why wait until now?"

"Because you were here alone. Or so he thought. You were an easy target."

Faith zoomed in on the obvious flaw in his theory. "And his motive for wanting me dead?"

"Maybe Nolan thinks you'll use your new job to come after him for the two murders. He might even think that's why you've come back."

She opened her mouth to deny it, but she couldn't. In fact, that's exactly the way Nolan would think.

Other than in confidence to her boss, Faith hadn't announced to anyone in Oklahoma that she had accepted the job in LaMesa Springs.

Not until this morning.

This morning, she'd also called LaMesa Springs' D.A. to tell him she would be arriving. She had arranged for renovations and a security system for the house. She'd made lots and lots of calls, and anyone could have found out her plans.

Anyone, including Nolan.

"Where's your daughter right now?" Beck asked. His tone alone would have alarmed her, but there was more than a sense of urgency in his expression.

"Aubrey's still in Oklahoma with her nanny. Why?"

"Because I was just trying to put myself in Nolan's place. If he came here to scare you off and it didn't work, then what will he do next?" His stare was a warning. "If he's got an accomplice or if it was his accomplice who just tossed those rocks, that means one of them could be here in LaMesa Springs and the other could be in Oklahoma."

Her heart dropped to her knees.

Beck took a step toward her. "Either Darin or Nolan might try to use your daughter to get to you."

"Oh, God."

Faith grabbed her phone from her purse and prayed that it wasn't too late to keep Aubrey safe.

Chapter Three

By Beck's calculation, Faith had been pacing in his office for three hours while she waited for her daughter to arrive. Even when she'd been on the phone, which was a lot, or while giving her official statement to him, she still paced. And while she did that, she continued to check her delicate silver watch.

The minutes were probably dragging by for her.

They certainly were for him.

Beck tried to keep himself occupied with routine paperwork and notes on his current cases. Normally he liked keeping busy. But this wasn't a normal night.

Faith Matthews was in his office, mere yards away, and sooner or later he was going to have to break the news to his family that she'd returned. Since it was going on midnight, Beck had opted for later, but he knew, with the gossip mill always in full swing, that if he didn't tell his father, brother and sister-in-law by morning—early morning, at that—then they'd find out from some other source.

As if she knew what he was thinking, Faith tossed him a glance from over her shoulder.

Despite the vigor of her pacing, she was exhausted. Her eyes were sleep-starved, and her face was pale and tight with tension. On some level he understood that tension.

Her daughter might be in danger, and she was waiting for the little girl to arrive with her nanny and the Texas Ranger escort from the Austin airport. Beck hadn't had the opportunity to be around many babies, but he figured the parental bond was strong, and the uncertainty was driving Faith crazy.

"You're staring at me," she grumbled.

Yeah. He was.

Beck glanced back at his desk, but the glance didn't take. For some stupid reason, his attention went straight back to Faith. To her tired expression. Her tight muscles. The still damp hair that she hadn't had a chance to dry after her shower.

Noticing her hair immediately made him uncomfortable. But then so did Faith. Dealing with a scrawny eighteen-year-old was one thing, but Faith was miles away from being that girl. She was poised and polished, even now despite the damp hair. A woman in every sense of the word.

Hell. That made him uncomfortable, too.

"I figure you're having second thoughts about accepting the A.D.A. job," he grumbled, hoping conversation would help. It was a fishing expedition since she'd kept her thoughts to herself the entire time she had been waiting for her daughter and the nanny to arrive.

"You wish," she tossed at him. "The D.A. and the city council want me here, and I have to just keep telling myself that not everyone in town hates me like the Tanners."

Okay. No second thoughts. Well, not any that she

would likely voice to him. She had dug in her heels, unlike ten years ago when she'd left town running. Part of him, the part he didn't want to acknowledge, admired her for not wavering in her plans. She certainly hadn't shown much backbone or integrity ten years ago.

She flipped open her cell phone again and pressed redial. Beck didn't have to ask who she was calling. He knew it was the nanny. Faith had called the woman at least every half hour.

"How much longer?" Faith asked the moment the woman apparently answered. The response made her relax a bit, and she seemed to breathe easier when she added, "See you then."

"Good news?" he asked when she didn't share.

"They'll be here in about fifteen minutes." She raked her hair away from her face. "I should have just gone to the airport to meet them."

"The Texas Rangers didn't want you to do that," Beck reminded her, though he was certain she already knew that. The Ranger lieutenant and her new boss, the D.A., had ordered her to stay put at the sheriff's office.

The order was warranted. It was simply too big of a risk for her to go gallivanting all over central Texas when there might be a killer on her trail.

"So what's the plan when your daughter arrives?" Beck asked.

"Since the Texas Rangers said they'll be providing security, we'll check in to the hotel on Main Street." She didn't hesitate, which meant, in addition to the calls and pacing, she'd obviously given it plenty of thought. "Then tomorrow morning, I can start putting some security measures in place."

He'd overheard her conversations with the Rangers about playing bodyguard and the other conversation about those measures. She was having a high-tech security system installed in her childhood home. In a whispered voice, she'd asked the price, which told Beck that she didn't have an unlimited budget. No surprise there. Faith had come from poor trash, and it'd no doubt taken her a while to climb out of that. She probably didn't have money to burn.

She made a soft sound that pulled his attention back to her. It was a faint groan. Correction, a moan. And for the first time since he'd seen her in the shower, there was a crack in that cool composure.

"I have to know if you're a real sheriff," she said, her voice trembling. "I have to know if it comes down to it that you'll protect my daughter."

Because the vulnerable voice had distracted him, it took him a second to realize she'd just insulted the hell out of him.

Beck stood and met her eye-to-eye. "This badge isn't decoration, Faith," he said, and he tapped the silver star clipped to his belt.

She just stared at him, apparently not convinced. "I want you to swear that you'll protect Aubrey."

Riled now, Beck walked closer. Actually, too close. No longer just eye-to-eye, they were practically toe-to-toe. "I. Swear. I'll. Protect. Aubrey." He'd meant for his tone to be dangerous. A warning for her to back down.

She didn't. "Good."

Faith actually sounded relieved, which riled him even more. Hell's bells. What kind of man did she think he was if he wouldn't do his job and protect a child?

Or Faith, for that matter?

And why did it suddenly feel as if he wanted to protect her?

Oh, yeah. He remembered. She was attractive, and mixed with all that sudden vulnerability, he was starting to feel, well, protective.

Among other things.

"Thank you," she added.

It was so sincere, he could feel it.

So were the tears that shimmered in her eyes. Sincere tears that she quickly blinked back. "For the record, I'm a good lawyer. And I'll be a good A.D.A." Now she dodged his gaze. "I have to succeed at this. For Aubrey. I want her to be proud of me, and I want to be proud of myself. I'll convince the people of this town that I'm not that same girl who tried to run away from her past."

She turned and waved him off, as if she didn't want him to respond to that. Good thing. Because Beck had no idea what to say. He preferred the angry woman who'd barked at him in the shower. He preferred the Faith who'd turned tail and run ten years ago.

This woman in front of him was going to be trouble.

His brother had once obviously been attracted to her. Beck could see why. Those eyes. That hair.

That mouth.

His body started to build a stupid fantasy about Faith's mouth when thankfully there was a rap at his door. Judging from Corey's raised eyebrow, he hadn't missed the way Beck had been looking at Faith.

"What?" Beck challenged.

Corey screwed up his mouth a moment to indicate his displeasure. "I took a plaster of one of the footprints like you said. It's about a size ten. That's a little big for one of the Kendrick kids."

Beck had never believed this was a prank. Heck, he wasn't even sure it was a scare tactic. Those rocks had been meant to send Faith running, and Beck didn't think the killer was finished.

"I'll send the plaster and the two rocks to the Rangers lab in Austin tomorrow morning." With that, Corey walked away.

Realizing that he needed to put some distance between him and Faith, Beck took a couple of steps away from her.

"My brother wears a size-ten shoe," Faith provided.

He stopped moving away and stared at her again. "So does your sister's ex, Nolan."

She blinked, apparently surprised he would know that particular detail.

"Even though the murders didn't happen here in my jurisdiction, I've been studying his case file," Beck explained.

Another blink. "I hope that means you're close to figuring out who killed my mother and sister."

"I've got it narrowed down just like you do." He shrugged. "You think it's Nolan. I think it's your brother, Darin, working with Nolan. The only other person I need to rule out is your daughter's father."

She folded her arms over her chest. Looked away. "He's not in the picture."

"So you said in your statement to the Rangers, but I have to be sure that he's not the one who put those rocks through the window."

"I'm sure he has no part in this," she snapped. "And

that brings us back to Darin and Nolan. Darin really doesn't have a motive to come after me—"

"But he does," Beck interrupted. "It could be the house and the rest of what your mother owned."

Faith shook her head. "My mother disowned Darin four years ago. He can't inherit anything."

"Does your brother know that?"

"Darin knows." There was a lot emotion and old baggage that came with the admission. The disinheritance had probably sparked a memorable family blowup. Beck would take her word for it that Darin had known he couldn't benefit financially from the murders.

"That leaves Nolan," Beck continued. "While you were on the phone, I did some checking. Your sister, Sherry, lived with Nolan for years, long enough for them to have a common-law marriage. And even though they hadn't cohabited in the eighteen months prior to her death, they never divorced. That means he'd legally be your mother's next of kin…if you and your daughter were out of the way."

Her eyes widened, and her arms uncrossed and dropped to her sides. "You think Nolan would kill me to inherit that rundown house?"

"Not just the house. It comes with three acres of land and any other assets your mother left. She only specified in her will that her belongings would go to her next of kin, with the exclusion of Darin."

"The land, the house and the furniture are worth a hundred thousand, tops," she pointed out.

"People have killed for a lot less. That's why I alerted every law-enforcement agency to pick up Nolan the moment he's spotted. I want him in custody so I can question him."

That caused her to chew on her bottom lip, and Beck wondered if she was ready to change her mind about staying in town. "I have to draw up my will ASAP. I can write it so that Nolan can't inherit a penny. And then I need to let him know that. That'll stop any attempts to kill me."

Maybe.

Unless there was a different reason for the murders.

The front door opened, and just like that, Faith raced out of his office and into the reception area. Corey was at the desk, by the dispatch phone, and Faith practically flew right past him to get to the three people who'd just stepped inside.

A Texas Ranger and a sixtysomething-year-old Hispanic woman carrying a baby in pink corduroy overalls and a long-sleeved lacy white shirt. Aubrey.

Faith pulled the little girl into her arms and gave her a tight hug. Aubrey giggled and bounced, the movement causing her mop of brunette hair to bounce as well.

Beck hadn't really known what to expect when it came to Faith's daughter, but he'd at least thought the child would be sleeping at this time of night. She wasn't. She was alert, smiling, and her brown eyes were the happiest eyes he'd ever seen.

"Sgt. Egan Caldwell," the Ranger introduced himself first to Beck and then to Faith.

"Sheriff Beck Tanner."

"Marita Dodd," the nanny supplied. Unlike the little girl, this woman's dark eyes showed stress, concern and even some fear. She was petite, barely five feet tall, and a hundred pounds, tops, but even with her demure size and sugar-white hair, she had an air of authority about her. "Aubrey's obviously got her second wind. Unlike the rest of us."

"Ms. Matthews," the Ranger said to Faith. "Could I have word with you?" He didn't add the word *alone,* but his tone certainly implied it.

"Of course." After another kiss on the cheek, Faith passed the child back to the nanny, and she and Sgt. Caldwell went to the other side of the reception area to have a whispered conversation.

Beck watched Faith's expression to see if she was about to get bad news, but if her brother had been caught or was dead, then why hadn't the Ranger told Beck as well? After all, Beck was assisting with the case.

"I really have to go the ladies' room," Marita Dodd said. That brought Beck's attention back to her.

"Down the hall, last room on the right," Beck instructed.

But Marita didn't go. She glanced at Aubrey, then at Faith, and finally thrust Aubrey in his direction. "Would you mind holding her a minute?"

Beck was sure his mouth dropped open. But if Marita noticed his stunned response, she didn't react. Aubrey reacted though. The little girl went right to him. Straight into his arms.

And then she did something else that stunned Beck.

Aubrey grinned and planted a warm, sloppy kiss on his cheek.

That rendered him speechless and cut his breath. Man. That baby kiss and giggle packed a punch. In that flash of a moment, he got it. He understood the whole parent thing and why men wanted to be fathers.

He got it, and he tried to push it aside.

This was the last child on earth to whom he should have an emotional response.

Aubrey babbled something he didn't understand and cocked her head to the side as if waiting for him to reply. She kept those doe eyes on him.

"I don't know," Beck finally answered.

That caused her to smile again, and she aimed her tiny fingers at the Ranger vehicle parked just outside the window. "Tar," she said as if that explained everything.

"Car?" Beck questioned, not sure what he was supposed to say.

"Tar," she repeated. Then added, "Bye-bye."

Another smile. Another kiss that left his cheek wet and smelling like baby's breath. And she wound her plump arms around his neck. The child obviously wasn't aware that he was a stranger at odds with her mother.

Beck was having a hard time remembering that, too.

Well, he was until he heard Faith storming his way. Her footsteps slapped against the hardwood floor. "Aubrey," she said, taking the child from his arms.

While Beck understood Faith's displeasure at having him hold her baby, Aubrey showed some displeasure, too.

"No, no, no," Aubrey protested and reached for Beck again. She waggled her fingers at him, a gesture that Beck thought might mean "come here."

"This won't take but another minute," the Ranger interjected. He obviously wasn't finished talking to Faith.

Faith huffed. Aubrey continued to struggle to get

back to Beck, and she clamped her small but persistent hand onto the front of his shirt. They were still in the middle of the little battle when the phone rang. The deputy, Corey, answered it, but immediately passed the phone to Beck.

"It's your brother," Corey announced.

Great. This was not a conversation Beck wanted to have tonight.

Faith practically snapped to attention, and despite Aubrey's protest, she carried the child back across the room and resumed her conversation with the Ranger.

"Pete," Beck greeted his brother. "What can I do for you?"

"You can tell me if what I heard is true," Pete stated. "Is Faith Matthews back in town?"

Because he was going to need it, Beck took a deep breath. "She's here."

With that, Faith angled her eyes in his direction. Hearing his brother's voice and seeing Faith was a much-needed reminder of the past.

"Why did she come back?" Pete didn't ask in anger. There was more dread in his voice than anything else.

"She's the new assistant district attorney. I didn't tell you sooner because I didn't think she was coming until next month. It wasn't my decision to hire her. It was the D.A.'s."

"It's for sure? The D.A. actually hired her?"

"Yeah. It's for sure."

"Then I'll have a chat with him," Pete insisted.

Beck had already had that chat, and the D.A. wouldn't budge. Pete wouldn't, either. His brother would talk and argue with the D.A., too, but in the end the results would be the same—Faith would still be the new A.D.A.

"In the meantime, you do whatever it takes to get Faith Matthews away from here," Pete continued. "I don't want her upsetting Nicole."

Nicole, Pete's wife of nearly a dozen years. This would definitely upset her. Nicole was what his grand-mother would have called high-strung. An argument would give Nicole a migraine. A fender bender would send her running to her therapist over in Austin.

This would devastate her.

"There's a lot to be resolved," Beck told his brother.

"What does that mean?"

Heck, he was just going to say it even though he knew Faith would overhear it. "It means Faith might change her mind about staying."

Yeah, that earned him a glare from her. He hadn't expected anything less. But then she glared at whatever the Ranger said, too. Her glare was followed by a look of extreme shock. Wide eyes. Drained color from her cheeks. Her mouth trembled, and he wasn't thinking this was a fear reaction. More like anger.

"I'll call you back in the morning," Beck continued with his brother. "In the meantime, get some sleep."

"Right." With that final remark, Pete hung up.

Beck hung up, too, and braced himself for the next round of battle he was about to have with Faith. But when he saw her expression, he rethought that battle. No more shock. Something had taken the fight right out of her.

Sgt. Caldwell stopped talking to Faith and made his way back to Beck. "I got a call on the drive over here.

The crime lab reviewed the surveillance disk you sent us. The one from Doolittle's convenience store. They were able to positively identify your suspect."

Beck let that sink in a moment. Across the room while holding a babbling happy baby, Faith was obviously doing the same.

"So Darin Matthews was in LaMesa Springs?" Beck clarified.

The Ranger nodded. "We can also place him just five miles from here. About four hours ago, he filled up at a gas station on I-35."

Everything inside Beck went still. "Any reason he wasn't arrested?"

"The clerk thought Darin looked familiar, but he didn't make the connection with the wanted pictures in the newspaper until Darin had already driven away. But the store had auto security feeds to the company that monitors them, and that means we had fast access to the surveillance video. That's how we were able to make such a quick ID."

So Darin had come back, and he might have thrown those rocks with the threatening messages through Faith's window. "You didn't see Nolan Wheeler on either surveillance feed?" Beck asked.

"No. But that doesn't mean he wasn't there. He could have been out of camera range."

Beck snared Faith's gaze. "Does this mean you're leaving?"

She didn't jump to defend herself. Her mouth tightened, she kissed the top of Aubrey's head and looked at Sgt. Caldwell. "They want me to be bait."

Beck repeated that, certain he'd misunderstood. "Bait?"

"An enticement," the Ranger clarified. "We believe there's only one person who can get Darin Matthews to surrender peacefully, and that's his sister."

True. But Beck could see the Texas-size holes in this so-called plan. "She's got a kid. Being bait isn't safe for either of them."

Sgt. Caldwell nodded. "We're going to minimize the risks."

"How?" Beck demanded.

"By making her brother think he can get to her. No matter where she goes, she'll be in danger. Her baby, too. My lieutenant thinks it's best if we make a stand. Here. Where we know Darin is."

Beck cursed under his breath, but he bit off the rest of the profanity when he realized Aubrey was smiling at him. "So what's the plan to keep her and that little girl safe?"

"The lieutenant wants to set up a trap to lure Darin back. We'll alert all the businesses in town and the surrounding area to be on the lookout for Matthews. Meanwhile, we'll put security measures in place for Ms. Matthews's house while she's at the hotel tonight."

"Her house?" Beck questioned. He didn't like anything about this plan. "You honestly expect her to stay there after what happened tonight? Someone threw rocks through her window."

Another nod. "She won't actually be staying at the house. She'll just make an appearance of sorts, but we'll tell everyone in town that's where she'll be staying."

Beck felt a little relief. "So Faith and her daughter will be going to a safe house?"

The sergeant glanced back at Faith, and it was she who continued. "Not exactly. I can't live in a safe house for the rest of my life, and Darin won't be able to find me if I'm hidden away. So the Rangers want to set up a secure place for Aubrey and the nanny. I'll be there, too, while making appearances at my house to coax out Darin. Obviously, we can't have Aubrey in harm's way, but my brother would know something was up if Aubrey's in one location and I'm in another. So we have to make it look as if she's with me even though she'll be far from danger." She paused, moistened her lips. "I'm hoping it won't take long for my brother to show, especially since he's already in the area."

So she agreed with this plan. But for someone in agreement, she certainly didn't seem pleased about it.

"If it weren't for Aubrey, I would have never gone along with this," she stated.

Confused, Beck shook his head. "Excuse me?"

"She means the protective custody issue," Sgt. Caldwell explained.

Beck sure didn't like the sound of this. "What about it? She doesn't want to be in the Rangers' protective custody?"

"No." Faith hesitated after her terse answer. "I don't want Aubrey to be in yours."

"Mine?" Beck felt as if someone had slugged him.

"Yours," Caldwell verified. "The Rangers will continue to provide you assistance on the case, but with a possible suspect in your jurisdiction, this is now your investigation, Sheriff Tanner."

"What are you saying exactly?"

The Ranger looked him straight in the eyes. "I'm saying we'll need your help. We can't risk it being leaked that Ms. Matthews really isn't staying at her place. And we can't keep her real whereabouts concealed if she's in the hotel for any length of time. There are too many employees there who could let it slip."

Beck's hands went on his hips. "So where do you propose her daughter and she go?"

"First, to the hotel to give us time to set up some security. Then, when everything's in place, they can go to your house. Her daughter will be in your protective custody." The Ranger didn't even hesitate.

It took Beck a moment to get his jaw unclenched so he could speak. "Let me get this straight. I'll become a bodyguard and babysitter in my own home?"

Sgt. Caldwell gave a crisp nod. "Protecting the child will be your primary task." The Ranger glanced at Faith again. Frowned. Then turned back to Beck. "Ms. Matthews has refused to be in your protective custody."

Her left eyebrow lifted a fraction when Beck's attention landed on her. "Yet you'd trust me with your daughter?" Beck asked.

"This wasn't her idea," Sgt. Caldwell interjected, though Faith had already opened her mouth to answer. "I had to convince her that this was the fastest and most efficient way to keep the child safe. And as for her not being in your protective custody, well, you can call it what you want, but it won't change what you have to do."

Beck stared at the Ranger. "And what exactly do I have to do?"

Sgt. Caldwell stared back. "Once we have this plan in place, Faith and her daughter's safety will be *your* responsibility."

Chapter Four

This was not the homecoming Faith had planned.

From the window of the third-floor "VIP suite" of the Bluebonnet Hotel, she stared down at the town's equivalent of morning rush hour. Cars trickled along the two-lane Main Street flanked with refurbished antique streetlights. The sidewalks were busy but not exactly bustling as people walked past the rows of quaint shops and businesses. Many of the townsfolk stopped to say "Good morning."

There were lots of smiles.

She wanted to be part of what was going on below. She wanted to dive right into her new life. But instead she was stuck inside the hotel, waiting for "orders" from Beck and the Texas Rangers, while one of Beck's deputies guarded the door to make sure no one got in.

The three-room suite was a nice enough place with its soothing Southwest decor. Her and Aubrey's room was small but tastefully decorated with cool aqua walls and muted coral bedding. Marita's room was similar, just slightly smaller, and the shared sitting room had a functional, golden-pine desk and a Saltillo tile floor.

It reminded Faith of a gilded cage.

Of course, anything less than getting on with her new life would feel that way.

She forced herself to finish the now cold coffee that room service had delivered an hour earlier. She already had a pounding headache, and without the caffeine, it would only get worse. She had to be able to think clearly today.

What she really needed was a new plan.

Or a serious modification of the present one.

Aubrey was now in Beck's protective custody and he was responsible for her safety. Right. What was wrong with this picture?

She went back to the desk, sank down onto the chair and glanced at the notes she'd made earlier. It was her list of possible courses of action. Unfortunately, the list was short.

Option one: she could immediately leave LaMesa Springs, and go into hiding. But that would be no life for Aubrey. Besides, she had to work. She couldn't live off her savings for more than six months at most.

Faith crossed off option one.

Option two: she could arrange for a private bodyguard. Again, that would eat into her savings, but it was a short-term solution that she would definitely consider. Plus, she knew someone in the business, and while things hadn't worked out personally between them, she hoped he could give her a good deal.

And then there was option three, and it would have to be paired with option two: try to speed up her brother's and Nolan's captures. The only problem was that other than making herself an even more obvious target, she wasn't sure how to do that. Maybe she could make an appeal on the local TV or radio stations? Or maybe she could just step foot inside her house a few times.

She already felt like a target anyway.

Frustrated, she set her coffee cup aside and grabbed a pen, hoping to add to the meager list. She sat, pen poised but unmoving over the paper, and she waited for inspiration to strike. It didn't.

The bedroom door opened, and Marita came out. Behind her toddled Aubrey, dressed in a pink eyelet lace dress, white leggings and black baby saddle oxfords. Just the sight of her instantly lightened Faith's mood.

"'i," Aubrey greeted her. It was her latest attempt at "hi" and she added a wave to it.

"Hi, yourself." Faith scooped her up in her arms and kissed her on the cheek.

"She ate every bite of her oatmeal," Marita reported. "And getting to bed so late doesn't seem to have bothered her." Marita patted her hand over a big yawn. "Wish I could say the same for my old bones."

"Yes. I'm sorry about that."

"Not your fault." Marita went to the window and looked out. "You warned me that some folks in this town wouldn't open their arms to you." She paused. "Guess Sheriff Tanner is one of those folks."

It wasn't a question, but Faith knew the woman wanted and deserved answers. After all, Marita had essentially been part of her family since Faith had hired her fifteen months ago as Aubrey's nanny. Faith had gotten Marita through an employment agency, but their short history together didn't diminish her feelings and respect for Marita.

"I left town ten years ago because of a scandal,"

Faith said, hoping she could get this out without emotion straining her voice. "Beck saw me coming out of a motel with his brother, Pete. His married brother. Word quickly got around, and his brother's wife attempted suicide because she was so distraught. Beck blames me for that."

Marita turned from the window, folded her arms over her chest and stared at Faith. "You *were* with the sheriff's married brother?"

Aubrey started to fuss when she spotted the stuffed armadillo on the settee, and Faith eased her to the floor so she could go after it.

"I was with him at the hotel." But Faith shook her head. She wasn't explaining this to Beck, who would challenge her every word. Marita would believe her. "But I didn't have sex with him. It didn't help that I couldn't tell the whole truth." She lowered her voice so that Aubrey wouldn't hear, even though she was much too young to understand. "It also didn't help that there were used condoms in the motel room. And when Beck found us, Pete was groping at me."

Marita made a sound of displeasure. "Beck was an idiot not to see what was really going on. You're not the sort to go after a married man." She glanced at the papers on the desk and frowned again. "Is that what I think it is?" Marita pointed to the document header, Last Will and Testament.

"I wrote it this morning." She noted the shocked look on Marita's face. "No, I'm not planning to die anytime soon. I just need to let someone know that he won't inherit anything in the event of my demise."

Faith didn't have time to explain that further because

her cell phone rang. Since she was expecting several important calls, she answered it right away.

"Zack Henley," the caller identified himself. "I'm the driver who took you from the airport to LaMesa Springs last night. You left a message with my boss saying to call you, that it was important."

"It is. I need to know if you told anyone that you'd taken me to my house."

"Told anyone?" he repeated. He sounded not only surprised but cautious.

Faith rephrased it. "Is it possible that someone in LaMesa Springs learned that you had driven me to my house?"

He stayed quiet a moment. "I might have mentioned it to the guy at the convenience store."

That grabbed her attention. "Which guy and which convenience store?"

"Doolittle's, I think is the name of it."

The same store where her brother had been sighted. "And who did you tell about me?"

"I didn't tell, exactly. I mean, I didn't go in the place to blab about you, but the guy asked me what a cab driver was doing in LaMesa Springs, and I told him I'd dropped someone off on County Line Road. He asked who, and I told him. I knew your name because you paid with your credit card, and you didn't say anything about keeping it a secret."

No. She hadn't, but she also hadn't expected to be threatened with those tossed rocks. Or with the possibility that her brother had been the one to do the threatening. "Describe the person you spoke to."

"What's this all about?" he asked.

"Just describe him please." Faith used her courtroom voice, hoping it would save time.

"I don't remember how he looked, but he was the clerk behind the counter. A young kid. Maybe nineteen or twenty. Oh, yeah, and he had a snake tattoo on his neck."

She released the breath she didn't even know she'd been holding and jotted down the description. That wasn't a description of her brother. But it didn't mean this clerk hadn't said something to anyone else. Or her brother could have even been there, listening.

"Thank you," she told the cab driver.

Faith hung up and grabbed the Yellow Pages so she could find the number of the convenience store. She had to talk to that clerk. But before she could even locate the number, there was a knock at the door. Faith reached for her pepper spray, only to remind herself that there was a deputy outside and that a killer probably wouldn't knock first.

"It's me, Beck," the visitor called out.

Faith groaned, unlocked the door and opened it. It was Beck all right. Wearing jeans, a blue button-up and a walnut-colored, leather rodeo jacket. The jacket wasn't a fashion statement, though on him it could have been. It was as well-worn as his jeans and cowboy boots.

"My deputy needed a break," Beck explained. He didn't move closer until Aubrey came walking his way.

"'i," Aubrey said, grinning from ear to ear. It was adorable. But in Faith's opinion that cuteness was aimed at the wrong person.

Beck, however, obviously wasn't able to resist that

grin either because he smiled and stepped around Faith to come inside the suite.

"Is she ever in a bad mood?" he asked, keeping his focus on Aubrey.

"Wait 'til nap time," Marita volunteered. Unlike Aubrey's cheerfulness, Marita's voice had an unfriendly edge to it.

When Aubrey began to babble and show Beck the armadillo, he knelt down so that he'd be at her eye level. "That's a great-looking toy you got there."

"Dee-o," Aubrey explained, giving him her best attempt to say "armadillo." She put the toy right in Beck's face and didn't pull it back until he'd kissed it.

Aubrey giggled and threw her arms around Beck's neck as if she'd known him her entire life. The hug was brief, mere seconds, before she pulled back and pointed to the silver badge he had clipped to his belt.

"See?" Aubrey said. "Wanta see."

And much to Faith's surprise, Beck unclipped it and handed it to her so she could "see."

Frustrated with the friendly exchange, Faith shut the door with more force than necessary. Beck seemed to become aware of the awkward situation, and he stood.

"We need to talk," he told her, suddenly sounding very sherifflike.

That was obviously Marita's cue to give them some privacy, so she came across the room and picked up Aubrey. However, she stopped and looked at Beck. "Maybe this time you'll be willing to see the truth," she snarled. She took the badge from Aubrey and handed it back to him.

"What does that mean?" Beck asked, volleying confused glances between Faith and Marita.

"Nothing," Faith said at the same time that Marita said, "She wasn't with your brother that night. Faith's not like that."

And with that declaration, which would be hard to explain, Marita started walking. Aubrey waved and said, "Bye-bye," before the two disappeared into the bedroom.

"Don't ask," Faith warned him.

"Why not?"

"Because you won't believe me."

He lifted his shoulder. "What's not to believe? Didn't you tell me the truth ten years ago?"

"I told you I hadn't slept with your brother. That's the truth."

"He said otherwise."

She huffed and wondered why she was still trying to explain this all this time later. "Pete was drunk, and he lied, maybe because he was too drunk to know the truth. Or maybe because he didn't want you to know what'd really happened. I didn't seduce him, and I didn't take him to that motel. The only thing I tried to do was get him out of there."

Faith stopped when she noted his stony expression. "You know what? Enough of this. I don't owe you anything." To give herself a moment to calm down, she went to the desk and glanced at the notes she'd taken earlier. "I need to question a clerk at Doolittle's convenience store. The cabbie who drove me home told this clerk that I was in town. I want to find out who else knew so I can figure out who threw those rocks."

Beck just stared at her.

Unnerved and still riled, Faith continued, "You said we had something to discuss, and I don't think you meant personal stuff."

"Why would Pete lie about being with you?" He walked closer, stopping just a few inches away.

Why didn't he just drop this? "Ask him. For now, stick to business, *Sheriff.*"

"The personal stuff between us keeps interfering with the business."

He caught her arm when she started to move away. Faith looked down at his grip, but he didn't let go of her. He kept those gunmetal-blue eyes nailed to her, and though she hadn't thought it possible, he got even closer. So close that she could smell coffee and sugar on his breath.

Faith hiked up her chin and met his gaze. "Be careful," she warned. She meant her voice to sound sharp and stern. It didn't quite work out that way.

Because something changed.

With his hand on her, with him so close, old feelings began to tug at her. She'd once been hotly attracted to him. A lifetime ago. But those years suddenly seemed to melt away.

She was still attracted to him. And this time, she didn't think it was one-sided.

She was toast.

"The Rangers installed some security equipment at your house," Beck said. His voice wasn't strained. Nor angry. He sounded confused, and the subject didn't fit the slow simmer in the air.

"Good," she managed to answer. She tried to step away, but he held on. And she didn't fight him.

She was obviously losing her mind.

"The Rangers dressed like security technicians so anyone looking wouldn't realize the authorities had staked out the place." He paused. His jaw muscles stirred. "There. That's what I came to say. Now, let's finish this." He shook his head. Cursed. Shook his head again. And finally, he let go of her and took a step back. "This can't happen between us."

"You're right. It can't."

Neither of them looked relieved.

And neither of them looked as if they believed it.

That tug inside her pulled harder. So hard that she moved away and returned to the window. She needed a few deep breaths before she could continue. "I want a different plan than the one the Rangers came up with."

He paused. Nodded. Nodded again. "I'm listening."

It took her a moment to realize that was all he was going to say. "Well, I don't *have* a different plan," she admitted. "I just *want* one."

"Welcome to the club. I sat up most of the night trying to make a list of options."

She huffed and glanced at her list. "Since Sgt. Caldwell made it clear that the Rangers don't have the manpower to provide protection for Aubrey, Marita and me, I was thinking of hiring a private bodyguard from Harland Securities in San Antonio. A friend owns the company."

"Ross Harland," Beck provided. "I've heard of him. He's your friend?"

"We used to date." Though she had no idea why

she'd just told him that, especially since things hadn't ended that well between Ross and her. Ross might not even want to talk to her, but that wouldn't stop her from trying. "I plan to call him this morning and ask if he can help."

"You mean so that Aubrey and you won't be in my protective custody?"

Suddenly, that made her feel a little petty, but she pushed the uncomfortable feeling aside. Who cared if he was insulted that she would look elsewhere for protection? "You said yourself the personal stuff keeps getting in the way."

His jaw muscles went to war. "I swore I'd protect Aubrey, and I will. I'll protect you and Marita, too. There's not enough personal stuff in the world to ever stop me from doing my job."

She believed him. More than she wanted to.

Their eyes met again, and something circled around them. A weird intimacy. Something forged with all the emotion of the bad blood. And this bizarre attraction that had reared its hot, ugly head.

Faith forced herself to look away. To move. She shook off the Beck Tanner hypnotic effect and reached for the phone to call Ross Harland. She pressed in the number to his office, hoping she remembered it correctly, and the call went straight to voice mail. It was still before normal duty hours.

"Ross, this is Faith," she said. "Please call me. I'm in LaMesa Springs, and my cell-phone service is spotty so if you can't get through, you can reach me at the Bluebonnet Hotel."

She read off the number of the hotel phone and her

room number and clicked the end call button just as the door to the suite burst open. The movement felt violent. And suddenly so did the air around them.

The woman who rushed into the room was Nicole Tanner.

Beck's sister-in-law. Pete's wife.

Faith hadn't seen the woman since the night of the motel incident, but Nicole hadn't changed much. Sleek and polished in her high-end, boot-length, black duster, London blue pants and matching top. Her shoulder-length honey-blond hair was perfect. Not a strand out of place. She looked like the ideal trophy wife.

Except for her eyes and face.

The tears had cut their way through her makeup, leaving mascara-tinged streaks on her porcelain cheeks.

"Nicole, what are you doing here?" Beck demanded.

"Taking care of a problem I should have taken care of years ago."

And with that, Nicole took her hand from her coat pocket and aimed a slick, silver handgun right at Faith.

Chapter Five

Hell.

That was Beck's first thought, right after the shock registered that his sister-in-law had obviously gone off the deep end. Now he had to diffuse this situation before it turned deadly.

Beck stepped in front of Faith. He didn't draw his weapon, though that was certainly standard procedure. Still, he couldn't do that to Nicole.

Not yet anyway.

He lifted his hands, palms out, in a backup gesture. "Nicole, put down that gun."

Nicole shook her head and swiped away her tears with her left hand. "I can't. I have to make her leave."

Beck could hear Faith's raw breath and knew she was afraid, but that didn't stop her from leaving the meager cover he'd provided her. She stepped out beside him.

"Get back," he warned her. "Nicole's not going to shoot me," he added. But he couldn't say the same about what she might do to Faith. He didn't want his sister-in-law to do anything stupid, and he didn't want bullets flying with Aubrey just in the next room.

He didn't want Faith hurt, either.

"I'm not leaving," Faith said, though her voice trembled slightly.

Man, it took courage to say that to an armed woman. Ill-timed courage.

"Let me handle this," he insisted. He then fastened his attention to Nicole. "You have to put the past behind you. Faith won't cause you any more trouble."

Nicole's hysteria increased. "She already has caused more trouble. Pete's been up all night talking about her. You know how he is when he gets upset. He shuts me out, and he drinks too much."

Beck did know. Like Nicole, Pete had a low tolerance for certain kinds of stress, and Faith's return would have set him off.

"Put down the gun, Nicole," Beck tried again. "And I'll talk to Pete."

"It won't do any good. I have to make Faith leave before it destroys my marriage."

"Your marriage?" Faith spat out. She obviously didn't intend to let him handle this in his own way. "You have a gun pointed at me, and my daughter is just one room away. You're endangering her as well as Beck, and yet your top priority is saving your marriage?"

Nicole blinked. She probably hadn't expected this. Faith hadn't stood up for herself ten years ago. "My marriage is in trouble because of you."

"No," Faith countered. "Your marriage is in trouble because of your cheating husband. Now, put down that gun, or I'll take it away from you myself."

Since this was quickly getting out of hand, Beck moved in front of Faith again. The new position wouldn't last long. Faith was already trying to maneuver herself to his side, but Beck didn't let that happen. It was a risk. He didn't want to push Nicole into doing something even more stupid.

"Give me the gun," he insisted. Beck didn't bolt toward her. He kept his footsteps even and unhurried. No sudden moves.

But Beck was just about a yard away when there was movement in the hall, just outside the suite. Nicole automatically glanced over her shoulder, and that split-second distraction was all Beck needed. He lunged at Nicole, snagged her by the wrist and latched on to the gun. The momentum sent them flying, and they landed against the two men who'd just arrived.

His brother, Pete, and his father, Roy.

"What the hell's going on here?" Pete shouted.

"I'm disarming your wife," Beck snarled. He took control of the gun and stepped back just in case anyone else decided to try to make a move toward Faith.

Pete shot Nicole a glance. Not of disapproval, either. The corner of his mouth actually lifted as if he were pleased that Nicole was in the process of committing a felony.

"I tried to get her to leave," Nicole volunteered.

"Well, this probably wasn't the way to go about it," her father-in-law interjected.

Good. Father was being reasonable about this. Beck needed another voice of support since Faith's and his didn't seem to be enough.

He checked Nicole's gun and discovered that it wasn't loaded. Beck showed Faith the empty chamber, causing her to groan again.

"I wanted to scare her into leaving," Nicole explained. "I didn't want to actually hurt her."

Well, that was something at least, but it didn't make this situation less volatile.

With emotion zinging through the air, his father and Pete stood side by side, and Pete glared at Faith. Roy only shook his head and mumbled something under his breath. The men were the same height, same weight, and with the exception of some threads of gray in Roy's hair, they looked enough alike to be brothers. That probably had something to do with the fact that Roy had only been eighteen years old when Pete was born.

Beck glanced back at Faith. He could tell she wasn't about to back down despite being outnumbered.

"Before this gets any worse, I want everyone to know that I'm not Beck right now. I'm *Sheriff* Tanner, and this is not going to get violent."

"Then she's leaving." That from Pete, and it was a threat aimed at Faith. Their father caught onto Pete's arm and stopped him from moving any closer.

"No. I'm not," Faith threatened right back. "Maybe it is time for an air clearing. For the truth. I'd planned to do it anyway, just not this soon."

That got everyone's attention, and the room fell silent.

Faith pointed to Pete. "I didn't sleep with you ten years ago. Or any other time."

There it was. The finale to the conversation that Faith and he were having shortly before Nicole arrived.

Beck pushed aside his own surprise and checked out the responses of the others. Nicole went still, the muscles in her arms going slack. The reactions of his father and brother, however, went in different directions. Pete's face flushed with anger, and it seemed as if Father had been expecting her to say just that. He didn't look surprised at all.

"You were drunk," Faith reminded Pete. "All the years I've told myself that maybe you actually didn't lie about what happened, that you simply couldn't remember what you'd done, but now I'm not so sure."

"I didn't lie." Pete's voice was low and tight. Dangerous.

Faith walked closer. "Well, it wasn't me in that motel room with you. It was my sister, Sherry."

"Sherry," Beck mumbled. Since Sherry had been the town's wild child, he didn't have any trouble believing that, but apparently two members of his family did: Pete and Nicole. His father was still just standing there as if all of this was old news.

And maybe it was to him.

Had his father known the truth this whole time?

Nicole shook her head. "If that's true, why didn't you say so sooner? No one put a gag on you when you were outside the motel."

All attention turned back to Faith.

She pulled in a long breath. "I didn't say anything because Sherry's boyfriend, Nolan, would have killed her if he'd found out she cheated on him with your husband or with any other man, for that matter."

That made sense, and it also made Beck wonder why he hadn't thought of it sooner. But he knew why—he'd believed his brother.

"So why were you even there that night?" Nicole

questioned Faith again. Judging from her expression, she wasn't buying any of Faith's account.

Faith took another breath. "When you came to the motel and started pounding on the door, Sherry called me. She was terrified word would get out that she'd been with Pete. I came over, hid on the side of the building and waited for you to leave. Then I took Sherry out of there. I was trying to get your husband out, too, when you and Beck showed up and accused me of seducing Pete."

"That's not the way I remember things," Pete insisted.

"Then your memory is wrong," Faith insisted right back.

Pete rammed his finger against his chest. "Why would I lie about which Matthews sister I'd slept with when I was drunk?"

"Only you can answer that, Pete." Faith volleyed glares at each one of them. "I want you all out of here. Now. If not, I intend to call the Texas Rangers and have you arrested."

He understood Faith's desire to be rid of his kin, but that riled Beck. Of course, he was already riled about this entire situation, so that was only frosting on the cake. "I don't need the Rangers to handle this," he assured Faith. "Do you want to file charges against Nicole?"

That earned him a fierce look from Pete, a raised eyebrow from his father and a surprised gasp from Nicole. Why, Beck didn't know. Nicole couldn't have possibly thought brandishing a gun, even an unloaded one, wouldn't warrant at least a consideration of arrest.

"I won't file charges at the moment," Faith said, pointing at Nicole. "But let's get something straight. I won't have you anywhere near my daughter or me with a weapon again. Understand?"

"But you ruined my life. *You.* It wasn't Sherry in that motel room. If it'd been your sister, my husband would have said so."

"Get them out of here," Faith mumbled, and she turned and walked into the adjoining room.

She didn't slam the door. She closed it gently. But Beck figured if she'd been wrongly accused and run out of town, that had to be eating away at her. Now add this latest incident with Nicole, and, oh, yeah, Faith was no doubt stewing.

"Go home, Nicole," Pete told his wife.

When Nicole didn't move, Roy caught onto his daughter-in-law's arm and led her toward the door. "I'm sorry about this, Beck. We'll talk later."

Beck nodded his thanks to his father and turned back to unfinished business. "Did you sleep with Faith or not?"

Pete glanced away. "What does it matter?"

Beck cursed under his breath. "That's not an answer to my question."

"Because it's not a question you should be asking. I'm your brother, for heaven's sake."

"Being my brother doesn't mean I'll gloss over your indiscretions. Especially if that indiscretion has put the blame on the wrong woman for all these years."

Pete looked him straight in the eye. "I was with Faith that night, not Sherry."

For the first time, Beck was seriously doubting that

his brother had told the truth. But if he was lying, why? What could be worse than letting everyone, especially Nicole, believe he'd had sex with Faith? Unless fear of Nolan did play some part of this. The problem was his brother wasn't usually the sort to fear anyone.

"So what happens now?" Pete asked. "Faith just stays in town like nothing ever happened?"

Beck didn't want to mention that Faith, Aubrey and the nanny would soon be going to his house. And that they were in his protective custody. Besides, he didn't want anyone to know that his place was now essentially a safe house for the three. He wanted to get Faith, Aubrey and Marita in there without anyone else noticing. Or knowing about it. That would mean hiding them in the backseat of his car, parking in his garage and getting them inside only after the garage door was closed.

Of course, there was the other part to the plan. The part he could tell Pete since he needed the gossip mill working for the bait plan to succeed.

"Faith plans to stay at her mother's old house," Beck informed him, and he watched carefully for his brother's reaction. There wasn't much of one, just a slight shift in his posture. "I tried to talk her out of it, but she insisted on staying there."

"Then she's an idiot," Pete declared. "Her brother's a killer, and he's out on the loose. Anything could happen to her at that house."

And it wasn't a surprise that Pete didn't seem torn up about that. He probably wanted Darin to go after Faith.

Beck nodded and tried to appear detached from the situation. He realized, much to his disgust, that he wasn't detached. He didn't like this plan, and he didn't like that he'd just used his brother to set it into motion.

"You need to leave," Beck said, unable and unwilling to keep the anger from his voice. "See to your wife and make sure she doesn't come anywhere near Faith again."

Beck practically shoved his brother out the door, and he locked it. He made a mental note to keep it locked in case Nicole or Pete returned for round two. He needed to do some damage control from round one first.

Because once Faith gave it some thought, she just might file those charges against Nicole.

And if so, he'd have to arrest his own sister-in-law. Beck didn't want to speculate what kind of powder keg that would create between Pete, Nicole and Faith.

The phone on the desk rang. Figuring that Faith was still too shaken to answer it, Beck snatched it up. "Sheriff Tanner," he answered.

He was greeted with several seconds of silence, and for a moment Beck thought this might be another threat, similar to the rocks.

"Ross Harland," the caller finally said. "I'm returning Faith's call."

Beck glanced at the closed bedroom door. "She's, er, indisposed at the moment."

"Is she okay?" It didn't sound like a casual question, which might mean this guy, this former boyfriend, still had feelings for her.

"Faith's fine, but she had a rough morning. And a rough night, too."

"What happened?" Another noncasual question.

Beck didn't intend to get into specifics, but for anyone who knew Faith, her background was no doubt common knowledge. "Faith's brother is suspected of murder and is still at large. Aubrey and Faith might be in danger because of him."

"Who's Aubrey?"

That caused Beck to pause a moment. "Faith's daughter."

"A daughter?" He sounded shocked.

"I figured you knew."

"No. Faith and I dated for a year or so, but we stopped seeing each other nearly two years ago."

He didn't want to, but Beck quickly did the math. Aubrey was sixteen months old, which meant she'd been conceived a little over two years ago.

Right about the time Faith had been with Ross Harland.

Beck mentally groaned. Had Faith kept it from this man that he'd fathered a child?

"How can I help Faith?" Harland asked.

The question stunned Beck. Here, Beck had just told him in a roundabout way that he likely had a daughter, and Harland hadn't even asked about Aubrey. Certainly Harland could do the math as well. And that riled Beck to the core. If Aubrey had been his child, he'd sure as hell want to know, and he'd want to be part of her life.

"I'm not sure you can help," Beck answered, trying not to launch into a rant about how Harland should step up to the plate and be a man. "But Faith wanted to ask about getting a bodyguard for Aubrey."

Harland made a sound of understanding. "Well, I do have someone on staff who might work. Her name is Tracy Collier, and she's trained as both a nanny and a bodyguard. How old is Faith's daughter?"

Now the guy might finally get it. "Sixteen months."

"Good. I was hoping we weren't dealing with a new-born here."

"No. Not a newborn." Beck hesitated, wondering how much he should say and knowing he couldn't stop himself. He had to know, because despite Faith's denial, her past lover could have a part in this. "I thought you might be Aubrey's father."

"Me? Not a chance."

Beck had to hesitate again. This conversation was getting more and more confusing. "But you were with Faith about the time Aubrey was conceived."

"Look, I don't know what Faith told you about our relationship, and I'm not even sure it's any of your business, but there's no way that child could be mine."

"Birth control isn't always effective," Beck pointed out.

He cursed. "I want to talk to Faith."

"Like I said, she's indisposed. She'll have to call you back. And for the record, she never said you were Aubrey's father. I just put one and one together."

"Well, you came up with the wrong answer. Faith and I weren't lovers."

Beck nearly dropped the phone. "Not lovers? And you were together for a year?"

"Her choice. Not mine. Now, what the hell does this have to do with your investigation, Sheriff?"

Maybe nothing. Maybe everything. "Faith doesn't believe her brother is trying to kill her, and it's possible the danger is linked to someone in her past. When relationships go bad, situations can turn dangerous. Aubrey's father might have some part in this."

"Well, I don't know who he is, but he must be someone pretty damn special."

"What do you mean?"

Harland cursed again, and he stayed silent so long that Beck thought maybe the call had been dropped. "Ask Faith why we never slept together," Harland finally said.

"Excuse me?" Beck said because he didn't know what else to say.

"You heard me. If you want answers, ask her." And with that, Harland hung up.

Beck glanced at the phone and then at Faith's bedroom door. He didn't know what the devil was going on, but he intended to find out.

Chapter Six

"Beck Tanner asked you what?" Faith demanded.

There was a groan from the other end of her cell-phone line. "He thought I was your daughter's father," Harland explained.

Faith slowly got up from the bed where she'd been sitting and started to pace across the guest room in Beck's house. "What did you say?"

"The truth, that the child couldn't be mine because we were never lovers."

Faith didn't groan, but she squeezed her eyes shut a moment and silently cursed a blue streak.

"The sheriff said this was pertinent to the investigation," Ross added. "He said he wanted to be certain that none of your previous relationships could have a part in you being in danger."

"Maybe, but he had no right to ask you about our sex life." Or the lack thereof. Mercy, she did not want to explain this to Beck.

The truth could ultimately put Aubrey in danger.

"Anyway, the bodyguard I'm sending over is Tracy Collier," Ross continued, obviously opting for a less volatile subject. "She's one of my best. She should be there any minute, and she's yours for as long as you need her."

"Thanks, Ross," Faith managed to say. She did appreciate this, truly, but it was hard to be thankful when Beck might learn the truth.

"I'm sorry I told Sheriff Tanner anything about our relationship," Ross continued. "Should I phone him and have a little chat with him?"

It wouldn't be a chat. More like a tongue-lashing. "No. I'll do that myself." She thanked her old friend again and ended the call.

How dare Beck ask Ross a question like that, and he hadn't even had the nerve to tell her. But then he hadn't exactly had a chance, she reluctantly admitted. Like her, he'd been tied up all day planning to make Aubrey as safe as possible.

And they had succeeded. For now, anyway.

She, Marita and Aubrey were at Beck's house on the edge of town, and it appeared that no one had been aware of the move. Beck had literally sneaked them out the back of the hotel and into his place. Once the bodyguard arrived, then the plan was for a Texas Ranger to pull backup bodyguard duty while she and Beck made an appearance at her own house.

But first, she wanted to let Beck have it for that phone conversation with Ross.

Faith jerked open the guest-room door and stormed toward the family room, where she could hear voices. Beck's house was large, especially for a single guy: three bedrooms, three baths and an updated gourmet kitchen. A real surprise. When Beck had given them the whirlwind tour, she'd wanted to ask if he actually used the brick-encased French stove or the gleaming, stainless cookware on the pot rack over the butcher's block island. But she hadn't said a word, because she hadn't wanted to intrude on his personal life.

He obviously hadn't felt the same about hers.

She nodded to Sgt. Sloan McKinney, a Texas Ranger who was sipping coffee while he stood by the kitchen door. Faith went straight to the family room and stopped dead in her tracks. Her temper didn't exactly go cold, but it did chill a bit when she saw what was going on. Marita was talking to a tall brunette. The bodyguard, no doubt. But it wasn't the bodyguard who snared her attention. Aubrey was on the floor, sitting in Beck's lap while he read *Chicka Chicka Boom Boom* to her.

Beck looked up at Faith, and his smile dissolved. Maybe because she looked angry. And was. And maybe because he knew the reason for her anger.

He'd changed clothes since they'd arrived and was now wearing black jeans and a white button-up long-sleeve shirt. Anything he could have worn would have made him look hot. But sitting there with Aubrey made him look hot and…extraordinary. It wasn't just his good looks now. It was that whole potential fatherhood thing. Beck seemed totally natural holding a child. Her child. And that created a bizarre ripple of emotions.

She had to remind herself to hang on to the anger.

"We'll go to your house when I'm done with the story," Beck let her know. Aubrey didn't take her eyes off the brightly colored pages.

"Faith, this is Tracy Collier," Marita said.

Faith shook the woman's hand. "Thank you for coming."

"No problem. Ross said it was important."

Yes, and Faith owed him for that. But not for what he'd volunteered to Beck.

"Sheriff Tanner checked my ID," Tracy volunteered. "And he ran a background check on me before I arrived." She didn't sound upset. More amused.

"She checked out clean," Beck informed Faith.

Though she was upset with him, she couldn't find fault with the extra security steps he'd taken with Tracy. But how could any man look that hot while jabbering nonsensical words like *chicka, chicka?*

Marita and Tracy resumed their conversation about sleeping arrangements. Apparently, Tracy had decided to take the sofa in the family room since it was near the front door. The Ranger would have a cot near the back door. Good. The arrangement gave Faith a little reassurance about leaving Aubrey, but it would still be tough.

Babbling, Aubrey tried to repeat the last line of the book that Beck read. He then did something else that shocked Faith. He brushed a kiss on Aubrey's forehead. There was genuine affection in his eyes. Aubrey's eyes, too.

Aubrey gave Beck a hug.

Beck's gaze met Faith's again, and he went from affection to a little discomfort. With Aubrey in his arms, he stood and walked to Faith.

"Ready to go to your house?" he asked.

No, but she was ready for that conversation. And ready to get her mind off Beck as a potential father.

Marita came to take Aubrey, and Faith gave the little girl a kiss. "Mommy won't be long."

Aubrey babbled something, reached for Beck again,

but Marita moved her away. Faith gave her a nod of thanks.

"You don't want me reading to Aubrey," Beck mumbled.

"Yes. I mean, no." Since she was starting to feel petty again, she headed toward the garage. "I'm just surprised, that's all."

"Me, too. But it's hard not to get attached to her."

"Oh, that should make your family really happy," she snarled.

He didn't respond to that. They went into the garage, got into his SUV. Even though the windows were tinted and it was dusky dark outside, he still had her slip down low in the seat so that none of his neighbors, or a killer, would spot her coming out of his place.

On the backseat, there was a doll wrapped in a blanket. Faith already knew what she would do with that doll. She'd carry it into her house so that anyone watching would think it was Aubrey. The little detail had been Beck's idea because he said he didn't want anyone questioning why Faith wouldn't have her daughter with her at her house, especially since everyone in town likely knew about the child's arrival the night before.

Beck looked down at her. "You talked to Ross Harland," he said. Apparently, that was an invitation to start the argument he guessed they were about to have.

"You had no right to ask him those questions," Faith accused.

"I beg to differ. You don't think your brother is guilty. But I'm trying to figure out the identity of a killer. Your previous relationships are relevant." He pulled out of the garage and immediately hit the remote control clipped to his visor to shut it. He didn't pull away from the house until the door was fully closed.

Faith just sat there. Stewing. And waiting. She didn't have to wait long.

"Harland said he couldn't possibly be Aubrey's father," Beck continued. "I don't guess you intend to tell me who is."

"No." She didn't even have to think about her answer.

"That's what I figured you'd say, though I don't have a clue why you'd keep something like that a secret. I'm repeating myself here, but I'm trying to find a killer, Faith."

"And knowing Aubrey's father won't catch that killer."

He cursed under his breath. "I had a friend at the FBI fax me a copy of Aubrey's birth certificate. The father's name isn't listed. Just yours."

That had been intentional, and it would stay that way. Her silence must have let him know that because he didn't say anything else about it. Silently, he drove through LaMesa Springs and down Main Street—Faith could tell from the tops of the streetlights, but she was too low in the seat to actually see anything.

"No one seems to be following us," he explained, checking the rearview and side mirrors. He made the turn into the hotel and went to the back parking lot. Beck glanced all around them. "You can sit up now. I want people to think I picked you up here."

"But what if someone on the hotel staff blabs that I wasn't here all afternoon?"

"No one knows. There's been a Do Not Disturb sign on the door and strict orders that no one goes into the room. Later, I'll phone the manager and tell him that I've moved you guys to your house."

Even though it was the plan, it still sent a chill over her. After that call, she'd officially be bait.

"So it was really Sherry in the motel with Pete?" Beck asked as he drove away from the parking lot. Except it didn't sound like a question.

But Faith answered it as if it'd been one. "What did your brother say?"

"He lied."

She glanced at him, and even in the darkness she had no trouble seeing his expression. A mixture of emotions. "How do you know that?"

"Because I could see it in his eyes."

Faith blew out a long breath. "Why didn't you see it ten years ago?"

"Because I wasn't looking. I just accepted what he told me as gospel."

"You accepted it because you already believed the worst about me."

He took a moment to answer. "Yes, and it's probably too little, too late, but I'm sorry."

She nearly laughed. For years, she'd wanted that apology. She'd wanted Beck to know the truth. But it seemed a hollow victory since she couldn't enjoy it. Well, not now anyway. But once the danger had passed it would no doubt sink in that this moment had been monumental.

Faith frowned.

She certainly hadn't expected an apology from Beck to feel so darn good. Maybe because she'd already written him off. She hoped it had nothing to do with this crazy attraction between them.

"I'll work on my father and Nicole," he continued, taking the final turn to her house. Even though the curtains all appeared to be closed, some lights were on. "Pete, too, eventually. Once they've accepted that you were the scapegoat in this, then your life here should be a little smoother."

"Thank you." That was a gift she certainly hadn't expected so soon. Then it hit her. "You're doing this for Aubrey."

"In part," he readily admitted. "I don't want her to feel any resentment from anyone. But I'm doing it for me, too. Because it's the right thing to do, and since Sherry is dead, I think this will help my family get past the hurt. You know that old saying—the truth will set you free."

"Not always," she said under her breath.

They came to a stop outside her house, directly in front of the porch. All she had to do was go up the steps, and she'd be inside.

Beck glanced at her again, and for a moment she thought he might have heard her and was going to question it. He didn't. He just looked at her.

He opened his mouth. Closed it. Shook his head. But he didn't explain why he was suddenly speechless. Instead, he picked up the doll, handed it to her and motioned for her to get out.

"Make it quick but not too obvious that you're trying to hurry," he instructed.

Faith did. While clutching the doll, she got out of

the SUV and went inside to find Sgt. Caldwell waiting for them.

Beck and he exchanged handshakes. "Let's hope we catch a killer tonight," Beck greeted him.

"We'll do our best." The Ranger pointed to the security keypad by the door. "Before I leave, I want to go over the updates. There are external motion detectors that'll alert you if anyone comes within twenty feet of the house."

"What about windows?" Beck asked.

"All doors and windows are wired for security, and if anything's tripped, the alarm will go off, and the keypad will light up the problem area."

Faith was certain she looked confused. "But won't the alarm scare off Darin if he shows?" She propped the doll against the wall.

"No. The alarm will be a series of soft beeps. You shouldn't have any trouble hearing them, but they won't be loud enough to be heard from outside."

Beck's cell phone rang, and he stepped aside to answer it.

"The keypad's easy to work," Sgt. Caldwell continued. "Just press in the numbers one, two, three and four to arm it after I leave. Oh, and don't stand directly in front of any windows."

She had no plans for that. "If Darin shows, how fast can you respond?"

"Less than two minutes. I'll be nearby, parked several streets over. I don't want to be any closer, because if he sees me, it might scare him off."

"Two minutes," she repeated. "I hope that's fast enough to catch him."

Sgt. Caldwell lifted his shoulder. "Best case scenario is that your brother will call you first before he shows up. If that happens, just stay on the line with him and have Beck contact us so we can make a trace."

Faith nodded. "I don't want Darin hurt."

"We'll try our best. But it might not be possible. For that matter, it might not even be your brother who shows up."

"Nolan Wheeler," she provided.

Yes, he might have tossed those rocks through the window. And if so, if he was the one who arrived on her doorstep, then he could be arrested and questioned. It wouldn't tie up the loose ends with her brother, but she believed it would get a killer off the street.

Beck ended his call and rejoined them. One glance at him, and Faith knew something was wrong.

"That was the manager of the convenience store," Beck explained.

She held her breath, waiting for him to say her brother had been spotted again.

"Not Darin," Beck clarified, obviously understanding the concern in her body language. "This is about the taxi driver who stopped there after dropping you here at your house. When the clerk asked him what he was doing in LaMesa Springs, the driver told him."

Which confirmed what the taxi driver told Faith. "Let me guess—Nolan Wheeler was in the store?"

Beck shook his head. Paused. "No, but my father was."

"Your father?" she mumbled.

She didn't have to clarify what that meant. If his father knew, then so had Nicole and Pete. And after that stunt Nicole had pulled in her hotel room, Nicole could have been the one who'd thrown those rocks.

Beck looked away from her and handed Sgt. Caldwell his car keys. "I turned off the porch light. Figured it'd help in case someone's already watching the place."

And that person would believe it was Beck leaving. That's why Beck had changed his clothes, so that he would be dressed like the Ranger. Since no one knew the Ranger was there, the killer or her brother would think Faith was alone and vulnerable. Well, she wouldn't be alone, but the vulnerable part still applied.

"This could end up lasting all night," the Ranger reminded him.

Faith had considered that, briefly. What she hadn't considered was staying in the house alone with Beck. That suddenly didn't seem like a smart idea. But she couldn't let something like attraction get in the way of catching the person responsible.

"Good luck," Sgt. Caldwell said, heading for the door. He turned off the light in the entry as well and waited until Beck and Faith stepped into the shadows before he walked out. She immediately went to the door, locked it and set the security alarm.

"I'll talk to my dad," Beck promised. "I'll see if he repeated any information he got from the taxi driver. Plus, the rocks and foot casting are still at the crime lab. Either might give us some evidence."

"If it's Nicole who threw those rocks, I intend to file charges for that and the empty gun incident." Faith couldn't let the woman continue her harassment. Of course, if it was Nicole, there was a problem with the size-ten shoeprint that'd been found. Though maybe that print had been left earlier by someone not involved in this.

"If it's Nicole, I'll arrest her."

Faith caught his gaze. And saw the determination there. The pain, too. She also saw concern for her, so she thought it best if she stepped away from him.

Keeping in the shadows, she walked into the living room. Someone had taken the sheets from the furniture, and the sofa and recliner had a stack of bedding and pillows on them. This was where she and Beck were supposed to sleep. If sleep was even possible.

Beck would only be a few feet away from her.

With that overdue apology out of the way, there didn't seem to be so many old obstacles standing between them. Too bad. Because it made her remember a time when she'd lusted after him.

Who was she kidding?

She was still lusting after him. At least she was when she wasn't riled at him.

He followed her into the living room and caught onto her arm. The contact surprised her so much that she jumped. Faith reeled around, expecting him to do God knows what, but he merely repositioned her farther away from the window. He let go of her quickly, but then looked down at his hand as if that brief touch had caused him to feel something more.

"You might as well just go ahead and slap me," he said.

"For what?" she asked cautiously.

"For what I'm about to say."

Oh. With both curiosity and some fear, she considered the possibilities of what he might say. Maybe he wanted a discussion about the attraction. Or to discuss something about the touch that was still tingling her arm. Maybe he even intended to kiss her. Could that have been wishful thinking on her part?

"What?" she prompted when he didn't continue. Mercy. Her voice had way too much breath in it. She sounded like a lovesick schoolgirl.

"It has to do with the conversation I had with Ross Harland."

Oh, that. Faith hated that she'd anticipated anything not dealing with the case.

Beck moved closer to her again. Too close. "He was so adamant about not being Aubrey's father that I figured he was telling the truth about you two not having had sex." His voice was smooth and easy. No pressure, no expectations. He shrugged. "You can slap me for asking, and I doubt you'll answer, but at least tell me if Ross Harland might have anything to do with the murders."

That easy drawl took away some of the sting. "He doesn't."

He nodded. That was it. Beck's only reaction. He even seemed to believe her, which he should, since it was the truth.

The silence came. It was suddenly so quiet she could hear her own heartbeat in her ears. Seconds passed. Very slowly. While Beck and she just stood there and stared at each other.

"Is Ross Harland gay?" Beck finally asked.

She had no idea why that made her laugh, but it did. Maybe because Beck had lost the battle with curiosity after all. "No. He's not gay. And I don't know whether to be angry or flattered that you'd want to know so much about my sex life."

"Be flattered," he said, his voice all sex and sin.

She was. Flattered and suddenly very warm.

He leaned in, letting his mouth come very close to hers. Breath met breath. Her heart kicked into overdrive. So did her body.

She knew she should say something flippant and move away. But she didn't. "Beck," she warned.

But it sounded more like an invitation than anything else.

He didn't back away. Didn't heed her warning. He moved in for the kiss. His mouth brushed against hers. It was gentle. Nonthreatening. No demands.

It hit her like a boulder.

Faith felt the jolt. New sensations mixed with old ones that she thought she would never feel again. Leave it to Beck and his mouth to accomplish the impossible.

She leaned into him. Deepening the kiss with the pressure. He slid his hand around her neck, easing her closer. Inch by inch. Slowly, as if to give her a chance to escape. Beck was treating her like fine crystal.

And that kiss was melting her.

Faith heard herself moan. She felt the strength of his body. The fire was instant. The impact was so hard that she nearly lost her breath. She'd apparently already lost her mind. But then she broke the intimate contact and stepped back.

"I don't kiss a lot," she said, the words rushing out.

He cocked his head to the side. "Well, you should because you're good at it."

"No. I'm not." She didn't know what to do with her hands so she folded them over her chest.

His easy expression faded a bit. By degrees. Until it was replaced by confusion.

"I like to kiss," she clarified. Well, she liked to kiss Beck, anyway. "But kissing leads to other things. Like sex. Which we aren't going to have."

He lifted his left eyebrow. "You're right. Our relationship is too complicated for sex."

"Yet you still kissed me."

He shook his head, cursed under his breath and dragged his hand through his hair. "I don't know why. Maybe because I haven't been able to get you out of my mind since I saw you naked in the shower. But I know that kiss can't go any further than it just did."

She blinked. "You honestly believe that?"

"I have to believe it. We can't deal with the alternative right now. Aubrey's safety has to come first. Then this investigation. Once we catch this killer, then we can…talk. Or kiss. Or do something we'll really regret like have great sex."

But he waved off that last part. Too bad she couldn't wave off the effect it had on her body. The image of them having sex sizzled through her.

"So *this* is on hold," he continued. "Unless there's something you want to tell me now."

She wanted to. But it wasn't that easy. The truth would give him some answers. More questions, too. And it would open Pandora's box.

Beck was right. Aubrey's safety came first.

Faith was about to repeat that, but a blast tore through the room.

Chapter Seven

Someone had fired a shot at them.

The moment the sound of the bullet registered, Beck reacted.

He hooked his arm around Faith's waist and dragged her to the floor. She was already headed in that direction anyway, and they landed on the pile of sheets that'd been removed from the furniture. That cushioned their fall a little, but the new position didn't take them out of the line of fire.

Another bullet came at them and slammed into the wall just above their heads.

Hell.

Beck drew his weapon. "We have to move."

But where and how?

His initial assessment of the situation wasn't good. There'd been no broken glass, and that meant no broken windows. And no tripped motion detector, either. So the shooter had to be more than twenty feet away from the house and was literally shooting through the wall.

Probably with a high-powered rifle.

But it was the accuracy of the shot that caused Beck's stomach to knot. Both bullets had come entirely too close, especially considering there was no way the shooter could have a visual on them.

So, was the guy pinpointing them through some kind of eavesdropping device or had he managed to rig surveillance cameras that had given him an inside view of the house?

The third shot slammed into the wooden floor next to them and sent splinters flying. That was it. They couldn't stay there any longer.

"Let's go." Beck latched on to Faith's arm and got them running out of the living room. He needed to put another wall between them and the shooter.

Staying low, they raced toward the kitchen, the nearest room, but the shooter stayed in pursuit, and the bullets continued. Each blast followed them, tracking them as they made their way across the living room.

Beck shoved Faith ahead of him so that his body would give her some small measure of protection. It wasn't enough. They needed a barrier, something wide and thick. He spotted the fridge. It was outdated and fairly small, but he hoped the metal would hold back those bullets. He hauled Faith in front of it and shoved her to the linoleum floor.

The bullets didn't stop.

They tore through the kitchen drywall and shattered the tiny window over the kitchen sink. That set off the alarm, and the soft beeps began to pulse through the room. If the shooter moved to the back of the house, they'd be sitting ducks with that broken window.

"Call Sgt. Caldwell," Beck instructed Faith. He handed her his cell phone and kept his gun ready just in case the shooter decided to bash through a window or door and try to come into the house.

Beside him, he felt Faith trembling, and her voice trembled, too, as she made the call to the Ranger and told him that someone was shooting at them from the front of the house. She asked him to come immediately.

Faith had no sooner made that request when the angle of the shots changed.

The next two rounds came right at the refrigerator. The bullets slammed into the metal but thankfully didn't exit out the front. The accuracy of the shots, however, told Beck that the gunman wasn't just using a high-powered, long-range rifle but that it was likely equipped with some kind of thermal scope or camera.

That thermal device could be a deadly addition.

It was no doubt picking up their body heat, and that heat had given away their exact location. That's why the shots were aimed so closely at them.

Faith ended her call with the Ranger. Even though the overhead light wasn't on, there was enough moonlight for Beck to see the terror on her face.

"Aubrey," she said, flipping open the phone again. She frantically stabbed in the numbers, and a moment later over the deafening blasts, she said, "Marita, is Aubrey okay?"

Beck hadn't been truly afraid until that moment. Faith was silent, and he watched her expression, praying that the gunfire had been only for them and a second shooter hadn't gone to his house to make a simultaneous attack there.

"They're fine," she finally said. Faith let out a hoarse sob. Fear mixed with relief.

Beck shared that relief. For just a moment. And then the anger took over. How dare this shooter put Faith through this. This was a blatant attempt to kill her, but the fear of harm to her child was far, far worse.

"I'll get this guy," Beck promised her.

The shots stopped.

Just like that, there were no more blasts. The only sounds were their sawing breaths, the hum of the central heating and the beeps from the security alarm.

"Is it over?" Faith asked.

He caught onto her arm to stop her from trying to get up. "Maybe."

Beck left it at that, but her widened eyes let him know that she understood. This could be a temporary cease-fire, a lure to draw them out away from the fridge.

Or it could mean the shooter was moving to the back of the house.

Where he'd have a direct shot to kill them.

"We'll stay put," he said, not at all sure of his decision. It was a gamble either way.

"I want to go to Aubrey," Faith mumbled.

"I know. So do I."

Waiting was hell, but this was the best way he knew to keep Faith alive.

His cell phone rang, the sound slicing through the room. Faith quickly answered it.

"Sgt. Caldwell's nearby," she relayed to him a moment later. "He'll turn on his sirens and an infrared scanner."

The sirens started to sound almost immediately. They would almost certainly scare off a shooter, if the shooter was still around, that is. But maybe, just maybe, the infrared would help Caldwell spot the shooter so he could be apprehended and arrested.

Beck wanted to be outside, to help with the search. He wanted to be the one to catch this piece of slime. But he couldn't leave Faith because the shooter could use that opportunity to go after her.

So he waited. It seemed endless. But it was probably only a couple of minutes before the phone rang again. This time, Beck grabbed it and answered it.

"It's Caldwell," the Ranger said.

"Did you get him?" Beck snapped.

"No. Nothing showed up on the infrared."

Beck groaned. This couldn't happen. They couldn't let this guy get away.

"I'm taking Faith back to my house to stay with the Ranger there and the bodyguard," he told the Ranger. "And then I'm going after this SOB."

FAITH CHECKED THE TIME on the screen of her cell phone. It was ten o'clock. Not that late, but Beck had been out looking for the shooter for well over an hour.

Each minute had seemed like an eternity.

She paced in the family room but kept her movements light so she wouldn't disturb Marita and Aubrey, who were already in bed and hopefully sleeping. Aubrey certainly was. Faith had verified that just five minutes earlier when she peeked in on them in the guest room. Marita had her eyes closed, but Faith doubted the woman was truly asleep.

The shooting had put them all on edge.

Tracy was on the sofa, reading. The Ranger, Sgt. McKinney, was standing guard in the kitchen. Everything was quiet, but the tension was thick enough to taste.

Where was Beck? And why hadn't he checked in?

The silence was driving her crazy. She was imagining all sorts of things. Like he was lying somewhere shot. Or that he was being held hostage.

Because she was so caught up in those nightmarish thoughts, the sound of the phone ringing caused her to jump. "Hello?" Faith said as quickly as she could get the phone to her ear.

Silence.

That brought on some more horrible thoughts, and then she checked the caller ID. The person had blocked their number, and there was no reason for Beck to have done that.

"Who is this?" she asked.

Her alarmed tone obviously alerted Tracy, who got to her feet. She put her hand on the butt of the pistol that rested in her shoulder holster.

"It's me," the caller finally said.

Faith had no trouble recognizing that voice.

Nolan Wheeler.

Her stomach dropped to her knees from the shock of hearing him, but she welcomed this call. It was the first contact she'd had in years with a man she thought was a cold-blooded killer.

"Nolan," Faith said aloud so that Tracy would know what was going on. Tracy reacted. She went racing into the kitchen to tell Sgt. McKinney. Hopefully, they could do something to trace this call and pinpoint Nolan's location. "Did you take shots at me tonight?"

"Me? Of course not." He used his normal cocky tone,

but that didn't mean he was telling the truth. "I called about Sherry."

"What about her? She's dead. And I think you might be responsible."

"Not a chance. I didn't want her dead. She owed me money. Lots of it."

Faith was instantly skeptical. "How did that happen? You've never been one to have extra cash to lend anyone."

"I didn't exactly lend it to her. She stole my car and left a note, saying she was in a bind. She needed cash and needed it fast."

"Did she say why she needed money?" Faith asked.

"To gussy up." Nolan snickered. "Said she had to impress somebody, and she needed to look her best and that she'd pay me back. Killing her wouldn't get me the money so I've got no motive."

"What about the house? Did you think you could inherit it? Because you can't. I made a will, and there's no way you can ever inherit anything that's mine."

He made a tsk-tsk sound. "But I can inherit what's mine. Well, what was Sherry's anyway. Half of the place should have been hers after your mother was killed. Guess what, Faith? I want that half."

She fought to hang on to her temper. Flying off the handle now wouldn't solve anything. Besides, she wanted to give the Ranger more time to locate Nolan.

"Sherry and you separated eighteen months before her death," Faith reminded him. Even though their marriage was common law, Nolan probably did have a right to half of whatever Sherry owned. "And after the hell you put her through, you don't deserve anything from her estate."

"In the eyes of the law, I do. And you know the law, don't you?"

"I know it well enough that you won't see a penny."

"Oh, I want more than pennies," Nolan gloated. "A lot more. So here's the deal. You give me a hundred thousand dollars, and I'll go away."

Oh, mercy. "That's more than the place is worth, and besides, I don't have that kind of money."

"Then get it. Bye, Faith."

"Wait!" she said in a louder voice than she'd anticipated. This call couldn't end yet. "I need to know about Darin. Have you seen him?"

Nolan took his time answering. "He's around."

That was chilling, and despite the simple answer, it sounded like some kind of threat. "Where?"

"Don't worry about your brother. He can take care of himself."

"I'm not so sure of that, especially if you're manipulating him in some way." And if Nolan was in contact with her brother, then he was almost certainly manipulating him. "Where are you, Nolan?"

"Just get me that money," he said, ignoring her question.

Faith tried again. "Where are you?"

"I'm closer than you think, sweet cakes."

With that, Nolan hung up.

Faith looked in the doorway of the family room, where Tracy and the Ranger were standing. Sgt. McKinney took her phone and relayed the numbers to someone on the other end of his own cell-phone line.

A moment later, the sergeant shook his head. "The guy was using a prepaid cell phone. We couldn't trace it."

Faith didn't have time to groan because she heard the garage door open. Beck was home. And she raced to meet him. One look at his face, however, told her that he didn't have any better news than she did.

Beck took off his muddy cowboy boots and dropped them on the laundry-room floor. "I couldn't find the shooter."

Because he looked exhausted and beyond frustrated, Faith motioned for him to go into the family room so he could sit down. He smelled like the woods and sweat, and there were bits of dried leaves and twigs on his clothes.

"What about the shell casings?" Sgt. McKinney asked. "Caldwell called and said you'd found some at the scene."

"We did. They're Winchester ballistic silver tips." Beck looked at her. "They're used for long-range shooting. Coupled with what was probably a thermal camera or scope, I'm guessing the shooter had what we call a hog rifle. It's used for hunting wild hogs or boars at night."

"This type of weapon is rare?" she asked hopefully.

"Not around here. I know of at least a half dozen people who own one. Wild boars can be dangerous to people and livestock so they're usually hunted when they show up too close to the ranches."

Maybe Nolan had gotten his hands on one of these rifles. "Nolan Wheeler called a few minutes ago," she filled him in. "We couldn't trace the call."

The fatigue vanished. The concern returned. "What did he want?"

"Money. A hundred grand to be exact. He wants me to give him more than half of my inheritance. But he didn't tell me how I could find him."

I'm closer than you think.

She pushed aside the chill from remembering Nolan's final remark. "He'll call back." Faith was certain of that. "He'll want that cash. And maybe we can use it to draw him out."

Beck hesitated a moment. Then nodded. "But you won't be the one who's drawing him out. No more playing bait."

Faith was still too shaky to argue with him. Nor did she argue when Beck reached out and pulled her closer. That was all it took. That bit of comfort. And Faith felt the tears well up in her eyes.

"I could use a cup of coffee," Tracy said, and she hitched her shoulder toward the kitchen. "Why don't you join me?" she asked Sgt. McKinney.

Faith didn't mind the obvious ploy to leave her and Beck alone because the tears started to spill down her cheeks.

"I'm sorry," she mumbled.

Beck pulled her even closer to him and closed his arms around her. She took everything he was offering her, even though it was wrong. Beck had been through that shooting, too, and he wasn't falling apart.

"I'm not ashamed of crying," she said, wiping away the tears with the back of her hand. Beck wiped away the other cheek. "But I wish I wasn't doing this in front of you."

"Why?" With his fingers still on tear-wiping duty, he caught her gaze, and the corner of his mouth hitched. "Because I'm the enemy?"

"No. Because you're Beckett Tanner."

The smile didn't fully materialize, and his fingers stayed in place. Warm on her cheek. "What would that have to do with it?"

"I always wanted to impress you. Or at least get your attention in a good way." She blamed the confession on the adrenaline crash and the fatigue.

"You succeeded. You got my attention. Even back then, before you left town." He slid his fingers down her cheek to her chin and lifted it slightly. As if he were readjusting it for a kiss. "You were about sixteen, and I saw you coming out of the grocery store on Main. You were wearing this short red dress. Trust me, I noticed."

Faith was stunned. "So why didn't you ask me out or something?"

"Because you were sixteen and I was twenty. The term *jailbait* comes to mind. I decided it'd be best to wait a couple of years."

For a moment, she got a glimpse of what life could have been if there hadn't been the incident at the motel. Of course, Beck's family would have never accepted her, and besides, the attraction would have run its youthful course and burned out.

She looked at him again.

Maybe not.

His mouth came to hers. Just a brush of his lips, and then he pulled back. When his gaze met hers again, the trip down memory lane was over. He drew her into his arms again. But it had nothing to do with kisses or sex. He eased her onto the sofa and simply held her.

For some reason, it seemed more intimate than a real kiss.

"I'm a good cop," he said, his voice hardly more than a whisper. "But I've made mistakes. I nearly let you get killed tonight."

So he was feeling guilty, too. "You couldn't have known that was going to happen."

"Yes, I did. I should have nixed that bait plan right from the start."

"It worked out all right," she assured him. Though they both knew that was a lie. They'd have nightmares about this for years. "I would just leave town, but I'm afraid this monster will follow me."

He made a sound of agreement.

Faith's phone rang again. She jolted. Her body was still on full alert. The caller had blocked the number.

"Nolan again," she mumbled. She answered the call and held the phone between Beck and her so he could hear as well.

"Hello, Faith."

It was a man all right. But not Nolan.

"Darin?" Though it wasn't a question. She knew it was her brother's voice. "God, I've been so worried about you. Where are you?"

"I can't say." He sounded genuinely sad about not being able to tell her that detail. "I called to warn you. You're in danger."

"Yes. From Nolan." She moved to the edge of the sofa. "I think he tried to kill me tonight."

"Maybe. But watch out for the Tanners. You can't trust them, Faith. They want to hurt you."

She wasn't exactly surprised after what had happened at the hotel. "Who, Nicole Tanner?"

"All of them. The whole family. If Sherry was alive, she'd tell you the same. It's about those letters. Something went wrong with the letters."

Now she was surprised. "Darin, I don't understand— what letters? What do you mean?"

He stayed silent for several long moments. "Just be careful."

"Don't go," she said when she thought he was about to hang up. "I want to see you. Can we meet somewhere?"

That earned her a sharp look from Beck.

"No meeting," Darin insisted. "Not yet. It isn't safe. Not for you. Not for Aubrey."

"Aubrey?" Her breath practically froze in her throat.

Beck had a slightly different response. She saw the anger wash over him, and he tried to take the phone. She shook her head and eased her hand over the receiver. "He'll hang up if he knows you're listening," she mouthed.

"Aubrey's in danger because of the letters," Darin continued a moment later.

"Who has these letters?" Faith asked. "Nolan?"

"I don't know. Maybe."

If those letters contained something sinister, then Nolan was almost certainly involved. "Then I need to find him. Where is he?"

"He's here in LaMesa Springs."

Here.

I'm closer than you think.

And that meant Darin was probably in town, too.

"Yes, but where in LaMesa Springs?" Faith pressed.

"He's in the attic."

Faith flattened her hand over her chest to steady her heart. *Mercy, was Nolan here at Beck's house?* "What attic?" And she held her breath, waiting.

"At the house. Your house. He said the lock on the back door was broken so he went inside and climbed into the attic so he could wait for you. He got there before the cops and Rangers and then stayed quiet so they wouldn't hear him moving around."

"Darin?" Faith forced herself to talk. Nolan could be dealt with later. "I want to see you. Please."

But she was talking to herself. Her brother had already hung up.

Beck pulled out his own phone and jabbed in some numbers. Since the room was so quiet, Faith had no trouble hearing the man who answered. It was Sgt. Caldwell.

"Are you still at the Matthews house?" Beck asked the Ranger.

"Yeah. Why?"

"Check the attic. But be careful. One of our suspects, Nolan Wheeler, might be up there."

"I'll call you back," Caldwell let him know.

Beck hung up and looked at her. "Do you know anything about those letters Darin mentioned?"

She shook her head. This wasn't something she wanted to discuss right now. She wanted to know what was going on in that attic. But at least the conversation would keep her mind off the wait. Plus, this was im-

portant. "It sounded as if he believed they were connected to your family."

"Yeah, it did. But this is Darin, remember? He might
not be mentally stable right now. Still," Beck continued before she could say anything, "I'll call my father
in the morning and set up a meeting. I want to ask him
about the convenience store anyway."

With everything else that was going on, she'd nearly
forgotten about that. "I think it's pretty clear that he told
Pete and maybe even Nicole that I was back in town.
After all, your brother called you when I was still at
your office. That was only a couple of hours after the
rock throwing incident."

He mumbled another "yeah" and checked his watch.

"Sgt. Caldwell will be careful," she said more to
herself than Beck.

But she prayed nothing went wrong and that the
Ranger didn't get hurt. Besides, her brother could have
been wrong. Beck was right about Darin possibly being
delusional. God knows how much of what he said was
real or a product of his mental illness.

Beck's phone rang, and he answered it immediately.
He clicked on the speakerphone function.

"There's no one in the attic," Sgt. Caldwell explained.
"But someone's been here. There's a discarded fast-food
bag and graffiti."

"Kids maybe?" Beck asked.

"I don't think kids did this." His comment and tone
upped the chill coursing through her. "I used my camera phone to take some pictures of the walls. I'm sending four of them to you now."

Beck went to the phone menu and pressed a few buttons. The first picture started to load on the screen.

Yes, it was definitely the attic. And though she couldn't see the fast-food bag the sergeant had described, she could see the wall that he'd captured in the photograph. Someone had taken red paint—at least she hoped it was paint—and written on the rough wood planks.

It was a calendar of sorts, crudely drawn squares, some blank, some with writing inside. The dates went back to a month earlier. She couldn't make out the writing and motioned for Beck to go to the next picture. It was the square with the date November 11th.

Inside the box someone had written:

Sherry dies.

Faith swallowed hard. That was indeed the day Sherry had been killed. But anyone who knew her sister would have had that information.

The next picture showed the date. November 12th. The caption inside:

Annie dies.

Her mother's name was Annie, and like the previous caption, it was correct. Her mother had been murdered then.

Picture three was dated January 12th with the words:

Faith's homecoming.

Yes, she had come home then. And someone had thrown rocks through her window.

God, had Nolan been there that whole time, waiting for her, watching her? The security had been set up to keep anyone from getting in, but what if he was already inside?

Beck clicked another button and the final picture loaded. There was a date: January 14th.

Tomorrow's date.

And beneath it were two words that caused her to gasp.

Faith dies.

Chapter Eight

Faith was not going to die today.

Beck wouldn't let that happen.

It riled the hell out of him to think of the death threat that'd been left in her attic. It had shaken Faith to the core. Immediately after seeing those pictures on the phone, she'd sat motionless in his arms while he rattled off how he was going to put an end to this.

The handwriting and fast-food bag would be analyzed. That was a given. As would the shell casings collected from the attack the night before. But there was something else Beck could do. He could keep Faith away from her house. If he didn't let her out of his sight, he could protect her.

He hoped that'd be enough.

So, after giving her all the assurance he could, he'd sent her off to bed, where he was sure she hadn't gotten any sleep. He certainly hadn't. But that didn't matter. He could sleep later. Right now, he had to solve the case. The devil was in the details, and there was one detail he could further investigate.

He'd already called his father at the family ranch and asked about the encounter with the taxi driver at the convenience store and the mysterious letters that

Darin had mentioned to Faith. His father had become defensive, saying that it wasn't a good time to talk, but Beck didn't think it was his imagination that his dad was confused about those letters. Surprised, even. Maybe that meant his family had nothing to do with any potential evidence.

Maybe.

Since Pete and Nicole also lived on the grounds of the ranch, Beck would extend his questions to them and have that chat about giving Faith a much-needed break.

Beck got up from the kitchen table and poured himself another cup of coffee. He could hear the TV in the family room, where Tracy was having her breakfast. She was alone since the Ranger had left to assist with the processing of the crime scene at Faith's house. Beck had wanted to be part of that, but not at the expense of leaving Faith and Aubrey.

Before he could return to his seat and his case notes, he heard soft uneven footsteps. A moment later, Aubrey appeared. She was wearing a yellow corduroy dress and no shoes, just socks with lace at the tops.

She smiled and waved at him.

Just like that, the weight of the world seemed to leave his shoulders. "Good morning," he told her.

She babbled something with several syllables and went straight to him. "Up, up," she said.

Beck set his coffee aside and out of her reach, and he picked her up. Aubrey rewarded him with a hug and kiss on the cheek.

"She's faster than she used to be," Marita said, hurrying in. The nanny stopped and eyed them. "And she seems to think you're her new best friend."

There was worry in the woman's tone. Beck understood that. Faith had probably told her about their bitter past, but as far as Beck was concerned, that wasn't going to play a part in how he felt about his new best friend.

"Anything come back on that stuff you found in her attic?" Marita asked, helping herself to a cup of coffee. "Faith just told me about all of that while she was getting dressed."

So that's where she was. Beck had hoped she was still in bed. "We'll try to link the writing to Nolan Wheeler."

Marita flexed her eyebrows and had a sip of coffee. "Or Faith's brother."

Beck nodded and realized that Aubrey was studying him with those intense, cocoa-brown eyes. The little girl finally reached out and pinched his nose. She giggled. And Beck wondered how anyone could be in a bad mood around this child.

From the doorway, Faith stepped into view, studying him. She'd put on a pair of dark brown pants and a coppery top that was nearly the same color as her eyes. She'd pulled her shoulder-length hair into ponytail, a style that made him think of fashion models.

And kissing her neck.

He frowned, hating how he couldn't control those thoughts that kept popping into his head.

"I fixed some eggs," Beck let Marita and Faith know. He considered asking Faith how she was, but he knew the answer. Her eyes said it all. She was troubled and weary. Fear and adrenaline could do that.

Marita went to the stove and lifted the lid to a terra-cotta server. "This looks good. Really good."

"I put in a little smoked sausage and Asiago cheese." He got a little uncomfortable when both women stared at him. "I left some plain for Aubrey. If she can eat eggs, that is. I wasn't sure."

Great. Now he was babbling and sounding like a contestant on some cooking or parenting show.

Thankfully, Marita quit staring at him as if he had a third eye. She dished up some eggs and sampled them. "Mmm. A man who can cook. I think I'm in love," she joked.

"It's a hobby," Beck explained.

Faith smiled. An actual real smile. And that made all of his discomfort worth it. He wasn't embarrassed about his hobby, but it wasn't exactly something a man with his true Texas upbringing liked to brag about. Barbecuing steaks was one thing, but stove cooking and a cowboy image didn't always mesh.

It didn't take long, however, for Faith's smile to fade. "Anything new on the investigation?"

Yeah. And it was news she wasn't going to like. "There were no prints on the rocks and no match on the shoe impression. The sole was too worn to come up with anything distinguishable. Also, the track could have been there a day or two. It wasn't necessarily made by the rock thrower."

Faith stayed quiet, processing that information.

Aubrey pointed to the window, obviously wanting to go closer and look out, but Beck moved her farther away from it. The danger was just too great to do normal things, and if a gunman could shoot into Faith's house, he could do the same to Beck's if he found out Faith and Aubrey were there. He couldn't let that happen.

Marita dished up a small plate of plain eggs, took a spoon from the drawer and reached for Aubrey. "Why don't I feed this to her in the family room so you two can talk?"

When the nanny took Aubrey from him, Beck immediately felt the loss. So did Aubrey—her mouth tightened into a rosebud pout as Marita carted her away.

"You look…disappointed," Faith commented.

"I think being around Aubrey makes me think about being a father. I'm thirty-two. Guess this weird gut feeling is the equivalent of my biological clock ticking."

Great. Now he was talking biological clocks after his cooking babble. He might have to go wrestle a longhorn to get back his manly image.

Faith lifted an eyebrow. "You want to be a father?"

Her astonished expression and tone stung. "You don't think I'd be a good dad?"

"No. I think you'd be very good at it." Faith walked closer and poured some coffee. She smelled like peach-scented shampoo. "I'm just a little surprised, that's all."

Another shrug. He tipped his head to the family room, where he could hear Aubrey babbling. "What can I say? I've decided I want a child."

Actually, he wanted Aubrey.

Why did he feel such a strong connection to that little girl? Maybe because he was starting to feel a strong connection to Aubrey's mother.

Beck looked at Faith then, just as her gaze landed on him. Uh-oh. There it was again. The reminder of that kiss.

She moistened her lips, causing his midsection to clench. He had to move away from her, or he was going to kiss her again. But Faith beat him to it. She leaned in and brushed her mouth over his.

"Mmm," she mumbled. That sound went straight through him. "I shouldn't want you."

He smiled. God knows why. There wasn't anything to smile about. He was getting daddy fever, and he wanted Faith in his bed. Or on the floor.

Location was optional.

Because he was crazed with lust, Beck did something totally stupid. He hooked his arm around her waist and eased her to him. Body against body. It was a good fit. The heat just slid right through him.

"Does saying 'I shouldn't want you' make you want me less?" he asked, making sure it sounded like a joke.

"No." That wasn't a joking tone. A heavy sigh left her mouth. "It's complicated, Beck."

He was aware of that. But something was holding her back other than what'd happened in their past. "Want to tell me about it?"

He saw the hesitation in her eyes. "You'll want to sit down for this," she finally said.

Beck silently groaned. This sounded like trouble.

Before either of them could sit at the kitchen table, he heard the doorbell. It was almost immediately followed by a knock.

Beck snatched his gun from the top of the fridge. "Take Marita and Aubrey and go into the bedroom," he instructed.

Faith gave a shaky nod and started toward the family room. She didn't have to go far. Marita was carry-

ing Aubrey, and she was headed back into the kitchen.
Tracy was right on their heels.

"Try to keep Aubrey quiet," Faith told them. She
began to pick up the toys that'd been left in the room.

There was another ring of the doorbell. Another
knock. Beck hurried to see who his impatient visitor
was, but before he could get to the door, the key slid into
the lock. He took aim. The door flew open.

His father was standing there.

Pete was behind him.

"Hell." Beck lowered his gun and cursed some more.
His father had obviously not waited and used his emer-
gency key to get in. "It's not a good time for a visit.
We'll have to get together later."

His father eyed the gun. Then Beck. But Pete looked
past Beck, and his attention landed on Faith. She had
various toys clutched in her hands and was apparently
headed to the bedroom. She froze.

"What's she doing here?" Pete demanded.

His father didn't let Beck answer, and he gave Pete
a sharp warning look. "Maybe this is a good thing. She
can probably clear up some of this mess."

Beck had no idea what *mess* his father was talking
about, but he had a massive problem on his hands. His
family now knew Faith's whereabouts, and unless he
could convince them to keep quiet—and trust them
to do so—then he was going to have to find a new location to use as a safe house. But he'd have to do that
later. Right now, he needed to deal with the situation.

"What's this about?" Beck asked.

His father and brother stepped in and shut the door.
"When you called earlier, you wanted to know if I knew

anything about some letters that had to do with Sherry Matthews," Roy said. "Well, I do."

Beck was poleaxed. This was another unwanted surprise. Beck had expected his father to have no idea about that particular subject. "What do you mean?"

Roy pulled out a large manila envelope he had tucked beneath his arm. "These letters."

Beck placed his gun on top of the cabinet that housed the TV. Hoping this wasn't something that would lead to his father's arrest, he grabbed a Kleenex from the box on the end table, and he used a tissue so that he wouldn't get his prints on what might be evidence.

Still clutching the toys, Faith walked closer and watched as Beck took out the letters.

"Two and a half months ago, Sherry came out to the ranch to see Pete and me," Roy explained. "He wasn't there so I talked to her alone. She wanted money."

"Two and a half months ago?" Beck repeated. "That was just a couple of weeks before she was murdered."

"A week," Roy corrected. "She was very much alive when she left, but she said she was in big trouble. That she owed someone some money."

"Nolan," Faith supplied. "She called me about that same time, and I told her I couldn't lend her any more. I told her to work it out with Nolan."

"She didn't," Roy informed her. "Sherry said if Pete didn't give her ten grand in cash, then she was going to tell Nicole that she was having an affair with him. She said she'd tell Nicole she was having an affair with me, too."

Beck felt every muscle in his body go stiff. He waited for his father to deny it. He didn't. But Pete did.

"They were bald-faced lies," Pete volunteered. "Sherry didn't wait around to say those lies to my face. She left, and a day later, the first letter arrived."

Roy nodded. "When I came out of the grocery store, it was tucked beneath the windshield wiper of my truck." He pointed to the letter in question.

The envelope simply had "Pete and Roy" written on it. No "to" or "from" address. Still using the tissue as a buffer, Beck took out the letter itself. One page. Typed. No handwritten signature. No date. No smudges or obvious fingerprints.

However, the envelope had obviously been sealed at one time, and since it was the old-fashioned lick-and-press kind, he might be able to have that tested for DNA to prove if Sherry had indeed sent it. At this point, he had no reason to doubt that she was the sender, but it was standard procedure to test that sort of thing.

Not that his family had followed procedure.

They should have brought the letters to him, and maybe he could have prevented the murders.

"I need that money," Beck read aloud. "You two owe it to me, and if I don't have that ten thousand dollars by Friday, I'm calling Nicole. Miss Priss won't be happy to hear you're both sleeping with me again, and this time I have proof. Sherry."

Again.

That word really jumped out at him. Maybe it was a reference to the motel incident. Or maybe this was something more recent. If his brother could lie about the first, he could probably lie about the second. But where did that leave his father? Had he slept with Sherry, too?

"Sherry called after the first letter," Pete explained.

"I told her I wasn't going to give her a dime. The next day, the second letter was in the mailbox."

The second letter was typed like the first, but this one contained a copy of a grainy photo. It appeared to be Pete, sleeping, his chest bare and a sheet covering his lower body. Sherry was also in the shot, and it was a photo she'd obviously taken herself since Beck could see her thumb in the image. She was smiling as if she knew that this photo would be worth big bucks.

"That's not me in the picture," Pete insisted. "It's some guy she got who looks like me."

Maybe. It wasn't clear. It, too, would have to be tested and perhaps could be enhanced to get a better image.

"This is your last chance," Beck read aloud from the second letter. "If I don't have the money by tomorrow at six o'clock, a copy of this picture will go to Nicole. Leave the cash with my mom at the liquor store."

"When he got the second letter, I told Pete that maybe we should just pay Sherry off," his father explained. "I didn't care what people thought about me, but I just didn't want Nicole involved in this."

Since blackmailers were rarely satisfied with one payoff, Beck ignored that faulty reasoning and went on to the third letter. It was similar to the others, but this time Sherry demanded fifty thousand dollars, not ten. There was no copy of a photo, only the threat to spill all to Nicole.

"Why didn't you tell me about these letters before?" Beck asked.

"Because I wouldn't let him," Pete spoke up. "I wanted to handle it myself. And I didn't want anyone to know. I didn't want this to get back to Nicole. All it would have taken is for one of your deputies to let it slip, and this wouldn't have stayed private very long."

"I wouldn't have shown this to my deputies." His family must have known that was true, which made Pete's excuse sound even less plausible. But Beck couldn't doubt Pete's motives completely. He would have done anything to prevent Nicole from knowing. His brother might have a loose zipper, but he was obsessed enough with his wife that he would do anything to keep her from being hurt.

Pete pointed to Faith. "I think she was in on this blackmail scheme of her sister's. I think she knew all about it."

"I didn't," Faith said at the same moment that Beck said, "She didn't."

His comment got him stares from all three. "Faith's been upfront with me about this case. Unlike you two," Beck added. "You should have come forward with these and told me about Sherry's visit."

Not that it would have helped him catch the killer. But it would have given Beck the whole picture. Of course, it would have also made his brother and father suspects in Sherry's and her mother's murders.

Hell.

First that gun incident with Nicole. Now this. He might have to arrest a Tanner or two before this was over.

"Faith's brainwashed you," his father decided.

"That's not brainwashing," Pete piped in. "She's using her body to blur the lines. It's what the Matthews women are good at."

Beck slowly laid the letter aside and stared down his brother. "How do you know that?"

"What the hell does that mean?" Pete's nostrils flared.

"Were you having an affair with Sherry?"

Pete cursed. "I won't dignify that with an answer."

"Why, because it's true?"

Roy caught onto Pete's arm when his son started to bolt toward Beck. "If your brother says he wasn't sleeping with that woman, then he wasn't."

The denial didn't answer the questions. "Then why would Sherry say it? Why would she have that picture? And why would she try to blackmail you?"

"Because she's a lying tramp, just like her sister." Pete jabbed his finger at Faith again.

That did it. Beck was tired of this. He put the letters aside, went to the door and opened it. "Both of you are leaving now. Once I've processed these letters, I'll let you know if I'm going to file any charges against you."

"Charges?" his father practically yelled. "For what, trying to be discreet? Trying to protect my family from a liar and schemer?"

Beck reminded himself that he was speaking to his father and tried to keep his voice level. "The Rangers could construe this as obstruction of justice."

Roy looked as if he'd slugged him. "Don't do this, son. Don't choose this woman over your own family."

"It's not about Faith. I'm the sheriff. It's my job to investigate all angles of a double murder." He ushered them out, closed the door and locked it.

Faith dropped Aubrey's toys onto the floor. She blew out a long breath and rubbed her hands against the sides of her pants. "I always say I'm not going to let your family get to me."

But they had. And Beck hated that.

Even though she had her chin high and was trying to look strong, Beck went to her and pulled her into his arms. He brushed a kiss on her forehead.

"I didn't know Sherry tried to blackmail Pete and Roy," she volunteered. "I didn't know anything about the letters until Darin mentioned them last night."

"I believe you. If you'd known, you would have told me."

He felt her go stiff, and she eased back to meet his gaze. She shook her head, and he got the sinking feeling that he was about to hear another confession that would cause his blood pressure to spike.

"I have to move Aubrey," she said. "Now that your father and brother know she's here, she can't stay."

She was right. Keeping Aubrey safe had to be at the top of their list.

He nodded. "I have a friend who's the sheriff over in Willow Ridge. I'll call him and see if he can set up a place for all of you there."

"No. Not me. I can't go with her. The danger is tied to me, not her. If I get her away from me, then she'll be safe. But if she stays with me, she could be hurt."

Beck wanted to shoot holes in that theory, but he couldn't. "Are you sure you can be away from her?"

"No. I'm not. I'll miss her. But I can't risk another shooting with her around." She blinked back tears. "You can trust this friend?"

"I can trust him," Beck assured her.

He let go of her so he could start making the necessary arrangements. Beck walked toward his office, and Faith went into the bedroom to tell the others that they'd be moving.

She was keeping something from him.

Damn it.

Here, he'd just blasted his family for withholding evidence and information. He'd given Faith a carte blanche approval when defending her. But she obviously had some kind of secret. Was it connected to the murders?

It must at least be connected to Sherry or Darin.

And that meant he'd have to deal with it as soon as he made arrangements for the safe house. He also needed to call the bank and find out if his father or brother had recently withdrawn a large sum of money. Beck hated to doubt them, but he had to think like a lawman.

It was possible that one of them had taken the cash to Sherry to pay her off. Maybe an argument had broken out. Maybe one of them had accidentally killed Sherry. Then maybe Sherry's mother had been killed because she suspected the truth. Or might she have been a witness to her daughter's murder?

Beck groaned and scrubbed his hand over his face. Oh, man. He hated to even consider that, but it was possible. He only hoped it didn't turn out to be the truth.

His phone rang, and when he checked the caller ID screen, he saw that it was from the sheriff's office.

"It's me, Corey," his deputy greeted him when Beck answered. "You're never going to guess who just showed up here at your office."

After the morning from Hades that he'd just had, Beck was almost afraid to ask. "Who?"

"Our murder suspect, Nolan Wheeler. And he's demanding to see you and Faith. Now."

Chapter Nine

Faith could feel her heart breaking. Letting her daughter go was not what she wanted to do. She wanted Aubrey with her.

But more than that, she needed her child to be safe.

For that to happen, she had to say goodbye, even if it made her ache.

"It'll be okay," Beck assured her. Again. He'd been saying that and other reassuring things for the past three hours, since they'd started the preparations to move Aubrey and Marita to a safer location.

Faith wanted to believe him, especially since she didn't feel as if she had a choice. The killer had seen to that.

She kissed Aubrey again and strapped her into the car seat in Beck's SUV. Marita and Tracy were already seated, as was Sgt. Caldwell, who would be driving them to the sheriff's house in Willow Ridge. The Ranger had already promised her that he would take an indirect route to make sure no one followed. Every precaution would be taken. And he'd call her as soon as they arrived.

Faith's heart was still breaking.

Aubrey waved, first to Faith. Then to Beck, who

was standing behind her. The little girl gave them both a grin, looked at Beck and said, "Dada."

Her words were crystal clear.

Faith stepped back and met Beck's gaze. "I have no idea why she said that."

He shrugged. "One of the books I read her yesterday had the word *daddy* in it. Guess she picked it up from there."

Relief washed through Faith. She didn't want Beck to think she'd coached Aubrey into saying that. Their lives were already complicated enough without adding those kind of feelings to the mix. But it was clear that her little girl was very fond of Beck.

Beck leaned in, kissed Aubrey's cheek. Faith added another kiss of her own, and Beck shut the door. They backed into the mudroom, and only then did the Ranger open the garage door.

Somehow, Faith managed not to cry when they drove away.

"We need to go to the station and deal with Nolan," Beck reminded her.

As much as she loathed the idea of seeing Nolan Wheeler, it'd get her mind off Aubrey, and would keep Nolan occupied while Aubrey was being transported to the new safe house.

"You don't have to see him," Beck said, heading toward the other vehicle, a police cruiser, that one of his deputies had driven over earlier. He had the manila envelope with Sherry's blackmail letters tucked beneath his arm, and he laid it on the console next to him. "You can wait in my office while I interrogate Nolan."

"Right," she mumbled. Faith got into the passenger's seat and strapped on the belt. "I'm doing this."

"You're sure?" Beck started the cruiser, drove out and closed the garage door behind him. "I told Corey to put Nolan in a holding cell and test him for gunshot residue. That was three hours ago. Nolan will be good and steamed by now that we didn't jump at his invitation to meet with him immediately."

Yes, but there was an upside to that. "With his short temper, maybe he'll be angry enough to tell us what we want to know."

And maybe that info would lead to an arrest. Preferably Nolan's. Faith wanted there to be enough physical evidence to prove Nolan had murdered her mother and sister. Then she could bring her little girl home and get on with her life.

Part of that included coming clean with Beck.

She needed to do that as soon as this meeting with Nolan was over and they had some downtime. She'd told Beck lies, both directly and by omission. He wouldn't appreciate that—it would put a wedge between them, just when they were starting to make some headway.

Faith touched her fingertips to her lips and remembered the earlier kiss. That kiss wasn't ordinary, but the truth was, it couldn't mean anything. It couldn't lead to something more serious. Still, she fantasized about the possibilities. What if all their problems were to magically disappear? And what if Beck could forgive her for lying to him?

Would they have a chance?

She silently cursed. She had enough on her plate without complicating things with a relationship.

"Having second thoughts?" Beck asked.

Faith looked at him. He glanced at her with those sizzling blue eyes and gave her a quick smile. He was very good with those smiles. They were part reassurance, all sex.

Wishing the attraction would go away wasn't working, and that meant she was fast on her way to a broken heart. She hadn't returned to town for that, but it seemed as inevitable as the white-hot attraction between them.

Beck pulled into a parking space directly in front of the back entrance to the sheriff's office. But he didn't reach for the door. He glanced around the parking lot before his eyes came back to her.

"I need to talk to you when we're done here," she said.

He stared at her, and for a moment she thought he was going to insist that conversation happen now. But he didn't. He glanced around the parking lot again and nodded. "Let's go inside. We'll talk later."

Beck ushered her into the break room and through the hall that led to the offices and the front reception.

Deputy Winston met them. "Glad you're here. Our *guest* is complaining."

"I'll bet he is," Beck commented. "What about the GSR test?"

"It was negative." Corey looked at her. "Probably means he wasn't the one who shot at you."

"Or it could mean he washed his hands in the past twelve hours," Beck disagreed.

Corey shrugged and hitched his thumb to the right. "I was watching the security camera and saw you drive up. I just took Nolan to the interview room. He's waiting for you."

Beck handed Corey the manila envelope. "I need you to process this as possible evidence in the Matthews murders. There are three letters inside. Use latex gloves when you handle them, then copy them and send the originals to the crime lab. I want the DNA analyzed and all the pages and envelopes processed for prints and trace."

Corey studied the envelope. "Where'd you get this?"

A muscle flickered in Beck's jaw. "My father and my brother. Once the letters are processed, I'll have them make official statements."

So there might be charges against his family members after all. Faith hated that Beck had to go through this and hated even more that she had to meet with Nolan. He wouldn't willingly give up anything that would incriminate himself. Still, a long shot was unfortunately their best shot.

Faith was familiar enough with the maze of rooms and offices that constituted the LaMesa Police Department. When she was sixteen, she'd had to come and pick up her mother after she'd been arrested for public intoxication. The holding cell had been in the center of the building, but this was Faith's first trip to the west corridor. The walls were stone-gray and bare, unlike Beck's office, which was dotted with colorful Texas landscapes, photos and books.

There were no books or photos in the interview room, either. Just more bare, gray walls and a heavy metal table where Nolan was seated. Waiting for them.

Nolan stood when they entered, and Faith caught just

a glimpse of his perturbed expression before it morphed into a cocky smile. The man hadn't changed a bit. His overly highlighted hair was too long, falling unevenly on his shoulders, and his stubble had gone several days past being fashionable. Ditto for his jeans, which were ripped at the knees and flecked with stains.

"You're looking good there, sweet cakes," he greeted her. Nolan's oily gaze slid over her, making her feel the urgent need to take a bath.

Faith didn't return his smile. "You're looking like the scum you are."

"Oh, come on." He pursed his mouth, bunched up his forehead and made a show of looking offended. "Is that any way to talk to your own brother-in-law?"

"My sister's abusive ex-live-in," she corrected. "You left a death threat for me in the attic of my house."

"It wasn't me. It was your brother." Nolan put his index finger near his right temple and made a circling motion. "Darin's loco."

Beck walked closer and stood slightly in front of her. Protecting her, again. Nolan didn't miss the little maneuver either. His cat green eyes lit up as if he'd witnessed something he might like to gossip about later.

"Have you two buried the hatchet?" Nolan asked.

"I rechecked your alibis for the nights of the murders," Beck said, ignoring Nolan's too-personal question. "They're weak."

Nolan shrugged and idly scraped his thumbnail over a loose patch of paint on the table. "I was at the Moonlight Bar in downtown Austin both times, nearly twenty miles from where Sherry lived. People saw me there."

"Yes, but those same people can't say exactly when

you left. You had time to leave the Moonlight and get to both locations to commit both murders." Beck met him eye-to-eye. "So did you kill Sherry and Annie Matthews?"

"No." Nolan smiled again and sank back down onto the chair. "And you must believe that or I would have been arrested, not just detained."

"The day's not over," Beck grumbled. He pulled out a chair for Faith and one for himself. Both of them sat across from Nolan. "Where were you last night?"

"Any particular time that interests you?" Nolan countered.

"All night."

"Hmm. Well, I got up around noon, ate and watched some TV. Around six, I dropped by the Moonlight and hung out with some friends. I left around midnight."

Beck shook his head. "Can anyone confirm that?"

"Probably not." Nolan winked at her. "You really think I'd want to put a bullet in you? I've always liked you, Faith." Again, he combed that gaze over her.

The glare that Beck aimed at the man could have been classified as lethal. "I want your clothes bagged. My deputy will give you something else to wear."

Nolan lifted his left eyebrow. "And if I say no?"

"I'll make a phone call to Judge Reynolds and have a warrant here in ten minutes. Then I'll have you stripped and searched—thoroughly. Ever had a body cavity search, Nolan?"

For the first time since they'd walked into the room, Nolan actually looked uncomfortable.

"I also want a DNA sample," Beck added.

Faith felt her stomach tighten.

"Why?" Nolan challenged. "I heard there was no unidentified DNA at the crime scenes."

There wasn't, but there might be DNA in her attic. However, it wasn't the prospect of that match that was making her squirm.

"I want to make some DNA comparisons." Beck made it seem routine. "If you're innocent, you have nothing to worry about."

Nolan shifted in the chair. "Are you taking Darin's DNA and his clothes to test them for *comparisons?*"

"I would if I could find him."

"Maybe I can help you with that." Nolan let that hang in the air for several snail-crawling seconds. "He calls me a lot. And, no, you can't trace the number. He bought one of those cheapskate disposable phones. But when he calls again, I think I can talk him into meeting with you." Nolan was looking at her, not Beck, when he said that.

"If you believed you could arrange a meeting, then why haven't you already done it?" Faith asked.

"No good reason to."

"He's a murder suspect," Beck pointed out. "The police and the Rangers have been looking for Darin for two months."

"No skin off my nose." Nolan turned to her again. "But I'll do it. I'll set up a meeting, as a favor to you."

He probably thought this would make her more amicable about splitting the inheritance with him. And maybe she would be. If her brother was guilty. And if it got Darin off the street. But Faith wasn't at all convinced that Darin had committed these crimes.

"Set up the meeting if you can," Faith finally said.

She stood. "Once I've talked with Darin, then and only then will I discuss anything else with you."

"Deal," Nolan readily agreed. "But one way or another, I'm getting that money. I don't care who I have to turn over to our cowboy cop friend here." Nolan flashed another smile before turning to Beck. "So am I free to go, after you get my clothes and my DNA?"

"Not just yet. Why don't you hang around for a while." It wasn't exactly a request.

Nolan's smile went south. "You can't hold me, Beckett Tanner. I got myself a lawyer, and she said there's not enough evidence for an arrest."

"Then I'll hold you here until your lawyer shows up," Beck informed him.

Faith didn't say anything until they were outside the room. "A good lawyer will have him out in just a few hours," she whispered.

"Well, that's a few hours that he won't be free to roam around and terrorize you." Beck walked to the reception, where Corey was waiting. "I want his clothes and his DNA, and I want it all sent to the crime lab ASAP."

"Will do. Are we locking him up?"

Beck nodded. "Until his lawyer shows. Maybe by then one of his alibis will fall through. The Rangers have put out feelers to see if anyone noticed Nolan leaving the bar in time to commit the murders. Or the shooting last night."

Corey grabbed an evidence kit from the supply cabinet behind him, and he strolled in the direction of the interview room.

Beck turned to Faith. "You really think Nolan can set up a meeting with your brother, or was that all hot air?"

"Maybe. Darin and Nolan aren't friends, but they did get along. Well, better than Nolan got along with the rest of us."

"Then maybe the meeting will pan out." Beck paused. "You flinched when I told Nolan I wanted a DNA sample."

"Did I?" Though she knew she had.

"You did." He blew out a deep breath and put his hands on his hips. "Nolan flirted with you in there. I thought there'd be more animosity. I thought I'd see more hatred in his eyes. But there wasn't any."

It took a moment for all that to sink in, and Faith was certain she flinched again. "What are you saying?"

But he didn't have time to answer. The front door flew open, and Nicole walked in. Faith automatically looked for a gun, but the woman appeared to be unarmed. Still, that didn't make this a welcome visit. She'd had more than enough of Beck's family today. Because of his father and brother's impromptu visit, Aubrey had had to go to a safe house.

"Her brother stole from me," Nicole announced.

That got Faith's attention, and she changed her mind about this visit. It might turn out to be a good thing. "You've seen Darin?"

But Nicole didn't answer her. Instead, she turned her attention to Beck. "That killer was at the ranch." She shuddered. "He was there and could have murdered us all."

"Let's go into my office," Beck suggested.

Faith silently agreed. Though they were the only ones

in the reception area, it still wasn't the place to have a private discussion.

"I don't want to go into your office," Nicole insisted, and she wouldn't budge. "I want you to make her tell us where her creepy brother is so you can arrest him before he murders me like he did his mother and sister."

Beck held up his hands. "Faith doesn't know where Darin is. No one does. Now what happened to make you think Darin wants to kill you, and what exactly did he steal?"

"He took a tranquilizer gun from the medical storage room in the birthing barn."

Faith pulled in her breath. A tranquilizer gun had been used to incapacitate both her mother and sister before they'd been strangled.

"I have proof," Nicole continued. She pulled a disk from her purse and slapped it onto the reception counter. "He's there, right on the security surveillance. He took it two and a half months ago, just days before the murders. He knew where it was because we've kept it in the same place for years, and as you well know, he used to work at the ranch part-time before all that mess at the motel."

Oh, mercy.

If this was true, it didn't sound good. Right up until the time of the murders, her brother had worked on and off as a delivery man for Doc Alderman, the town's only vet. The police had investigated the vet's supplies, but he could account for both of the tranquilizer guns in his inventory. Neither of those guns had prints or DNA from her brother. It was the bit of hope that Faith had clung to that Nolan had perhaps used a tranquilizer gun to set up Darin.

"And you just now noticed this tranquilizer gun was missing?" Faith asked.

Nicole still didn't look at her. She aimed her answer at Beck. "We haven't had to use it in ages. One of the ranch hands went in there to get it this morning to sedate one of the mares, and that's when we realized it was missing. Darin Matthews took it."

"That's on this disk?" Beck picked it up by the edges.

"It's there. It took me a while to find it. The security system in the storage room is motion-activated, and since the ranch hands hardly go in there, the disk wasn't full. I played it, and I saw Darin."

"You're sure it was him?" Beck asked before Faith could.

"Positive. You can see his face as clear as day."

"And you can see him take the tranquilizer gun?" Beck pressed.

Nicole dodged his gaze. "Not exactly. He moved in front of the camera, but what else would he have been doing in there?"

"Maybe delivering something for Dr. Alderman?" Faith immediately suggested. "Did you check with the vet to find out if he'd sent Darin out there to the ranch?"

"He had," Nicole said through clenched teeth. "Even though I'd told Alderman that I didn't want Darin anywhere near us."

"So maybe Darin was just delivering supplies," Beck concluded.

"Then what happened to the tranquilizer gun?"

"It could have been misplaced. Or someone else could have stolen it."

Anger danced through Nicole's cool blue eyes. "You're standing up for her again."

"I'm standing up for the truth," Beck corrected.

Her perfectly manicured index finger landed against his chest. "You're standing up for the Matthews family. I don't understand why. You know what they've done to us. The cheating, the lies."

"Pete cheated that night, too," Beck countered.

The color drained from Nicole's face, and she dropped back a step. "I expected this from the likes of her. But not from you." And with that, Nicole turned on her heels and hurried out the door.

Faith stood there silently a moment and tried to hold on to her composure. "Thank you," she said to Beck.

He turned and faced her. But he seemed unmoved by her gratitude. "I'll look at this disk," he said, his words short and tight. "And if there's any hint that Darin or anyone else stole that gun, I'll send it to the crime lab."

She nodded. "I expected that. I never expected you to give my brother a free ride. If Darin's guilty, I'll do whatever's necessary to catch him, and I'll support your decision to arrest him."

He searched her eyes, as if trying to decide if she was telling him the truth. Then he motioned for her to follow him to his office.

Faith did, and her heartbeat sped up with each step. The moment he made it into his office, Beck turned around to face her again.

"After watching the way Nolan reacted to you, I need to know." But he didn't ask it right away. He waited a moment, with the tension thick between them. "Is Nolan Aubrey's father?"

There it was. The question she'd been dreading.

Well, one of them anyway.

"Is he Aubrey's father?" Beck demanded when she didn't answer.

Faith shook her head, stepped farther inside and shut the door. "Maybe."

"Maybe? Maybe!" That was all he said for several seconds. Seconds that he spent drilling her with those intense and suddenly angry eyes. "You don't know who fathered your own child?"

"No, I don't."

Faith took a deep breath and braced herself for the inevitable fallout that would follow. "Because I'm not Aubrey's biological mother."

Chapter Ten

Beck dropped into the chair behind his desk, squeezed his eyes shut and groaned.

"I know, I should have told you sooner," Faith said. "But I had my reasons for keeping it a secret."

He slowly opened his eyes and pegged her gaze. "I'm listening." Though he was almost positive he wouldn't like what he heard.

Faith sat first. She eased into the chair as if it were fragile and might break. "Sixteen months ago, Sherry showed up at my apartment in Oklahoma. I hadn't seen her in months, but she was pregnant and needed money. I gave her what cash I had, and when she left, I realized she'd stolen my wallet. It had my ID and driver's license in it."

Beck didn't say a word because he'd already guessed how this had played out.

"The following day when Sherry went into labor, she used my name when she admitted herself to the hospital. She even put my name on Aubrey's birth certificate. I didn't know," Faith quickly added. "Not until after she checked out of the hospital two days later. She broke into my apartment and left Aubrey and a letter on my bed."

"Hell," he mumbled. He had guessed the part about Sherry being the birth mom. But not this. "She left a newborn alone?"

Faith nodded and swallowed hard. "Aubrey was okay. Hungry, but okay. Needless to say, I was a little shaken when I realized what Sherry had done."

Beck leaned closer, staring at her from across the desk. "Why didn't you tell anyone?"

"Because of the letter Sherry left. I have it locked away in a safety deposit box in Oklahoma if you want to read it for yourself. But Sherry told me in the letter that Aubrey would be in danger if her birth father found out she existed. 'He'll kill her,' Sherry wrote. 'You have to protect her. You can't tell anyone or she'll die.'" Faith shuddered. "I believed Sherry."

Yeah. Beck bet she had. He would have, too.

"You covered for your sister, again, just like you did ten years ago outside the motel with Pete."

Faith nodded. "I had to protect Aubrey. I loved her from the moment I laid eyes on her."

He understood that, too.

Beck wanted to be angry with Faith. He hated being lied to. He hated that she hadn't trusted him with something this important. But if their situations had been reversed, he might have done the same thing. All he had to do was look at the things he'd done to protect his own family.

"I'm sorry I let you believe she was mine." Faith swiped away a tear that slid down her cheek. "But she is mine, in every way that counts."

He didn't want to deal with Aubrey's paternity just

yet. But he had to find out if this was connected to the case.

"Nolan could be the father," Beck said more to himself than to Faith. "But if he knew, he would have already tried to use her to get money."

Faith mumbled an agreement. "Sherry told me she'd kept her pregnancy a secret. That no one knew, except our mother and Darin. She left Austin when she starting showing and stayed in Dallas until the day before she came to see me."

Beck wasn't sure he could take Sherry's account at face value, but something must have happened to make her want to hide the pregnancy and her child. Or maybe the woman simply didn't want to play mother and conned Faith with that sob story. It felt real.

"If Aubrey's father is someone other than Nolan, he hasn't made any contact with me," Faith continued. "And if he'd talked to Sherry, she probably would have let me know. She was so worried about him finding out about Aubrey."

Beck thought that through. If Aubrey's birth father was the person responsible for the attempt to kill Faith, then why had he shot at her? If he wanted something—money, for instance—then why hadn't he gotten in touch with her so he could blackmail her?

"I don't think this is connected to the case," she added, her voice practically a whisper now.

"Maybe not, but we need to know for sure."

She shook her head and looked more than a little alarmed. "How can we do that without endangering Aubrey?"

"Do you have something of hers that would have her DNA on it?"

She stood, and he could see the pulse pounding on her throat. "I have her hairbrush in my purse, but I don't want her DNA tested. I believed Sherry when she said Aubrey could be in danger."

"I'm taking that threat seriously, too. But we have to know who Aubrey's father is. He could have killed Sherry and your mother. We have to rule him out as a suspect. Or else find him and arrest him."

"I know." A moment later she repeated it, and the fear and frustration made her voice ragged. "Sherry often had affairs with married men."

"And one of those men might not want the world to know he has a child." Beck stood, too, and walked closer to her. "So here's what we do. I'll package the hairbrush myself so that no one, including my deputies, will see it. Then I'll seal it and send it to the lab in Austin. I'll ask them to compare the DNA to Nolan's. And to mine."

Her eyes widened. "Yours?"

He obviously needed to explain this. "I'll ask Sgt. Caldwell to give the results only to me. But I want him to leak information that he did some DNA testing and that I'm Aubrey's father."

"What?" Her eyes widened even more.

From the moment the idea had popped into his head, he figured she'd be shocked. Still, this was a solution. Time would tell if the solution was a successful one. "If everyone believes I'm Aubrey's father, that'll stop Nolan or anyone else from being concerned that they've produced an unwanted heir."

With her eyes still wide, she shook her head. "Beck, this could backfire. What happens when your family finds out?"

Oh, they would find out. No way to get around that. "They won't be happy about it, but it doesn't matter. This will keep Aubrey safe."

He hoped.

But there was another reason he wanted his DNA compared to Aubrey's. Beck was positive he wasn't the little girl's biological father, but he couldn't say the same for his brother. Or even his own father.

If Aubrey was his niece or his halfsister, then the test would prove it.

And if Aubrey was the primary motive for murder, that might mean there was a killer in his family.

FROM WHERE IT LAY on the coffee table, Beck's cell phone softly beeped again. An indication that he had voice mail. He didn't get up from the sofa and check it. Didn't need to. He'd already looked at the caller ID and knew the voice mails were from his father and brother.

He did check his watch though. It'd been six hours since he told Sgt. McKinney to get out the word that Beck was Aubrey's father. To make the info flow a little faster, Beck had told his deputy, Corey, the same necessary lie. The Rangers knew the truth. Corey didn't. He hoped Corey had leaked the little bombshell all over town, especially since Beck hadn't said anything about keeping it a secret.

Those two calls wouldn't be the only attention he'd get from his family. If he didn't answer their calls, they'd drop by for a visit—maybe even tonight. This time though, Beck had put the slide lock on. His father wouldn't be able to just walk inside as he'd done that morning. He'd also set the security system so if anyone tried to get in through any of the doors, the alarm would sound. Hopefully no one in his family would be desperate enough to try to crawl through a window.

He glanced at the numbers he'd written down when the bank manager had called him just minutes earlier. It was one of two other calls that brought bad news. Beck wasn't sure what to do about the second, but as for the first, he needed to investigate the bank figures from his father's account. Those numbers added up to trouble. They were yet another piece of a puzzle that was starting to feel very disturbing.

"Mommy misses you so much," he heard Faith say.

She was sitting on one of the chairs in the family room, just a few feet from him, with her phone pressed to her ear. She had her fingers wound in her hair and was doing some frequent chewing on her bottom lip. She was obviously talking to Aubrey, and it was the third call she'd made since the Ranger, Marita, Tracy and Aubrey had arrived at the safe house.

It wouldn't be the last.

This separation was causing her a lot of grief. Grief that Beck felt as well. But this arrangement was necessary. And hopefully only temporary. Once he'd caught the killer, then Faith could bring Aubrey home.

Wherever home was.

He doubted she could go back to her house, not with the attic death calendar and the shooting incident.

Faith got up from the chair and made her way to

him. She held out the phone. "I thought you'd want to tell Aubrey 'Good night.'"

He did, but Beck knew all of this was drawing him closer and closer to a child he should be backing away from. He needed to stay distanced and objective.

But he took the phone anyway. "Hi, Aubrey," he told her.

She answered back with her usual "'i" and babbled something he didn't understand, but Beck didn't need to understand the baby words to know that Aubrey was confused. She was probably wondering why her mother wasn't there to tuck her into bed.

"Your mommy will be there soon," he added.

The next syllables he understood. She strung some Da-da-da's together. Such simple sounds. Sounds Aubrey didn't even comprehend, but they were powerful.

"Good night," he said and handed the phone back to Faith.

"Good night," she repeated to Aubrey. "I love you."

Faith hung up, stood there and blew out a long breath. "It's hard to be away from her."

Beck settled for a "yeah."

She put her phone on the coffee table next to his and then looked around as if she didn't know what to do with herself. "I cringe when I think of the prenatal care Sherry would have gotten when she was pregnant. She wouldn't have taken care of herself. But thankfully, Aubrey turned out just fine."

"You've done a good job with her. You're a good mother, Faith."

Her eyes came to his. "I'm sorry about lying to you. For what it's worth, I'd planned to tell you today."

He believed her. It riled him initially, but ultimately brought them closer.

Like now.

She stood there, just a few feet away, wearing dark jeans and a sapphire-blue stretch top, something she'd put on after showering when they'd returned from his office. Her hair was loose, falling in slight curls past her shoulder.

She looked like the answer to a few of his hot fantasies.

His body wanted him to act on the fantasies, to haul her onto his lap so he could kiss her hard and long. Of course, because this was his fantasy, the kiss would be just the beginning.

And all that energy would be misplaced because he needed to do everything to make sure there wasn't another attempt on her life.

Forcing his mind off her body, he picked up copies of the three blackmail letters and spread them out over the coffee table so that Faith could see them. "With everything else that's happened today, I haven't had a chance to go over these. They could be important."

She made a sound of agreement, sat down on the floor near his feet and picked up the first one. "I find it interesting that Sherry sent the letters to both your father and brother. By doing so, she implicates both, which means she could have had a recent affair with either of them."

"Or neither."

Faith didn't look offended by that. She stayed quiet a moment, apparently giving that some thought. "True, but then why would she think she could get money from them unless there'd been some kind of inappropriate relationship? Because Nicole hated Sherry so much and blamed her for her emotional problems, an affair with either would have upset her. Both Roy and Pete would have wanted to prevent Nicole from finding out."

She paused, and her gaze snapped to his. Her eyes widened. "The DNA tests," she said. "You wanted to compare Aubrey's DNA to yours so you'd know if Roy or Pete is Aubrey's father."

He nodded.

"Beck, this could be a nasty mess if one of them is."

He nodded again.

"Oh, mercy." She dropped the letter on the table and tunneled her hands through the sides of her hair again. "What happens if it's true, if one of them is a DNA match?"

"Then I'll deal with it." Which was his way of saying that he didn't know what he'd do. Still, he and Faith had to know the truth, and this was one way of getting it. DNA could also exclude his relatives and hone right in on Nolan.

Shaking her head, she leaped up from the floor. "I'm not giving up custody. I've raised Aubrey since birth. I love her—"

"You're not going to lose her," Beck promised, though he had no idea how he'd keep that promise. If necessary, he'd just continue the lie that he was Aubrey's father.

He felt as if he were anyway.

Because he was losing focus again, Beck forced himself to look at the letters. "The third letter is different from the other two," he continued.

It took her a moment to regain her composure, but then she glanced at all three letters. "Yes. Sherry asks for more money in the third one. Maybe because Nolan pressed her for more. Ironic, since his car was probably worth less than a thousand bucks. He would have tried to get everything he could from her, all the while threatening to go to the police to report her for car theft. With her priors, she would have gone to jail."

That made sense, but he wasn't sure that the rest of it did. "Why would Sherry have typed the letters, especially since she put her name on them, visited my father and told him what she wanted? These letters are physical evidence and prove attempted extortion."

Faith lifted her shoulder. "Who knows why Sherry did what she did. Maybe she thought she could bluff her way out of extortion charges if she was arrested. She could claim she didn't type the letters." Faith paused. "You think someone else did?"

Now it was Beck's turn to shrug. But he also stood so he could deliver this news when they were closer to eye level. "The bank manager called when you were on the phone with Aubrey. It took some doing, but he found that my father had taken money from his various investment accounts. A little here, a little there, but it all added up to ten grand."

She walked closer and stopped right in front of him. "That's the exact amount Sherry was demanding in the first two letters."

"Yes. And she might have gotten it." His father might have paid Sherry off. He'd deal with that later, after he'd put more of this together.

"But if your father gave her the money, then why the third letter?" Faith asked.

"My theory is that someone else might have continued the blackmailing scheme."

"You mean Nolan." She didn't hesitate.

Neither did he. "Or your brother. Or even your mother. All it would have taken is knowledge of Sherry's plan and a computer to type the letters."

She bobbed her head, took another deep breath. "Nolan could have done this, and when Sherry threatened to expose him, he could have killed her."

That's what Beck thought, too. Nolan could have killed Sherry's mother if the money had been left with her. She would have known Nolan had a part in the scheme.

Because he was watching her, he saw Faith go still. "Is Nolan still being held at the sheriff's office?"

Hell. He hated to tell her this. "No. His lawyer showed up, and he was released about a half hour ago."

"I see." The words were calm enough, but the emotion was there in her expression and in her body.

"If I can get just one person at the Moonlight Bar to say they saw Nolan leave early on any of the three nights in question, then I should have enough to ask the D.A. to take this to a grand jury."

"In the meantime, Nolan is a free man. And he might stay that way. There's enough reasonable doubt, especially with the security disk of Darin in that barn."

Her voice didn't crack. Her eyes didn't water. He didn't touch her, but he did move closer.

"Some homecoming," she mumbled. She tried to

smile at him, but it turned into a stare that ran the gamut of emotions. "But at least we're on the same side."

Oh, yeah. And more. They'd moved from being enemies to being comrades. To being…something else that Beck knew he should avoid.

But he didn't.

When Faith stepped closer, he didn't step back. He just watched her as she reached out and touched his arm lightly with the tip of her fingers.

"How badly would this screw things up?" she asked.

"Bad," he assured her.

She nodded. Didn't step back. She didn't take her caressing fingers from his arm.

"I'm not good at this." Her voice dropped to a silky whisper. "But I'll bet you are."

Beck couldn't help it. He smiled.

And reached for her.

Chapter Eleven

Beck's mouth came to hers, and just like that, Faith melted. The intimate touch, the gentle I'm-in-control-here pressure of his lips. The heat. They all combined to create a kiss that went straight through her.

She couldn't move. Couldn't think. Couldn't breathe. The kiss claimed her, just as Beck did when he bent his arm around her waist and pulled her to him. The sweet assault continued, and Faith could only hang on for the ride.

Or so she thought.

But then he stopped and eased back just a bit. That's when Faith realized her heart was pumping as if she were starved for air. She blamed it on the intense heat Beck had created with his kiss.

"You need a minute to rethink this?" he asked.

Did she?

Beck stood there, waiting. Breathing hard as well. Looking at her.

Faith looked at him, too. At those sizzling blue eyes. At that strong, ruggedly hot face. And she looked at his body. Oh, his body. That was creating more firestorms inside her.

Because her right hand was already on his chest, she

slid it lower and along the way felt his muscles respond. They jerked and jolted beneath her touch. It was amazing that she could do that to him.

Beck didn't touch her. He stood there with his intense eyes focused on her and his body heat sending out that musky male scent that aroused her almost as much as his kiss had done.

Her hand went lower, while their gazes stayed locked. A muscle flickered in his jaw. His heart was pounding. Hers, too. So much so that she wasn't sure if that was her own pulse in her fingertips or if it was Beck's.

When she made it to his stomach, she slipped her fingers inside the small gap between the buttons of his shirt and had the pleasure of touching his bare skin.

You can do this, she told herself. She wanted to do this.

"You still need time to think?" Beck asked her. She was surprised he could speak with his jaw clenched that tight.

"No." She eased her fingers deeper inside his shirt, loosening a button until it came undone. "I don't need any more time."

Before the last syllable left her mouth, he kissed her. It was hard and hungry. If it hadn't fueled the need inside her, it would have been overwhelming. Suddenly, she wanted to be overwhelmed. She wanted everything she knew Beck was capable of giving her.

With their bodies still facing each other, he scooped her up in his arms. Faith wrapped her legs around him, and he immediately started toward his bedroom. They bumped into some furniture along the way. And a wall.

Neither of them were willing to break the kiss so they could actually see where they were going.

Beck used his foot to shove open the door. The room was dark, with only the moonlight filtering through the blinds and thin curtain.

Several steps later, Faith felt herself floating downward. Her back landed against his mattress. And Beck landed against her with his sex touching hers through the barrier of their jeans.

She didn't want any barriers. She kicked off her shoes and went after his shirt.

Beck went after hers, stripping it over her head and tossing it onto the floor.

Everything became urgent. Frantic. A battle against time. She cursed her fumbling fingers but then gave a sigh of pleasure when she got his shirt off and put her hands on him. He was all sinew and muscle. All man.

And for the moment, he was hers for the taking.

So Faith took.

She kissed his chest and explored some of those muscles. Not for long though. Beck had other ideas. He unhooked the clasp of her bra, and her breasts spilled out. He fastened his mouth onto her left nipple and sent her flying.

Mercy, was all she could think.

He kept kissing her breasts and lightly nipped her with his teeth; all the while he worked to get her jeans off. She worked to get his off, too, though she had to keep stopping to catch her breath.

Her jeans surrendered and landed somewhere on the floor where Beck tossed them. Faith shoved down his zipper. He shoved down her panties. And for only a moment, she felt the cool air on the inside of her thighs.

The coolness didn't last.

Beck kissed her. The heat from his mouth warmed her all right and had her demanding that he do something about the fire he'd created inside her.

He stood and rid himself of his boots and jeans. She wished the light had been on so she could see him better, but the moonlight did some amazing things to his already amazing body. The man was perfect.

Beck reached in the nightstand drawer and pulled out a foil-wrapped condom. Safe sex. She was glad he'd remembered. She certainly hadn't.

He tugged off his boxers while he opened the condom. She got just a glimpse of him, huge and hard, before he came back to her, moving between her legs.

Faith forced herself not to think. She wanted this to happen. With Beck. Right here, right now.

Their eyes met. The tip of his erection touched her in the most intimate way and sent a spear of pleasure through her. She gasped and gasped again when he pushed deeper.

Wow.

With just that pressure, that movement, that sweet invasion, she was certain this was as much of the tangle of heat that she could take. She felt on the verge of unraveling.

But Beck stopped.

In fact, he froze.

Faith wanted no part of that. She hooked her leg around his lower back and shoved him forward.

There was a flash of pain. But it was quickly over-shadowed by a flood of pleasure.

Beck didn't move. He stayed frozen.

She focused, trying to see his face, and the confused expression she saw there probably matched her own. He had questions.

"You're a virgin?" he asked.

Now it was her turn to freeze. "Sort of."

Sort of? Sort of! She wanted to kick herself for that stupid response. And she wanted to kick herself again because the moment was gone. Even though the need was still there, racing through her, she knew this wasn't going to continue until Beck got an explanation.

She caught onto him when he tried to move off her. "I tried to have sex with my boyfriend in college, but it didn't work out. I panicked."

"You're twenty-eight," he reminded her. This time, he did move off her. He landed on his back next to her and groaned. "There would have been other opportunities since college."

"One other, a few years ago. I panicked then, too." Faith hesitated, wondering how much she should say, but since she'd already messed this up, she went for broke. "When I was fourteen, one of Sherry's drunk boyfriends sneaked into my bedroom one night and tried to rape me. He didn't succeed, obviously. Darin came in and hit the guy with an alarm clock. Anyway, it took me a long time to get over that."

Beck cursed under his breath. "You're over it now?" he asked, staring up at the ceiling.

"I'm over it." Beck seemed to have cured her. Amazing that he could do what therapy hadn't.

He turned on his side and faced her. "Why didn't you tell me before I got you onto this bed?"

"I didn't want to explain what'd happened in my past. I wanted to have sex with you. And besides, I didn't think you'd notice."

"I noticed." It sounded as if he'd worked hard to keep the emotion and maybe even some sarcasm out of his voice. "Did I hurt you?"

"No." Since that sounded like a lie, she tried again. "Just a little, that's all."

This time the cursing didn't stay under his breath. "I'm sorry."

"No need to be. I'm not."

He stared at her, groaned and looked up at the ceiling again. "You just turned my life upside down. Now I've got positive proof that my brother's been lying all these years about what happened in the motel. And everything I'd ever thought about you was wrong."

"You thought I was a slut." She put her hand over his mouth so he wouldn't have to confirm that. "Everyone did. Because everyone believed I was just like my mother and Sherry. Guilt by association. But the truth is, I went in the opposite direction. I didn't want to be anything like either of them."

He stayed quiet a moment, before he reached for her and pulled her to him gently, and just held her.

"I never wanted to be any woman's first lover," he said. "It was sort of a badge of honor for some guys in high school. Not me. I figured it created some kind of permanent bond that I wasn't sure I wanted."

That stung a little. Was he saying he was sorry this

had happened? Apparently. Because he wasn't doing anything to continue what they'd started.

"You don't owe me anything, Beck," she assured him.

"Oh, I owe you. An apology for starters for the way I've treated you." He kissed the top of her head. Cursed softly. And looked down at her. "What the hell am I going to do with you now?"

Though he probably didn't want her to answer, she considered pointing out that they were naked on his bed. But a soft thump stopped her from saying anything. The small sound came from the direction of the window. It sounded as if someone had bumped against the glass.

Beck shot off the bed.

"Get down on the floor," he told her.

Her heart banged against her rib cage, and Faith did as he said. Beck ran into the bathroom and seconds later emerged with his boxers on. He gathered up his jeans and started to put them on while he reached for something in his nightstand drawer.

A gun.

That got her moving.

She hurriedly crawled around, collected her clothes and got dressed. Once Beck had on his jeans, shirt and boots, he raced to the window. Pressing himself against the wall, he peered out the edge of the blinds.

"Hell, someone's out there," he let her know.

Her heart banged even harder. "Who is it?"

"Can't tell. He's dressed all in black, and he's crouched down near the rosemary bush in the side yard."

A ringing sound sliced through the silence. It was her cell phone. She'd left it in the family room.

"Stay put," Beck instructed. But a moment later, he

cursed again. "The guy looks like he's trying to sneak away."

Oh, mercy. She didn't want him to get away. If it was Nolan, they could use this to arrest the man for trespassing. If he had a weapon, even better, because they could possibly charge him with criminal intent.

Beck started for the bedroom door. "My cell's not in here either. Use the phone by the bed and dial nine-one-one. Ask for backup. But I don't want sirens. I want a quiet approach so we don't scare this guy off."

She dialed the number as he asked. The dispatcher answered right away, and she relayed what Beck had told her. The dispatcher said he would send the night deputy immediately.

"Are you thinking about going out there?" she asked Beck the moment she hung up.

"I need to catch this guy," was his uneasy answer.

The silence lasted several seconds. "I have another gun on the top shelf in the closet," he instructed. "Get it and then stay low while you follow me to the back door. Lock it when I leave and set the security system. I won't be long."

"You don't know that. This guy could shoot you."

"I'm the sheriff," he reminded her. Plus, if he could end this tonight, then Aubrey wouldn't be in danger.

Her little girl could come back home.

"I'm doing this," Beck insisted.

Faith considered arguing with him, but she knew it would do no good. She hurried to the closet and took the .38 from the shelf. They crouched down and hurried to the back door.

"Be careful," she told him. But that was it. All she had time to say.

"Six-eight-eight-nine," he explained, disarming the security system so it wouldn't go off when he made his exit. He shoved a set of keys into his jeans pocket. "Lock the door, reset it and then get back into the bedroom. Stay on the floor. I'll let myself back in when I'm finished."

And just like that, he hurried out.

Faith followed his instructions to a tee, added a prayer that he would be okay and headed to the bedroom. She hadn't even made it there when the house phone rang. Five rings and the answering machine kicked in.

"Sheriff Beck Tanner," the machine announced. "I'm not here, so leave a message. If this is an emergency, hang up and call nine-one-one."

She waited, her mind more on Beck than the caller. And then she heard the voice.

"Faith?"

It was Darin.

She scrambled across the room and picked up the phone. "Darin, it's me. I'm here."

"I'm here, too. Outside Beck's house. I need to see you. I have something to show you."

Oh, God. Beck was out there expecting to catch a killer. He might shoot Darin by mistake. Of course, there was that possibility that Darin was the killer.

"I'm in the yard," Darin continued. "By some rose-bushes. There's a window nearby."

So he wasn't by the rosemary. He'd moved from the side yard to the back, where Beck had just exited. They'd probably just missed each other. She needed to tell Beck what was going on, but he didn't have his cell phone with him.

"I won't hurt you," Darin promised. And for a moment, she remembered her brother, the one who'd saved her from Sherry's drunken boyfriend. The brother she loved.

With the cordless phone in one hand and the gun gripped in the other, Faith crawled back toward the kitchen. Toward the window with the roses.

"What do you need to show me?" she asked Darin.

"Sherry had some pictures of her with a man. I found them, and I think they're important."

It was likely the photo that Sherry had sent Pete and Roy, the one that proved she'd had the affair that might earn her some blackmail money.

When she reached the kitchen window, Faith lifted her head a little and looked out. She didn't spot her brother. "Darin, listen. Beck's out there, and if he sees you, he might shoot first and ask questions later. So I want you to stay put. Don't run. Don't make any sudden moves."

She saw something then. Was that a shadow in the shrubs or was it Beck?

She couldn't tell.

"Stay down," she told her brother in a whisper. She waited until Darin had gotten to the ground. Then she opened the window several inches, and in a slightly louder voice, she said, "Beck?"

Nothing. Not even from the other end of the phone, and she wondered if Darin had hung up.

Faith lifted the window a little more. The shadow didn't move. "Beck?" she called out.

She waited. Not long. Seconds, maybe. And a swishing sound came right at her. It happened in the blink of an eye.

Something tore through the mesh window screen.

There was a stab in her neck. Sharp and raw. But she didn't even have time to scream.

Faith felt herself falling, losing consciousness, and there was nothing she could do to stop it.

BECK STAYED CLOSE TO the house so he could use it for cover in case something went wrong and so he could make sure no one got inside to go after Faith.

The figure he'd seen in the yard might be a kid playing a stupid game, but with everything else that'd happened in the past two days, he couldn't take the chance. He also didn't want to leave Faith alone much longer, so that meant he had to find this guy and take care of the situation—fast.

He hoped it was Nolan so he could arrest him. Or beat him senseless, whichever came first.

Hurrying but keeping his gun aimed and ready, Beck went to the front of the house and looked around the corner. No one was there so he moved across the porch toward the side yard where he'd first seen the figure.

He silently cursed when he didn't see anyone there.

Had Nolan or Darin gotten away?

From up the street, he saw a cruiser approaching. The siren was off, but the deputy had his headlights on. He turned them off when he was about a half block away, parked the cruiser and got out. It was Deputy Mark Gafford. Beck motioned that he was going to go back around the house.

Beck stepped down from the porch and into the side yard where his bedroom extended to just a few feet from that rosemary bush. He glanced inside the bedroom window but couldn't see Faith. Good. That hopefully meant the killer couldn't see her either.

With the deputy now covering his back, Beck got moving again. Staying in the shadows. Keeping watch. He half expected someone to ambush him at any moment. Because after all, Sherry and her mother had been ambushed. But with each step, he heard nothing, saw nothing.

Until he made it to the backyard.

Someone was on the back porch at the door, dressed all in black. Could it be the same shadowy figure that'd been in the rosemary?

"Hold it right there!" Beck called out. He ducked partly behind the corner of the house to use it as cover in case the person fired.

But there was no shot.

The person bolted off the porch and began to run.

"Stop!" Beck yelled.

The guy didn't. Beck jumped on the porch in pursuit. From the corner of his eye, he saw Faith. On the kitchen floor.

His heart fell to his knees.

He called out her name, the sound ringing through his head, and he got a glimpse of the darkly clad figure rounding the corner, out of Beck's sight.

Beck didn't chase after him. Instead, he raced to the back door, forgetting that it was locked. God, he had to get to her.

There was blood on her neck.

"Watch out for a gunman," Beck yelled to his deputy, hoping the man would hear him.

He fumbled through his pocket for his keys. It seemed to take an eternity before he got the right one into the lock. Finally, it opened, and despite the fact he'd triggered the security system and it started to blare, he ran to her.

She wasn't moving.

Trying to keep watch to make sure the gunman didn't return, Beck pressed his fingers to the side of her neck that wasn't bleeding.

He felt her pulse. It was faint. But it was there. She was alive.

For now.

He reached up, yanked the wall phone from its cradle and jabbed in nine-one-one.

"Sheriff Tanner," he said, the second the dispatcher answered. "Get an ambulance out to my place now. Faith Matthews has been shot."

He tossed the phone aside and checked her injury to see what he could do to help her. She wasn't bleeding a lot, and he soon realized why.

The injury wasn't from a bullet.

Beck reached down and plucked the tiny dart from her neck. And he felt both relief.

And fear.

Because someone had shot her with a tranquilizer gun.

Just the way her sister and mother had been shot, right before someone had murdered them.

Chapter Twelve

Faith forced her eyes open. No easy task, because her eyelids felt as heavy as lead. Actually, her entire body felt that way.

She glanced around and saw she was in a bed in a sterile white room. A hospital. That's when she remembered what had happened in Beck's kitchen.

Someone had shot her.

Her hand flew to her neck, to the thin bandage that was there. The skin beneath it was sore, but she wasn't actually in pain.

"Someone used a tranquilizer gun on you," a man said. "You're going to be okay." It was Beck. He was there. It was his voice she'd heard, and next to him stood Corey, his deputy.

"We didn't catch him," Beck added with a heavy, frustrated-sounding sigh.

"But you saved me. I didn't die," she mumbled.

Beck shook his head and walked closer. "You didn't die." His face was etched with worry, and judging from his bloodshot eyes, he hadn't slept in a while. Faith had no idea how long it might had been.

"How long have I been here?" she wanted to know.

Beck eased down on the side of the bed beside her

and pushed her hair away from her face. His touch was gentle. "All night. It's nearly ten o'clock. There was enough tranquilizer in that dart to knock out someone twice your size. That's why you had to stay the night here in LaMesa Hospital."

"Ten o'clock?" That was too long. She had to find out who'd done this to her. She also had to check on Aubrey. Faith tried to get up, but Beck put his hand on her shoulder to make her lie back down.

"How are you feeling?" Corey asked.

So that it would speed things along and get her out of that bed, Faith did a quick assessment. Well, as quickly as her brain would allow. It felt as if her thoughts were traveling through mud. "I'm not in pain." She touched her throat and looked at Beck. "I guess you got to me before the killer could try to strangle me?"

"I got to you," Beck assured her, though that had not been easy for him to say. His jaw was tight again.

He was blaming himself for this.

Deciding to do something about that, Faith sat up. Beck tried to stop her again, but this time she succeeded. "How soon can I leave?"

He didn't look as if he wanted to answer that. "The doctor should be here any minute to talk to you."

She hoped he didn't hassle her about getting out of here. She wanted to get in touch with Marita and check on Aubrey. And her brother. She had to talk him into surrendering, or he was going to end up getting himself killed.

"Darin called me last night after you went outside," she explained to Beck. "He was there in your yard, but

I don't think he's the one who shot me with the tranquilizer gun. I think someone else was out there."

Beck nodded. "There were two sets of tracks. I'm hoping I can match one of the sets to Nolan."

Good. That was a start and might finally lead to Nolan's arrest.

"I also had your neck photographed so the crime lab can compare your puncture wound to Sherry's and your mother's. The killer didn't leave the actual darts at those scenes so the lab can't make that comparison. But if the puncture wounds match, then we know the same person's responsible for all three attacks. Plus, they might be able to get some DNA from the dart I pulled from your neck."

And she prayed that DNA wouldn't belong to her brother. "Any sign of Darin or Nolan?"

Beck and Corey exchanged an uneasy glance. "No." Corey handed him an envelope that he'd been holding, and in turn Beck gave the envelope to her. "Darin left this by the rosebushes."

"Are these the pictures?" she asked, opening the envelope. "When he called last night, he said he had Sherry's pictures."

"And he obviously did," Corey mumbled. "I found them when I was processing the crime scene." He hitched his thumb toward the door. "I'll get back to the office and see if there's been any news about the case."

Faith waited until Corey was gone before she took out the first photograph. It was blurry and similar to the one in the blackmail letter. In the shot, there was a man lying asleep on a bed, and he was covered from the waist down with a white sheet. Maybe it was Pete, or even Roy, but it could have been Nolan with a wig.

In the second photo, someone had moved the sheet to expose the man's bare leg. Faith saw the spot on his thigh. A birthmark, she decided. She looked up at Beck for an explanation.

"Pete, my father and I all have that same birthmark."

Oh, no. Since she was dead certain that wasn't Beck in Sherry's bed, that left Roy and Pete. "The birthmark could be fake," she pointed out. "Nolan could have learned about the birthmark from Sherry and then painted it on to incriminate them."

Beck gave a crisp nod, an indication he'd already considered that. So why did he look as if that was a theory he didn't want to accept?

Faith tucked the second picture behind the third one. The last one. Again, it was a blurry shot, not of the man in the bed. This one was taken from long range, and it took Faith a moment to realize it wasn't Sherry.

It was a shot of her and Aubrey.

It'd been taken at the park about two months earlier. Right about the time the blackmail letters had been sent to Roy and Pete.

Faith drew in a sharp breath. "You think Sherry planned to use Aubrey to blackmail someone?"

But she didn't need an answer. She knew. This was exactly the kind of reckless thing Sherry would do.

"I have to go check on Aubrey," Faith insisted. She got out of the bed, and Beck looped his arm around her to steady her. If he hadn't, she would have fallen—her legs felt like pudding.

"Aubrey's fine," Beck assured her. "I talked to Sheriff Whitley less than a half hour ago. No one has attempted to get into the safe house. You can't go check on her. It's too risky. Someone might try to follow you."

The disappointment was as strong as her concern for her daughter. But he was right. Faith couldn't take the danger to her child's doorstep. However, that didn't mean she had to stay put.

She was wearing a hospital gown, but Faith spotted her clothes draped over a chair. Wobbling a bit, she reached for the jeans and top.

Beck had her sit on the bed while he put on her jeans. It was a reminder that he'd done the exact opposite the night before when they were on his bed, and despite the hazy head and the punch of adrenaline, she remembered the heat they'd generated.

When she met Beck's gaze, she realized that he remembered it, too.

"Are you *really* okay?" he asked.

"I'm really okay." She was still wearing her bra, and he slipped off her gown and eased her stretchy blue top over her head so that she could put it on. "This wasn't your fault."

"Like hell it wasn't."

Because he looked as if he needed it, Faith put her arms around him. She would have done more. She would have kissed him for reassurance, both hers and his, if the door hadn't flown open.

Pete and Roy.

Apparently, there wasn't much security at the small-town hospital if anyone was allowed to march right into her room. That in itself was alarming enough. But her alarm skyrocketed when she spotted the blood on Roy's shirt. The man also had what appeared to be several fresh stitches on his forehead.

"Well, isn't this cozy?" Pete barked.

Faith stepped away from Beck as quickly as she could. But Beck didn't step away from her. He stood by her side and slipped his arm around her waist.

"What happened?" Beck asked his father.

Roy looked at her. "I had a run-in with your brother about a half hour ago."

Oh, God. "Are you hurt? Is Darin hurt?"

"My father's obviously hurt," Pete interjected before Roy could answer. "Darin is a sociopath and a killer."

"What happened?" Beck repeated, sounding very much like a cop now.

Unlike Pete, there was no anger in Roy's expression or body language. Just fatigue and spent adrenaline, something Faith could understand.

"I went out to the stables to check on a mare, and Darin was there," Roy explained. "He said he wanted to talk to me, but I didn't think that was a good idea. I grabbed my cell phone from my pocket to call you, and Darin tried to stop me." Roy lifted his shoulder. "I don't think he meant to hurt me. He just sort of lunged at me, and we both fell."

"Dad cut his head on a shovel and needed stitches," Pete supplied.

"What about Darin? What happened to him?" Beck wanted to know.

"He ran off, but I think he was hurt." Roy touched his wounded head and winced. "He was limping pretty badly."

As much as Faith hated to hear that, she hoped it

would make Darin seek medical attention, and then maybe, finally, she could talk to him.

Roy looked at her. "I heard what happened to you. Could have been worse."

"Much worse," she supplied. "I'm sorry about what went on with my brother. He's scared, and he needs help."

"He needs to go back to the loony bin," Pete jabbed. "And maybe you do, too." But he didn't aim that last insult at her but rather Beck. "What's this I hear about you being the father of her kid?"

So the info had indeed been leaked, though it was ironic that the first question about it had come from Pete, the man who might very well be Aubrey's biological father. Faith didn't want to know what kind of problems that was going to create if he was. Of course, the alternatives were Roy and Nolan. Nolan was a jerk. Possibly even a killer. And Roy seemed too decent not to own up to fathering a child.

But then maybe Sherry hadn't told him.

"You didn't mention a word to us about the baby," Roy continued where Pete had left off. "Or about being with Faith."

"Because I knew you wouldn't approve." Not exactly a lie. They wouldn't have.

Pete's hands clenched into fists. "So you're saying it's true, that you are the kid's father?" But then he relaxed a bit. "Oh, wait. I get it. You slept with her on a down and dirty whim, and then she claimed you got her pregnant. And you actually believed her?"

Roy caught onto Pete's arm. "If Beck thinks the little girl is his, he must have a good reason to believe it."

"I do," Beck supplied. "I also have a good reason to believe that Pete lied ten years ago. You didn't sleep with Faith."

The anger flushed Pete's face. "You're taking her word over mine?"

"No. I'm taking what I know over what you said. I think you lied because you thought Nolan would pound you to dust if he found out you'd been with Sherry."

She expected Pete to return fire, but he didn't. He went still, and it seemed from his expression that he was giving it some thought. Several moments later, he scrubbed his hand over his face.

"I wasn't afraid of Nolan," Pete finally said. "And I don't remember what went on in that motel room."

Pete seemed to be on the brink of an apology, or at least an honest explanation, but Beck's cell phone rang. Pete shook his head again, and she could tell that he'd changed his mind about saying anything else.

"What?" Beck snapped at the caller.

That got everyone's attention. So did Beck's intensity. He cursed and slapped the phone shut.

"That was Nicole," he explained. "She said she just found a dead body in the west barn at the ranch."

BECK CAUGHT ONTO FAITH'S arm to stop her from bolting from the cruiser when he brought it to a stop in front of the west barn at his family's ranch.

"I have to see if it's Darin," she insisted.

Not that she needed to tell him that. From the moment he'd relayed Nicole's message, Faith had been terrified that the body belonged to her brother.

Beck figured it did, but he didn't say that to her.

Still, he couldn't discount the altercation Darin had had with Roy just an hour or so earlier. His father had even said that Darin was injured. Maybe he'd hit his head, and that had caused his death.

That wouldn't make it any easier for Faith to accept.

This was going to hurt, and Beck wasn't sure she would let him help pick up the pieces.

Nicole was there, standing in front of the dark red barn, waiting. There wasn't a drop of color in her face, despite the cold wind whipping at her.

"I have to go in first," he instructed Faith. He drew his weapon, just in case. "I have to do my job."

He didn't wait for her to acknowledge that. Behind him, Pete and Roy pulled up. And behind them was Corey. All three men barreled from their vehicles.

Beck got out and held out his hands to stop them from going any farther. "Corey, I need you to wait here with Faith. Pete and Dad, you wait with Nicole. As soon as I've checked it out, I'll let you know what's going on."

None of them argued, maybe because none of them were anxious to have a close encounter with a dead body.

"I couldn't see his face," Nicole volunteered. "But it's a man, and he's dead in the back stall. There's blood, a lot of it," she added in a hoarse whisper.

Pete pulled her into his arms, and Beck gave Corey one last glance to make sure he was guarding Faith. He was. So Beck went inside.

The overhead lights were on, so he had no problem seeing. The barn was nearly empty, except for a paint gelding in the first stall. He snorted when Beck moved past him. Beck walked slowly, checking on all sides of him.

With the exception of six stalls and a tack room at the back, there weren't many places a killer could hide.

If there was a killer anywhere around.

But Beck figured Darin would be the only person he'd find inside. That meant he'd have to interview his father about the fight he had with the man, and Beck only hoped that he had told the truth. He didn't want to find out his father had shot an unarmed man.

Beck spotted a pair of boots sticking out from the back stall. Judging from the angle, the guy was on his back. He wasn't moving, and there was a dark shiny pool of blood extending out from his torso. Nicole had been right—there was a lot of it. Too much for the person to have survived.

Keeping his gun ready and aimed, Beck went closer. There was a piece of paper on the open stall door. The top of the page was slightly torn where it'd been pushed against a raised nail head that was now holding it in place. Beck decided he would see what that was all about later, but first he needed to ID the body and determine if this person was truly dead or in need of an ambulance.

More blood was on the front of the man's shirt. And in his lifeless right hand, there was a .38. The barrel of the gun was aimed directly beneath his chin.

Yeah, he was dead.

Blood spatter covered his face, too, and it took Beck a moment to pick through what was left of the guy and figure out who this was.

"Hell," Beck mumbled.

He looked at the paper then. Hand-scrawled with just three sentences.

I killed them. God forgive me. I can't live with what I've done.

He left the note and body in place so the county CSI crew and the Rangers would have a pristine scene to process. That was if Nicole hadn't touched anything. He wanted them to find proof that this was indeed a suicide or if someone had staged it to look that way.

Everyone was waiting for Beck when he came back out, including Sgt. McKinney, the Ranger who was still investigating the tranquilizer gun incident from the night before. But it was Faith that Beck went to.

"It's not Darin," he told her.

Her breath broke, and she shattered. He felt the relief in her when he pulled her into his arms. "It's Nolan Wheeler."

Blinking back tears of relief, she looked up at him. "Nolan?" she repeated.

So did Pete and Nicole. "What was Nolan Wheeler doing here?" Pete asked.

"Apparently killing himself. There's a suicide note."

"I'll have a look," the Ranger insisted, going inside.

Faith shook her head. "Nolan committed suicide?"

Beck couldn't confirm that. "According to the note, he couldn't live with himself because of the murders he committed."

He saw the immediate doubt in Faith's eyes and knew what she was thinking. On the surface, Nolan wasn't the suicide type.

So did the man have some "help"?

"Why would he have done this?" Corey questioned.

Beck was short on answers. "Maybe he thought we were getting close to arresting him."

That was the only thing he could think of to justify suicide. But why choose the Tanners' barn to do the deed? As far as Beck knew, Nolan wasn't familiar with the ranch.

"What were you doing in the barn?" he heard his brother ask Nicole.

Beck pushed aside his questions about Nolan because he was very interested in her answer.

Nicole, however, didn't seem pleased that all eyes were suddenly on her. "I was looking for my riding jacket. I thought I left it in there." Pete didn't jump to confirm her answer, so she sliced her gaze at Beck. "Why would I do anything to Nolan Wheeler? I hardly know him."

"You went to high school with him," Corey pointed out, earning him a nasty glare from both Pete and Nicole.

"I won't have Nicole accused of this or anything else," Pete snapped.

Nicole nodded crisply. "There's only one person here who had a reason to kill Nolan, and that's Faith."

Beck was about to defend her the way Pete had Nicole, but he spotted the Ranger walking back toward them. "I used my camera phone to take a picture of the suicide note and sent it straight to the crime lab. They'll compare it to Nolan's handwriting. We've got some samples on file that we've been comparing to the threats written in the attic."

"And did Nolan write those threats?" Faith wanted to know.

Sgt. McKinney shook his head. "The results are inconclusive, but we might have better luck with this suicide note since whoever wrote it didn't print."

Before the last word left the Ranger's mouth, Beck saw a movement out of the corner of his eye. He turned, automatically drawing his weapon. So did the Ranger and Corey. Pete shoved Nicole behind him.

Darin Matthews was walking straight toward them.

"Darin?" Faith called out.

Beck caught her arm to keep her from running toward her brother. Darin was limping and looked disheveled, maybe from the altercation he'd had with Roy.

"Don't shoot," Darin said. He lifted his hands in a show of surrender.

"Are you hurt?" Faith asked.

"Just my ankle. I think I sprained it when I was here earlier."

Roy took a step closer to the man. "You mean when I ran you off or when you killed Nolan?"

Darin froze, and his eyes widened. "Nolan's dead?" And he looked to Faith for confirmation.

"He's dead."

"I didn't do it. I came here because I've been sleeping in one of the barns while I've been in town looking for evidence to clear my name. I didn't kill anyone, and I didn't help Nolan do it, either." He took in a weary breath. "But I'm tired now. I need to rest."

"You'll have to get your rest at the sheriff's office," Beck let him know. He walked closer and patted Darin down. He wasn't armed, but in addition to the limp, there was a nasty gash on the back on his head. It was no longer bleeding, but it looked as if it could use some stitches.

The Ranger's cell phone rang, and he stepped aside to take the call.

"Darin will have to be cuffed," Beck let Faith know, and he kept a grip on her until after Corey had done that.

When he let go of her, Faith ran to Darin and hugged him. "I want to go with him."

Beck didn't even try to argue with her. He knew it would do no good. He motioned for Corey to get Darin into the cruiser. He and Faith would follow it, first to the emergency room and then to his office, where he'd eventually have to lock up Darin.

"I'll do whatever you need me to do," Darin insisted. He looked at Faith. "You're not in danger anymore. Nolan can't hurt you."

"And I'll help you," Faith promised. "I have attorney friends who can defend you if you're charged with anything. There's a lot of evidence, and when it's all examined and processed, I think it'll prove you're innocent."

Beck hoped the same thing.

Nicole walked closer to them. "Now that this is over, and the killer's been caught, there's no reason for Faith to stay at your house any longer. We can finally get back to the way things were."

Beck shook his head. "This case isn't settled." And Faith would stay with him until it was.

He didn't want to think beyond that.

"We might be one step closer to getting things settled," the Ranger announced, rejoining them. "That was the crime lab. We'll need to do more analysis, of course, but the handwriting expert says the suicide note appears to be a match to Nolan Wheeler's."

"So he did write that note," Nicole concluded.

Beck considered a different theory. "Perhaps he wrote it under duress?" While a gun was pointed to his head?

The Ranger shrugged. "Maybe, but according to the expert, there are no obvious indications of hesitation. There probably would have been if he'd been forced to write it."

Well, that put a new light on things. Nolan had confessed to the murders in that note. Maybe Darin had been telling the truth about his lack of involvement? Maybe he wasn't a killer, and Nolan had been the one to orchestrate all of this so he could get the money from Sherry's blackmail scheme and her estate.

"We should go." Beck caught Faith's arm and led her toward his cruiser.

With her barely out of the hospital, he didn't like the idea of her having to accompany him to the station, but he didn't want her alone, either. Besides, she would want to be there when Beck questioned Darin. And when the questioning was done, the loose ends would be tied up into a neat little package.

So why did Beck have this uneasy feeling in the pit of his stomach?

Why did he feel that Faith was in even more danger than ever?

Chapter Thirteen

Faith's mind was racing. She was mentally exhausted after spending most of the afternoon with her brother. But she was also hopeful.

Because soon she'd get to see her little girl.

She'd already called Marita, and the nanny had told her they would be on their way back when they got everything packed up. With luck, Aubrey would be home within the next three hours.

Well, not home exactly. But back at Beck's house, where they'd stay another day or two until she could decide something more permanent.

She climbed out of the cruiser, went inside the house and into the kitchen. Because it suddenly seemed to take too much energy to go any farther, she leaned against the wall and tried to absorb everything.

So much had happened in the past twenty hours. Too much to grasp at once.

Nolan was dead and no longer a threat to Aubrey and her. Her brother was at the LaMesa Springs hospital receiving treatment for the head wound he'd gotten from the altercation with Roy. Once the doctor released him, Darin would still have to undergo an intense interrogation. Maybe the evidence against him would even have to go to a grand jury. But Beck had promised her that Darin would be given fair treatment and that he personally was going to recommend that any assessment come from the county mental health officials.

Her brother might finally get the help he needed.

Beck came in behind her, took off his jacket and hung it on the hook on the mudroom door. "How's your neck?" he asked.

It took her a moment to realize what he meant. The tranquilizer dart wound. Even though it hadn't been that long since the injury, she'd forgotten all about it. "It's fine," she assured him.

The corner of his mouth lifted. A weary smile. "You're not feeling any pain because Aubrey will be here soon."

Faith couldn't argue with that, so she returned the smile. She took off her coat and hung it next to his. "Thank you for letting us stay with you."

It seemed as if he changed his mind a dozen times about what to say. "You're welcome."

His response was sincere, she didn't doubt that, but there was something else. Something simmering beneath the surface. "Your family won't like me being here. I'll make plans to leave tomorrow."

No smile this time. He took off his shoulder holster, and with the weapon inside, he placed it on top of the fridge. "No hurry. I don't want you to make any decisions based on my family. Truth is, I'm fed up with them. And I'd like for Aubrey, Marita and you to stay here for as long as you like. Or until at least we have everything sorted out with your brother. It's a big place, lots of room, and we can get to know each other better."

"You've known me for years," she pointed out.

He lowered his head. Touched his lips to hers. "But I want to know you *better*."

The kiss was over before it even started. It was hardly more than a peck. But it slid through her from her lips all the way to her toes.

"That sounds sexual." Or maybe that was wishful thinking on her part.

"It is," he drawled. "But the invitation isn't good for tonight. Tonight, you'll rest, take a hot bath and spend time with Aubrey when she gets here. In a day or two, I'll work on getting you into my bed again."

There it was. More heat. She'd been attracted to men before but never like this. Nothing had ever felt like this. It scared her, but at the same time, she wanted more.

"Don't look at me like that," he warned.

She touched the front of his shirt with her fingertips. "Like what?"

"Like you want to get naked with me."

"Oh." Maybe she looked that way because that's exactly what she wanted. "I'm at a disadvantage here. I've spent my entire adult life pulling back from men. I don't know how to stop you from treating me like glass. I don't know how to make you take me the way you would a woman with lots of experience. I don't know how to seduce you."

He shrugged. "Breathe."

Faith blinked. "Excuse me?"

He leaned in, whispered in her ear, "This is all about you, Faith. Just you. To seduce me, all you have to do is breathe and say yes."

"Yes." She pulled in a loud breath, and with that, his mouth came to hers.

This time, it wasn't a peck, it was a full-fledged kiss. His mouth moved over hers as if he knew exactly what to do to set her on fire.

It worked.

Faith leaned against him—until she could no longer do the thing that had set all of this into motion. She couldn't breathe. And she didn't care. She'd take Beck's kisses over breathing any day.

His left arm went around her waist, and he pulled her to him. The embrace was gentle. Unlike the kiss that had turned French and a little rough.

Faith broke the intimate contact so he could see her face. "No treating me like glass," she reminded him. "And I'd rather not rest tonight if you don't mind."

He stared at her, and she could see the debate that stirred the muscles in his jaw. "All right."

That was the only warning she got before he hoisted her up. Face-to-face. Body against body. And he delivered some of those kisses to the front of her neck and then into the V of her top.

Faith automatically wrapped her arms and legs around him. His sex touched hers and sent a shiver of heat dancing through her. She wanted him naked, now.

She went after his shirt as he carried her toward his bedroom. Buttons popped and flew, pinging on the floor, and her frenzy of need for him only fueled the fire. She got his shirt off and kissed his neck. Then his chest.

He made a throaty sound of approval and, off balance, he rammed his shoulder into the doorjamb. Faith wanted to ask if he was okay, but he obviously was.

Beck kissed her even harder, and instead of taking her to the bed, he stopped just short of it, and with her pressed between him and the mattress, he slid them to the floor. While he kissed her blind, he unzipped her jeans and peeled them off her. Bra and panties, too, leaving her naked. He quickly covered her left nipple with his mouth.

The sensation shot through her.

His hand went lower, between her legs, and his fingers found her. He slipped his index finger through the slippery moisture of her body and touched her so intimately that Faith could have sworn she saw stars.

"Breathe," he reminded her.

She thought she might be breathing, but couldn't tell. The only thing she knew for sure was that she wanted him to continue with those slippery, clever strokes.

And he did.

He touched and created a delicious friction that brought her just to the edge.

Faith caught her breath and caught onto his hand. "You, inside me," she managed to say, though she didn't know how she'd gotten out the words. Speech suddenly seemed very complex and not entirely necessary.

She shoved down his zipper, which took some doing. He was huge and hard, making it difficult for her to free him from his jeans and boxers.

Even though her need was burning her to ash, she took a moment to fulfill a fantasy she'd had for years. She got him out of those jeans, took Beck in her hand

and slid her fingers down the length of him, all the while guiding him right to where she wanted him to go.

He reacted with a male sound deep within his chest. He buried his face in her hair. His breath, hot against his skin. His mouth, tense now, muffled a groan, and he kissed her. His tongue parted the seam of her lips as his hard sex touched the softness of hers.

Her vision blurred. She reached to pull him closer. Deeper into her. But he stopped and cursed.

"Condom," he gutted out.

Still cursing, he reached over, rummaged through his nightstand drawer and produced a condom. He hurried, but it still seemed an eternity. The moment he had it on, Faith pulled him back to her.

Despite the urgency that she could feel in every part of him, Beck entered her slowly. Gently. Inch by inch. While he watched her. That wasn't difficult to do since they were face-to-face with her straddling him. He was watching to see if he was hurting her.

He wasn't.

The only pain she felt was from the hard ache of un-filled need. A need that Beck was more than capable of satisfying.

She could see how much this gentleness was costing him. Beck didn't want to hold back anything, and Faith made sure he didn't. She thrust her hips forward.

Beck cursed again.

"It's better than I thought it'd be," she mumbled. A shock since she'd been positive it would be pretty darn good.

"Yeah," he said.

He stilled a moment to let her adjust to this intimate invasion, but the stillness only lasted a few seconds and a kiss. He moved, sliding into her. Drawing back. Then sliding in even deeper. Each motion took her higher. Closer. Until her focus honed in on the one thing she had to have.

Release.

Beck had taken her to this hot, crazy place. He'd made her feel things she'd only imagined. And he just kept making her feel.

He slid his hand between their bodies, and with him sliding in and out of her, he touched her with his fingers, matching the frenetic stokes of his sex. He kept touching. Kept moving. The need got stronger. Until she was sure she couldn't bear the heat any longer.

Beck seemed to understand that. He kissed her. Touched her. Went deep inside her. A triple assault. And it happened. In a flash. Her orgasm wracked through her, filling her and giving her primal release.

Breathe, Faith reminded herself. *Breathe.*

There were no barriers. No bad blood. Nothing to stop her from realizing the truth.

She was in love with Beckett Tanner.

WELL, FAITH WAS BREATHING all right.

Her chest was pumping as if starved for air, and each pump pushed her sweat-dampened breasts against his chest. There was a look of total amazement on her face.

She was practically glowing.

Beck knew he was somewhat responsible for giving her that look, and when his brain caught up with the now sated part of his body, he might try to figure out what he was going to do about that look. And about what'd just happened.

For now though, he just held her and tried not to make any annoying male grunts when the aftershocks of her climax reminded him that he was still inside her. Not that he needed such a reminder.

"That was worth waiting for," she mumbled.

He kissed her, tried to think of something clever to say and settled for another kiss. But he would have to address this sooner or later. Faith obviously wasn't a casual sex kind of person. Neither was he. But it suddenly felt as if he had more than a normal responsibility here. A commitment, maybe.

After all, he was her *first*.

He certainly hadn't expected to have that title once he was past the age of twenty. Maybe she'd have some emotional fallout from this.

Maybe even some regrets.

Beck realized she was staring at him. Her breathing had settled. There were no more aftershocks. But she had her head tilted to the side, and she was studying him.

"What?" he prompted.

"I'm just trying to get inside your head." She smiled. It was tentative. Perhaps even a facade. "Don't worry. This doesn't mean we're going steady or anything." Still smiling, she moved off him and stood.

Beck caught onto her hand before she could move too far from him. All in all, it wasn't a bad vantage point. He was still sitting. Looking up at her. She was naked. Beautiful. Glistening with perspiration. And his scent was on her.

He wanted her all over again.

"I need a drink of water," she let him know. She leaned down and kissed him. "Then I think I'll take a bath before Aubrey gets here."

He had some cleaning up to do, too, and rather than sit there and watch her dress, Beck got up, gathered his clothes from the floor and went into the adjoining bathroom.

While he cleaned up and put his jeans back on, he glanced at the tub. Should he run her a bath? Probably not. It would only lead to more sex. Once was enough for her tonight. Plus, despite her "going steady" remark, she had some feelings she needed to work through.

He certainly did.

The house phone rang, and he went back into the bedroom to answer it. "Sheriff Tanner."

"It's Corey. Is Darin Matthews with you?" His words were harried and borderline frantic.

That put a knot in Beck's stomach. "No. He's supposed to be at the hospital with you."

Corey cursed. "Darin was sedated so I went to the vending machine to get a Coke. When I got back, he wasn't in his bed. I guess he wasn't sedated as much as I thought. I've looked all through the building and the parking lot. He's not here."

Darin couldn't have gotten far with that injured leg. Beck hoped. Unless he stole a car.

"Don't put out an APB just yet, but if one of the Rangers is still around, let him know so he can look for him. Faith and I will drive around, too, and see if we can spot him. Darin's probably looking for her anyway."

"One more thing," Corey said before Beck could

end the call. "The Ranger lab in Austin put a rush on that DNA test you ordered. They faxed the results over, and the dispatcher brought it to me while I was looking for Darin."

Great. He needed those results, but he had to resolve this problem with Darin first. "The results will keep," Beck let him know.

Cursing under his breath, Beck hung up and reached for his boots. He should probably call Marita and Tracy and delay Aubrey's homecoming, just in case Darin had some kind of psychotic episode.

Beck reached for the phone again, but stopped when he heard the soft sound. A thud. He stilled and listened. But there wasn't another sound. Just the uneasy feeling that all was not right.

"Faith?" he called out.

Nothing.

That knot in his stomach tightened. Hell. Why hadn't she answered?

The answer that came to mind had him grabbing the gun from the nightstand.

Beck started for the kitchen.

Chapter Fourteen

Faith opened the cupboard and reached for a glass. But reaching for it was as far as she got.

The lights went out.

She heard footsteps behind her. Before she could pick through the darkness to see who was behind her, an arm went around her neck, putting her in a choke hold.

A hand clamped over her mouth, and she felt the cold steel of a gun barrel shoved against her right temple.

Oh, God. What was happening?

Nolan was dead. The danger was over. Who was this person, and what was going on?

She didn't wait for the answers. Faith rammed her elbow into her attacker's belly. She might as well have rammed it into a brick wall because other than a soft grunt, the person didn't react.

"What do you want?" she tried to say, but his hand muffled any sound.

Still, there were sounds. Footsteps, both his and hers, as he started to drag her in the direction of the back door. Beck would likely hear the sounds, even though he might still be on the phone dealing with the call that'd come in. Once that call was finished, he would begin to wonder what was taking her so long to get a drink of water.

Then Beck would come looking for her.

And this person might shoot him.

He jammed the gun even harder against her temple when she started to struggle, and Faith had to try to come to terms with the fact that she might be murdered tonight. She thought of Aubrey, of her precious little girl. And of Beck. He would blame himself for this because he hadn't been there to protect her. But Faith didn't want him there. She wanted to live, but not at the expense of Beck being killed.

The man opened the back door, and cold air rushed inside, cutting what little breath she had. He tried to push her outside, but Faith dug in her heels. If he got her out of the house and away from Beck, he'd just take her to a secondary crime scene where he'd do God knows what to her.

But why?

And that brought her back to the question of whom.

Had Nolan hired someone to do this last deed? A way of reaching out from beyond the grave to settle an old score with her?

Of course, there was another possibility. One she didn't want to consider—maybe somehow her brother had gotten free. Maybe he really was a killer after all and had come to eliminate the last member of their family.

"Faith?" she heard Beck call out.

Her attacker froze for just a moment and then resumed the struggle to get her out the door. She tried to warn Beck, but her assailant's hand prevented that.

"What the hell's going on?" Beck called.

Though it was pitch-dark, she spotted him in the hallway opening just off the kitchen. She also saw him lift his gun and take aim.

The attacker stopped trying to shove her out the door, and he pivoted, placing her in front of him. He even crouched slightly down so that his head was partially behind hers.

She was now a human shield.

"Who are you?" Beck demanded. He squinted, obviously trying to adjust to the darkness. He reached out for the light switch on the wall next to him.

"Don't," her attacker growled. He kept his voice throaty and low, but there were no doubts that this was a man. A strong one. He had her in a death grip, and the barrel of the gun cut into her skin.

Beck didn't turn on the light, but he kept his gun aimed.

"I'm leaving with her," the man said. He was obviously trying to disguise his voice. That meant Beck and she probably knew him.

Inching sideways and with her still in front of him to block Beck's shot, the man started dragging her back to the door.

Faith didn't know whether to fight or not. If she did resist, he might just shoot Beck. However, the same might happen if she cooperated.

Beck inched closer as well, and because she was watching him, she saw his eyes widen. He didn't drop his gun, but he did lower it.

"Pete?" Beck called out.

The man's muscles went stiff, and he stopped. She heard every word of his harshly whispered profanity.

"What the hell do you think you're doing?" Beck demanded. He came even closer.

"Stop," the man said. Not a muffled whisper this time. She clearly heard his voice.

It was indeed Pete, Beck's brother.

"Well?" Beck prompted. "What the hell are you doing?"

"What's necessary." With that, Pete jammed the gun even harder against her. She could smell the liquor on his breath, but he wasn't drunk. He was too steady for that.

"What's necessary?" Beck spat out. "How did you even get in here?"

"You gave Dad the codes to disarm the security system and I used the key you gave me for emergencies. I didn't want you to be part of this," Pete said to Beck. "I wanted to take care of her before you noticed she was missing. She's a loose end."

Beck shook his head, and his expression said it all. He couldn't believe this was happening. "Put down your gun."

"I can't. I have to fix this." Pete groaned and took his hand from her mouth. "I've made a mess of my life."

"You can fix things the legal way," Beck insisted. His voice was calm, and he took another step toward them. "Put down the gun."

"It's too late for that. I killed them, Beck. I killed them all."

Oh, God. It was true. Pete was a killer, and he had her in his grips.

"You mean you killed Sherry and Annie?" Beck clarified.

"Yeah, I did. But it was all Sherry's fault. I swear she tricked me into that affair. When I saw her at the Moonlight Bar, she came onto me, got me drunk and then took pictures of me when I was sleeping. She blackmailed me. And I gave her the money. I gave her exactly what she wanted—ten thousand dollars that I got from Dad's accounts. Look where it got me."

"Start from the beginning. What happened?" Beck asked.

"The beginning? I'm not sure when it all started. But killing Sherry was an accident. I swear. I used the tranquilizer gun from the stables and drugged her so I could reason with her. But the drug wore off too soon, and when she started struggling, I had to strangle her."

"It wasn't premeditated," Beck explained. "You could maybe plea down to manslaughter. That's why you need to put down the gun so we can talk."

"Talking's not going to save me. Sherry's death might not have been premeditated, but the others were."

Until that statement, Beck had managed to maintain some of his cop's persona, but the grim reality of Pete's confession etched his face with not just concern but shock. "What do you mean?"

"After I killed Sherry, I tried to get the money back so Dad and Nicole wouldn't find out, but Annie wouldn't give it to me. She said she wanted it and more. A lot more. She wanted fifty thousand dollars. That's when I had to kill her. I couldn't keep paying her off, and I knew she'd tell Nicole."

It was so hard for Faith to hear all of this. She hadn't

been close to Sherry or her mother, but both of them had been killed for money. For greed. And to cover up an affair that Sherry had probably orchestrated just so she could blackmail Pete. If he hadn't been thinking from below the belt, Pete might have figured it out before things got this far.

"I thought after I killed Annie that it'd be over," Pete continued, his voice weary and dry. "But I got another letter demanding more money. I thought it came from Nolan. That's why I put a gun to his head and made him write that suicide note. But he insisted right up to the end that he hadn't sent any blackmail letters."

"You killed him anyway," Beck said. It wasn't a question.

"Nolan Wheeler deserved to die." Pete's voice was suddenly defiant. "He'd been skirting the law for years. I did the world a favor."

"The world might not agree," Beck countered. "I certainly don't. You killed three people, and you're holding a gun on your brother and the assistant district attorney. Where's the justice in that?"

Pete stayed quiet a moment. "It'll be my own form of justice. I can't let either of you live. Especially Faith. This afternoon there was another blackmail letter in the mailbox. She put it there. I know she did. There couldn't be anyone else."

"You don't know that. It could be one of Sherry's friends. Besides, Faith's been with me all day. She couldn't have put the letter in the mailbox."

"I don't believe you," Pete practically shouted. "You're covering for her because you're sleeping with her. You chose her over your own family."

"Maybe I did," Beck conceded. Unlike Pete, he kept his voice level and calm though Faith didn't know how he managed to do that. "But it's my job to protect her." He took another step toward them. "Put the gun down, Pete, and let's talk this out."

"No. No more talking. I'd wanted to do this clean and nearly succeeded last night. I got the tranquilizer in her, but then you came to the rescue. Just like tonight. But the difference is, tonight I'll kill you, too."

"I'm your brother," Beck reminded him. "Think what killing me would do the family."

"I can't think about that. I have to protect Nicole. She's my first and only concern. I have to make sure she never learns about any of this. The only way for that to happen is for you to die."

Pete re-aimed his gun.

At Beck.

Faith felt the muscles in Pete's arm tense. She saw the realization of what was about to happen on Beck's face. He couldn't shoot at his brother because he might hit her. Pete, however, had no concern about that since he intended to kill them both anyway.

She yelled for Beck to get down. With the sound of her voice echoing through the house, Faith turned, ramming her shoulder into Pete. He hardly budged from the impact, but it was enough to shake his aim.

The bullet that Pete fired slammed into the wall next to the fridge.

Beck lunged at them, and the hard tackle sent all three of them to the floor. Beck's own gun went flying, and it skittered across the floor. And the race was on to see which one would come up with Pete's gun.

Faith managed to untangle herself from the mix. She got to her feet and slapped on the light. Pete and Beck were practically the same size, and they were in a life-and-death struggle.

She waited until she spotted Pete's hand. And the gun. Faith went for it, dropping back to the floor, and she latched on to his wrist. Somehow, she had to keep that gun pointed away from Beck.

Beck drew back his fist and slammed it into Pete's face. The man was either tough as nails or the adrenaline had made him immune to the pain because he hardly reacted. In fact, Pete twisted his body and slammed his forearm into her jaw. The impact nearly knocked the breath from her, but somehow Faith managed to hang on to his wrist. She dug in her nails and clawed at any part of his flesh that she could reach.

Beck threw another punch. And another. The third one was the charm. Pete's head flopped back onto the tile floor. Dazed and bleeding from his mouth and nose, he groaned and mumbled something indistinguishable.

"The gun," Beck said.

Beck wrenched it from his brother's hand. He pulled in a hard breath and reached again, this time to roll Pete on his stomach so he could subdue him.

"Call nine-one-one," Beck told her.

"You're sure?" she asked, though she knew he had no choice. This was attempted murder. But Pete was still his brother. A lesser man would have wanted to try to resolve this without the law and tried to keep it a family secret.

Beck nodded. "I'm sure. Make the call."

She got up to do that, but before Faith even made it to

her feet, the back door flew open, hitting her squarely in the back and sending her plummeting into Beck.

"Oh, my God," someone said.

Nicole.

Pete used the distraction of his wife's arrival to ram his elbow into Beck and grab his gun.

Faith couldn't scramble away from him in time. Pete latched on to her hair and dragged her in front of him again.

"January fourteenth," Pete said as if in triumph. "Faith dies."

HIS BROTHER'S WORDS WERE like stabs from a switch-blade. It was the threat written in the attic. A threat Beck hadn't announced to anyone other than law enforcement, which meant Pete had been the one to paint that threat on Faith's attic walls.

Oh, man. Things had really gone crazy. And worse, it might turn deadly if he didn't do something now to stop all of this.

Beck's gaze connected with Faith's. She was scared. And shocked. But he could also see determination. She wasn't just going to stand there and let Pete kill them. She was a fighter, but this fight might cause Pete to pull that trigger even faster.

"Pete, what's going on?" Nicole asked.

Nicole looked at Beck, her eyes searching for a logical answer. But he couldn't give her one. There was no logic in any of this. Another of Pete's affairs had gotten him into trouble, and he'd been willing to kill to keep his secret.

"Pete killed Annie and Sherry Matthews. Nolan

Wheeler, too," Beck explained to Nicole. "Now he's going to put his gun down so we can deal with this."

Beck hoped.

"I killed them for you, Nicole," Pete insisted.

She gasped and stepped back. Good. So Nicole wasn't in on this. Maybe, just maybe, she could talk Pete into surrendering.

"Tell Pete to put his gun down," Beck instructed Nicole.

She gave a choppy nod. "Please, Pete. Do as Beck says."

"Faith's blackmailing me. She sent me a letter today. Left it in the mailbox—"

"No. She didn't." Nicole shook her head. "I sent the last two letters."

Beck hadn't thought there could be any more surprises tonight, but he'd obviously been wrong. "You?" he questioned. "Why?"

Tears filled Nicole's eyes. "Sherry called me two months ago and told me about her affair with Pete. She faxed me copies of the pictures of them together."

"Oh, God." Pete groaned. "I'm sorry. So sorry."

"I know." Nicole blinked back the tears, and her voice was eerily calm. "But I was upset, and I wanted to leave you—after I punished you. So, after Sherry and Annie were killed, I sent a third letter. This afternoon, I put the fourth one in the mailbox. I wanted you to suffer. I wanted you to think that your indiscretion would be punished for a long, long time."

Pete cursed. He glanced at Faith and then cursed some more.

"Faith didn't do anything wrong," Beck said. "You need to let her go."

"Yes," Nicole agreed. "Let her go. Let Beck handle this."

"I can't. Don't you see what has to happen here? I've already put the plan in place. I waited at the hospital until I could get Darin alone, and I forced him to leave with me. There are no security cameras in the entire place so it was easy. Then I left him on the side of the road about a mile from here."

"No," Faith mumbled.

Beck silently mumbled the same. With Darin hurt and possibility medicated, he shouldn't be out on his own on a cold winter night. It was a cliché, but he could literally die in a ditch somewhere.

"Darin will try to go home, but he won't have an alibi," Pete continued. "He'll be blamed for Beck's and Faith's murders. Then we can start over, Nicole. I swear, no more affairs."

That just pissed Beck off. His brother was willing to kill Faith and him rather than take responsibility for what he'd done. Somehow, he had to get Faith out of harm's way and subdue Pete.

"Do you hear yourself?" Beck snapped. "I knew you were self-centered and egotistical, but I had no idea you'd stoop to this. Think it through. You plan to kill me and Faith in front of Nicole? What kind of future can you have with that hanging over your heads?"

"Beck's right," Nicole added. "I could never stay with you after what you've done."

"You tricked me with those letters!" Pete shouted.

"Letters?" Nicole threw right back at him. "I didn't

murder anyone. Nor would I. Did you honestly think I could live with a killer?"

Pete slowly aimed his attention at Nicole. The change in his brother's expression wasn't subtle. Rage sliced through his eyes, and the muscles corded on his face. "I did this all for you, and this is how you treat me?"

"You didn't do this for Nicole." Beck wanted to get Pete's attention off Nicole and Faith and back onto him. Because it looked as if his brother was about to start shooting at any minute. "You did this to cover up what you'd done. Well, the covering up has to stop."

"Who says?" He pushed Faith onto her knees and put the gun to the back of her head.

She looked up. Her eyes met Beck's. "I love you," she said, silently mouthing the words.

Oh, man. Oh. Man. That hit him, hard, but he knew he couldn't think about it. Later—and there would be a later—he'd deal with her confession.

A sound shot through the room.

Beck was certain he lost ten years of his life. It took him a moment to realize that Pete hadn't fired. The phone was ringing.

"Don't answer that," Pete ordered. "You," he said to Nicole. "Get down on the floor next to her."

Nicole frantically shook her head. "You're going to shoot me?"

"Yeah." This was no longer the voice of his brother. It was the voice of a cold, calculated killer. "I love you, Nicole. I always will. But I won't give up my life for you. I'm not going to jail for you."

The answering machine kicked in on the fifth ring. "Faith, it's Marita. Pick up."

"No," Faith whispered. She repeated it as Marita's cheerful voice poured through the room.

"I guess you're celebrating, but I wanted you to know we'll be there in about ten minutes. Aubrey's sacked out, but I'll wake her when we arrive so you can get some hugs and kisses."

Hell. Ten minutes. He couldn't have Marita, Tracy and especially Aubrey walking into this.

"I gave Marita an emergency key," Beck let Faith know. And that meant if they didn't answer the door, which they wouldn't be able to do at this point, then Marita might let herself in.

"You couldn't hurt a child," Beck told Pete, trying one last time to reason with him.

Pete met him eye-to-eye. "I'm fighting for my life. I can and will hurt anyone who gets in my way."

Beck believed him. This wouldn't end with a successful surrender. It would end only when he managed to stop Pete. He might even have to kill his own brother. But he would if it came down to that.

He wouldn't allow Pete to hurt anyone else.

"Go ahead," Beck instructed Nicole. "Get on the floor."

The tears were spilling down her cheeks now, and her eyes were wide with terror.

"Trust me," Beck added. "Get on the floor."

Nicole gave a shaky nod. Using her right hand to steady herself, she started to lower herself to her knees.

Beck waited.

Watching Pete.

His brother glanced at Nicole. Just as Beck had

figured he would do. It was just a glance. But in that glance, Pete took his attention off Beck and Faith.

That was the break Beck had been waiting for.

He dove at Pete.

Though Beck was moving as fast as he could, everything seemed to slow to a crawl. He saw the split-second realization in Pete's eyes. And then Pete reacted. He didn't turn the gun on Beck.

But on Faith.

Pete lowered the barrel of the semiautomatic right toward the back of Faith's head.

And he fired.

Chapter Fifteen

Faith moved as quickly as she could, but she figured it wasn't nearly fast enough. She braced herself.

Death would come before she even knew if Beck had heard her. "I love you," she'd said. It might be the last time she ever had a chance to say that to anyone.

She was feeling and hearing way too much for Pete's bullet to have killed her. Instead, she realized that it'd smacked into the tile floor less than two feet from her.

Pete's bullet had missed her.

The sound of the fired shot was deafening, and it roared through her head, stabbing into her eardrums. It was excruciating, but since she could feel it, she knew she was very much alive.

So was Beck, thank God.

With his momentum at full speed, Beck crashed into Pete, and into her. Pete's gun dislodged from his hand and landed somewhere behind them.

"No!" Nicole yelled. She scrambled to the side to get away from the collision.

However, because Faith was directly in front of Pete, she wasn't so lucky. She was caught in the impact, again. Caught in the middle of the struggle. But this time, the stakes were even higher.

Aubrey was on her way there.

"Run!" Beck told her.

From the corner of her eye, she saw Nicole do just that. She threw open the back door and rushed out into the night. Maybe the woman would call the deputy. But as distraught as Nicole was, Faith couldn't rely on her for help. She and Beck had to stop Pete.

"Now!" Beck snarled to her. "Get out of here."

Faith wiggled her way out of the fight and somehow managed to get to her feet. But before she could run, Pete latched on to her ankle and tried to pull her back down. She fought, kicking at him, but he was pumped on adrenaline now and was fighting like a crazy man with triple his normal strength.

Then things got worse. The doorbell rang.

"We're here," Marita called out.

Marita's announcement nearly caused Faith to panic, but she forced herself to concentrate on the task. She gave Pete another hard kick, and that broke the vising grip he had on her. She felt him reach for her, and he groped at the floor.

Faith ran. But not out the back as Nicole had done.

Frantically, she looked around for Beck's gun. She didn't see it, and it took her a moment to figure out why.

Pete had it.

Oh, God.

Pete had the gun.

"Come in!" Pete shouted to Marita, dodging a fist that Beck had tried to send his way. "Beck needs help."

"No," Faith countered. "Stay back." And she hoped they'd heard her and would do as she said.

She looked around the floor for another weapon and

remembered Beck's service pistol. Faith grabbed it from the top of the fridge, where he'd put it right after they'd returned from seeing Darin.

"Stop!" she yelled.

Pete didn't. Neither did Beck. Pete managed to land a hard punch on Beck's jaw, and the momentum sent him backward. The two men weren't separated for long because Beck dove at him.

The doorbell rang again, and it was followed by a knock. "What's going on in there?" Tracy asked.

Faith hurried to him and held out his service revolver. Beck snatched it from her hand and got up off the floor.

Pete did the same.

And the two brothers met gun-to-gun.

"Don't," Beck warned, his voice a threatening growl.

The corner of Pete's mouth lifted. A twisted, sick smile. "You think a bullet can go through your front door?" He didn't wait for Beck to answer. "Because I do. God knows what a bullet would hit…"

Pete didn't have to aim in that direction. Faith realized his gun was already pointed there. Just to Beck's right. And that put it in line with the door.

Oh, God. That nearly brought Faith to her knees. Her baby was in danger.

"Try to warn them and I'll shoot through the door," Pete warned. "I have nothing to lose."

Faith didn't cower. "And you have nothing to gain from hurting my child."

"True. But it'll be nice to see you suffer."

Every inch of Beck was primed for the fight, and his face was dotted with sweat from the struggle. "Faith did nothing to you."

"Yes, she did. She came back. She made me think she'd written that blackmail letter. She made me believe I had to stop her. The woman's just bad luck, Beck. She always has been."

Faith saw Beck's finger tense on the trigger, and he had his attention fastened to his brother's own trigger finger. One move, and Beck would shoot him. Faith didn't doubt that. But what she did fear was that even if Beck shot him that Pete would still manage to shoot.

Aubrey could still be in danger.

She heard the scrape of metal, a key being inserted into a lock, and she glanced at the front door.

Just as it opened.

"No!" Faith shouted. And she automatically turned in the direction of the door. She had to block any shot that Pete might take.

She only made it one step before the bullet rang out.

BECK DIDN'T EVEN WAIT to see where Pete's bullet had hit.

Or who.

He couldn't think about that. Right now, he had to stop Pete from firing again. Each shot could be lethal.

Still, Beck couldn't stop the rage that roared through him. Pete had put Aubrey and Faith in danger. To save his own butt, his brother had been willing to hurt a child.

Beck grabbed Pete's right arm. He wanted to shoot his brother. To end this here and now. But Beck couldn't risk another shot being fired.

Not with Aubrey and Faith so close.

Faith yelled something, but the blood crashing in

Beck's ears made it impossible to hear. Besides, Beck only wanted to concentrate on the fight.

Beck dropped his gun so he could use both hands to try to gain control of Pete. His brother was fighting him, trying to re-aim his gun in the direction of the door. Beck wasn't able to get his finger off the trigger.

Pete fired again. The shot landed somewhere in the ceiling, and white powdery plaster began to rain down on them. Good. As long as that shot wasn't near the others.

Beck heard the sound then. A cry.

Aubrey.

Every muscle in his body turned to iron. *God, was the child hurt?* Or maybe it was Faith who'd taken the bullet. Maybe both were injured. Hell. He could lose them and all because of his selfish SOB of a brother.

"You can't save them," Pete growled.

It was exactly what Beck needed to hear. Not that he needed a reminder of what was at stake, but his brother's threat was the jolt that gave Beck that extra boost of adrenaline. Nothing was going to stop him from saving Aubrey and Faith.

Nothing.

From the corner of his eye, Beck saw Faith running toward the front door. There was no color in her face, and she appeared to be trembling. But she was headed in Aubrey's direction. Hopefully, she'd take the child and run. He wanted them as far away from there as possible.

With both his hands clamped onto Pete's right arm and wrist, Beck used his body and strength to maneuver Pete backward. Toward the wall. Pete didn't go willingly. He cursed, kicked and spat at Beck, all the while using his left fist to pound any part of Beck that he could reach.

Beck slammed him against the wall. The impact was so hard that it rattled the nearby kitchen cabinets. Still, Pete didn't stop struggling. Beck didn't stop, either. He bashed Pete's right hand against the granite countertop. The first time he didn't dislodge the gun.

But the second time he did. Pete's gun fell onto the granite.

Even though he was unarmed, Pete was still dangerous. So Beck didn't waste even a second of time. He caught onto his brother's shoulder and whirled him around, jamming his face and chest against the wall between the cabinets and the mudroom door. There wasn't much room to maneuver, but Beck wanted to get Pete onto the floor, facedown, so he could better subdue him.

Pete didn't cooperate with that, either, but Beck had the upper hand. With his forearm against the nape of Pete's neck, he put pressure on the backs of his brother's knees until he could get him belly down onto the tile floor.

By the time it was done, both Pete and he were fighting for air. Both of them were covered in sweat and blood from their cuts and scrapes.

But it was finally close to being over.

"Faith, are you all right?" Beck called out.

Since he'd expended most of his breath in the fight, he had to repeat it before it had any sound. And then he waited.

Praying.

He didn't hear her say anything. No reassurance that she was okay. But he could hear footsteps. Frantic ones.

Something was going on in the living room. Before he could call out to Faith again, there was another sound.

The back door opened.

It was Nicole.

"Let Pete go," she said. Her voice was trembling as much as her hand.

And she had a gun in her hand.

Beck cursed. He didn't need another battle when he hadn't even finished the first one.

"Nicole," Pete said through his gusting breath. "I knew you'd come back for me."

"I didn't do this for you. What you did was stupid, Pete, but I can't let you go to jail. Despite what you've done, you're still my husband. Part of me still loves you." She turned her teary eyes to Beck and pointed the gun right at him. "I'm a good shot," she reminded him. "Now let him go."

"Go where? Pete's a killer. What if he turns his anger on you?"

"He won't. I'm the reason he killed."

"He could hurt someone else," Beck reminded her. "You'd be responsible for that."

"What do I care if Faith Matthews and her bastard child are hurt?" Her attention went back to Pete. "I'll get you out of this, and then we'll be even. I want you to leave and never come back."

That wouldn't be good enough. Beck knew Pete wouldn't stay away. As long as his brother was alive and free, Faith and Aubrey would be in danger.

"I can't let him go," Beck insisted.

"Then I'll have to shoot you," Nicole insisted right back.

And she would.

Beck could see it in her eyes.

She'd already crossed over and left reason behind. She was going to save Pete whether he deserved it or not.

Nicole adjusted her aim so that it was right at Beck's shoulder. She wasn't going for the kill, but it didn't matter. The shot could still be deadly, and even if it only incapacitated him, it would leave the others vulnerable.

Cursing under his breath, Beck readied himself to take evasive action. He'd roll to the right, dropping to Pete's side. It might cause Nicole to think twice about shooting. But then it would give Pete the opportunity to break free.

"Nicole!" someone yelled.

Faith.

Hell. She'd come back.

Nicole automatically looked in the direction of Faith's voice. Beck couldn't see her. She was behind him.

But he saw the movement of something flying through the air.

Nicole tried to adjust her aim. But it was too late. A coffee mug slammed right into Nicole's hand. Maybe it was the impact or the surprise of the attack, but Nicole dropped the gun.

Pete went after it.

So did Beck.

Both of them scrambled across the floor toward it.

Above them, Nicole moved as well. Faith, too. Beck could hear Faith's footsteps, and he knew she was going after Nicole.

And Faith might get hurt in the process.

Beck caught onto Pete and slammed him against the floor. Nicole reached down, to help Pete or get the gun. But reaching was as far as she got. Faith grabbed Nicole and with a fierce jerk, she yanked her back. It was the break that Beck needed. His hand clamped around the gun, and this time, he came up ready to fire.

"Move back," Beck told Faith.

Nicole reached for her to try to use her as a shield, but Faith darted across the room just out of Nicole's reach.

"Don't move," Beck warned Pete when he tried to get up. His brother turned his head, and their gazes connected.

Beck made sure there were no doubts or hesitation in his eyes. Because there certainly wasn't any of that in his heart.

"I will kill you," Beck promised.

Pete laid his head on the floor and put his hands on the back of his head. Finally surrendering.

Chapter Sixteen

Faith frantically checked Aubrey again.

She hadn't seen any blood, or even a scratch, but she had to be sure that Pete's shots hadn't harmed her child.

"No, no, no," Aubrey fussed, batting Faith's hands away. The little girl rubbed her eyes and yawned. She was obviously sleepy and didn't want any more of this impromptu exam.

Deputy Winston rushed in the door. He had his weapon drawn, and he hurried past them and into the kitchen. A moment later, the Ranger, Sgt. McKinney, followed. Then Deputy Gafford.

Finally!

Even though it'd been only minutes since her nine-one-one call, Beck now had the backup he needed. And once she had the all clear that it was safe to check on him, she would. Well, she would after Marita had taken Aubrey into the bedroom away from Nicole and Pete.

She prayed Beck was all right.

In the distance she heard the sirens from an ambulance. And she heard footsteps. Faith looked up from her now fussy daughter and spotted Beck.

Oh, God. He was bleeding. There was a gash on his forehead. His left cheek. And both hands were bloodied.

"The ambulance will be here any minute," Faith told him.

He looked at her. Then at Aubrey. He seemed to make it to them in one giant step, and he pulled them both into his arms. Faith's breath shattered, and she was afraid she wouldn't be able to hold back the tears of relief.

"Is she hurt?" Beck asked. His voice was frantic. "Are you hurt?"

Faith pulled back so she could meet his gaze. "We're not hurt. You are. I called the ambulance for you."

His breath swooshed out. "You're not hurt." He repeated it several times and drew them back into his embrace.

Aubrey rubbed her eyes again and babbled something. It sounded cranky, and Faith figured she was about to cry, but her daughter maneuvered her way into Beck's arms and dropped her head on his shoulder.

"I'll see if I can be of assistance in the kitchen," Tracy volunteered, trying to give them some privacy.

"Want me to take Aubrey?" Marita asked.

"No," Faith and Beck said in unison.

"All right then. I'll just go outside and let the EMTs know what's going on." Marita took a step and then stopped. Her forehead was bunched up. "What exactly is going on?"

He and Faith exchanged glances. He didn't let go of her. But then she had no plans to let go of him either.

"My brother is about to be arrested for three murders," Beck explained. "Nicole will be taken into custody as well since she tried to assist him with his escape.

And we need to look for Darin. He's out there some-where and needs medical attention."

"Oh. I see." Marita turned pale. She waggled her fin-gers toward the sound of the sirens. "What should I tell the EMT guys? They'll be here any minute."

"Have then come in and check out Faith," Beck in-sisted.

Other than some bruises and maybe a scrape or two, Faith knew she was fine. She couldn't say the same for Beck. He'd need stitches for that gash.

"And I want them to check out Beck," Faith added as Marita went out the door.

"I'm okay," he insisted, kissing Aubrey's cheek. He kissed Faith's, too. "At least now I am. For a minute there, I thought I'd lost you."

"Me, too," she managed to say. Her emotion was too raw to talk about.

There was movement from the kitchen, and a mo-ment later, Pete appeared. Handcuffed. Corey had a hold on him. The other deputy had Nicole cuffed and was walking her to the front door.

Pete stopped, and Beck automatically turned so that Aubrey wouldn't be near the man. "There's nothing we have to say to each other," Beck insisted.

But Pete didn't speak right away. He stood there, vol-leying glances among Beck, Aubrey and Faith. "You fell hard for her, didn't you?" He didn't wait for Beck to confirm it. "That's how I feel about Nicole."

"You were ready to kill her," Faith pointed out.

"I wouldn't have. *Couldn't* have," he corrected. "Love really messes you up." His attention landed on Aubrey again. "I know she's Sherry's kid. Sherry showed me her picture. One she'd taken in a park, and she tried to convince me that I was the one who got her pregnant."

That gave Faith another jolt of adrenaline. "Did you?"

Pete shook his head. "Not a chance."

Faith desperately wanted to believe him. "And since you've been so truthful in the past, I should just take you at your word?"

"He's telling the truth," Corey volunteered. "This time, anyway. I saw the DNA results from the Ranger lab. He's not the father. Neither are you, Beck. It's Nolan Wheeler."

Nolan. In hindsight, it didn't surprise her. Not really. Sherry had spent most of her life breaking up and then getting back together with Nolan.

"He might have fathered her," Beck mumbled. "But Nolan was never her father."

Faith couldn't have agreed more. If the man hadn't been dead, his DNA connection to Aubrey would have caused her stomach to go into a tailspin. Because Nolan would have spent the rest of his life trying to figure out ways to use Aubrey to get what he wanted.

"Get my brother out of here," Beck instructed the deputy.

Pete didn't protest. He looked straight ahead as he was escorted out. Nicole was next. She didn't even try to say anything. Tears were streaming down her cheeks, and she made a series of hoarse sobs.

However, Deputy Gafford did stop. "On the way over, I got a call from the hospital. Darin Matthews is back there. He's not hurt, and he wanted me to check on Faith, to make sure she was all right."

Faith was so glad that Beck was holding on to her. Her brother was safe. Pete hadn't hurt him. And better yet, he was receiving the medical treatment he needed. She would check on him as soon as things had settled down.

Whenever that might be.

It might take her years to forget how close she'd come to losing Beck and Aubrey.

"The other Texas Ranger is with Darin now," the deputy continued. "Will there be any charges filed against him?"

"No," Beck quickly answered. "But I want him to have a thorough psychiatric evaluation."

The deputy nodded and escorted Nicole out.

Faith looked around and realized they were alone. The house was quiet. Her heart rate was slowly returning to normal.

"Are you really okay?" Beck asked.

But the silence didn't last. Before she could answer, there was the sound of hurried footsteps, and she automatically braced herself for the worst.

Roy came rushing through the front door.

He looked at Beck. At Aubrey. Then at her. He'd no doubt passed his other son and daughter-in-law and knew they were under arrest. But his concern seemed to be aimed at Beck.

"Son, you're bleeding," Roy greeted him.

"Just a scratch," Beck assured him.

"He needs stitches," Faith insisted.

Roy agreed with a nod, and he put his hands on his hips. He looked around, as if he didn't know what to say or do. "I just spoke to Corey and the nanny, Marita. They told me what happened in here."

"Yeah," was all Beck said.

"'i," Aubrey babbled to Roy.

There were tears in Roy's eyes, but he forced a smile when he returned the "hi." He hesitated. "I'm sorry. So sorry for what Pete did. I knew about the blackmail and the payoff, but I swear I didn't know he'd killed those people. And I didn't know he would come after the three of you. I'm sorry," he repeated, aiming this one at Faith.

She gave his arm a gentle squeeze. "Thank you."

Roy turned those tearful eyes to Beck. "What can I do? Give me something to do. I can't go home and sit there."

"You can go to my office and call Pete and Nicole a lawyer. They're going to need one."

"Of course. I'll do that. And if you need anything, just let me know."

"I will."

"Make sure he sees the medics," Roy whispered to Faith. He gave her arm a gentle squeeze as well and went back out the door just as the medics were coming in.

Beck held up his hand to stop them. "Could you give me a few minutes?" he asked.

That halted the two men in their tracks, and they looked at her for verification. "Just a few minutes," she bargained. But only a few. She wanted that gash checked.

Aubrey fussed and babbled, "Bye-bye," but Faith didn't think she wanted to go with Roy or the medics.

She smeared her fist over her eyes again and whimpered.

"It's okay," Beck said to Aubrey, and he lightly circled his fingers over her back.

"Da, Da, Da, Da," Aubrey answered. Not in a happy tone, either. But it was a tone Faith recognized. Her baby was on the verge of a tired tantrum.

Beck must have sensed that because he caught onto Faith's arm and led them to the sofa. Once he'd sat down, he moved Aubrey so that her tummy was against his chest. She dropped her head onto his shoulder and stuck her thumb in her mouth. Within seconds, her eyelids were already lowering.

Faith smiled. "Tantrum averted," she whispered. Good. She didn't have any energy left to deal with anything. "I might have to call you the next time she gets fussy."

Beck angled his eyes in her direction and stared at her. She'd thought the light comment would have given him some relief. It was certainly better than the alternative of her falling apart.

"You said you loved me," Beck reminded her.

That kicked up her heart again. She'd planned on having this discussion later. After some of the chaos had settled. "Yes, I did say that." Because she wanted to dodge eye contact with him, she checked Aubrey. Sound asleep.

"You meant it?"

But before he let her answer, he leaned in and kissed her. He winced because his lip was busted. Hers, too, she realized when his mouth touched hers. She didn't care. That kiss was worth a little pain, and it was the ultimate truth serum. She was going to lay her heart out there and let him know exactly how she felt about him.

She hoped he wouldn't laugh.

Or run the other direction.

"I meant it," she answered. "I love you." Beck and Aubrey were two things in her life that she was certain of. "I'm crazy in love with you."

His face relaxed a bit. The corner of his mouth even lifted in a near smile. "Good. Because I'm crazy in love with you, too."

A sharp sound of surprise leaped from her mouth. "Really?" She heard her voice. Heard the shock. "You're sure it's not just the lust talking?"

"The lust is there," he admitted. He reached out and pushed her hair away from her face. "But so is the love. You did me the honor of letting me be your first lover. Now I'm asking if you'll let me be your last."

Mercy. That was not a light tone. Nor a light look in his eyes. Still, Faith approached that comment with caution. "Are you asking me to go steady?" she joked.

"No. I'm asking you to marry me."

Oh. *Wow.*

Her heart went crazy. So did her stomach. Her breathing. Her entire body.

Was this really happening? She wanted it to happen. Desperately wanted it, she realized. But she hadn't expected it.

As if to convince her, he kissed her again. And again. Until he was the only thing she could think of. Beck had that kind of effect on her. He could make even the aftermath of chaos seem incredible. Heat and love just rippled through her.

"I don't want you to call me when Aubrey's fussy because I want to be there, close by, to hear her myself. I want to be her father, and I want to be your husband."

"You're already her father," Faith said. And it was true. "Aubrey chose you herself." She had to blink back happy tears. "She made a good choice."

"I'm glad you think so. Now to the rest. I want to be your last lover. Your only lover. What do you think about that?"

Faith didn't have to think. She knew. There was only one answer. "Yes."

* * * * *

EXPECTING TROUBLE

To Tom, thanks for all the support.

Prologue

A deafening blast shook the rickety hotel and stopped Jenna cold.

With her heart in her throat, Jenna raced to the window and looked down at the street below. Or rather what was left of the street, a gaping hole. Someone had set shops on fire. Black coils of smoke rose, smearing the late afternoon sky.

"Ohmygod," Jenna mumbled.

There was no chance a taxi could get to her now to take her to the airport. And worse were rebel soldiers, at least a dozen of them dressed in dark green uniforms. She'd heard about them on the news and knew they had caused havoc in Monte de Leon. That's why by now she'd hoped to be out of the hotel, and the small South American country. She hadn't succeeded because she'd been waiting on a taxi for eight hours.

One of the soldiers looked up at her and took aim with his scoped rifle. Choking back a scream, Jenna dropped to the floor just as the bullet slammed through the window.

She scurried across the threadbare rug and into the bathroom. It smelled of mold, rust and other odors she didn't want to identify, and Jenna wasn't surprised to see roaches race across the cracked tile. It was a far cry from the nearby Tolivar estate, where she'd spent the past two days. Of course, there'd been insects of a different kind there.

Paul Tolivar.

Staying close to the wall, Jenna pulled off one of her red heels so she could use it as a weapon and climbed into the bathtub to wait for whatever was about to happen.

She didn't have to wait long.

There was a scraping noise just outside the window. She pulled in her breath and waited. Praying. She hadn't even made it to the please-get-me-out-of-this part when she heard a crash of glass and the thud of someone landing on the floor.

"I'm Special Agent Cal Rico," a man called out. "U.S. International Security Agency. I'm here to rescue you."

A rescue? Or maybe this was a trick by one of the rebels to draw her out. Jenna heard him take a step closer, and that single step caused her pulse to pound in her ears.

"I know you're here," he continued, his voice calm. "I pinpointed you with thermal equipment."

The first thing she saw was her visitor's handgun. It was lethal-looking. As was his face. Lean, strong. He had an equally strong jaw. Olive skin that hinted at either Hispanic or Italian DNA. Mahogany-brown hair and sizzling steel-blue eyes that were narrowed and focused.

He was over six feet tall and wore all black, with various weapons and equipment strapped onto his chest, waist and thighs. He looked like the answer to her un-finished prayer.

Or a P.S. to her nightmare.

"We need to move now," he insisted.

Jenna didn't question that, but she still wasn't sure what she intended to do. Yes, she was afraid, but she wasn't stupid. "Can I trust you?"

Amusement leapt through his eyes. His reaction was brief, lasting barely a second before he nodded. And that was apparently all the reassurance he intended to give her. He latched on to her arm and hauled her from the tub. He allowed her just enough time to put back on her shoe before he maneuvered her out of the bathroom and toward the door to her hotel room.

"Extraction in progress, Hollywood," he whispered into a black thumb-size communicator on the collar of his shirt. "ETA for rendezvous is six minutes."

Six minutes. Not long at all. Jenna latched on to that info like a lifeline. If this lethal-looking James Bond could deliver what he promised, she'd be safe soon. Of course, with all those rebel soldiers outside, that was a big *if*.

Cal Rico paused at the door, listening, and eased it open. After a split-second glance down the hall, he got them out of the room and down a flight of stairs that took them to the back entrance on the bottom floor. Again, he looked out, but he must not have liked what he saw. He put his finger to his lips, telling her to stay quiet.

Outside, Jenna could still hear the battery of gun-fire and the footsteps of the rebels. They seemed to be moving right past the hotel. She was in the middle of a battle zone.

How much her life had changed in two days. This should have been a weekend trip to Paul's Monte de Leon estate. A prelude to taking their relationship from friendship to something more. Instead, it'd become a terrifying ordeal she might not survive.

Jenna tried not to let fear take hold of her, but adrenaline was screaming for her to run. To do something. *Anything.* It was a powerful, overwhelming sensation. Fight or flight. Even if either of those options could get her killed.

Cal Rico touched his fingers to her lips. "Your teeth are chattering," he mouthed.

No surprise there. She didn't have a lot of coping mechanisms for dealing with this level of stress. Who did? Well, other than the guy next to her.

"Try doing some math," he whispered. "Or recite the Gettysburg Address. It'll help keep you calm."

Jenna didn't quite buy that. Still, she tried.

He moved back slightly. But not before she caught his scent. Sweat mixed with deodorant soap and the faint smell of the leather from his combat boots. It was far more pleasant than it should have been.

Stunned and annoyed with her reaction, Jenna cursed herself. Here she was, close to dying, only hours out of a really bad relationship, and her body was already reminding her that Agent Cal Rico smelled pleasant. Heaven help her. She was obviously a candidate for therapy.

"I'll do everything within my power to get you out of here," he whispered. "That's a promise."

Jenna stared at him, trying to figure out if he was lying. No sign of that. Just pure undiluted confidence. And much to her surprise, she believed him. It was probably a reaction to the testosterone fantasy he was weaving around her. But she latched on to his promise.

"All clear," he said before they started to move again.

They hurried out the door and into the alley that divided the hotel from another building. Cal never even paused. He broke into a run and made sure she kept up with him. He made a beeline for a deserted cantina. They ducked inside, and he pulled her to the floor.

"We're at the rendezvous point," he said into his communicator. "How soon before you can pick up Ms. Laniere?" A few seconds passed before he relayed to her, "A half hour."

That was an eternity with the battle raging only yards away. "We'll be safe here?" Jenna tried not to make it sound like a question.

"Safe enough, considering."

"How did you even know I was in that hotel?"

Cal shifted his position so he could keep watch out the window. "Intel report."

"There was an intelligence report about me?" But she didn't wait for him to answer. "Who are you? Not your name. I got that. But why are you here?"

He shrugged as if the answer were obvious. "I'm a special agent with International Security Agency—the ISA. I've been monitoring you since you arrived in Monte de Leon."

Still not understanding, she shook her head. "Why?"

"Because of your boyfriend, Paul Tolivar. He is bad news. A criminal under investigation."

Judas Priest. This was about Paul. Who else?

"My ex-boyfriend," she corrected. "And I wish I'd known he was bad news before I flew down here."

Maybe it was because she was staring craters into him, but Agent Rico finally looked at her. Their gazes met. And held.

"I don't suppose someone could have told me he was under investigation?" she demanded.

He was about to shrug again, but she held tight to his shoulder. "We couldn't risk telling you because you might have told Paul."

Special Agent Rico might have added more, if there hadn't been an earsplitting explosion just up the street. It sent an angry spray of dirt and glass right at them. He reacted fast. He shoved her to the floor, and covered her body with his. Protecting her.

They waited. He was on top of her, with his rock-solid abs right against her stomach and one of his legs wedged between hers. Other parts of them were aligned as well.

His chest against her breasts. Squishing them.

The man was solid everywhere. Probably not an ounce of body fat. She'd never really considered that an asset, but she did now. Maybe all that strength would get them out of this alive.

Since they might be there for a while, and since Jenna wanted to get her mind off the gunfire, she forced herself to concentrate on something else.

"I believe Paul might be doing something illegal. He uses cash, never credit cards, and he always steps away from me whenever someone calls him on his cell. I know that's not really proof of any wrongdoing."

In fact, the only proof she had was that Paul was a jerk. When she refused to marry him, he'd slapped her and stormed out. Jenna hadn't waited around to see if he'd return with an apology. She hadn't even waited when Paul's driver had refused to take her into town. She'd walked the two miles, leaving everything but her purse behind.

Agent Rico smirked. "Tolivar was under investigation for at least a dozen felonies. The Justice Department thought you could be a witness for their case against him."

"Me?" She'd said that far louder than she intended. Then she whispered, "But I don't know anything." Oh, mercy. She hadn't thought things would be that bad. "What did Paul want with me? Not a green card. He's already a U.S. citizen."

Cal nodded. "The Justice Department believes he wanted your accounting firm so he could use it to launder money."

"Wait, he can't have my accounting firm. According to the terms of my father's will, I'm not allowed to sell or donate even a portion of the firm to anyone that isn't family."

He had no quick response, and his hesitation had her head racing with all sorts of bad ideas.

"We believe Paul Tolivar planned to marry you one way or another this evening," Cal said. "He had a phony marriage license created, in case you turned down his proposal. Intel indicates that after the marriage, he planned to keep you under lock and key so he could control your business and your money."

A sickening feeling of betrayal came first. Then

anger. Not just at Paul, but at herself for believing him and not questioning his motives. Still, something didn't add up. "If Paul planned to keep me captive, then why didn't he come after me when I left his estate?"

"He had someone follow you. I doubt he intended to let you leave the country. He contacted the only taxi service in town and told them to stall you."

So she'd been waiting for a taxi that would never have shown up. And it was probably just a matter of time before Paul came after her.

"I slept with him," Jenna mumbled. Groaned. She pushed her fists against the sides of her head. "You must think I'm the most gullible woman in the world."

"No. I think you're an heiress who was conned."

Yes. Paul had given her the full-court press after she'd met him at a fund-raiser. Phone calls. Roses. *Yellow* roses, her favorite. And more. "He told me he was dying of a brain tumor."

Rico shook his head. "No brain tumor."

It took Jenna a moment to get her teeth unclenched. "The SOB. I want him arrested. I want—"

"He's dead."

She had to fight through her fit of rage to understand what he'd said. "Paul's dead?"

Cal Rico nodded. "He was murdered about an hour ago. That's why I'm here—to stop the same thing from happening to you."

Her heart fell to her knees. "Wh-what?"

"We have reason to believe that Paul left instructions. In the event of his death, he wanted others dead, too. You included. Those rebel soldiers out there are after you. And they have orders to kill you on sight."

Chapter One

International Security Agency Regional Headquarters
San Antonio, Texas
One year later

Special Agent Cal Rico checked his watch—again. Only three minutes had passed since the last time he'd looked. It felt longer.

A lot longer.

Of course, waiting outside his director's door had a way of making each second feel like an eternity.

"Uh-oh," he heard someone say. Cal saw a team member making his way up the hall toward him. Mark Lynch was nicknamed Hollywood because of his movie-star looks. He was a Justice Department liaison assigned to the regional headquarters. "What'd you screw up, Chief?" Lynch asked.

Chief. Cal had been given his moniker because of his aspirations to become chief director of the International Security Agency. Except they weren't just aspirations. One day he *would* be chief. Since that was his one and only goal, it made things simple.

And in his mind, inevitable.

"Who said I screwed up anything?" Cal commented. But he was asking himself the same thing.

Lynch arched his left eyebrow and flashed a Tom Cruise smile. "You're outside Kowalski's office, aren't you?"

Cal had been assigned to the Bravo team of the ISA for well over a year, and this was the first time he'd ever been ordered to see his director. Since he'd just returned from a monthlong assignment in the Middle East and wouldn't receive new orders within seven duty days, he was bracing himself for bad news.

He'd already called his folks and both of his brothers to make sure all was well on the home front. That meant this had to do with the job. And that made it more personal than anything else could have been.

"If you have a butt left when Kowalski quits chewing it," Hollywood continued, "then show up at the racquetball court at 1730 hours. I believe you promised me a rematch."

Cal mumbled something noncommittal. He hated racquetball, but after this meeting he might need a way to work out some frustrations. Pounding Hollywood might just do it.

The door to the director's office opened, and Cal's lanky boss motioned for him to enter.

"Have a seat," Director Scott Kowalski ordered. There was no mistake about it. His tone and demeanor confirmed that it was an order. "Talk to me about Jenna Laniere."

Cal had geared up to discuss a lot of things with his boss, but she wasn't anywhere on that list. Though he'd certainly thought, and dreamed, about the leggy blonde heiress. "What about her?"

"Tell me what happened when you rescued her in Monte de Leon last year."

That was a truly ominous-sounding request. Still, Cal tried not to let it unnerve him. "As best as I can recall, I entered the hotel where she'd checked in, found her hiding in the bathroom. I moved her from that location and got her to the rendezvous point. About a half hour later or so, the transport took her away, and I rejoined the Bravo team so we could extract some American hostages that the rebels had taken."

Kowalski put his elbows on his desk and leaned closer. "It's that half hour of unaccounted-for time that I'm really interested in."

Hell.

That couldn't be good. Had Jenna Laniere filed some kind of complaint all these months later? If so, Cal had her pegged all wrong. She had seemed too happy about being rescued to be concerned that he'd used profanity around her.

"Wait a minute," Cal mumbled, considering a different scenario. One that involved Paul Tolivar, or rather what was left of Tolivar's regime. "Is Jenna Laniere safe?"

Translation: had Tolivar's cronies or former business partners killed her?

The FBI had followed Jenna for weeks after her return to the States. When no one had attempted to eliminate her, they'd backed off from their surveillance.

As for Tolivar's regime, there hadn't been enough hard evidence for the Monte de Leon or U.S. authorities to arrest Tolivar's partners or anyone else for his murder. In fact, there hadn't been any evidence at all except for Justice Department surveillance tapes that couldn't be used in court since they would give away the identities of several deep-cover operatives. A move that would almost certainly cause the operatives to be executed. The Justice Department wasn't about to lose key men to further investigate a criminal's murder. Especially one that'd happened in a foreign country.

"Ms. Laniere's fine," Kowalski assured him.

The relief Cal felt was a little stronger than he'd expected. And it was short-lived. Because something had obviously happened. Something that involved her. If Jenna had indeed filed a complaint, there'd be an investigation. It could hurt his career.

The one thing he valued more than anything else.

He would not fail at this. He couldn't. Bottom line— being an operative wasn't his job, it was who he was. Without it, he was just the middle son of a highly decorated air force general. The middle son sandwiched between two brothers who'd already proven themselves a dozen times over. Cal had never excelled at anything. In his youth, he'd been average at best and at worst been a screwup—something his father often reminded him of.

His career in the ISA was the one way he could prove to his father, and more important to himself, that he was worth something.

"After you rescued Ms. Laniere, the Justice Department questioned her for hours. Days," Kowalski corrected. "She didn't tell them anything they could use to build their case against Tolivar's business partners. In fact, she claims she never heard Tolivar or his partners speak of the rebel group that they'd organized and funded in Monte de Leon. The group he ordered to kill her. She further claimed that she never heard him discuss his illegal activities."

"And the Justice Department believes she was telling the truth?"

Kowalski made a sound that could have meant anything. "Have you seen or spoken with her in the past year?"

"No." Cal immediately shook his head, correcting that. "I mean, I tried to call her about a month ago, but she wasn't at her office in Houston. I left a message on her voice mail, and then her assistant phoned back to let me know that she was on an extended leave of absence and couldn't be reached."

The director steepled his fingers and stared at Cal. "Why'd you try to call her?"

Cal leaned slightly forward as well. "This is beginning to sound a little like an interrogation."

"Because it is. Now back to the question—why did you make that call?"

Oh, man. That unnerving feeling that Cal had been trying to stave off hit him squarely between the eyes. This was not something he wanted to admit to his director. But he wouldn't lie about it, either.

No matter how uncomfortable it was.

"I was worried about her. Because I read the investigation into Tolivar's business partners had been reopened. I just wanted to see how things were with her."

Judging from the way Director Kowalski's smoke-gray eyes narrowed, that honest answer didn't please him. He muttered a four-letter word.

"Mind telling me what this is about?" Cal asked. "Because last I heard it isn't a crime for a man to call a woman and check on her."

But in this case, his director might consider it a serious error in judgment.

Since Jenna had a direct association with an international criminal like Paul Tolivar, no one working in the ISA should have considered her a candidate for a friendship. Or anything else.

Kowalski aimed an accusing index finger at Cal. "You know it violates regulations to have intimate or sexual contact with someone in your protective custody. And for those thirty minutes in Monte de Leon, Jenna Laniere was definitely in your protective custody."

That brought Cal to his feet. "Sexual contact?" Ah, hell. "Is that what she said happened?"

"Are you saying it didn't?"

"You bet I am. I didn't touch her." It took Cal a few moments to get control of his voice so he could speak. "Did she file a complaint or something against me?"

Kowalski motioned for him to take his seat again. "Trust me, Agent Rico, you'll want to sit down for this part."

Cal bit back his anger and sank onto the chair. Not easily, but he did it. And he forced himself to remain calm. Well, on the outside, anyway. Inside, there was a storm going on, and he could blame that storm on Jenna.

"As you know, I'm head of the task force assigned to clean up the problems in Monte de Leon," Kowalski explained. "The kidnapped American civilians. The destruction of American-owned businesses and interests."

Impatient with what had obviously turned into a

briefing, Cal spoke up. "Is any of this connected to Ms. Laniere?"

"Yes. Apparently, she's still involved with Paul Tolivar's business partners. That's why we started keeping an eye on her again."

That took the edge off some of Cal's anger and grabbed his interest. "Involved—how?"

Kowalski pushed his hands through the sides of his graying brown hair. "She's been staying in a small Texas town, Willow Ridge, for the past couple of months. But prior to that while she was still in Houston, one of Tolivar's partners, Holden Carr, phoned her no less than twenty times. They argued. We're hoping that during one of their future conversations, Holden might divulge some information. That's why the Justice Department has been monitoring Ms. Laniere's calls and emails."

In other words, phone and computer taps. Not exactly standard procedure for someone who wasn't a suspected criminal. Of course, Hollywood would almost certainly have been aware of that surveillance and monitoring, and it made Cal wonder why the man hadn't at least mentioned it. Or maybe Hollywood hadn't remembered that Cal had rescued Jenna.

"What does all of this have to do with alleged sexual misconduct?" Cal insisted.

Kowalski hesitated a moment. Then two. Just enough time to force Cal's anxiety level sky-high. "It's come to our attention that Jenna Laniere has a three-month-old daughter."

Oh, man.

It took Cal a few moments to find his breath, while

he came up with a few questions that he was afraid even to ask.

"So what does that have to do with me?" Cal tried to sound nonchalant, but was sure he failed miserably.

"She claims the baby is yours."

Chapter Two

Cal finally spotted her.

Wearing brown pants and a cream-colored cable-knit sweater, Jenna came out of a small family-owned grocery store on Main Street. She had a white plastic sack clutched in each hand. But no baby.

One thing was for sure—she didn't look as if she'd given birth only three months earlier.

But she did look concerned. Her forehead was bunched up, and her gaze darted all around.

Good. She should be concerned about the lie she'd told. It probably wasn't a healthy thought to want to yell at a woman. But for the entire hour-long drive from regional headquarters to the little town of Willow Ridge, Texas, he'd played around with it.

She claims the baby is yours.

Director Kowalski's words pounded like fists in Cal's head. Powerful words, indeed.

Career-ruining words.

That's why he had to get this situation straightened out so that it couldn't do any more damage. Before the end of the week, he was due for a performance review, one that would be forwarded straight to the promotion board. If he had any hopes of making deputy director two years early, there couldn't even be a hint of negativity in that report.

And there wouldn't be.

That's what this visit was all about. One way or another, Jenna was going to tell the truth and clear his name. He'd worked too damn hard to let her take that early promotion away from him.

Cal stepped out of his car, ducked his head against the chilly February wind and strolled across the small parking lot toward her. He figured she was on her way to the apartment she'd rented over the town's lone bookstore. Judging from the direction she took, he was right.

Even though she kept close to the buildings, she was easy to track. Partly because there weren't many people out and about and partly because of her hair. Those shiny blond locks dipped several inches past her shoulders. Loose and free. The strands seemed to catch every ray of sun.

That hair would probably cause any man to give her a second look. Her body and face would cause a man to stare. Which was exactly what he was doing.

She must have sensed his eyes on her because she whirled around, her gaze snaring him right away.

"It's you," she said, squinting to see him in the harsh late afternoon sun. She sounded a little wary and surprised.

However, Cal's reactions were solely in the latter category.

First, there were her eyes. That shock of color. So green. So clear. He hadn't gotten a good look at her eyes when he rescued her in that dimly lit hotel, but he did now. And they were memorable. As was her face.

She wore almost no makeup. Just a touch of peachy color on her mouth. She looked natural and sensual at the same time. But the most startling reaction of all was that he wasn't as angry at her as he had been five minutes before.

Well, until he forced himself to hang on to that particular feeling awhile longer.

"We have to talk," Cal insisted. And he wasn't about to let her say no. He took one of her grocery sacks so he could hook his arm through hers.

She looked down at the grip he had on her before she lifted her eyes to meet his. "This is about Paul Tolivar's business partner, isn't it? Is Holden Carr the one who's having me followed?"

That stopped Cal in his tracks. There was a mountain of concern in her voice and expression. Much to his shock, he wasn't immune to that concern.

He didn't like this feeling. The sudden need to protect her. This sure as heck wasn't an ISA-directed mission.

He repeated that to himself. "Someone is following you?" he asked.

She gave a surreptitious glance around, and since their arms were already linked, she maneuvered him into an alley that divided two shops.

"I spotted this man on my walk to the grocery store. He stayed in the shadows so I wasn't able to get a good look at him." Her words raced out, practically bleeding together. "Maybe he's following me, maybe he's not. And there's a reporter. Gwen Mitchell. She introduced herself a couple of minutes ago in the produce aisle."

Cal made note of the name. Once he was done with

this little chat, he'd run a background check on this Gwen Mitchell to see if she was legit. "What does she want?"

Jenna dismissed his question with a shrug, though tension was practically radiating from her. The muscles in her arm were tight and knotted. "She claims she's doing some kind of investigative report on Paul and the rebel situation in Monte de Leon."

That in itself wasn't alarming. There were probably lots of reporters doing similar stories because of the renewed investigation. "You don't believe her?"

"I don't know. Since the incident in Monte de Leon, I've been paranoid. Shadows don't look like shadows anymore. Hang-up calls seem sinister. Strangers in the grocery line look like rebel soldiers with orders to kill me." She shook her head. "And I'm sorry for dumping all of this on you. I know I'm not making any sense."

Unfortunately, she was making perfect sense. Cal had never met Paul's business partner, the infamous Holden Carr, but from what he'd learned about the man, Holden wasn't the sort to give up easily. Maybe he wanted to continue his late partner's quest to get Jenna's accounting firm and trust fund. Jenna's firm certainly wasn't the only one enticing to a potential money launderer, but Holden was familiar with it, and it had all the right foreign outlets to give him a quick turnover for the illegal cash.

Or maybe this was good news, and those shadows were Justice Department agents. Except Director Kowalski hadn't mentioned anything about her being followed. It was one thing to monitor calls and emails, but tailing a person required just cause and a lot of manpower. Since Jenna wasn't a suspect in a crime, there shouldn't have been sufficient cause for close surveillance.

And that brought them right back to Holden Carr.

"You've heard from Holden recently?" he asked. A lie detector of sorts since he knew from the director's briefing that she'd been in contact with the man in the past twenty-four hours.

"Oh, I've heard from him all right. Lucky me, huh? He's called a bunch of times, and right after I got back from Monte de Leon, he visited my office in Houston. And get this—he says he's always been in love with me, that he wants to be part of my life. Right. He's in love with my estate and accounting firm, and what he really wants is to be part of my death so he can inherit it." She paused. "Please tell me he'll be arrested soon."

"Soon." But Cal had no idea if that was even true.

"Good. Because as long as he's a free man, I'm not safe. That's why I left Houston. I thought maybe if I came here, Holden wouldn't be able to find me. That he'd stop harassing me. Then yesterday afternoon he called me again, on my new cell phone." She moistened her lips. And looked away. "He threatened me."

That didn't surprise Cal. Holden wouldn't hesitate to resort to intimidation to get what he wanted. Still, that was a problem for the back burner. He had something more pressing.

"Holden didn't make an overt threat," Jenna continued before Cal could speak. "He implied it. It scared me enough to decide that I need professional security. A bodyguard or something. But I don't know anyone

I can trust. I don't know if the bodyguard I call might really be working for Holden."

Unfortunately, that was a real possibility. If Holden knew where she was, then he would also know how to get to her.

She paused and blew out a long breath. "Okay, that's enough about me and my problems. Why are you here?" She conjured a halfhearted smile. "Gosh, that's a déjà vu kind of question, isn't it? I remember asking you something similar when you were rescuing me in Monte de Leon. Is that why you're here now—to rescue me?"

"No." But why the heck did he suddenly feel as if he wanted to do just that?

From that still panicked look in her eyes, it wasn't a good time to bring up his anger, but Cal wasn't about to let her off the hook, either.

"Why did you lie about who your baby's father is?" he demanded.

Jenna blinked, and then her eyes widened. "How did you know?"

"Well, it wasn't a lucky guess, that's for sure. This morning my director called me into his office to demand an explanation as to why I slept with someone in my protective custody."

"Ohmygod." Jenna leaned against the wall and pulled in several hard breaths. "I had no idea. How did your director even find out I'd had a baby?"

Because she already had a lot to absorb, Cal skipped right over the Justice Department eavesdropping on her, and gave her a summary of what Director Kowalski had relayed to him. "You told Holden Carr that the baby was mine."

Jenna nodded, and with her breath now gusting hard and fast, she studied his expression. It was as icy as the Antarctic. "This could get you into trouble, couldn't it?"

"It's *already* gotten me into trouble. Deep trouble. And it could get worse."

He would have added more, especially the part about Director Kowalski demanding DNA proof that Cal wasn't the baby's father. But he caught some movement from the corner of his eye. A thin-faced man in a dark blue two-door car. He drove slowly past them.

"That's the guy," Jenna whispered, tugging on the sleeve of Cal's leather jacket. "He's the one who followed me to the grocery store."

The words had hardly left her mouth when the man gunned the engine and sped away. But not before Cal made eye contact with him.

Oh, hell.

Cal recognized him from the intel surveillance photos.

He cursed, dropped the grocery bag and slipped his hand inside his jacket in case he had to draw his gun. "How long did you say he's been following you?"

Jenna shook her head and looked to be on the verge of panicking. "I think just today. Why? Do you know him? Is he a friend of yours?"

There was way too much hope in her voice.

"Not a friend," Cal assured her. "But I know *of* him." He left it at that. "Where's your baby?"

"In the apartment. My landlord's daughter is watching her. Why?"

Cal didn't answer that. "Come on. We'll finish this conversation there."

And once they had finished the discussion about the paternity of her child, he'd move on to some security measures he wanted her to take. Maybe the Justice Department could even provide her with protection or a safe house. He'd call Hollywood and Director Kowalski and put in a request.

Cal tried to get her moving, but Jenna held her ground. "Tell me—who's that man?"

Okay, so that wasn't panic in her eyes. It was determination. She wasn't about to drop this. Not even for a couple of minutes until they could reach her apartment.

"Anthony Salazar," Cal let her know. "That's his real name, anyway. He often uses an alias."

She stared at him. "He works for Holden Carr?"

"He usually just works for the person who'll pay him the most." Cal hadn't intended to pause, but he had to so he could clear his throat. "He's a hired assassin, Jenna."

Chapter Three

Jenna was glad the exterior wall of the café was there to support her, or her legs might have given way.

First, there was Cal's out-of-the-blue visit to deal with.

Then the news that he knew about the lie she'd told.

And now this.

"An assassin?" she repeated.

Somehow she managed to say aloud the two little words that had sent her world spinning out of control—again. She'd had a lot of that lately and was more than ready for it to stop.

Cal cursed under his breath. He picked up the grocery bag he'd dropped and then slipped his arm around her waist.

Jenna thought of her baby. Of Sophie. She couldn't let that assassin get anywhere near her daughter.

She started to break into a run, but Cal maneuvered her off the sidewalk and behind the café. They walked quickly into the alley that ran the entire length of Main Street. So they'd be out of sight.

"You didn't know that guy was here?" she asked as they hurried.

"No."

That meant Cal had come to confront her about naming him as Sophie's father. That alone was a powerful reason for a visit. She owed him an explanation.

And a Texas-size apology.

But for now, all Jenna wanted to do was get inside her apartment and make sure that hired gun, Anthony Salazar, was nowhere near her baby. And to think he might have been following her on her entire walk to the grocery store. Or even longer. He could have taken out a gun and fired at any time, and there wouldn't have been a thing she could do to stop it.

He could have hurt Sophie.

Maybe because she was shaking now, Cal tightened his grip around her, pulling her deeper into the warmth of his arm, while increasing the pace until they were jogging.

"I didn't name you as my baby's father to hurt your career," she assured him. "I didn't think anyone other than Holden would hear what I was saying."

A deep sound of disapproval rumbled in Cal's throat. He didn't offer anything else until they reached the bookstore. Her apartment was at the back and up the flight of stairs on the second floor.

"You have a security system?" he asked as they hurried up the steps.

"Yes."

She unlocked the door—both locks—tossed the groceries and her purse on the table in the entry and bolted across the room. The sixteen-year-old sitter, Manda, was on the sofa reading a magazine. Jenna raced past her to the bedroom and saw Sophie sleeping in her crib.

Exactly where she'd left her just a half hour earlier at the start of her afternoon nap.

"Is something wrong?" Manda asked, standing.

Jenna didn't answer that. "Did anyone come by or call?"

Manda shook her head, obviously concerned. "Are you okay?"

"Fine," Jenna lied. "I just had a bad case of baby separation. I had to get back and make sure Sophie was all right. And she is. She's sleeping like…well, a baby."

Still looking concerned, Manda nodded, and her gaze landed on Cal.

"He's an old friend," Jenna explained. She purposely didn't say Cal's name. Best not to give too much information until she knew what was going on. Besides, she'd already caused Cal enough trouble.

Jenna took the twenty-dollar bill from her pocket and handed it to Manda. "But I was barely here thirty minutes," the teen protested. "Five bucks an hour, remember?"

"Consider the rest a tip." Jenna put her hand on Manda's back to get her moving. She needed some privacy so she could find out what was going on.

"Why didn't the alarm go off when we came in?" he wanted to know as soon as Manda walked out with her magazine tucked beneath her arm. It wasn't a question, exactly. More like the start of a cross-examination.

"It's connected to the bookstore." She shut the door and locked it. "The owner turns it on when she closes for the evening."

That didn't please him. His disapproving gaze fired around the apartment, but it didn't have to too far. It was one large twenty-by-twenty-five-foot room with an adjoining bath and a tiny nursery. The kitchenette and dining area were on one side, and the living room with its sofa bed was on the other. It wasn't exactly quaint and cozy with the vaulted, exposed beam ceiling, but it was a far cry from her massive family home near Houston.

"Why this place?" he asked after he'd finished his assessment.

"It has fewer shadows," she said, not wanting to explain about her sudden fear of bogeymen, assassins and rebel fighters.

She could still hear the bullets.

She'd always be able to hear them.

Cal nodded and eased the grocery bag onto the tile-topped table.

"You want a drink or something?" Jenna motioned to the fridge.

"No, thanks." There was an unspoken warning at the end of that. That was her cue to start explaining this whole baby-daddy issue.

She was feeling light-headed and was still shivering, so Jenna snagged the trail mix from her grocery bag and went to the sofa so she could sit down.

"First of all, I didn't know what I said about the baby would even get back to you. To anyone." She popped a cashew into her mouth and offered him some from the bag. He shook his head. "Yesterday, when Holden called, I'd just returned from Sophie's three-month checkup with the pediatrician. Right away, he started yelling, saying that he knew that I'd had a child."

"How did he know?"

"That's the million-dollar question." But then, Jenna

rethought that. "Or maybe not. I stopped by my house on the outskirts of Houston to pick up some things before I went to the appointment. Holden probably had someone watching the place and then followed me. I was careful. You know, always checking the rearview mirror and the parking lot at the clinic. But he could have had that Salazar guy following me the whole time."

In hindsight, she should have anticipated Holden would do something like this. In fact, she should have known he would. He was as tenacious as he was ruthless.

"So Holden confronted you about the baby?" Cal asked.

"Oh, yes. Complete with yelling obscenities. And that was just the prelude. No more facade of being in love with me. He demanded to know if Paul was Sophie's father. If so, he said he would challenge me for custody."

"Custody?" Cal didn't hide his surprise very well.

"Apparently, Paul had some kind of provision in his will that would make Holden the legal guardian to any child that Paul might have—if I'm proven unfit, which Holden says he can do with his connections. After he threatened me with that, I stalled him, trying to think of what I should say, and your message was still in my head. It made the leap from my brain to my mouth before I could stop it, and I just blurted out your name."

Cal walked closer and slid onto the chair across from her. Close enough for her to see all the scorching blue in his eyes. And close enough to see the emotion and the anger, too. "My message?"

She swallowed hard. "The one you left on my voice

mail at my office about a month ago. My assistant sent it to me, and I'd recently listened to it."

A lot. In fact, she'd memorized it.

She'd found his voice comforting, and that's why she'd replayed it. Night after night. When she couldn't sleep. When the nightmares got the best of her. But his voice wasn't comforting now, of course. Coupled with his riled glare, there wasn't much comforting about him or this visit.

Well, except that he'd put his arm around her when he thought she was cold.

A special kind of special agent.

He still looked the part, even though he wasn't in battle gear today. He wore jeans, a dark blue button-down shirt that was almost the same color as his eyes and a black leather jacket.

"Anyway, after I realized it was stupid to give Holden your name," she continued, "I thought about calling him back and making something up. But I figured that'd only make him more suspicious."

Because Cal wasn't saying anything and because she suddenly didn't know what to do with her hands, Jenna offered him the trail mix again, and this time he reached into the bag and took out a few pieces.

"I've done everything to keep my pregnancy and delivery quiet. *Everything,*" Jenna said, aware that her nerves were causing her to babble. It was either that, humming or reciting something, and she didn't want to launch into a neurotic rendition of the Preamble to the Constitution. "I don't have any family, and none of my friends know. No one here in Willow Ridge really knows who I am, either."

She didn't think it was her imagination that he was hesitant to say anything. Under the guise of eating trail mix, Cal sat there, letting her babble linger between them.

Since she had to know what was going on in his head, Jenna just went for the direct approach. "How did your director find out that I'd told Holden about my baby?"

His jaw muscles began to stir against each other. "The Justice Department has kept tabs on you."

"Tabs?" She took a moment to consider that. "That's an interesting word. What does it mean exactly?"

More jaw muscles moved. "It means they were keeping track of you in case Holden decided to divulge anything incriminating they could use in their case against him."

So it was true. Her fears weren't all in her head. The authorities thought Holden might be a danger as well.

Or maybe they didn't.

Maybe they were just hoping Holden would do something stupid so they could use that to arrest him.

"I was bait?" she asked.

"No." But then he lifted his shoulder. "At least I don't think so."

Jenna prayed that was true. The thought wasn't something she could handle right now.

"The baby is Paul Tolivar's?" Cal asked.

She nodded. And waited for his reaction. She didn't get one. He put on his operative's face again. "Just how much trouble will this cause for you?" she wanted to know.

"The ISA has a morality clause." His fingers tightened around a dried apricot, squishing it. "Plus, the regs forbid personal contact during a protective custody situation."

That was not what she wanted to hear. "You could be punished."

Again, it took him a moment to answer. "Yeah."

"Okay." Jenna took a deep breath, and because she couldn't stay still, she got up to pace. There was a solution to this. Not necessarily an appetizing solution, but it did exist. "Will my statement that I lied be enough to clear you, or will you need a paternity test?"

"My director wants a test." He stood as well, and caught her arm when she started to go past him. His fingers were warm. Surprisingly warm. She could feel his touch all the way through her thick sweater. "But I think that's the least of your worries right now."

"Because of Anthony Salazar." Jenna nodded. "Yes. He's definitely a worry. His being here means I'll need to leave Willow Ridge and go into hiding."

"You're already in hiding," Cal pointed out. "And he found you. He'll find you again. He's very good at what he does. You need more protection than a bookstore security system or a hired bodyguard can give you. I'll make some calls and see what I can do."

Pride almost caused her to decline his offer. But she knew that it wouldn't protect her baby. And that was the most important thing right now. She had to stay safe because if anything happened to her, it would happen to her precious daughter as well.

"Thank you," Jenna whispered. She repeated it to make sure he heard her. "I really am sorry about dragging you into my personal life."

"We'll get it straightened out," he assured her. But there was a lot of skepticism in his voice.

And annoyance, which she deserved.

"Okay, while you make those calls, I'll arrange to have the paternity test done," Jenna added.

Somehow, though, she'd have to keep the results a secret from anyone but Cal and his director.

Because she didn't want Holden to learn the truth. Jenna moved away from Cal and started to pace again, mumbling a poem she'd memorized in middle school. She couldn't help it. A few lines came out before she could stop them.

"What you must think of me," she said. "For what it's worth, Paul and I only had sex once, and we used protection. But I guess something went wrong…on a lot of levels. Honestly, I don't really even remember sleeping with him." Jenna mumbled that last part.

"You don't remember?" he challenged.

She shook her head. "One minute we were having dinner, and the next thing I remember was waking up in bed with him. I obviously had too much to drink. Or else he drugged me. Either way, it was my stupid mistake for being there. Then I made things so much worse by telling Holden that you're my daughter's father. And here we didn't even have sex. Heck, we never even kissed on the floor of that cantina."

A clear image formed in her mind. Of that floor. Of Cal on top of her to protect her from the explosion. It wasn't exactly pleasurable. Okay, it was. But it wasn't supposed to be.

Not then.

Not now.

She'd already done enough damage to Cal's career without her adding unwanted sexual attraction that could never go beyond the fantasy stage.

He opened his mouth to say something, but didn't get past the first syllable. There was a knock at the door, the sudden sound shattering the silence.

Cal reacted fast. He reached inside his jacket and pulled out a handgun from a shoulder holster. He motioned for her to move out of the path of the door.

Jenna raced across the room and took a knife from the cutlery drawer. It probably wouldn't give them much protection, but she didn't intend to let Cal fight alone. Especially since the battle was hers.

With his hands gripped around his weapon, he eased toward the door. Every inch of his posture and demeanor was vigilant. Ready. Lethal.

Cal didn't use the peephole to look outside, but instead peered out the corner of the window.

He cursed softly.

"It's Holden Carr."

Chapter Four

This was not how Cal had planned his visit.

It was supposed to be in and out quickly. He was only on a fact-finding mission so he could get out of hot water with the director. Instead, he'd walked right into a vipers' nest. And one viper was way too close.

Holden Carr was literally pounding on Jenna's door.

Cal glanced back at her. With a butcher knife in a white-knuckled death grip, Jenna was standing guard in front of the nursery. She was pale, trembling and nibbling on her bottom lip. *Bam!* There were his protective instincts.

There was no way he could let her face Holden Carr alone. From everything Cal had read about the man, Holden was as dangerous as Paul, his former business partner. And Paul had been ready to commit murder to get his hands on Jenna's estate.

"Go to your daughter," Cal instructed while Holden continued to pound.

She shook her head. "You might need backup."

He lifted his eyebrow. She wasn't exactly backup material. Jenna Laniere might have been temporarily living in a starter apartment in a quaint Texas cowboy town, but her blue blood and pampered upbringing couldn't have prepared her for the likes of Holden Carr.

"I'll handle this," Cal let her know, and he left no room for argument.

She mumbled something, but stepped back into the nursery.

With his SIG Sauer drawn, Cal stood to the side of the door. It was standard procedure—bad guys often like to shoot through doors. But Holden probably didn't have that in mind. It was broad daylight and with the door-pounding, he was probably drawing all kinds of attention to himself, but Cal didn't want to take an unnecessary risk.

Once he was in place, he reached over. Unlocked the door. And eased it open.

Cal jammed his gun right in Holden's face.

Holden's dust-gray eyes sliced in the direction of the SIG Sauer. There was just a flash of shock and concern before he buried those reactions in the cool composure of his Nordic pale skin and his Viking-size body. He was decked out in a pricy camel-colored suit that probably cost more than Cal made in a month.

"I'm Holden Carr and I need to see Jenna," he announced.

Cal didn't lower his gun. In fact, he jabbed it against Holden's right cheek. "Oh, yeah? About what?"

"A private matter."

"It's not so private. From what I've heard you're threatening her. It takes a special kind of man to threaten a woman half his size. Of course, you're no stranger to violence, are you? Did you murder Paul Tolivar?"

Holden couldn't quite bury his anger fast enough. It rippled through his jaw muscles and his eyes. "Who the hell are you?"

"Cal Rico. I'm Jenna's…friend." But he let his tone indicate that he was the man who wouldn't hesitate to pull the trigger if Holden tried to barge his way in. "Anything you have to say to Jenna, you can say to me. I'll make sure she gets the message."

"The message is she can't hide from me forever." Holden enunciated each word. "I know she had a baby. A little girl named Sophie Elizabeth. Born three months ago. That means the child is Paul's."

It didn't surprise Cal that Holden knew all of this, but what else did he know? "Paul, the man you murdered," Cal challenged.

There was another flash of anger. "Not that it's any of your business, but I didn't murder him. His housekeeper did. She was secretly working for a rebel faction who had issues with some of Paul's businesses."

"Right. The housekeeper." Cal made sure he sounded skeptical. He'd already heard the theory of the runaway housekeeper known only as Mary. "I don't suppose she confessed."

Holden had to get his teeth apart before he could respond. "She fled the estate after she killed him. No one's been able to find her."

"Convenient. Now, mind telling me how you came by this information about Jenna's child?"

"Yes. I mind."

Cal hadn't expected him to volunteer that, since it almost certainly involved illegal activity. "Hmmm. I smell a wire tap. That kind of illegal activity can get you arrested. Your dual citizenship won't do a thing to protect you, either. If you hightail it back to Monte de Leon, you can be extradited."

Though that wasn't likely. Still, Cal made a note to discover the source of that possible tap.

Holden looked past him, and because they were so close, Cal saw the man's eyes light up. Cal didn't have to guess why. Holden was aiming his attention in the direction of the nursery door and had probably spotted Jenna. He tried to come inside, but Cal blocked the door with his foot.

"She'll have to talk to me sooner or later," Holden insisted. "Call off your guard dog," he yelled at Jenna.

"What do you want?" Jenna asked. Cal silently groaned when he heard her walking closer. She really didn't take orders very well.

"I want you to carry out Paul's wishes. In his will, he named me guardian of his children. He didn't have any children at the time he wrote that, but he does now."

"You only want my daughter so you can control me," Jenna tossed out.

Holden didn't deny it. "I've petitioned the court for custody," he said.

Jenna stopped right next to Cal, and she reached across his body to open the door wider. "No judge would give you custody."

"Maybe not in this country, but in Monte de Leon, the law will be on Paul's side. Even in death he's still a powerful man with powerful friends."

"Sophie's an American," Jenna pointed out. "Born right here in Texas."

"And you think that'll stop Paul's wishes from being

carried out? It won't. If the Monte de Leon court deems you unfit—and that can easily happen with the right judge—then the court will petition for the child to be brought to her father's estate."

"Sophie is not Paul's child." She looked Holden right in the eye when she told that lie.

But Holden only smiled. "I've seen pictures of her. She looks just like him. Dark brown hair. Blue eyes."

Pictures meant he had surveillance along with taps. This was not looking good.

Cal could hear Jenna's breath speed up. Fear had a smell, and she was throwing off that scent, along with motherly protection vibes. But that wouldn't do anything to convince this SOB that he didn't have a right to claim her child.

From the corner of his eye, Cal spotted a movement. There was a tall redheaded woman with a camera. She was about forty yards away across the street and was clicking pictures of this encounter. Gwen Mitchell no doubt. And she wasn't the only woman there. He also spotted a slender blonde making her way up the steps to Jenna's apartment.

"That's Helena Carr," Jenna provided.

Holden's sister and business partner. Great. Now there was an added snake to deal with, and it was all playing out in front of a photographer with questionable motives. Cal could already hear himself having to explain why he was in small-town America with his standard-issue SIG Sauer smashed against a civilian's face.

"This meeting is over," Cal insisted. He lowered his gun, but he kept it aimed at Holden's right kneecap.

"It'll be over when Jenna admits that her daughter is Paul's," Holden countered.

"We just want the truth." That from Helena, who was a feminine version of her brother without the Viking-wide shoulders. Her stare was different, too. Nonthreatening. Almost serene. "After all, we know she slept with Paul, and the timing is perfect to have produced Sophie."

Cal hoped he didn't regret this later, but there was one simple way to diffuse this. "I have dark brown hair, blue eyes. Just like Sophie's." He hoped, since he hadn't actually seen the little girl.

Helena blinked and gave him an accusing stare. Holden cursed. "Are you saying you're the father?" he asked.

"No," Jenna started to say. But Cal made sure his voice drowned her out.

"Yes," Cal snarled. "I'm Sophie's father."

"Impossible," Holden snarled back.

Cal gave him a cocky snort. "There is nothing impossible about it. I'm a man. Jenna's a woman. Sometimes men and women have sex, and that results in a pregnancy."

And just in case Jenna was going to say something to contradict him, Cal gave her a quick glance. She was staring at him as if he'd lost his mind.

"You won't mind taking a DNA test," Holden insisted.

"Tell you what. You send the request for a DNA sample through your foreign judge and let it trickle its way through our American judicial system. Then I'll get back to you with an answer."

Of course, the answer would be no.

Still, that wouldn't stop Holden from trying. If he controlled Jenna's child, then he would ultimately have access to a vast money-laundering enterprise. Then he could fully operate his own family business and the one he'd inherited from Paul.

"This isn't over." Holden aimed the threat at Jenna as he stalked away.

Cal was about to shut the door and call his director so he could start some damage control, but Helena eased her hand onto the side to stop it from closing.

"I'm sorry about this." Helena sounded sincere. Or else she'd rehearsed it enough to fake sincerity. Maybe this was the brother-sister version of good cop/bad cop. "I just want the truth so I can make sure Paul's child inherits what she deserves."

Jenna didn't even address that. "Can you stop your brother?"

Cal carefully noted Helena's reaction. She glanced over her shoulder. First at her brother who was getting inside their high-end car. Then at the photographer.

"Could I step inside for just a moment?" That sincerity thing was there again.

But Cal wasn't buying it.

Jenna apparently did. With the butcher knife still clutched in her hand, she stepped back so Helena could enter.

"That reporter out there might have some way to eavesdrop on us," Helena explained. "She has equipment and cameras with her."

Maybe. But Cal hadn't seen anything to suggest long-range eavesdropping equipment. Still, it was an unnecessary risk to keep talking in plain view. Lipreading was a possibility. Plus, anything said here could ultimately put Jenna in more danger and get him in deeper trouble with the director. Not that her paternity claims were exactly newsworthy, but he didn't want to see his and Jenna's names and photos splashed in a newspaper.

"Well?" Cal prompted when Helena continued to look around and didn't say anything else.

"Where do I start?" She seemed to be waiting for an invitation to sit down, but Cal didn't offer. Helena sighed. "My brother is determined to carry out Paul's wishes. They've been friends since childhood when our parents moved to Monte de Leon to start businesses there. Holden was devastated when Paul was killed."

Cal shrugged. "Paul isn't the father of Jenna's child, so there's no wish to carry out."

The last word had hardly left his mouth when he heard a soft whimpering cry sound coming from the nursery.

"Sophie," Jenna mumbled.

"Go to her," Cal advised. "I'll finish up here."

Jenna hesitated. But not for long—the baby's cries were getting louder.

"I do need to talk to Jenna," Helena continued. She opened her purse and rummaged through it. "Do you have a pen? I want to leave my cell number so she can contact me."

That was actually a good idea. He might be able to get approval to trace Helena's calls and obtain a record of her past ones.

Cal didn't have a pen with him, and he looked around before spotting one and a notepad on the kitchen countertop. He got it and glanced into the nursery while he was on that side of the room. Jenna was leaning over the crib changing Sophie's diaper.

"Someone was following Jenna." Cal walked back to Helena and handed her the pen and notepad.

She dodged his gaze, took the pen and wrote down her number. "You mean that reporter across the street? She approached us when we drove up and said she was doing an article about Paul. She said she recognized Holden from newspaper pictures."

Cal shook his head. "Not her. Someone else. A man." He watched for a reaction.

Helena shrugged and handed him the notepad. "You think I know something about it?"

"Do you? The man's name is Anthony Salazar."

Her eyes widened. "Salazar," she repeated on a rise of breath. "You've seen him here in Willow Ridge?"

"I've seen him," Cal confirmed. "Now, mind telling me how you know him?"

Her breath became even more rapid, and she glanced around to make sure it was safe to talk. "Anthony Salazar is evil," she said in a whisper.

He caught her arm when she turned to leave. "And you know this how?"

She opened her mouth but stopped. "Are you wearing a wire?" she demanded.

"No, and I'm not going to strip down to prove it. But you *are* going to give me answers."

Her chin came up. Since he had hold of her arm, he could feel that she was trembling. "You're trying to make me say something incriminating."

Yeah. But for now, Cal would settle for the truth.

"What's your connection to Salazar? Does he work for your brother? For you?"

She reached behind her and opened the door. "He worked for Paul."

He hadn't expected that answer. "Paul's dead."

"But his estate isn't."

"What does that mean?" Cal asked cautiously.

"Yesterday was the first anniversary of Paul's death. Early this morning his attorney delivered emails of instruction to people named in his will. I saw the list. Salazar got one."

Cal paused a moment to give that some thought. "Are you saying Paul reached out from the grave and hired this man to do something to Jenna?"

"That's exactly what I'm saying." Helena turned and delivered the rest from over her shoulder as she started down the steps. "Neither Holden nor I can call off Salazar. No one can."

Chapter Five

After Jenna changed Sophie's diaper, she gently rocked her until her daughter's whimpers and cries faded. It took just a few seconds before her baby was calm, cooing and smiling at her. It was like magic, and even though it warmed her heart to see her baby so happy, Jenna only wished she could be soothed so easily.

Not much of a chance of that with Holden, his sister and that assassin lurking around. She kept mumbling the poem "The Raven," and hoped the mechanical exercise would keep her calm.

She heard Cal shut and lock the door, and Jenna wanted to be out there while he was talking to Helena. After all, this was her fight, not Cal's. But she also didn't want Holden or Helena anywhere near her baby.

With Helena gone, Jenna went into the kitchen so she could fix Sophie a bottle. Cal glanced at her, but he had his phone already pressed to his ear, so he didn't say anything to her.

"Hollywood, I need a big favor," Cal said to the person on the other end of the phone line. "The subjects are Holden Carr, Jenna Laniere and Anthony Salazar." He paused. "Yes, the Holden and Jenna from Monte de Leon. I need to know how he found out where she's living. Look for wiretaps first and then dig into her employees. I want to know about any connection with anyone who could have given him this info or photos of Jenna Laniere's baby."

Well, that was a start. Hopefully Cal's contacts would give them an answer soon. It wouldn't, however, solve her problem with Salazar.

She and Sophie needed protection.

And she needed to clear up the paternity issue with Cal's director. And amid all that, she had to make arrangements to move. The apartment was no longer safe now that Holden and Helena Carr knew where she was. Packing wouldn't take long—for the past year, she'd literally been living out of a suitcase, anyway.

With Sophie nestled in the crook of her arm, Jenna warmed the formula, tested a drop on her wrist to make sure it wasn't too hot, and carried both baby and bottle to the sofa so she could feed her. Sophie wasn't smiling any longer. She was hungry and was making more of those whimpering demands. Jenna kissed her cheek and started to feed her.

Once it was quiet, it was impossible to shut out what Cal was saying. He was still giving someone instructions about checking on the reporter and where to look for Holden Carr's leak, and Cal wanted the person to learn more about some emails that might have recently been sent out by Paul's attorney.

She didn't know anything about emails, but a leak in communication could mean someone might have betrayed her. There was just one problem with that. Before the trip to the pediatrician, no one including her own household staff and employees had known where she was.

Now everyone seemed to know.

Cal ended his call and scrubbed his hand over his face. He was obviously frustrated. So was Jenna. But she had to figure out a way to get Cal out of the picture. He didn't deserve this, and once she was at a safe location, she could get the DNA test for Sophie.

"So, this is Sophie," he commented, walking closer. "She's so little for someone who's caused a lot of big waves."

"I'm the one who caused the waves," Jenna corrected.

Cal shrugged it off, but she doubted he was doing that on the inside. "She seems to like that bottle."

"I couldn't breast-feed her. I got mastitis—that's an infection—right after she was born. By the time it'd run its course and I was off the antibiotics, Sophie decided the bottle was for her." Jenna cringed a little, wondering why she'd shared something so personal with a man who was doing everything he could to get her out of his life.

Cal walked even closer, and Sophie responded to the sound of his footsteps by turning her head in his direction. She tracked him with her wide blue-green eyes and fastened her gaze on him when he sat on the sofa next to them. Even with the bottle in her mouth, she smiled at him.

Much to Jenna's surprise, Cal smiled back.

It was a great smile, too, and made him look even hotter than he already was. That smile was a lethal weapon in his arsenal.

"She looks like you," Cal said. "Your face. Your eyes."

"Paul's coloring, though," she added softly. "But when I look at her, I don't see him. I never have. I loved her unconditionally from the first moment I realized I was pregnant." Sheez. More personal stuff.

Why couldn't she stop babbling?

"Helena left you her cell number," Cal said, dropping the notepad onto the coffee table, switching the subject. "She said you're to call her."

Jenna glanced at it and noticed that it had a local area code. "What does she want?"

"Honestly? I don't know. All I know is I don't trust her or Holden." Sophie kicked at him, and he brushed his fingers over her bare toes. He smiled again. But the smile quickly faded. "Helena said that early this morning Salazar received an email from Paul's estate. It might have something to do with why he's here."

Paul again. "It doesn't matter why he's here. I plan to call the Willow Ridge sheriff and see if he can arrest him."

"That's one option. Probably not a good one, though. Salazar won't be easy to catch."

"But we both saw him, right there on Main Street," Jenna pointed out.

Cal nodded. "Unless the local sheriff is very good at what he does, and very lucky, he could get killed attempting to arrest a man like Salazar."

Oh, mercy. She hadn't even considered that. "Then I have to move sooner than I thought. As soon as Sophie's finished with her bottle, I'll—"

But she stopped there because it involved too many steps and a lot of phone calls.

Where should she start?

"We'll have some information about Holden soon," Cal finished for her. "Once we have that, we'll go from there. It's best if we arrange for someone else to pick up Salazar, not the local sheriff."

"We?" she challenged, wondering why he wasn't excusing himself from this situation.

He kept his attention on Sophie and reached out and touched one of her dark brown curls. "We, as in someone assigned from the International Security Agency."

But not him. A coworker, maybe.

Jenna thought about that for a moment and wondered about the man sitting next to her. She hadn't forgotten the way he'd bashed through a window to save her. "Are you a spy?"

He didn't blink, didn't react. "I'm an operative."

"Is that another word for a spy?"

"It can be." Still no reaction. "The ISA is a sister organization to the CIA. We have no jurisdiction on American soil. We operate only in foreign countries to protect American interests, mainly through rescues and extractions in hostile situations." He took his eyes off Sophie and aimed them at her. "I'm not sure how much I can get involved in your situation."

"I understand." Sophie was finished with her bottle, and Jenna put her against her shoulder so she could burp her. "Besides, I've caused you enough trouble."

He didn't disagree. But there was some kind of debate stirring inside him. "I hadn't expected to want to protect you," he admitted.

Oh. She was surprised not just by his desire to help her, but also by the admission itself. "Why?"

"Why?" he repeated.

She searched his eyes, looking for an answer. Or at least a way to rephrase the question so that it didn't imply the attraction she felt for him. An attraction he probably didn't feel.

"Why did you call my office in Houston last month?" It was something Jenna had wanted to ask since she'd received the message.

Cal shrugged. "The ISA was reopening the investigation into Paul's business dealings and murder. I wanted to make sure you were okay."

"And that's all?" She nearly waved that off. But something in his eyes had her holding her tongue. She wanted to know the reason.

He didn't dodge her gaze. "I was going to see if you'd gotten over Paul. I'd planned to ask you out."

Jenna went still. So maybe the attraction was mutual after all.

She doubted that was a good thing.

"I was over Paul the moment he slapped me for refusing his marriage proposal," Jenna let him know.

His jaw muscles went to war again. "I heard that slap. I was monitoring you with long-distance eavesdropping equipment."

She felt her cheeks flush. It embarrassed her to know that anyone, especially Cal, had witnessed that. The whole incident with Paul was a testament to her poor judgment.

"I've been a screwup most of my life," she admitted.

He made a throaty sound of surprise. "You think that slap was your fault?"

"I think being at Paul's estate was my first mistake. I should have had him investigated before I went down there. I shouldn't have trusted him."

He leaned closer. "Is this where I should remind you about hindsight and that Paul was a really good con artist?"

"It wouldn't help. I've been duped by two other losers. One in college—my supposed boyfriend stole my credit cards and some jewelry. And then there was the assistant I hired right before this mess with Paul. He sold business secrets to my competition." She paused, brought her eyes back to his. "That's why I'm not jumping for joy that you wanted to ask me out."

Cal flexed his eyebrows. "You think I'm a loser like those other guys?"

"No." Shocked that he'd even suggest it, she repeated her denial. "I know you're not. But I have this trust issue now. On top of the damage I've caused your career, I know I'd be bad for you."

He didn't say a word, and the silence closed in around them. Seconds passed.

"Remember when you were lying beneath me in that cantina?" he asked.

"Oh, yes." She winced because she said it so quickly. And so fondly.

"Well, I remember it, too. Heck, I fantasize about it. I was hoping once I saw you, once I got out my anger over the lie you told, that the fantasies would stop."

Oh, my. Fantasies? This wasn't good. She'd had her own share of fantasies about Cal. Thankfully, she didn't say or do anything stupid. Then Sophie burped loudly, and spit up. It landed on Jenna's shoulder and the front of her sweater.

The corner of Cal's mouth lifted. There was relief in his expression, and Jenna thought he was already regretting this frank conversation.

She glanced down at Sophie, who was smiling now. Jenna wiped her mouth, kissed her on the forehead, put her in the infant carrier seat on the coffee table and buckled the safety strap so that she couldn't wiggle out.

"Could you watch her a minute while I change my top?" Jenna asked.

"Sure." But he didn't look so sure. It was the first time he'd ever seemed nervous. Including when he'd faced gunfire during her rescue.

Jenna stood. So did Cal, though he did keep his hand on the top edge of the carrier. "Forget about that fantasy stuff," he said.

"I will," she lied. "I don't want to cause any more problems for you."

But she had already caused more problems. Jenna could feel it. The attraction was stirring between them. It was a full-fledged tug deep within her belly. A tug that reminded her that despite being a mom, she was still very much a woman standing too close to a too-attractive man.

She fluttered her fingers toward the nursery. "I won't be long." But even with that declaration, she gave in to that tug and hesitated a moment.

Cal cursed softly under his breath. "We'll talk about security plans after you've changed your top."

That should have knocked her back to reality. But

while his mouth was saying those practical words, his eyes seemed to be saying, *I want to kiss you*.

Maybe that was wishful thinking.

Either way, Jenna turned before she said something they'd both regret.

She hurriedly grabbed another sweater from the suitcase in the nursery. She shut the door enough to give herself some privacy, but kept it ajar so she could hear if Sophie started to cry. Jenna peeked out to see Cal playing with her daughter's toes while he made some funny faces. The interaction didn't last long—Cal's phone rang, and he answered it.

"Hollywood," Cal greeted. "I hope you have good news for me."

So did Jenna. They desperately needed something to go their way.

She peeled off the soiled sweater, stuffed it into a plastic bag and put it in the suitcase. It would save her from having to pack it in the next hour or two. Then she put on a dark green top and grabbed some other items from around the room to pack those as well.

When she'd finished cramming as much in the suitcase as she could, she took a moment to compose herself. And hated that she didn't feel stronger. But then, it was hard to feel strong when her past relationship with Paul might endanger her daughter.

She peeked out to make sure Sophie was okay. She was. So Jenna waited, listening to Cal's conversation. It was mostly one-sided. He grunted a few responses, and started to curse, but he bit it off when he looked down at Sophie. The profanity and his expression said it all.

"Bad news?" Jenna asked the moment he hung up.

"Some." He looked at Sophie and then glanced around the room. "It's best if you stay put while arrangements are being made for you and Sophie to move."

She walked back to the sofa and sat down across from her daughter. Just seeing that tiny face was a reminder that the stakes were massive now. "Staying put will be safe?"

Cal nodded. "As safe as I can make it."

"You?" she questioned. Not we. "Your director approves of this."

"He approves."

Which meant the situation was dangerous enough for the director to break protocol by allowing her to be guarded by Cal despite the inappropriate conduct that he believed had happened between them.

"How bad is the bad news?" she asked.

He pulled in his breath and walked closer. "Our communications specialist is a guy we call Hollywood. He's very good at what he does, and he can't find an obvious leak, so we don't know how Holden located you. Not yet, anyway. But we were able to get more information about the emails sent out by Paul's attorney. Each one was sent from a different account, and one went to your office in Houston. Holden, Helena and Anthony Salazar each got one. The final one went to your reporter friend, Gwen Mitchell."

Gwen Mitchell? So Paul had known her. Funny, the woman hadn't mentioned that particular detail when she'd introduced herself at the grocery store.

Jenna reached for the phone. "Well, my email didn't come to my private or business addresses. I check those several times a day. I'll call my office and see if it arrived in one of the other accounts."

Cal caught her arm to stop her. "The ISA has already retrieved it and taken it off your server. It's encrypted so we'll need the communications guys to take a look at it."

That sounded a bit ominous, so she settled for nodding. "What's in these emails?"

"We've only gained access to yours and Salazar's. His email was encrypted as well, but we decided to focus on it first. The encryption wasn't complex, and the computer broke the code within seconds. We're not sure if all the emails are similar, but this one appears to be instructions that Paul left with his attorney shortly before his death."

"Instructions?" The content of that email was obviously the bad news that had etched Cal's face with worry. "Paul gave Salazar orders to kill me?"

"Not exactly."

His hesitation caused her heart rate to spike.

"Then what?" she asked, holding her breath.

"We're piecing this together using some files we confiscated from Paul's estate and the email sent to Salazar. Apparently before you rejected Paul's proposal and he decided to kill you, he tried to get you pregnant."

Oh, mercy. She'd known Paul was a snake, but she hadn't realized just how far he'd gone with his sinister plan.

"Paul used personal information he got from your corrupt assistant, the one who sold your business secrets," Cal continued. "With some of that information, Paul invited you to his estate when he estimated that you'd be ovulating. He drugged you. That's why you don't remember having sex with him."

She groaned. This just kept getting worse and worse. Everything about their relationship had been a cleverly planned sham. "Paul ditched the plan after I said there was no way I'd marry him."

Cal shrugged. "He intended to kill you, but he also planned for your refusal and your escape."

Jenna felt her eyes widen. "He knew I might escape?"

"Yeah." He let that hang in the air for several seconds. "He also took into account that he might have succeeded in getting you pregnant. In his email to Salazar, Paul instructed the man to tie up loose ends, depending on how your situation had turned out."

"So what exactly is Salazar supposed to do?" Jenna didn't even try to brace herself.

Cal glanced at Sophie. Then stared at her. "In the event that you've had a child, which you obviously have, Salazar has orders to kidnap the baby."

Chapter Six

Cal waited for a call while Jenna bathed Sophie. Jenna was smiling and singing to the baby, but he knew beneath that smile, she was terrified.

A professional assassin wanted to kidnap her baby and do God knows what to both her and Sophie in the process. They'd dodged a bullet—Salazar had indeed followed Jenna to the grocery store and hadn't just headed for the apartment to grab Sophie. Maybe he hadn't had the address of the apartment. Or perhaps he wanted to get Jenna first. Maybe he thought if he eliminated the mother, then it'd be a snap to kidnap the child.

That plan left Jenna in a very bad place. She couldn't go on the run, though every instinct in her body was shouting for her to do just that. Running was what Salazar hoped she would do.

She'd be an easy catch.

Cal didn't intend to let that happen. Correction. He had to arrange for someone else to make sure that didn't happen. For the sake of his career, he was going to take these initial steps to keep Sophie and Jenna safe, and then he was going to extract himself from the picture.

He checked his phone to make sure it wasn't dead. It wasn't. And there was still no call from headquarters or Hollywood, who was on the way with some much needed equipment. Cal needed some answers. They were seriously short on those.

Sophie made an "ohhh" sound and splashed her feet and hands in the shallow water that was dabbed with iridescent bubbles. Cal glanced at her to make sure all was okay, and then turned his attention back to the phone.

"Ever heard the expression a watched pot doesn't boil?" Jenna commented. "It's the same with a cell phone. It'll never ring when you're sitting there holding it."

She lifted Sophie from the little plastic yellow tub that Jenna had positioned on the sole bit of kitchen counter space, and she immediately wrapped the dripping wet baby in a thick pink terry-cloth towel.

Cal stood from the small kitchen table and slipped his phone into his pocket in case Jenna needed a hand. But she seemed to have the situation under control. She stood there by the sink, drying Sophie and imitating the soft baby sounds her daughter was making.

He went closer to see the baby's expression. Yep, she was grinning a big gummy grin. Her face was rosy and warm from the bath, and she smelled like baby shampoo. Cal had never thought a happy, freshly bathed baby could grab his complete attention, but this little girl certainly did.

Deep down, he felt something. A strange sense of what it would actually be like to be her father. It would be pretty amazing to hold her and feel her unconditional love.

When he came out of his daddy trance, he realized Jenna was looking at him. Her right eyebrow was slightly lifted. A question: what was he thinking? Cal had no intention of sharing that with her.

"Want to hold her while I get her diaper and gown?" Jenna asked.

Cal felt like someone had just offered to hand him a live grenade. "Uh, I don't want to hurt her."

Jenna smiled and eased Sophie into his arms. He looked at Jenna. Then Sophie, who was looking at him with suddenly suspicious eyes. For a moment, he thought the baby was going to burst into tears. She didn't, though he wouldn't have blamed her. Instead, she opened her tiny mouth and laughed.

Cal didn't know who was more stunned, Jenna, him or Sophie. Sophie jumped as if she'd scared herself with the unexpected noise from her own mouth. She did more staring, and then laughed again.

"This is a first," Jenna said, totally in awe. Cal knew how she felt. It was like witnessing a little miracle. "I'll have to put it in her baby book." She disappeared into the bedroom-nursery for a moment and came back with Sophie's clothes. "First time you've ever held a baby?" she asked.

He nodded. "My brother, Joe, has a little boy, Austin. He's nearly two years old, but I was away on assignment when he was born. I didn't see him until he was already walking."

"You missed the first laugh, then." She took Sophie from him and went to the sofa so she could sit and dress the baby. "You're close to your family?"

"Yes. No," he corrected. "I mean, we keep in touch, but we're all wrapped up in our jobs. Joe's a San Antonio cop. My other brother is special ops in the military. I started out in the military but switched to ISA."

Jenna had her attention fastened on diapering Sophie and putting on her gown, but Cal knew where her attention really was when he noticed she was trembling. He caught her hand to steady it and helped her pull the gown's drawstring so that Sophie's feet wouldn't be exposed. Sophie didn't seem to mind. The bath had relaxed her, and it seemed as if she was ready to fall asleep.

"Why is Paul sending Salazar after us now?" Jenna asked. She stood and started toward the nursery. "Why wait a year?"

Cal tried not to react to the emotion and fear in her voice. "Could be several reasons," he whispered as he followed her. "Maybe it took this long for his will to get through probate. The courts don't move quickly in Monte de Leon. Or maybe he figured the emails would cause a big splash, something to make sure everyone remembers him on the first anniversary of his murder."

"Oh, I remember him." She eased Sophie into the crib, placing the baby on her side, and then after kissing her cheek, Jenna covered her lower body with a blanket. "I didn't need the emails or Salazar to do that."

She kissed Sophie again and walked just outside the door, and leaned against the door frame.

A thin breath caused her mouth to shudder.

There was no way he could not react to that. Jenna was hurting and terrified for her daughter. Cal was worried for her, too. The ISA might not be able to stop Salazar before he tried to kidnap Sophie.

Since Jenna looked as if she needed a hug, Cal

reached out, slid his arm around her waist and pulled her to him. She didn't resist. She went straight into his arms.

She was soft. *Very* soft. And it seemed as if she could melt right into him. Cal felt his hand move across her back, and he drew her even closer.

Her scent was suddenly on him. A strange mix of baby soap and her own naturally feminine smell. Something alluring. Definitely hot. As was her body. He'd never been much of a breast man, but hers were giving him ideas about how those bare breasts would respond to his touch.

"This isn't a good idea," she mumbled.

Cal knew exactly what she meant. Close contact wasn't going to cool the attraction. It would fuel it.

But it felt right soothing her on a purely physical level. When he was done here, after Jenna and Sophie were no longer in danger, he needed to spend some time getting a personal life.

He needed to get laid.

Too often he put the job ahead of his needs. Jenna had a bad way of reminding him that the particular activity shouldn't be put off.

She pulled back and met his gaze. The new position put their mouths too close. All he had to do was lean down and press his lips to hers, and Cal was certain the result would be a mind-blowing kiss that neither of them would ever forget.

Which was exactly why it couldn't happen.

Still, that didn't stop his body from reacting in the most basic male way.

With their eyes locked, Jenna put her hand on his

chest to push him away. Her middle brushed against his. She froze for a split second, and then went all soft and dewy again. He saw her pupils pinpoint. Felt her warm breath ease from her slightly open mouth. Her pulse jumped on her throat.

She was reacting to his arousal. Her body was preparing itself for something that couldn't happen.

"I'm flattered," she said, her voice like a silky caress on his neck and mouth.

Uh-oh. She probably meant it to be a joke, a way of breaking the tension. But it didn't break anything. That breath of hers felt like the start of very long French kiss. A kiss he had to nix. He didn't have the time or inclination to deal with a complicated relationship.

Besides, she wasn't his type.

He didn't want a woman who was fragile, so prissy. No, he wanted a woman like him, who liked sex a little rough and with no strings attached. A relationship with Jenna would come with strings longer than the Rio Grande. And he couldn't see her having down-and-dirty sex with him whenever the urge hit.

Her breath brushed against his mouth again, and Cal nearly lost the argument he was having with himself. Knowing he had to do something, fast, he stepped away from her.

In the same instant, there was a knock at the door.

His body immediately went into combat mode, and he drew his gun from his shoulder holster.

"It's me, Hollywood," their visitor called out.

He pushed aside the jolt of adrenaline. "He works for the ISA," Cal clarified to Jenna.

However, he didn't reholster his weapon until he

looked out the side window to verify that it was indeed his coworker and that Hollywood wasn't being held at gunpoint. But the man was alone.

Cal opened the door and greeted him. "Thanks for coming." He checked the area in front of the bookstore but didn't see Gwen, the reporter, or either of the Carrs.

"No problem." Hollywood stepped inside and handed Cal a black leather equipment bag. "I brought a secure laptop, a portable security system, an extra weapon and some clothes. I didn't know how long you'd be here so I added some toiletries and stuff."

"Good." Cal didn't know how long he'd be there, either. "Has anyone picked up Salazar?"

"Not yet. We're still looking." Hollywood's attention went in Jenna's direction, and with his hand extended in a friendly gesture, he walked toward her. "Mark Lynch," he introduced himself. "But feel free to call me Hollywood. Everyone does."

"Hollywood," she repeated. She sounded friendly enough, but she was keeping her nerves right beneath the surface.

Cal hoped to do something to help with those nerves, something that didn't involve kissing, so he took out the laptop and turned it on. They needed information, and he would start by reviewing the message traffic on Salazar to see if anyone had spotted him nearby. By now, Salazar knew who Cal was. He would know that the ISA was involved. However, Cal seriously doubted that would send the man running. Salazar wasn't the type.

"We're working on trying to contain Anthony Salazar," Cal heard Hollywood tell Jenna.

"And I'm to stay put until that happens?" she spelled

out. She shoved her hand into the back pockets of her pants.

Cal frowned and wondered why he suddenly thought he knew her so well. Jenna and he were practically strangers.

Hollywood glanced at him first and then nodded in response to Jenna's question. "The local sheriff has been alerted to the situation, and the FBI is sending two agents to patrol through the town. Cal can keep things under control here until we can make other arrangements." He took out a folder from the bag and handed it to Cal.

Cal opened it and inside was a woman's picture. "Kinley Ford?" he read aloud from the background investigation sheet that he took from the envelope. He glanced through the info but didn't recognize anything about the research engineer.

"That file is a little multitasking," Hollywood explained. "The FBI sent her info and picture over this afternoon. She's not associated with Jenna or Salazar, but she's supposedly here in town. She disappeared from Witness Protection, and there are lot of people who want to find her."

Cal shook his head. "Please don't tell me I'm supposed to look for her."

"No. But if anyone asks, that's why you're here. It's the way the director is keeping this all legitimate. He can tell the FBI that you're here in Willow Ridge to try to locate Kinley Ford, as a favor for a sister agency. Don't worry. I'll be the one looking for the missing woman, but your name will be on the paperwork."

Cal breathed a little easier. He wanted to focus on Jenna and Sophie right now.

"I'll set up this temporary security system," Holly-wood continued. "And then I'll get out of here so I can stand guard until the FBI agents arrive."

Cal approved of that. The local sheriff would need help with Salazar around. "What about the background check on Gwen Mitchell?"

"Still in progress, but Director Kowalski found some flags. According to her passport, she was in Monte de Leon during Jenna's rescue."

That grabbed Cal's attention. "Interesting."

"Maybe. But it could mean nothing. She is a reporter, after all. There's nothing to link Gwen to Paul or the Carrs. She appears to have been doing a story on one of the rebel factions."

"And she got out alive." That in itself was a small miracle. Unless Gwen had had a lot of help. The ISA hadn't rescued her, that was for sure, so she must have had other resources to get her out of the country.

"We'll keep digging," Hollywood explained. His voice was a little strained as if he was tired. He rum-maged through the bag and came up with several pieces of equipment. "Are these the only windows?" he asked, tipping his head to the trio in the main living area.

"There's a small one in the bathroom," Jenna let him know.

Hollywood nodded and went in that direction to get started. Cal was familiar with the system Hollywood was using. It would arm all entrances and exits so that no one could break in undetected, but it could also be used to create perimeter security to make sure Salazar didn't get close enough to set some kind of explosive or fire to flush them out.

Once the laptop had booted up, Cal logged in with his security code and began to scan through the messages. One practically jumped out at him.

"Here's the email that Paul sent you," Cal told her. "ISA retrieved it and kept it in our classified in-box so I could look at it."

She took a step toward him, but then turned and checked on the baby first. "Sophie's sleeping," Jenna let him know, as she hurried to the sofa to sit beside him.

Cal was positive this email was going to upset her, but he was also positive that they needed to read it. Besides, there might be clues in it that only she would understand, and they might finally make some sense of all of this.

"Jenna, if you've received this email, then I must be dead," she read aloud. *"I doubt my demise has caused you much grief, but it should. Once I have a plan, I don't give up on it. Ever. Our heir will inherit your vast wealth and mine, and will continue what I've started here in Monte de Leon. What the plan doesn't include is you, my dear."*

She stopped, took a deep breath and continued. *"So put your affairs in order, Jenna. I'll be the first person to greet you in the hereafter. See you in a day or two. Love, Paul."*

There were probably several Justice Department and ISA agents already examining the email, but it appeared to be pretty straightforward. A death threat, one that Salazar had probably been paid to carry out.

She groaned softly. "Paul planned for all possibilities. Like a baby. I'm sure the email would have been different if I hadn't had a child." Jenna scrubbed her hands over her face. "And when I woke up this morning, I thought my biggest threat was Holden Carr."

Maybe he still was. Cal was eager to get a look at those other emails. All he needed was some kind of evidence or connection that could prompt the FBI to arrest Holden or his sister.

Cal glanced at the notepad on the coffee table. Helena's number was there, and she'd wanted Jenna to call her. While it wouldn't be a pleasant conversation, it might be a necessary one.

Jenna must have followed his gaze. She reached for the notepad and retrieved her cell phone from her purse on the table next to the front door. But before she could press in the numbers, Hollywood came back into the room.

"All secure back there," he informed them. He went to the windows at the front of the apartment and connected a small sensor to each. He put the control monitor on the kitchen table and checked his watch. "I'll be parked on the street near here until I get the okay from the FBI."

Cal stood and went to him to shake his hand. "Thanks, for everything."

"Like I said, no problem. If you need anything else, just give me a call."

Cal let Hollywood out, then closed and locked the door. While he set the security monitor to arm it, Jenna sat on the sofa, dialed the call to Helena and put her cell on speaker.

The woman answered on the first ring. "Jenna," Helena said, obviously seeing the name on her caller ID. Cal made a note to switch Jenna to a prepaid phone that couldn't be traced.

"Why did you want to talk to me?" Jenna immediately asked.

Helena's answer wasn't quite so hasty. She paused for several long moments. "Is your friend, Cal, still there with you?"

"He's here," Cal answered for himself.

It was a gamble. Helena might not say anything important with him listening. But he also didn't want Helena to think that Jenna was alone. That might prompt her to send in Salazar for Sophie—if the man was actually working for Helena, that is. But perhaps the most obvious solution was true—that Salazar was being paid by Paul's estate.

Helena paused again, longer than the first time. "Why didn't you tell us you're an American operative?"

Cal groaned softly. She shouldn't have been able to retrieve that information this quickly. "Who said I am?"

"Sources. *Reliable* ones."

"There are no reliable sources for information like that," Cal informed her. She or Holden had paid someone off. Or else there was a major leak somewhere in the ISA.

"What did you want to talk to me about?" Jenna prompted after a third round of silence.

"Holden," Helena readily answered. "The Justice Department and the ISA have contacted me. They want me to give them evidence so they can arrest my brother for illegal business practices and for Paul's murder."

Jenna glanced at him before she continued. "Is there evidence?"

"For his business dealings. Holden isn't a saint. But there couldn't be evidence for Paul's murder. The house-keeper's responsible for that."

Ah, yes. That mysterious housekeeper again. Cal had monitored Paul's estate for the entire two days of Jenna's visit, and while he'd heard the voices of many of Paul's employees, he hadn't heard of this housekeeper named Mary. Not until after Paul's body had been found with a single execution-style gunshot wound to the head. It'd been the local authorities who'd pointed the finger at the housekeeper, and they had based that on the notes they'd found on Paul's computer. He'd apparently been suspicious of the woman and had decided to fire her. But those notes had been made weeks before his death.

"Did you agree to help the Justice Department and the ISA?" Cal asked, though he was certain he knew the answer.

But he was wrong.

"Yes. I intend to help the authorities bring down my brother," Helena announced.

Jenna's eyes widened, but Cal figured his expression was more of skepticism than surprise. "Are you doing that to get Holden out of the way so you can inherit both Paul's and his estates?"

"No." She was adamant about it. That didn't mean she was telling the truth. "I want the illegal activity to stop. I want the family business to return to the way it was when my parents were still alive."

"Admirable," Cal mumbled. He didn't believe that, either, though he had to admit that it was possible Helena was a do-gooder. But he wasn't about to stake Jenna's and Sophie's safety on that.

"What was in Paul's email to you?" Jenna asked the woman. Cal moved closer to the phone and grabbed the notepad so he could write down the message verbatim.

"The email was personal," Helena explained. "Though I'm sure it won't stay that way long. Cal will see to that."

Yes, he would. "If that's true, then you might as well tell me what it says."

This was the longest silence of all. "Paul said he would see me in the hereafter in a day or two."

Almost identical wording to Jenna's email, but Cal jotted it down anyway. "Why would Paul want you dead?"

"I don't know." Helena sighed heavily, and it sounded as if she had started to cry. "But he obviously believes I wronged him in some way. Maybe Paul wanted Holden to inherit everything, and this is his way of cutting me out of his estate."

Or maybe Holden had gotten a death threat, too. But then with plans to have Sophie kidnapped, that left Cal with a critical question. Whom had Paul arranged to raise the child? Certainly not an assassin like Salazar.

He thought about that a moment and came full circle to the fifth recipient of one of Paul's infamous emails.

Gwen Mitchell.

He needed a full background report on her ASAP. It was possible that she was connected to Paul.

"Jenna, we're both in danger," Helena continued. "That's why we have to work together to stop this person that Paul has unleashed on us."

"Work together, how?" Jenna asked.

"Meet with me tomorrow morning. Alone. No Holden and no Cal Rico."

That wasn't going to happen. Still, Cal had to keep this channel of communication open. "Jenna will get back to you on that," he answered.

"Be at the Meadow's Bed-and-Breakfast tomorrow morning at ten," Helena continued as if this meeting was a done deal. "It's a little place in the country, about twenty miles from Willow Ridge. I'll see you then." And with that, she hung up.

Jenna clicked the end-call button. She wasn't trembling like before. Well, not visibly, anyway. "Do you think she wants to kill me, too?"

He considered several answers and decided to go with the truth. "Anything's possible at this point." But he did need to get a look at all the emails to get a clearer picture.

"I'm scared for Sophie," she whispered.

Yeah. So was he. And being scared wasn't good. It meant he'd lost his objectivity. He blamed that on holding Sophie. On that first laugh. Oh, and the cuddling session with Jenna. None of those things should have happened, and they'd sucked him right in and gotten him personally involved.

Jenna swiveled around to face him, blinking back tears, and moved closer into his arms.

And Cal let her.

"I'm not a wimp," she declared. "I run a multimillion-dollar business. And if the threats were aimed just at me, I'd be spitting mad. But my baby is in danger."

Cal couldn't refute that. Heck, he couldn't even reassure her that Salazar wouldn't make a full-scale effort to kidnap Sophie. All he could do was sit there and hold Jenna.

A single tear streaked down her cheek, and Cal caught it with his thumb, his fingers cupping her chin. And he was painfully aware that he was using his fingers to lift her chin. Just slightly.

So he could put his mouth on hers.

And that's exactly what he did.

The touch was a jolt that went straight through him like a shot. It didn't help that Jenna made a throaty, feminine sound of approval. Or that she slid her arms around his neck and drew him closer.

Cal cursed himself for starting this. And worse, for continuing it and deepening the kiss. French-kissing Jenna was the worst idea he'd ever had, but that jolt of fire that her mouth was creating overruled any common sense he had left. She tasted like silk and sin, and he wanted a whole lot more.

He heard a ringing sound and thought it was another by-product of the jolt. But when the ringing continued, Cal realized passion wasn't responsible. His cell phone was. He untangled himself from Jenna and checked the caller ID screen.

It was Director Kowalski.

"Hell," he mumbled. Cal quickly tried to compose himself before he answered it. "Agent Rico."

"We might have a problem," the director started. That wasn't the greeting Cal wanted to hear. "First of all, I just read the email that Paul Tolivar supposedly sent Jenna. You think it's legit?"

Cal had given that some thought. He should have

given it more. "I'm not sure. Anyone close to Paul could have composed those emails and sent them out. Anyone with an agenda." He glanced at Jenna. There was no surprise in her eyes, which meant she'd already come up with that theory.

"You have someone in mind?"

This was easy. Cal didn't even have to think about it. "Helena or Holden Carr. Both inherited a lot of money from Paul. Also, those flags on Gwen Mitchell might turn out to be a problem."

"Yes, we're working on her. But something else has popped up." The director took in an audible breath. "We might be wrong, but there are new flags. Ones within the department."

Everything inside Cal went still. This was worse than bad news. "What's wrong?"

"We think we might have a leak in communications who could have been responsible for alerting Gwen Mitchell and the Carrs as to Jenna Laniere's whereabouts."

"A leak might not have been necessary for that. Holden or Helena Carr could have been watching Jenna's estate and then followed her when she went there." Of course, that didn't explain how they'd known about Sophie, unless the person watching the estate had seen the baby in the car. That was possible, but it sounded as if the director thought someone or something else might have been responsible. "Who do these flags point to?"

"Not to anyone specific, but if it's true, the source of the information has to be in ISA."

Oh, man. The bad news just kept getting worse. They might have a traitor within the organization. "Who in

ISA would have access to the pool of information that would affect all the players in this case?"

Kowalski blew out an audible breath. "Mark Lynch is a possibility."

That was not the name he'd expected to hear the director say. "Hollywood," Cal mumbled.

"I know he's on the way there with equipment. And I know you two are friends. I didn't learn about the flags until a few minutes ago."

And that in itself could be a problem because it meant someone was trying to cover their tracks. Or else set someone up. "What exactly are these flags?"

"Hollywood monitored the message traffic pertaining to Jenna Laniere. Faxes, emails, telephone calls. The info in question went from Paul Tolivar to his lawyer. It was her detailed financial data, including passwords and codes for her business accounts."

Cal knew about those messages that'd been sent a year ago while Jenna was in Monte de Leon. Paul had gotten into Jenna's laptop the first day she was at his estate and had copied her entire hard drive. Though Paul had only sent those messages to his lawyer, it didn't mean that someone else couldn't have learned the contents, saved them and now sent them out again. But why do it now, especially since the information was a year old?

That led Cal to his next question. "Why do you think Hollywood's the one who compromised this information?"

"Because we intercepted an encrypted message that was meant for him. The message was verification of receipt of Ms. Laniere's info and details about the payment for services rendered. We checked, and there has been money sent to an account in the Cayman Islands."

Cal tried not to curse. He didn't want a gut reaction to make him accuse his friend of a crime he might not have committed. "That still doesn't mean Hollywood's guilty. One or both of the Carrs could be trying to set him up to make it look as if he sold Jenna's financial information. And they might be doing that to get us to focus on Hollywood and not them."

"Could be." But the director didn't sound at all convinced of that. "It's a lot of money, Cal. If the Carrs had wanted to set someone up, why wait until now?"

That timeline question kept coming up, and Cal still didn't have an answer for it. Was it tied to Sophie? And if so, how?

"There's a final piece to this mess," the director continued. "We accessed Hollywood's personal computer, and we found several encrypted messages from Anthony Salazar. In the most recent one, Salazar asks Hollywood to help him with the kidnapping."

Cal couldn't fight off the gut reactions any longer. He felt sick to his stomach. Yes, it could all be a setup, but it was a huge risk to take if it wasn't. Hell. Had he been that wrong about a man he considered a friend?

"We tried to stop Hollywood before he left to go see you. But when he gets there, tell him he's to report back to me immediately. Don't let him in," Kowalski warned.

Cal groaned. "He's already been here. He installed the equipment and left."

The director cursed. "He wasn't supposed to be there yet. He had instructions to arrive at 9:00 p.m."

Cal got to his feet and glanced around. At the equipment bag. At the laptop he'd used to read the email Paul sent Jenna. At the security systems that Hollywood had activated a full hour ahead of schedule.

"What are my orders?" Cal asked. He motioned for Jenna to get Sophie.

"We might have a rogue agent on our hands. Get Ms. Laniere and her daughter out of there," the director ordered. *"Now."*

Chapter Seven

The nightmare was back.

This time, she wasn't in Monte de Leon, and there were no rebel soldiers. Jenna knew this was much worse—her precious baby was in danger.

"Bring as little as possible," Cal instructed in a whisper. He stuffed diapers and some of Sophie's clothes into her bag and added a flashlight. "Hurry," he added.

Not that she needed him to remind her of that. Everything about his movements and body language indicated they had to move fast.

"What kind of flags did you say the director found on Hollywood?" Jenna whispered. Cal had told her that Hollywood might have bugged the place. He might be listening to their every word.

"They don't have a full picture yet." Cal looped the now full diaper bag over his shoulder and motioned for her to pick up Sophie. "You'll have to carry her. I need at least one hand free."

So he could shoot his gun if it became necessary.

"Does your car have an infant seat already in it?" he mouthed.

She nodded and scooped the sleeping baby into her

arms. Thankfully, Sophie didn't wake up. "I'm parked just behind the bookstore. The keys are in my purse."

Jenna wanted to ask if it was safe to take her car. But maybe it didn't matter. They had to take the risk and get out of there.

Cal drew his gun while she swaddled Sophie in a thick blanket. The moment she finished, she motioned for them to go. He paused a moment at the door. Then he opened it and glanced around outside.

"Let's go," he ordered.

Jenna grabbed her purse. She stuffed her cell phone into it, extracted her keys and stepped out into the cold night air. It was dark, and there was no moon because of the cloudy sky, but the bookstore had floodlights positioned on the four corners of the building.

Cal kept her behind him while they made their way down the stairs. He stopped again and didn't give her the signal to move until he'd glanced around the side of the store. Once he had them moving again, he kept them next to the exterior wall.

It seemed to take a lifetime to walk the twenty yards or so to her car. She unlocked the door with her keypad, but instead of letting her get in, Cal motioned for her to stand back. She did. And he used the flashlight to check the undercarriage for explosives.

God. What a mess they were in.

After Cal had gone around the entire perimeter of the car, he caught onto her and practically shoved them in through the passenger's side. Jenna turned to put Sophie in the rear-facing car seat, but a sound stopped her cold.

Footsteps.

Standing guard in front of her, Cal lifted his gun and took aim.

"Don't shoot," someone whispered. It was a woman's voice, and Jenna expected to see Helena step from the shadows.

Instead, it was Gwen Mitchell.

She lifted her hands in a show of surrender. She didn't appear to be armed and unlike the meeting in the grocery store, the woman didn't have a camera.

"I have to talk to you," Gwen said.

"This isn't a good time for conversation." Cal kept his gun aimed at Gwen, and he shut the car door. However, he didn't leave her side to get in. He stood guard, and Jenna made use of his body shield. She leaned over and put Sophie in the infant seat. She strapped her in and then climbed into the backseat with her in case she had to do what Cal was doing—use her body as a final defense.

"It's important," Gwen added.

Everything was important right now, especially getting out of there. Jenna glanced around and prayed that Salazar wasn't using Gwen as a diversion so he could sneak up on them and try to kidnap Sophie.

"We should go," Jenna reminded Cal.

Gwen fastened her attention on Jenna. "A few minutes ago I sent you a copy of the email that I got from Paul. Read it and you'll know why it's important that we talk. Then get in touch with me."

Jenna hadn't brought her laptop, but she thought maybe her BlackBerry was in her purse. Once they were on the road and away from there, she'd check and see if the email had arrived into her personal account.

But for now, she continued to keep watch and wished that she had a weapon to defend Sophie and herself with.

"Keep your hands lifted," Cal instructed Gwen, and he began to inch his way to the driver's side of the car.

"Don't trust anyone," Gwen continued. "There's something going on. I don't know what. But I think Paul's left instructions for someone to play a sick game. I think he wants to pit each of us against the other."

Then Paul had succeeded. Five emails. Five people. And there wasn't any trust among them. It was too big of a risk to start trusting now.

"Did he say anything about me in the email he sent to you?" Gwen asked.

"No," Jenna assured her.

"You're sure? Because I'm trying to figure out why he contacted me. Do you have any idea?"

Cal didn't answer. He'd had enough, and got into the car and started the engine. He drove away, fast, leaving Gwen to stand there with her question unanswered.

"The way she said Paul's name makes me think she knew him well," Jenna commented. She kept her eyes on the woman until she was no longer in sight.

"How well she knew him is what I need to find out. Right after I get you and Sophie to someplace safe."

With all the rush to leave her apartment, she hadn't considered where to go. First things first, they had to make sure no one was following them, or there wouldn't be any safe place to escape to.

Cal sped down Main Street. Thankfully, there was no traffic. It wasn't unusual for that time of night—Willow Ridge wasn't exactly a hotbed of activity. He took the first available side road to get them out of there.

Jenna continued to keep watch around them. She wanted to get her BlackBerry, but that could wait until she was sure they weren't in immediate danger. However, maybe she could get some answers to other questions. After all, her baby's life was in danger, and Jenna wanted to know why.

"What made your director think we couldn't trust Hollywood?" she asked.

Like her, Cal was looking all around. "He thinks Hollywood transferred some information he obtained through official message traffic that he was monitoring."

"Information about me?"

"Yeah," he answered as if he was thinking hard about that.

She certainly was. "I met Hollywood for the first time tonight. He doesn't even know me." But that didn't mean he couldn't be working for one of the other players in this. "You don't think Paul got to him, too?"

"I don't know. He was in Monte de Leon during your rescue, and he had access to any and all information flowing in and out of Paul's estate. There are plenty of people who would have paid for that information."

She considered that a moment while she stared back at the dark road behind them. The lights of Willow Ridge were just specks now. "Do you trust Hollywood?"

"Before tonight I thought I did." He shook his head. "But I can't risk being wrong. It's possible he got greedy and decided to sell your financial information to someone. If he's innocent, then what we're doing is just a waste of time."

But it didn't feel like a waste. It felt like a necessity.

"I changed all my passwords and account information after Paul was killed," Jenna explained. "So, unless someone's gotten their hands on the new info, those old codes won't do them any good." Of course, maybe Hollywood didn't know they were old.

"If someone were using this to set him up, it wouldn't matter if the codes were outdated. The unauthorized message traffic is enough to incriminate him."

So Hollywood could be innocent. Still, they were on the run, and that meant someone had succeeded in terrifying her.

"Any idea where we're going?" she asked.

Cal checked his watch and the rearview mirror. "I'm sure the director is making arrangements for a safe house. All previous arrangements will be ditched because Hollywood would have had access to the plans."

"So it could take a while." Jenna believed Cal would do whatever it took to keep Sophie safe, but she wasn't certain that would be enough.

"How far is your estate?" he asked.

She'd hoped there wouldn't be any more surprises tonight. "About two hours." But Jenna shook her head. "You're thinking about going there?"

"Temporarily."

Oh, mercy. She hated to point out the obvious, but she would. "The reason I'm not there now is the threats from Holden."

"Holden might be the least of our worries," Cal mumbled. And she knew it was true. "How good is the estate's security system?"

"It's supposed to be very good." Her surprise was replaced by frustration. "In hindsight, I should have stayed put there, beefed up security and told Holden where he could shove his threats. Then we wouldn't be running for our lives."

Cal met her gaze in the mirror. "You were scared and pregnant. I don't think your decision to leave was based solely on logic."

"Pregnancy hormones," she said under her breath. She couldn't dismiss that they hadn't played a part in her going on the run. But hiding had made her pregnancy more bearable, and it'd saved her from having to explain to her friends that she'd gotten pregnant by an accused felon.

"I've spent a lot of my life running," she commented. Why she told him that she didn't know. But she suddenly felt as if she owed him an explanation as to why she'd left the safety of the estate and headed for a small town where she knew no one. "Before my parents were killed in a car accident, when we'd have an argument, I'd immediately leave and take a long trip somewhere."

He shrugged. "There's nothing wrong with traveling."

"This wasn't traveling. It was escaping." Heck, she was still escaping. And this time, she might not succeed. Sophie might have to pay the ultimate price for Jenna's bad choices. "I have to make this right for Sophie. I can't let her be in danger. She's too important to me."

"I understand," he said. "She's important to me, too."

And for some reason, that wasn't like lip service. He wasn't just trying to console her.

Cal had only known Sophie a few hours. There was no way he could have developed such strong feelings for her. Was there? Maybe the little girl had brought out Cal's paternal instincts. Or maybe he was just protecting them. Either way, it was best not to dwell on it. Once they got to her estate, Cal would leave. After all, he had a career to salvage.

Jenna checked on Sophie again. She was still asleep and would probably stay that way for several hours. With no immediate threat, it was a good time to check for that BlackBerry. Jenna climbed over the seat, buckled up and grabbed the purse that she'd tossed onto the floor.

It took several moments for the BlackBerry to load and for her to scroll through the messages. There was indeed one that Gwen had forwarded to her.

"Gwen, I expect you're surprised to hear from me," Jenna read aloud. *"When I was considering whom to give this particular task, I thought of several candidates, but you're the best woman for the job. Yes, this is a job offer. You see, I've been murdered, and if you're reading this, then my killer is still out there. I want you to use your skills as an investigative journalist and find proof of who that person is. Once you have the proof, contact Mark Lynch at the International Security Agency."*

"Mark?" Cal repeated. "Why would Paul want her to contact Hollywood?"

Jenna exchanged puzzled glances with him. "Obviously, Paul knew him. Or knew *of* him. But why would Paul trust Hollywood with that kind of information? Why not just turn it over to Holden or Salazar?"

Cal didn't say anything for several seconds. "Maybe he's giving each person one task. Or maybe Gwen is right and this is his way of dividing and conquering. If you're all at odds and suspicious of each other, then he'll get some kind of postmortem satisfaction. He sends Salazar after Sophie. Gwen, after the person who murdered him. And he somehow turns Helena against her own brother."

Yes. Jenna would have loved to know what Paul had written to Helena. Or to Holden. If they had all the e-mails, they might be able to figure out what Paul was really trying to do.

"Did you read the entire email?" Cal asked.

"No. There's more." She scrolled down the tiny screen. *"If you find my killer, then my attorney will wire the sum of one million dollars to a bank account of your choice. I'm giving you one week. If you don't have the proof, the job will go to someone else."*

So this wasn't going to stop. If Gwen failed, then the investigation would continue.

"Maybe Hollywood will be offered the job," Cal speculated. "Or Salazar."

She heard him, but her attention was on the last lines of the email. *"To make things easier for you, I want you to focus your efforts on my number-one suspect,"* she continued reading aloud. *"Actually, she's my only suspect. Her name is Jenna Laniere."*

That was it. The end of Paul's instructions.

Jenna had to take a moment to absorb it. "Paul obviously didn't trust me right from the start, or he wouldn't have written this email."

"If he's the one who wrote it."

She turned in the seat to face Cal. "What are you thinking?"

"I'm thinking Gwen, Holden or Helena could be behind these messages from the grave." He hissed out a breath. "Even Hollywood could have done it. This could all be some kind of ploy to get Paul's estate."

Maybe. After all, Holden and Helena had shared Paul's money. Maybe one of them wanted it all. Or if Gwen was the culprit, maybe this was her way of ferreting out a story.

But how did Hollywood fit into this? Unless the man was just an out-and-out criminal, she couldn't figure out a logical scenario where he'd be collecting any of Paul's money.

"Maybe your friend's innocent," Jenna said, thinking out loud. "What if someone is setting him up so you can't trust him? That way, it would be one less person you could turn to for help."

Cal lifted his shoulder. "It's possible, I suppose. Once the director has gone through all the message traffic, we should know more."

Yes, but would that information stop her daughter from being in danger? Jenna couldn't shake the fear that Sophie was at the core of all of this.

Something caught her eye.

Headlights in the distance behind them.

Cal noticed it, too. His attention went straight to the rearview mirror. Neither of them said anything. They just sat there, breaths held, waiting to see what would happen.

He kept his speed right at fifty-five, and the headlights got closer very quickly. The other car was speeding. Still, that in itself was no cause for alarm. Combined with everything, however, her heart and mind were racing with worst-case scenarios.

"Get in the backseat and stay down," Cal insisted.

Jenna tried to keep herself steady. This could be just a precaution, she reminded herself, but she did as he asked. She climbed onto the seat with Sophie and positioned her torso over the baby so that she could protect her still-sleeping baby. But she also wanted to keep watch, so she craned her neck so she could see the side mirror.

The car was barreling down on them.

Jenna prayed it would just pass them and that would be the end to this particular scare. She could see Cal's right hand through the gap of the seats, and because of the other car's bright headlights, she could also see his finger tense on the trigger of his gun. He had the weapon aimed at the passenger's window.

The lights got even brighter as the car came upon them. Too close. It was a dark SUV, much larger than her own vehicle. Jenna braced herself because it seemed as if the SUV was going to ram right into them.

"Is it Salazar?" she asked in a raw whisper. Her heart was pounding now. Her breath was coming out in short, too-fast jolts.

"I can't tell. Just stay down."

Jenna didn't have a choice. She had to do whatever she could to protect Sophie. As meager as it was, her body would become a shield if the driver of that vehicle started shooting.

The headlights slashed right at the mirror when the car bolted out into the passing lane. She prayed it would continue to accelerate and go past them.

But it didn't.

With her heart in her throat, Jenna watched as the

car slowed until it was literally side by side with them. Cal cursed under his breath and aimed his gun.

"Brace yourself," he warned her a split second before he slammed on the brakes.

She saw a flash of red from the other car. The driver had braked as well, and the lights lit up the darkness, coating their shadows with that eerie shade of bloodred.

Cal threw the car into Reverse and hit the accelerator. She didn't know how he managed, but he spun the car around so they were facing in the opposite direction, and gunned the engine.

There was another flash of brake lights from the SUV. The sound of the tires squealed against the asphalt. Jenna squeezed her eyes shut a moment and prayed. But when she looked into the mirror, her worst fear was confirmed.

The SUV was coming at them again.

If it rammed them or sideswiped them, it'd be difficult for Cal to stay on the road. It was too dark to see if there were ditches nearby or one of the dozens of creeks that dotted the area. But Jenna didn't need to see things like that to know the danger. If the SUV driver managed to get them off the road, he could fire shots at a stationary target. They wouldn't be hard to hit.

"Should I call the sheriff?" she asked. She had to do something. *Anything.*

"He wouldn't get here in time."

The last ominous word had hardly left Cal's mouth when there was a loud bang. The SUV rammed into the back of her car, and the jolt snapped her body. Jenna caught Sophie's car seat and held on, trying to steady it and brace herself for a second hit.

It came hard and fast.

The front bumper of the SUV slammed into them. The motion jostled Sophie, and she stirred, waking.

"Get all the way down," Cal instructed. "Put your hand over Sophie's ears and cover her as much as you can with the blanket."

She did, though Jenna had to wonder how that would help. A moment later, she got her answer. He didn't slow down. Didn't try to turn around again. He merely turned his gun in the direction of the back window and the SUV. Cal used the rearview mirror to aim.

And he fired.

The blast was deafening. Louder than even the impact of the SUV. That sound rifled through Jenna, spiking her fear and concern for her child. Even though she had clamped her hands around Sophie's ears, the sound got through and her baby shrieked.

Cal fired again and again.

The bullets tore through the back window, the safety glass webbing and cracking, but it stayed in place. Thank God. Even though the glass wasn't much protection, she didn't want it tumbling down on Sophie.

Cal fired one more shot and then jammed his foot on the accelerator to get them out of there.

Chapter Eight

Cal sped through the wrought-iron gates that fronted Jenna's estate.

He'd spent most of the trip watching the road, to make sure that SUV hadn't followed them. As far as he could tell, it hadn't, even though they had encountered more traffic the closer they got to Houston. And then the traffic had trailed off to practically nothing once he was on the highway that led to Jenna's house.

Though the estate was only twenty miles from Houston city limits and there were other homes nearby, it felt isolated because it was centered on ten pristine acres.

The iron gates were massive, at least ten feet tall and double that in width. Fanning off both sides of the gate was a sinister-looking spiked-top fence that appeared to surround the place.

Even though there was no guard in the small redbrick gatehouse to the left, the builder had obviously planned for security, which made Cal wonder why Jenna had ever left in the first place. Yes, she'd told him she had a tendency to take off when things got rough, but the estate was as close to a stronghold as they could get. Somehow, he'd have to make Jenna understand that this was their best option. For now. He'd have to try to soothe her flight instinct so she wouldn't be tempted to run.

He stopped in the circular drive directly in front of the house and positioned the car so that Jenna would only be a few steps away from getting inside. He didn't want her exposed any longer than necessary. Salazar had expert shooting skills with a long-range assault rifle.

Like the rest of the property, the house was huge. There was a redbrick exterior and a porch with white columns that stretched across the entire front and sides. The carved oak front door opened, and he immediately reached for his gun.

"It's okay," Jenna assured him. "That's Meggie, the housekeeper. She's worked here since I was a baby."

The woman was in her mid-sixties with graying flame-red hair. Short, but not petite, she wore a simple blue-flowered dress. She didn't rush to greet them, but she did give them a warm smile when Jenna stepped from the car with a sleeping Sophie cradled in her arms.

"Welcome home. I have rooms made up for all of you," Meggie announced. Her words came out in a rushed stream of excitement. "When you called and said you were on the way, I got the crib ready in the nursery. The bedding is already turned down for the little angel. And I put your guest in the room next to yours."

"Thank you," Jenna muttered.

Once they were inside and the door was shut, Meggie patted Jenna's cheek and eased back the blanket a bit so she could see Sophie. She smiled again, and her aged blue eyes went to Cal. "She looks like you."

He wasn't sure what to say to that, so he didn't say anything. Meggie thought Sophie was his.

Cal forced himself to assess his surroundings. He'd expected luxury, and wasn't disappointed. Vaulted ceilings. Marble floors. Victorian antiques. But there were also a lot of windows and God knows how many points of entry. It would be a bear to keep all of them secure.

"We're exhausted," Jenna said to the woman, her voice showing her nerves. Maybe the nerves were from Meggie's comment about Sophie's looks but more likely from the inevitable adrenaline crash. "We'll get settled in for the night and we can talk tomorrow. There are things I should tell you."

Meggie nodded, and lightly kissed Sophie's cheek.

"Where's the main security panel?" he asked before Meggie could walk away.

She pointed to a richly colored oil landscape painting in the wide corridor just off the foyer. "The access code is seven, seven, four, one." Then she made her exit in the opposite direction.

Jenna let out a deep breath. A shaky one. Now that she was safe inside, the impact of what'd happened was hitting her. She was ready to crash, but Cal needed to take a few security measures before he helped her put Sophie to bed.

He aimed for some small talk so he could get some information about the place. And maybe get her mind off the nightmare they'd just come through.

"You were born here?" Cal asked, going to the monitor. The painting had a hinged front, and he opened it so he could take a look at what he had to work with.

"Literally. My mother didn't trust hospitals. So my

dad set up one here. In fact, he set up a lot of things here, mainly so that we'd never have to leave."

"They were overly protective?" Cal armed the system and watched as the lights flashed on to indicate the protected areas.

"Yes, with a capital Y. My mother was from a wealthy family, and she'd been kidnapped for ransom when she was a child. Obviously it was a life-altering experience for her. She was obsessed with keeping me safe, and over the years, Dad began to share that obsession. What they failed to remember was that my mother had been kidnapped from her own family's house."

Jenna followed his sweeping gaze around the room before her eyes met his. "There really is no place that's totally safe. Sometimes this estate felt more like a prison than a home."

That explained her wanderlust and maybe even the reason she'd gone to Monte de Leon. For months Cal had seen that trip as a near fatal mistake, but then he glanced at Sophie. That little girl wouldn't be here if Jenna hadn't made that trip. Maybe it was the camaraderie he'd developed with Jenna as they'd waited on that cantina floor. Whatever it was, that bonding had obviously extended to the child in her arms.

"Is the security system okay?" she asked.

"It looks pretty good." The back of the faux painting had the layout of the estate and each room was thankfully labeled not just for function but for the type of security that was installed. "The perimeter of the fence is wired to detect a breach. You have motion detectors at every entrance and exit. And all windows. This is a big place," he added in a mumble.

"Yes," she said with a slight tinge of irony. "Any weak spots you can see?"

"Front gate," he readily supplied. "Is it usually open the way it was when we came in?"

She nodded. "But it can be closed by pressing the button on the monitor or the switch located just inside the grounds." Jenna reached over and did just that. "There's an automatic lock and keypad entry on the left side of the gate."

Which wasn't very safe. Keypads could be tampered with or bypassed. Hollywood certainly knew how to do those things. Salazar likely did, too.

"What's this?" he asked, tapping the large area on the south side of the house that was labeled Gun Room.

"My father was an antique gun collector. He built an indoor firing range to test guns before he bought them."

Interesting. He hadn't expected that, but he would add it to his security plan. "You can shoot?"

"Not at all. The noise always put me off. But I'm willing to learn. In fact, I want to learn."

He just might teach her. Not so he could use her as backup. But it might make her feel more empowered. Plus, the room might come in handy, because it was almost certainly bulletproof. If worse came to worst, then he might have to move them in there. For now, though, he looked for a more comfortable solution.

"Where are the rooms we're supposed to stay in?" he asked. When Jenna shifted a little, he realized that Sophie was probably getting heavy. He holstered his gun and gently took the baby from her. The little girl was a heavy sleeper. She didn't even lift an eyelid.

"Thanks." Jenna touched her index finger to a trio of

rooms on the east side of the house. "That's the nursery, my room's next to it and that's the guest room."

He put his finger next to hers. Touching her. She didn't move away. In fact, she slipped her hand over his. It was such a simple gesture. But an intimate one. It was a good thing Sophie was between them, or he might have done something stupid like pull Jenna into his arms.

"There's a problem," he let her know.

The corner of her mouth lifted for just a second. "I think we're too tired to worry about another kissing session."

There was no such thing as being too tired to kiss. But Cal didn't voice that. Instead, he moved his hand away to avoid further temptation. "Your bedroom has exterior doors."

"Two of them. And another door leads to the pool area. The guest room has an exterior door as well."

From a security perspective, that wasn't good. "How about the nursery?"

"No exterior doors. Four windows, though."

He'd take the windows over the doors. "That's where we'll be spending the night."

She didn't question it. Jenna turned and started walking in that direction. Cal followed her, trying to keep his steps light so he wouldn't wake Sophie. Jenna led him down a corridor lined with doors and stopped in front of one.

"Don't turn on the lights," Cal told her when she opened the door. It was possible that Holden or someone else was doing some long-range surveillance, and Cal didn't want to advertise their exact location in the estate.

He took a moment to let his eyes adjust to the darkness, and he saw the white crib placed against an interior wall well away from the windows. That was good. Cal went that direction and eased Sophie onto the mattress. She moved a little and pursed her lips, sucking at a nonexistent bottle, and he braced himself for her to wake up and cry. But her eyes stayed closed.

"There isn't a bed in here," Jenna whispered. "Just that."

He spotted a chaise longue in the small adjacent sitting room just off the nursery. The chaise wasn't big enough for two people, but hopefully it would be comfortable enough for Jenna to get some sleep.

"I can have a bed brought in," she suggested.

"No. Best not to have any unnecessary movement." Nor did he want to alert anyone else in the household to their sleeping arrangements. Tomorrow, they'd work out something more comfortable.

Jenna walked mechanically to a closet and took out two quilts. The rooms were toasty warm, but she handed him one and draped the other around herself. Since she didn't seem steady on her feet, Cal helped her in the direction of the chaise.

"Get some sleep," he instructed.

She moved as if she were about to climb onto the chaise, but then she stopped. There was just enough moonlight coming through the windows that he could easily see her troubled expression.

"I've really made a mess of things," she said.

Oh, no. Here it was. The adrenaline crash. Reality was setting in, and she started to shake. He couldn't see any tears, but he had no doubt they were there.

She moved again. Closer to him. Until they were touching, her breasts against his chest. That set off Texas-size alarms in his head, and the rest of his body, but it didn't stop him from putting his arms around her.

She sobbed softly, but tried to muffle it by putting her mouth against his shoulder. Her warm breath fluttered against his neck.

"You'll get through this," he promised, though he knew it wouldn't be easy. She was in for a long, hard night. And so was he.

"You're not trembling," she pointed out.

"I'm trained not to tremble. Besides, I only shot an SUV tonight. Trust me, I've done worse." He tried to make it sound light. Cocky, even. But he failed miserably. The attack couldn't be dismissed with bravado.

She pulled back and blinked hard, trying to rid her eyes of the tears. "Have you ever killed anyone?"

Cal was a little taken aback with the question, and he kept his answer simple. "Yeah."

"Good."

"Good?" Again, he was taken aback.

Jenna nodded. "I want you to stop Salazar if he comes after Sophie."

Oh. Now he got it. Cal pushed her hair away from her face. "I won't let him hurt her. Or you."

Hell. He hadn't meant to say that last part aloud. It was too personal, and it was best if he tried to keep some barrier between them.

Her mouth came to his, and all that barrier stuff suddenly sounded like something he didn't want after all. He wanted her kiss.

Since it was going to be a major mistake, Cal decided

to make the most of it. Something they'd both regret. And maybe that would stop them from doing it again. So he took far more than he should have.

He hooked his arm around her, just at the top of her butt. He drew her closer so that it wasn't only their chests and mouths that were touching. Their bodies came together, and the fit was even better than his fantasies.

The soft sound Jenna made was from a silky feminine moan of pleasure. A signal that she not only wanted this but wanted more. She wrapped her arms around him and gently ground her sex against his.

While the body contact was mind-blowing, Cal didn't neglect the kiss. This last kiss. Since he'd already decided there couldn't be any more of them, he wanted to savor her in these next few scorching moments. To brand her taste, her touch, the feel of her into his memory.

The kiss was already hot and deep. He deepened it even more. Because he was stupid. And because his stupidity knew no boundaries, he followed Jenna's lead.

Oh, man. Their clothes weren't thick enough. A wall wouldn't have been thick enough.

He could feel the heat of her sex. And his. The brainless part of him was already begging him to lower Jenna to that chaise and strip off her pants. Sex would follow immediately. Great hot sex. Which couldn't happen, of course. Sophie was just in the adjoining room and could wake up at any minute.

Cal repeated that, and he forced himself to stop. When he stepped back from her, both of them were gasping for breath.

"Good night," he managed to say.

"That was your idea of a good-night kiss?" Jenna challenged.

No. It was his idea of foreplay, but it was best not to say that out loud. "We can't do it again."

Why did it sound as if he was trying to convince himself?

Because he was.

Still, he was determined to make this work. He was a pro. A rough-around-the-edges operative. He could stop himself from kissing a woman.

He hoped.

She trailed her fingers down his arm and then withdrew her touch. "I wanted to kiss you on the floor of that cantina," she admitted. "Why, I don't know." Jenna shook her head. "Yes, I do. You're hot. You're dangerous. You're all the things that get my blood moving."

His pulse jumped. "So you like hot dangerous things?" he asked.

"I like you," she said, her voice quivery now. She sank down onto the chaise and looked up at him. "But liking you isn't wise. I've made a lot of bad choices in my life, and I can't do that anymore now that I have Sophie. If I fall for a guy, then it has to be the right guy, you know?"

"Sure." He wouldn't tell her that soon his job wouldn't be that dangerous. If he got that deputy director promotion, he'd be doing his shooting from behind a desk. On some level Cal would miss the fieldwork, but the deputy director job was the next step in his dream to be chief. Maybe it was best that Jenna thought his dangerous work would continue. Maybe this was the barrier they needed between them.

"Sleep," he reminded her.

Jenna lay down on the chaise and covered up. Cal was about to do the same on the floor, but his cell phone rang. He yanked it from his pocket and answered it before it could ring a second time and wake up Sophie.

"It's Kowalski," his director greeted. "What's your situation?"

Cal got up, walked across the room and stepped just outside the door and into the hall. "Is this line secure?"

"Yes. I'm using the private line in my office."

Good. That meant if there was a leak or threat from Hollywood, then at least this call wouldn't be overheard. Cal had called Kowalski right after the SUV incident, but he hadn't wanted to say too much until he knew the info would stay private.

"I'm at Ms. Laniere's estate. Were you able to get anything on that SUV that tried to run us off the road?"

"Nothing. The Texas Rangers are investigating. There was a team of them nearby searching for that missing woman, and they got there faster than the FBI."

Well, Cal wasn't holding his breath that they'd find anything related to Salazar. If the assassin had been the driver, then the first thing he would have done was ditch the vehicle. He wouldn't have wanted to drive it around with bullet holes in it.

"And what about Salazar?" Cal asked, hoping by some miracle the man had been picked up.

"He's still at large."

Cal didn't bother to groan since that was the answer

he'd expected. "What about the plates?" He had made a note of them and had asked the director to run them.

"The plates weren't stolen. They were bogus."

Strange. A pro like Salazar would normally have just stolen a vehicle and then discarded it when he was done. Bogus plates took time to create. "And Hollywood? Anything new to report?"

"Nothing definitive on him, either."

Cal was afraid of that. "How did he take the news that he's under investigation?"

The director took several moments to answer. "He doesn't know."

"Excuse me?" Cal was certain he'd misunderstood the director.

"Lynch doesn't know he's being monitored. I want to let him have access to some information and see what he does with it. If he does nothing, then maybe someone has set him up."

Or maybe Hollywood knew about the monitoring and was going to play it clean for a while.

"How's Ms. Laniere?" Kowalski asked, pulling Cal's thoughts away from all the other questions.

She's making me crazy. "She's shaken up, of course." Cal used his briefing tone. Flat, unemotional, detached. Unlike the firestorm going on inside him. "My plan was to stay here with her and her child until we can make other arrangements."

"Of course." The director paused, which bothered Cal. Was Kowalski concerned about this whole paternity issue? Was he worried that Cal was going to sleep with her? Cal was worried about that, too.

"Ms. Laniere is the main reason I'm calling," Kowalski explained. "We might have another problem."

This didn't sound like a personal issue. It sounded dangerous. Besides, they didn't need another problem, personal or otherwise. They already had a boatload of them. "What's wrong now?"

"The Ranger CSI unit is at Ms. Laniere's apartment in Willow Ridge now. About a half hour ago they found a listening device near the front door. It wasn't government issue. It was something you could buy at any store that sells security equipment. Still, Lynch could have put it there."

Holden or Helena could have done the same. All three had been there. Or maybe even Gwen had done it after Jenna and he had left.

"There's more," the director continued. "I had the CSI check your car as well, and they just called to say they'd found a vehicle tracking system taped to the undercarriage."

Cal cursed. "Someone wanted to follow me." He carried that through one more step. "And that means someone could have done the same to Jenna's car."

"Probably."

"But I checked the undercarriage when I looked for explosives." Cal started for the front of the house.

"You could easily have missed it. It's small, half the size of a deck of cards. But don't let the size fool you. It might be wireless and portable, but it's still effective even at long range."

"Stay put," he called out to Jenna. "I have to go outside and check on something."

Cal hurried toward the front of the house, disengaged

the security system, unlocked the front door. He drew his weapon before he hurried out into the cold night. No one seemed to be lurking in the shadows waiting to assassinate him, but he rushed. He didn't want to leave Jenna and Sophie alone for too long.

Thankfully, the overhead porch lights were enough for him to clearly see the car. Staying on the side that was nearest to the house, he stooped and looked underneath. There was no immediate sign of a tracker. But then he looked again at a clump of mud. He touched it and realized it was a fake. Plastic. He pulled it back and looked at the device beneath.

His heart dropped.

"Found it," Cal reported. "Someone camouflaged it."

"So someone wired both cars," the director concluded. "The bad news is that anyone with a laptop could have monitored your whereabouts."

Cal's heart dropped even further. Because that meant someone had tracked them to Jenna's estate.

Salazar and maybe God knows who else knew exactly where they were.

Chapter Nine

Jenna checked her watch. It was nearly 6:00 a.m. Soon, Sophie would wake up and demand her breakfast bottle.

She took a moment to gather her thoughts and to reassure herself one last time that everyone was okay. The security alarm hadn't gone off. No one had fired shots into the place. That SUV hadn't returned.

But all of those things might still happen.

Cal hadn't come out and said that, but after he'd discovered the tracking device on her car, they both knew anything was possible. He'd considered moving them again, but had decided to stay put and hope their safety measures were enough to keep out anyone who might decide to come after them.

After Cal had disarmed and removed the tracking device, every possible function of the security system had been armed. Cal had even alerted all three members of the household staff, and the gardener, Pete Spears, had assured them that he'd keep watch from the gatehouse.

All those measures had been enough. They were still alive and unharmed. But the day had barely started.

With that uncomfortable thought, Jenna eased off the chaise and moved as quietly as she could so she wouldn't wake Cal. He hadn't slept much. She knew that because he'd been awake when she finally fell asleep around midnight. He was still awake when she'd gotten up at 2:00 a.m. to feed a fussing Sophie. He'd even gone with them to the kitchen when she fixed the bottle, and he'd taken his gun with him.

But he was thankfully asleep now.

He was sitting with his legs stretched out in front of him, so his upper back and neck were resting on the chaise. His face looked perfectly relaxed, but he had his hand resting over the butt of the gun in his shoulder holster.

She reached for her shoes, but Cal's hand shot out. Before Jenna could even blink, he grabbed her wrist, turned and used the strength of his body to flatten her against the chaise.

Their eyes met.

He was on top of her with his face only several inches away from hers. In the depths of those steel-blue eyes, she saw him process the situation. There was no emotion in those eyes. Well, not at first. Then he cursed under his breath.

"Sorry. Old habits," he mumbled.

It took her a moment to get past the shock of what'd just happened. "You mean combat training, not intimate situations?" She meant it as a joke, but it came out all wrong. Of course it did. His kisses could melt paint, and he was on top of her in what could be a good starting position for some great morning sex.

But there wouldn't be any.

Cal got off her with difficulty. He dug his knee into the chaise to lever himself up, but that created some interesting contact in their midsections.

"Dreams," he explained when he noticed that she was looking at the bulge behind the zipper of his jeans.

About me? she nearly asked but thankfully held her tongue. It was wishful thinking. Yes, he'd kissed her, but he hadn't wanted to. It'd been just a primal response. Now he wanted some distance between them. He wanted Sophie and her safe so he wouldn't feel obligated to help. And after all the trouble she'd caused for him, she couldn't blame him one bit.

Sophie's soft whimpers got her moving off the chaise but not before Cal and she exchanged uncomfortable glances. She really needed to make other security arrangements so he could leave. But that was the last thing on earth she wanted.

"Good morning, sweetheart," she greeted Sophie.

Jenna scooped her up into her arms and stole a few morning kisses. Sophie stopped fussing and gave her a wide smile. It wouldn't last, though. Soon her baby would want her bottle, so Jenna started toward the kitchen.

Cal was right behind her.

Meggie was ahead of them in the hall. The woman was walking straight toward them. "A fax just arrived for you." She handed Cal at least a dozen pages, but her attention went straight to Sophie. "I've got a bottle waiting for you, young lady."

Sophie looked at her with curious eyes and glanced up at Jenna. Jenna smiled to reassure her, and it seemed to work because Sophie smiled, too, when Meggie took her and headed for the kitchen.

Since Cal had stopped to look at the fax and since

it seemed to have grabbed his complete interest, Jenna stopped as well. "Bad news?"

"It could be." He glanced through the rest of the pages and then handed her the first one. "These are reports I requested from my director. I asked for a background on Gwen Mitchell and I also wanted him to look for any suspicious activity that could be linked back to you."

She skimmed through the page and groaned. "There was a break-in at the pediatrician's office. Sophie's file was stolen." Jenna smacked the paper against the palm of her hand. "Holden is responsible for this. He's trying to prove that Paul's the father."

"What would have been in that file?" Cal asked.

"Well, certainly no DNA information, but her blood type was listed. It's O-positive."

Cal actually looked conflicted. "O-positive is the most common. It's my blood type."

Jenna immediately understood his mixed emotions. This might make Holden think she was telling the truth about Cal being Sophie's father. But this would also make his director have more doubts. She really did need to get a DNA test done right away.

Cal made his way toward the kitchen while he continued to read the fax. "Gwen Mitchell's been a freelance investigative reporter for ten years." He shuffled through the pages. "She's gotten some pretty tough stories, including one on a mob boss. And a Colombian drug dealer."

So they weren't dealing with an amateur. "She doesn't sound like the type of person to back off."

"She's not," Cal confirmed. He stopped again just

outside the kitchen entrance. "According to this, when Gwen was working on that story in Colombia, a woman was killed."

Jenna nearly gasped. "Gwen murdered her?"

"Not exactly, but she was responsible for the woman's death. Gwen made the drug lord believe this woman had revealed sensitive information. The drug lord had her killed. Gwen managed to record the actual murder and that became the centerpiece of her story."

"Oh, God." So this was what they were up against. A ruthless woman who'd do whatever was necessary to get her story. And in this case her story was getting Jenna. Gwen would do anything to collect the one million dollars that Paul had offered her.

Cal walked ahead of her and checked the security system. It was identical to the check he'd made before and after Sophie's 2:00 a.m. feeding. When he was satisfied that everything was still secure, they went to the kitchen.

Meggie had Sophie in the crook of her arm and was trying to feed her a bottle while she checked something on the stove. Jenna went to take the child, but Cal caught her.

"I'll take her. You need to eat something."

Jenna's stomach chose that exact moment to growl. She couldn't argue with that. But she was more than a little surprised when Cal so easily took Sophie from Meggie. He sat down at the kitchen table and readjusted the bottle so there'd be an even flow of formula.

Jenna and Meggie exchanged glances.

"You're sure you haven't done baby duty before?"

Jenna asked. She poured herself a cup of coffee, and Meggie dished her up some scrambled eggs.

"Nope," he assured her.

He was a natural. He seemed so at ease with Sophie. And willing to help. It made Jenna feel guilty—his willingness could be costly for him. If she hadn't told that lie to Holden, Cal would never have come to Willow Ridge, and he wouldn't be in this dangerous situation now. Of course, Jenna was thankful he was there. For Sophie's sake. But she hated what she'd done to him.

Jenna had only managed to eat one bite of the eggs when a shrill beep pulsed through the room. It brought Cal to his feet. He handed Sophie to her and drew his gun.

Just like that, her heart went into overdrive, and her stomach knotted. Jenna passed her daughter to Meggie so she could go with Cal and see what had happened to trigger the surveillance system.

Cal hurried to the security panel just as his cell phone rang. He answered it while he opened the panel box.

"You're here at the estate?" he asked a moment later. That sent him to the side windows by the front door, and he looked out. "Something's wrong."

It wasn't a question, but he must have gotten an answer because he hung up.

"Director Kowalski just arrived," Cal relayed to her. "He found Holden and Helena Carr outside. They were trying to get in the front gate."

CAL HAD HOPED that today wouldn't be as insane as the day before, but it wasn't off to a good start. Here it was, barely dawn, his director had arrived for an impromptu visit, and two of their suspects were only yards away. Cal didn't want those two in the same state with Jenna and Sophie, yet here they were.

Had they been the ones to put the tracking devices on Jenna's and his vehicles? Maybe. Or maybe they'd merely benefited from what someone else had done.

"Can your director arrest Holden and Helena?" Jenna asked.

"Probably not. I'm sure they'll have a cover story for their attempt to get through the front gate."

But maybe they could call the local authorities and have them picked up for trespassing. It wouldn't keep the duo in jail long since they'd have no trouble making bail, but it would send a message that they couldn't continue to intimidate Jenna without paying a consequence or two.

Cal grabbed his jacket and disarmed the security system so he could go outside and *greet* their visitors. Jenna picked up her jacket as well.

"I want to talk to them," she said before he could object to her going with him.

"That wouldn't be wise."

"On the contrary. I want them to know I won't cower in fear or hide. I want them out of my life."

Cal wasn't sure this was the way to make that happen, but he didn't want to take the time to argue with her. Director Kowalski might need backup.

"Wait on the porch," he instructed. "That way, they can see you, but you can get back inside if things turn ugly."

He hoped like the devil that she obeyed.

Cal walked down the steps and spotted the gardener,

Pete, in the gatehouse. He was armed with a shotgun. Good. He'd take all the help he could get.

There were three cars just on the other side of the gate. Two were high-end luxury vehicles, no doubt belonging to Holden and Helena. Cal wondered why they hadn't driven together. The third vehicle was a standard-issue four-wheel-drive from ISA's motor pool.

The three drivers were at the gate, waiting. Cal didn't like the idea of his director being locked out with the Carrs, but he couldn't risk Sophie's and Jenna's safety. He needed to keep that gate closed until he was sure this visit wasn't going to lead to an attack.

Before he approached the gate, Cal glanced over his shoulder. Amazingly, Jenna was still on the porch. He doubted she'd stay there, but he welcomed these few minutes of safety.

"I didn't try to break in," Helena volunteered. "I merely wanted to speak to Jenna, and I was trying to find an intercom or something when that man with the shotgun sounded the alarm."

Kowalski was behind her. He had his weapon drawn in his right hand and held an equipment bag in his left. He rolled his eyes, an indication he didn't buy Helena's story.

Holden's eyes, however, were much more intense. He had his attention fastened to Jenna on the porch. "I need to talk to her, too," he insisted.

I, not *we.* Given the fact that the siblings had arrived in separate vehicles, perhaps they were in the middle of a family squabble. Considering what Helena had said at Jenna's apartment in Willow Ridge, that didn't surprise Cal.

"Jenna's not receiving visitors," Cal said sarcastically. "But I'll pass along any message."

Holden continued to watch Jenna. "The message is that she's in grave danger." His voice was probably loud enough for her to hear.

Cal shrugged. "Old news."

"Not exactly," Holden challenged. He glanced at his sister.

Now it was Helena's turn to show some intensity. Anger tightened the muscles on her face. "My brother broke into my personal computer and read the email Paul's attorney sent me. Holden seems to think that I'd be willing to do whatever Paul wants me to do."

Well, this had potential. "And what does Paul want you to do?"

Helena came closer and hooked her perfectly manicured fingers around the wrought-iron spindles that made up the gate front. "Paul seemed to believe that I would tie up loose ends if Salazar failed."

Holden stepped forward as well. "My sister's orders are to kill us all once Salazar has Sophie."

Oh, hell. Paul really had put together some plan. Kidnapping and murder.

"I'm not a killer," Helena said, her voice shaky now. "I have no idea why Paul thought I would do this."

"Don't you?" Holden again. He aimed his answer at Cal. "My sister was sleeping with Paul. She didn't think I knew, but I did. And I also knew that they had plans to kill Jenna if she turned down his marriage proposal."

"That's not true," Helena protested.

Cal heard footsteps behind him and groaned. A glance over his shoulder confirmed that Jenna wanted to be part of this conversation. He didn't blame her. But he also wanted to keep her safe. He positioned himself in front of her, hoping that would be enough if bullets started flying.

"Paul didn't love me," Helena said to Jenna. She shook her head. "He didn't love you, either."

"I know," Jenna readily agreed. "He wanted my business. And you were in on his plan to get it?"

"Only the business." Helena's face flushed as if she was embarrassed by the admission of her guilt. "I never would have agreed to murder."

Cal wasn't sure he believed her. A flushed face could be faked. "How does Gwen Mitchell fit into the picture?" he asked.

Helena's eyes widened. "The reporter?"

"Yeah. Paul was sleeping with her, too." It was a good guess. After reading Gwen's background, Cal figured she'd do anything to get a story.

Helena shook her head again and a thin stream of breath left her mouth. "I didn't know."

"So Paul slept around," Holden snarled. If he had any concern for his sister's reaction, he didn't show it. "I don't think that's nearly as important as the fact that he's put bounties on our heads." Holden cursed. "He was my friend. Like a brother to me. And this is what he does?"

Kowalski came closer. "What exactly did Paul say in the email he sent you?" he asked Holden.

Holden sent a nasty glare the director's way. "Well, he didn't ask me to kill anyone, that's for sure. He asked me to check on some accounts and old business connections. Nothing illegal. Nothing sinister. Obviously,

Helena can't say the same. Paul made some kind of arrangement with my sister—"

"He didn't," Helena practically shouted. "And I didn't agree to do what he asked." She caught her brother's arm and whirled him around so he was facing her. "Have you ever considered that he could be doing this for some other reason? To get us at each other's throats? Paul had a sick sense of humor, and this might be his idea of a joke."

"My daughter is in danger," Jenna said, drawing everyone's attention back to her. "It's not a joke. Salazar is out there, and Paul is the one who sent him after Sophie."

Cal glanced at Holden and Helena to see their reactions. They were still hurling daggers at each other. It was a good time to interject some logic in this game of pointing fingers.

"If Paul wanted Sophie, but he also wanted all of you dead, then who would be left to raise her?" the director challenged. "Who would be left to manage his estate? Why would he want to eliminate the very people who could give him some postmortem help?"

Dead silence.

"Maybe he expected Gwen Mitchell to help him," Jenna mumbled. "Maybe they were more than just lovers."

That was exactly what Cal was considering. Gwen's ruthlessness would have endeared her to Paul. And for that matter, the emails could be a hoax. A way to drive them all apart. Gwen could have further instructions that Paul could have given her before he was murdered.

And that brought Cal back to something he wanted to

ask. "How exactly did you two know that Jenna would be here?"

Holden shrugged and peeled off the leather glove on his left hand. "It wasn't a lucky guess, was it, Helena?"

The woman's shoulders snapped back, but she didn't answer her brother. She looked at Cal instead. "Salazar called me a few hours ago to tell me that he'd put a tracking device on Jenna's car. He said she was here."

Cal silently cursed and glanced around to make sure Salazar wasn't lurking somewhere. "Go back in the house," he instructed Jenna in a whisper. "Arm the security system."

"But if it isn't safe for me, it isn't safe for you," Jenna pointed out, also in a whisper.

"I won't be long," he promised, knowing that didn't really address her concerns. Still, he had some unfinished business. Concerns about his personal safety could wait.

"What else did Salazar say?" Kowalski demanded from Helena once Jenna started for the house.

"Nothing. I swear. He told me about the tracking device, said Jenna was at the estate, and that was it. He hung up." She slid an icy glance at her brother. "I didn't know Holden had tapped my calls. Not until I arrived here and realized that he'd followed me."

Cal stared at Holden, to see if he would add anything, or at least offer an explanation as to why he'd eavesdropped on his sister's conversations. But maybe this was the way it'd always been between them.

"You're not getting into the estate," Cal assured both of them. "You're trespassing."

Holden smacked the glove against the gate. "Arrest

me, then. Go ahead. Waste your time when what you should be doing is stopping Salazar."

"Oh, I intend to do that." And he intended to stop Gwen if she was as neck deep in this as he thought she was.

"I don't think it'll be a waste of time if you report to the local FBI office for questioning," the director interjected.

"When there's a warrant for my arrest, I'll show up," Holden snarled. He headed for his car, got in and drove away. His tires squealed from the excessive speed.

"I'll go in for questioning," Helena told Kowalski. Her eyes watered with tears. "I'll do whatever's necessary to keep us all alive."

"Paul asked you to kill us," Cal reminded her. "What makes you think you're in danger?"

She glanced at her brother's car as it quickly disappeared down the road. "Holden won't show me the email he got from Paul. My brother doesn't trust me. And why should he? Because of Paul, Holden thinks I'll try to kill him, and he's no doubt trying to figure out how to kill me first before I can carry through with Paul's wishes."

With that, she walked to her car. Her shoulders were slumped, and she swiped her hand over her cheek to wipe away her tears.

"Any idea what was in Holden's email?" Cal asked once Helena had driven away.

Kowalski shook his head. "We're still working on that. But Helena didn't lie when she said what was in hers. Paul did leave orders to kill Jenna, Holden and anyone else who got in the way of Salazar taking the baby."

Anyone else. That would be Cal. Somehow he would stop Salazar and unravel this mess that'd brought danger right to Jenna's doorstep.

He reached over and hit the control switch to open the gate. Kowalski walked closer and handed him an equipment bag. "I figured you might need this. There's an extra weapon, ammo and a clean laptop."

Cal appreciated the supplies, but knowing Salazar could be out there, he continued to keep watch. So did Pete. The lanky man with sandy blond hair shifted his shotgun and wary gaze all around the grounds. There weren't many places Salazar could take cover and use an assault rifle. Unless he actually made it onto the property. Then there were a lot of places he could use to launch an attack.

Cal glanced down into the unzipped bag and then looked at Kowalski. "Does this mean I'll be here for a while?"

"For now." He paused. "I know it's not protocol. Hell, it's not even legal. That's why you can't be here in a professional capacity. This is personal, understand? You're on an official leave of absence."

"I understand."

It was the truth. This had become personal for Cal.

"Last night after we talked, I worked to set up a safe house for Ms. Laniere and her child," Kowalski explained. "But then the communications monitor at headquarters informed me that my account might have been compromised. There was something suspicious about the way info was feeding in and out of what was supposed to be a secure computer. That means someone might have seen the message traffic on the safe house."

Cal cursed. "Hollywood?"

"Maybe. But it could also be a false alarm caused by a computer glitch. That's why I decided to come in person and tell you to stay put for now."

That's what Cal was afraid he was going to say. "But Salazar knows where Jenna is."

Kowalski nodded. "You might have to take him out if we can't stop him first. The FBI and the Rangers are looking for him. They know he's probably in the area."

Yeah. And for that reason, Cal didn't want to leave Jenna alone for too long. "I'll do what's necessary."

Another nod. The director glanced around uneasily. "What about the paternity issue? Did you get that DNA test done to prove you aren't the baby's father?"

Cal hadn't forgotten about that, but it was definitely on the back burner. "I figured it could wait until all of this is over. Besides, I want Holden and Salazar to believe the child is mine. That might get them to back off."

Though that was more than a long shot. Things had already been set into motion, and it would take a miracle to stop them.

Kowalski met him eye-to-eye. "You're sure that's the only reason you're putting off a DNA test?"

Cal stared at him and tried not to blast the man for accusing him of lying. "I've never given you a reason to distrust me."

"You have now." The director turned and started for his vehicle. "Clear up this paternity issue, Cal, before it destroys everything you've worked so hard to get."

There was just one problem with clearing it up. Well, two.

Jenna and Sophie.

He closed the gate and stood there watching his boss drive away. Cal wondered if his chances at that promotion had just driven away, too. Without Kowalski's blessing, Cal wasn't going to get that deputy director job. Not a chance. He wouldn't even have a career left to salvage.

Cal grabbed the equipment bag and went back to the house. Jenna was there, waiting for him just inside the door. A few feet behind her was Meggie. She had Sophie cradled in her arms. The little girl smiled at him. She was too young and innocent to know the danger she was in.

Seeing Jenna and the baby was a reminder that his career was pretty damn small in the grand scheme of things.

"So, are we going on the run again?" Jenna began to nibble on her bottom lip.

"No." He hoped that was the right thing to do.

Still, he wasn't going to put full trust in his director's decision for them to stay put because Hollywood might still be getting access to any- and everything.

"I need backup," Cal mumbled to himself. More than just a gardener with a shotgun.

And it had to be someone he trusted.

His brother Max was his first choice. If Max was on assignment, then he'd call a friend who owned a personal protection agency. One way or another he wanted someone reliable on the grounds ASAP, and these were men he could trust with his life.

"So we stay put," Jenna concluded. She paused. "And then what?"

"We prepare ourselves for the worst."

Because the worst was on the way.

Chapter Ten

"Rule one," Cal said to Jenna. He slipped on her eye goggles and adjusted them so they fit firmly on her face. "Treat all firearms as if they're loaded."

He positioned the Smith & Wesson 9 mm gun in her hand and turned her toward the target. It was the silhouette of a person rather than a bull's-eye. Jenna didn't like the idea of aiming at a person, real or otherwise, but she also knew this was necessary. Cal was doing everything humanly possible to keep her and Sophie safe. She wanted to do her part as well.

"Rule two," he continued. "Never point a weapon at anything or anyone you don't intend to destroy."

There it was in a nutshell. Her biggest fear. She'd have to kill someone to stop all of this insanity.

Every precaution was being taken to prevent anyone, especially Salazar, from gaining access to the estate. Cal's friend Jordan Taylor had arrived an hour earlier. He was an expert in security. Jenna hadn't actually met or seen the man because he'd immediately gotten to work on installing monitoring equipment around the entire fence. Jordan had brought another man, Cody Guillory, with him, and the two were going to patrol the grounds. In the meantime, Director Kowalski and the FBI had assured Cal they were doing everything to catch Salazar and neutralize the threat.

However, Cal had insisted she learn how to shoot, just in case.

Jenna hadn't balked at his suggestion, but she had waited until Sophie was down for her morning nap. Meggie and the baby were in the nursery with the door locked, Meggie was armed and the rest of the house was on lockdown. No one was to get in or out.

"Rule three—don't hold your gun sideways. Only stupid people trying to look cool do that. It'll give you a bad aim and cause you to miss your target." Cal moved behind her.

Touching her.

Something he'd been doing since this lesson started. Of course, it was impossible to give a shooting lesson without touching, but the contact made it hard for her to concentrate. It reminded her of their kiss and the fact that she wanted him to touch her. She needed therapy. How could she be thinking about such things at a time like this?

Quite easily, she admitted.

It was Cal and his superhero outfit. Camo pants, black chest-hugging T-shirt. Steel-toed boots. The clothes had been in the equipment bag that the director had delivered, and in this case, the clothes made the man. Well, they made her notice every inch of his body, anyway.

"Okay, here we go," he said, pulling her attention back to the lesson. "Feet apart." He put his hand on the inside of her thigh, just above her knee, to position her.

A shiver of heat went through her.

"Left foot slightly in front. Right elbow completely straight. Since you're new at this, look at the target with your right eye. Close your left one. It'll make it easier to aim." He stopped with his hand beneath her straight elbow and his arm grazing her breasts. "You're shaking a little. Are you cold?"

The room was a little chilly, but that wasn't it. Jenna knew she should just lie. It was right there on the tip of her tongue, but she made the mistake of glancing at him. Even through the goggles, he had no trouble seeing her expression.

"Oh," he mumbled. "Some women get turned on from shooting. All that power in their hands."

Jenna continued to stare at him. "I don't think it's the gun." She probably should have lied about that, too.

Cal chuckled. It was husky, deep and totally male. He dropped his hands to her waist to readjust her stance. At least that's how it started, but he kept his hands there and pressed against her. His front against her back.

That didn't help the shaking. Nor did it cool down the heat.

He grabbed two sets of earmuffs, put one on her and slipped the other on himself. "Take aim at the center of the target," he said, his voice loud so that she could hear him. "Squeeze the trigger with gentle but steady pressure."

Which was exactly what he was doing to her waist.

"Now?" she asked.

"Whenever you're ready." He brushed against her butt.

Sheez. Since this lesson was turning into foreplay, Jenna decided to go ahead. She thought through all of Cal's instructions and then pulled the trigger. Even with the earmuffs, the shot was loud, and her entire right arm recoiled.

She pulled off the earmuffs and goggles and had a look at where her shot had landed.

"That'll work," Cal assured her.

Jenna looked closer at the target and frowned. "I hit the guy in his family jewels."

Cal chuckled again. "Trust me, that'll work."

She replaced the earmuffs and goggles so she could try more shots. She adjusted her aim but the bullet went low again. It took her three more tries before she got a shot anywhere near the upper torso.

"I think you got the hang of it," Cal praised. He took off his own muffs and laid them back on the shelf. He did the same to hers and then took the gun from her. It wasn't easy—her fingers had frozen around it.

"You did good," he added, making eye contact with her.

His hand went around the back of her neck, pulling her to him, and his mouth went to hers.

Yes! she thought. *Finally!*

Maybe it was the fact she was a new mother and had learned to appreciate what little free time she had, but Jenna wanted to make the most of these stolen moments.

Cal obviously did, too. He kissed her, hungry and hot, as if he'd been waiting all morning to do just that.

He ran his hand into her hair so that he controlled the movement of her head. She didn't mind. He angled her so that he could deepen the kiss. And just like that, she was starved for more of him.

With his hands and mouth on her, Jenna's back

landed against one of the smooth, square floor-to-ceiling columns that set off the firing lane. Cal landed against her. All those firm sinewy muscles in his chest played havoc with her breasts. It'd been so long since she'd been in a man's arms, and this man had been worth the wait.

His mouth teased and coaxed her. The not so gentle pressure of his chest muscles and pecs made her latch on to him and pull him even closer, until they were fitted together exactly the way a man and woman should fit. They still had their clothes on, but Jenna had no trouble imagining what it would be like to have Cal naked and inside her.

Her need for him was almost embarrassing. She'd never been a sexually charged person. She preferred a good kiss to sex, probably because she'd never actually had good sex. But something told her that she wouldn't have to settle for one or the other with Cal. He was more than capable of delivering both.

He slid his hand down her side, to the bottom of her stretchy top, and lifted it. His fingers, which were just as hot and clever as his mouth, were suddenly on her bare skin, making their way to her breasts and jerking down the cups of her bra.

Everything intensified. His touch. The heat. That primal tug deep within her.

Cal pulled back from the kiss, only so he could wet his fingertips with his tongue. For a moment, she didn't understand why. But then his mouth came back to hers, and those slick wet fingers went to her nipples. He caressed her, and gently pinched her nipples, bringing them to peaks.

Jenna nearly lost it right there.

Frantically searching for some relief to the pressure-cooker heat, she hooked her fingers through the belt loops of his camo pants and dragged him to her, so that his hard sex ground against the soft, wet part of her body.

It was good. Too good.

Because it only made her want the rest of him.

She reached for his zipper, but Cal clamped his hand over hers. Stopping her. "No condom," he reminded her.

Jenna cursed, both thankful and angry that he'd managed to keep a clear head. She didn't want a clear head. She wanted Cal. But she also knew he was right. They couldn't risk having unprotected sex.

She tried to calm down. She'd been ready to climax, and her body wasn't pleased that it wasn't going to get what it wanted.

Cal, however, didn't let her come down. He pinned her in place against the column and shoved down her zipper. He didn't wait to see how she would react to that. He kissed her again. And again, the heat began to soar.

While he did some clever things with his mouth, he tormented her nipples with his left hand. But it was his right hand that sent her soaring. It slid into her jeans. Underneath her panties. He wasn't gentle, wasn't slow. His middle and index fingers eased into the slippery heat of her body and moved.

It didn't take much. Just a few of those clever strokes. Another deep French kiss. He nipped her nipple with his fingertips.

Their kiss muffled the sound she made, and his fingers continued to move, to give her every last bit of pleasure he could.

CAL CAUGHT HER to make sure she didn't fall. Jenna buried her face against the crook of his neck and let him catch her. Her breath came out in rough, hot jolts. Her body was trembling, her face, flushed with arousal.

She smelled like sex.

It was a powerful scent that urged his body to do a lot more than he'd just done. Of course, what he'd done was too much. He'd crossed lines that shouldn't have been crossed. In fact, he'd gone just short of what his director already suspected him of doing.

A husky laugh rumbled in Jenna's throat, and she blinked as if to clear her vision. Cal certainly needed to clear his. He made sure she was steady on her feet, and then he zipped up her jeans so he could step away from her.

She blinked again. This time, she looked confused, then embarrassed. "Oh, mercy. You could get into trouble for that."

He shrugged and left it at that.

"I keep forgetting that this has much stiffer consequences for you than it does for me." Still breathing hard, she pushed the wisps of blond hair from her face. A natural blonde. He'd discovered that when he unzipped her pants and pushed down her panties.

Now he needed to forget what he'd seen.

Hell. He just needed to forget, period.

"Of course, I'll get a broken heart out of this," she mumbled, and fixed her jeans.

A broken heart?

Did that mean she had feelings for him?

"Forget I said that," she mumbled a moment later.

She looked even more embarrassed. "I'm not making sense right now."

So no broken heart. But still Cal had to wonder....

He didn't have long to wonder because his phone rang. The caller ID screen indicated it was Jordan.

"I was beefing up security by the front gate when a car pulled up," Jordan explained in the no-nonsense tone that Cal had always heard him use. "You have a visitor. She says her name is Gwen Mitchell and that she *must* talk to you."

"Gwen Mitchell's out front," Cal relayed to Jenna.

He wasn't exactly surprised. Everyone seemed to know where they were. But how should he handle this visit? He needed to question Gwen, but he didn't want to do that by placing Jenna and Sophie at risk.

"She says she has some new information you should hear," Jordan added. "She's refused to give it to me, but I can get it if you like. What do you want me to do with her?"

From Jordan, it was a formidable question. If Gwen had any inkling of the dangerous man that Jordan could be, she probably would have been running for the hills. Jordan was loyal to the end. He and Cal were close enough that he would trust Jordan to kill for him. Of course, he hoped killing Gwen wouldn't be necessary.

"Make sure she's not armed," Cal instructed. "And then escort her to the porch. I'll meet you at the front door."

"You're not going to let her in the house?" Jordan challenged.

"Not a chance."

Cal believed Gwen wanted one thing. A story. And

even though he could relate to her devotion to duty, he was beginning to see that as a huge risk.

"You're meeting with her?" Jenna asked, following right behind him.

Cal locked the gun room door, using the key that Jenna had given him earlier. "I have a hunch that Gwen knows a lot more than she's saying. Plus, I want to hear what she considers to be important information."

"It could be a trap," Jenna pointed out.

"It could be, but if so, it's suicide. Jordan won't let an armed suspect make it to the door. Still, I want you to wait inside."

She huffed. For such a simple sound, it conveyed a lot. Jenna didn't like losing control of her life. But one way or another he was going to protect her.

"I'll stay in the foyer," she bargained. "Because you aren't actually going outside, are you?" She didn't wait for him to confirm that. "Besides, any information she has would pertain to me. Paul sent her after me because he thought I planned to murder him. I deserve to hear what she has to say."

He stopped at the front door, whirled around and stared at her. He had already geared up for an argument about why she shouldn't be present at this meeting, but Jenna pressed her fingers over his mouth.

"Don't let sexual attraction for me get in the way of doing what's smart," she said. Except it sounded like some kind of accusation.

"The sexual attraction isn't making me stupid."

"If you didn't want me in your bed," Jenna continued, "then you wouldn't be so protective of me. You'd let me confront Gwen." She frowned when he scowled at her.

"Or you'd at least let me listen to what she has to say. I can do that as safely as you can. You already pointed out that Jordan will make sure Gwen isn't armed."

True. So why did he still feel the need to shelter Jenna from this conversation?

Hell. The attraction he felt for her could really complicate everything.

Cal scowled and threw open the front door.

Gwen was there, looking not at all certain of what she might have gotten herself into. Jordan probably had something to do with that. At six-two and a hundred and ninety pounds, he was no lightweight. He stood behind Gwen, looming over her. He was armed and had an extra weapon on his utility belt. In addition, he had a small communicator fitted into his left ear. He was no doubt getting updates from an associate somewhere on the grounds.

Jordan seemed to be doing a good job of neutralizing any threat from Gwen, but Cal took it one step further and made sure he was in front of Jenna.

"There's someone else waiting by the gate," Jordan informed them. "Archie Monroe. His ID looks legit. Says he's from Cryogen Labs."

Cal went on instant alert, and motioned for Jordan to come inside. He shut the door, leaving Gwen standing outside, and lowered his voice to a whisper. "Could it be Salazar?"

"Not unless he's had major cosmetic surgery. This guy's about sixty, gray hair and he's got a couple of spare tires around his middle."

"It's not Salazar," Jenna provided. Jordan and Cal stared at her. "He's a lab technician. I called Cryogen this morning and asked them to send out someone to do a DNA test on Sophie."

Cal choked back a groan and geared himself up for an argument.

Jenna beat him to it. "The DNA issue is hurting your career. I can't let it continue."

Cal opened his mouth. Then he closed it and tried to get hold of his temper. "I will not let you put my job ahead of Sophie's safety. Got that?" Then he turned to Jordan. "Tell him there's been a misunderstanding, that his services are not needed."

Jordan nodded and opened the door to hurry toward the front gate. Jenna didn't say anything else, but she did send Cal a disapproving look. He knew she didn't want this test. Not really. She wouldn't want to do anything to increase the risk of danger for Sophie. That's what made it even more frustrating.

She was doing this for him.

That attraction had *really* screwed up things between them.

"Is there a problem?" Gwen asked, glancing over her shoulder at Jordan, who was making his way to the lab tech.

"You tell me," Cal challenged. "Why are you here?"

Gwen's attention went to Jenna. "I know you didn't murder Paul."

Not exactly a revelation.

"That's why you came?" Jenna stepped closer. "To tell me something I already know?"

"I have proof. I got Paul's attorney to email me surveillance videos. There's not any actual footage of Paul being killed, but there is footage of you leaving the estate. Fifteen minutes later, there's footage of Paul coming out of his office to get something and then returning."

Cal knew all about that surveillance. The ISA had studied and restudied it. Well, Hollywood had. And Cal had reviewed it to make sure Jenna hadn't been the killer. The surveillance hadn't captured images of the person who'd entered Paul's office and shot him in the back of the head. Thermal images taken with ISA equipment had shown a person entering through a private entrance. No security camera had been set up there. Of course, the killer had to have known that.

"You could have called Jenna to tell her this," Cal pointed out.

Gwen shook her head. Her eyes showed stress. They were bloodshot and had smudgy dark circles beneath. "I think someone's listening in on my conversations. Someone's following me, too. I think it's because I'm getting close to unraveling all of this."

"Or maybe you're faking all this to cover your own guilt," Jenna countered.

Gwen didn't look offended. She merely nodded. "I could be, but I'm not." She gave a weary sigh. "I think there's a problem with the emails Paul wanted us all to receive."

"I'm listening," Cal said when she paused.

"I've been talking to Paul's attorney, and he told me that Paul wrote many emails and left instructions as to which to send out. For instance, if Jenna had had a baby, he was to send out set three. If any one of us, Jenna, Holden, Helena or Salazar, was dead by the time of the send-out date, then a different set was to be emailed."

"So?" Cal challenged. This wasn't news, either.

"So it wasn't the lawyer who determined which set was to go out. It was Holden."

"Holden?" he and Jenna said in unison. Whoa. Now *that* was news.

"I asked him, and he confirmed it. But he said he had no idea what was in the other emails. He claims that they were encrypted when they went out and that in Paul's instructions to him, he asked Holden not to try to decode them, that he wanted each email to be personal and private."

Well, that added a new twist, not that Cal needed this information to suspect Holden. Holden had a lot to gain from this situation, especially if he wanted to make sure he didn't have to share Paul's estate with his sister or any potential heirs.

But then, Gwen had motive, too. It could be that she just wanted a good story from all of this, but Paul had offered her a million dollars to find his killer. That was a lot of incentive to put a plan together. And there was another possibility: that Gwen hadn't just been involved in Paul's life but also his death.

Cal decided to go with an old-fashioned bluff.

"You didn't have any trouble getting Paul's lawyer to cooperate." He made a knowing sound. "Did you meet him when you were pretending to be Paul's maid? Are you the infamous Mary? And before you think about lying to me, you should probably know that I just read a very interesting intel report from an insider in Monte de Leon." That was a lie, of course, but Cal thought it would pay off.

Gwen's eyes widened, and she went a little pale.

"Yes, I was Mary. I faked a résumé to get a job at Paul's estate, but he quickly figured out who I was."

The bluff had worked. Cal continued to push. "Is that when you killed him?"

"No." More color drained from her face, and she repeated that denial. "I didn't kill Paul."

"And why should I believe you?" Cal pressed.

"Because killing him wouldn't have helped me get a story. I wanted the insider's view to Paul's business. With him dead, my story was dead, too."

"Now you've resurrected it with a new angle. You don't care that you're putting Jenna and her daughter in danger?"

"I don't know what you mean." Gwen's voice wavered. "I haven't put them in danger."

"Haven't you?" Jenna asked, stepping closer so that she was practically in Gwen's face.

"Not intentionally." She seemed sincere. Of course, she was a reporter after a story, so Cal wasn't buying it.

Cal saw something over Gwen's shoulder, and he re-aimed his gun. But it was Jordan, who was quickly making his way back to the porch.

"Hell. It's like Grand Central Terminal around here," Jordan grumbled. "I sent the lab guy on his way, but someone else just drove up. He says his name is Mark Lynch. Hollywood. And he wants to see all three of you."

Gwen flattened her hand on her chest. "Me?"

"Especially you."

Chapter Eleven

Jenna didn't know which surprised her more—that Hollywood had shown up or that he wanted to see Gwen. It was definitely a development that she hadn't seen coming. It could be very dangerous.

Her first instinct was to tell Jordan to stop Hollywood from getting any closer to the house. Sophie would be waking from her nap at any minute, and even though Meggie had instructions not to leave the nursery until she checked with them, if they let Hollywood in the gate, he would be too close to her baby.

Gwen was already too close.

"We could take this meeting to the gatehouse," Jenna suggested. That way, they could ask Hollywood how he knew Gwen and why he wanted to see her. Or why he wanted to see Cal and her, for that matter. Even though he didn't know it, he was a suspect.

Cal glanced at her. She knew that look. He was trying to figure out how to make this meeting happen so that she wasn't part of it.

"Hollywood asked to see me, too," Jenna reminded him.

"People don't always get what they want," Cal responded.

Before Jenna could challenge that, Gwen interrupted. "I don't want to see him." She managed to look indignant. Angry, even. "He's going to tell you that I'm behind the attempt to kill you. It's not true."

"Why would he tell us that?" Jenna demanded.

Silence. Gwen glanced over her shoulder as if to verify that Hollywood's car was indeed there.

"We'll go to the gatehouse," Cal insisted. "I'm interested in what Hollywood has to say about you. And himself." He turned to Jenna and took his backup weapon from an ankle holster. Cal handed it to her. "Stay close to me."

She nodded, taking the weapon as confidently as she could. Jenna didn't want Gwen to know that she didn't have much experience handling a gun.

Jenna also silently thanked Cal for not giving her a hassle about attending this impromptu meeting. That couldn't have been easy for him. His training made him want to keep her tucked away so she'd be safer. Part of Jenna wanted that, too. But more than her own safety, she wanted to get to the truth that would ultimately get her daughter out of danger.

Cal locked the front door before they stepped away from it. The chilly wind whipped at them as they went down the porch steps and across the front yard. Both Cal and Jordan shot glances around the estate, both of them looking for any kind of threat. However, Jenna felt their biggest threat was the man waiting on the other side of the gate.

Hollywood was there with his hands clamped around the wrought-iron rods. He stepped back when Jordan entered the code to open the gate.

"Thanks for seeing me," Hollywood greeted Cal. He volleyed glances at all of them, except for Gwen. He tossed her a venomous glare.

Jordan stepped forward, motioning for Hollywood to lift his arms, and searched him. He extracted a gun from a shoulder holster hidden beneath Hollywood's leather jacket. Hollywood didn't protest being disarmed. He merely followed Cal's direction when Cal motioned for him to go inside the gatehouse.

The building was small. It obviously wasn't meant for meetings, but Cal, Gwen and Jenna followed Hollywood inside. Jordan waited just outside the door with his body angled so that he could see both them and the house. Good. Jenna didn't want anyone trying to sneak in.

Hollywood aimed his index finger at Gwen. "Anything she says about me is a lie."

"Funny, she said the same thing about you," Cal commented.

"Of course she did. She wants to cover her butt."

"And you don't?" Gwen challenged.

Jenna decided this was a good time to stand back and listen. These two intended to clear the air, and that could give them information about what the heck was going on.

"I slept with her last year in Monte de Leon," Hollywood confessed to Cal. "And when I told her it couldn't be anything more than a one-night stand, she didn't take it well. I figured she'd be out to get me. She's the one who's setting me up. She wants to make it look as if I've been feeding information to Salazar."

"Don't flatter yourself." Gwen took a step closer and

got right in Hollywood's face. "I wasn't upset about the breakup. I was upset with myself that I let it happen in the first place."

Hollywood cursed. "You planned it all. You came on to me with the hopes I'd give you information about the ISA's investigation into Paul's illegal activities."

"I slept with you because I'd had too much to drink," Gwen tossed back.

Hollywood didn't have a comeback for that. He stood there, seething, his hands balled into fists and veins popping out on his forehead.

"So you slept with both Paul and Hollywood around the same time?" Jenna asked the woman.

Gwen nodded and had the decency to blush, especially since her affair with Paul had been a calculating way to get her story. That meant Hollywood might be telling the truth about Gwen's motives. But he still could have leaked information.

"How exactly could Gwen have set you up?" Cal asked, taking the words out of Jenna's mouth.

"I think she stole my access code and password while she was in my hotel room in Monte de Leon."

Jenna looked at Gwen, who didn't deny or confirm anything. But she did dodge Jenna's gaze.

"You reported that the code and password could have been compromised?" Cal asked.

"No. I didn't know they had been. Not until yesterday when I figured out that someone was tapping into classified information. I knew it wouldn't take long for Kowalski to think I was the one doing it."

"And you aren't?" Jenna asked point-blank.

"I'm not." There was no hesitation. No hint of guilt.

Just frustration. But maybe Hollywood was true to his nickname—this could be just good acting.

"There's a lot going on," Hollywood continued. "Someone is pulling a lot of strings to manipulate this situation. Gwen wants a story, and she wants it to be big. That's why she's stirring the pot. That's why these crazy things are happening to all of us."

"Someone is out to get us," Cal clarified. "Someone tried to run me and Jenna off the road last night. And someone planted a tracking device on her car. You think Gwen is responsible for that?"

"Well, it wasn't me. I stayed back in Willow Ridge to look for that missing woman, Kinley Ford. Heck, I even called the FBI from town to let them know I'd learned the woman had been there. You can check cell tower records to confirm that."

Not really. Because with Hollywood's expertise, he could have figured out a way around that.

Hollywood swore under his breath and shook his head. "Gwen has the strongest motive for everything that's happening. She wants that story."

Gwen stepped forward, positioning herself directly in front of Hollywood. "Holden or Helena could be paying you big bucks for information. For that matter, the money could be coming directly from Paul's estate."

"I wouldn't take blood money," Hollywood insisted, ramming his finger against his chest. "But you would. So would Holden or Helena."

So this could all come down to money. That didn't shock Jenna, but it sickened her to know that her daughter could be in danger simply because someone wanted to get rich.

Cal glanced at Jordan to make sure the area was still safe. He waited until Jordan nodded before he continued the conversation with Hollywood. "Any reason you didn't tell me yesterday that you'd had sex with a person of interest in this investigation?"

The frustration in Hollywood's expression went up a significant notch. His chest pumped with his harsh breaths. "Before you judge me, I think you should remind yourself why you're here. You slept with Jenna while she was in your protective custody."

Jenna wanted to set the record straight for Cal's sake, but he caught her hand and gave it a gentle warning squeeze.

"I can't trust either of you," Cal said to Hollywood and Gwen. "I don't care what your motives are. I want you to back off and leave Jenna and Sophie alone."

"You should be telling the Carrs this," Gwen pointed out.

"Maybe you'll do that for me." Cal didn't continue until Gwen looked him in the eye. "You can also tell them that Jenna, Sophie and I are leaving the estate within the hour. We're already packed and ready to go."

Jenna went still. Had Cal really planned that, or was this a ruse to get everyone off their trail?

"You think that's a wise move?" Hollywood asked.

"I think it's a *safe* move. And this time, I'll check and make sure there aren't any tracking devices on the vehicle we use."

Gwen turned and faced Jenna. Her expression wasn't as tense as Hollywood's, but emotion tightened the muscles in her jaw. "No matter where you go, the Carrs will find you."

"And you, too?"

Gwen shrugged and folded her arms over her chest. "I plan to write a story about Paul's murder."

"Then this meeting is over," Cal insisted. He put his hand on Hollywood's shoulder to get him moving out the door.

"I'm innocent," Hollywood declared. "But I don't expect you to trust me. Just hear this, I'll do whatever's necessary to clear my name."

"If you do that, I'll be overjoyed. But for right now, I don't want you anywhere near Jenna or Sophie. Got that?" It was an order, not a request.

Hollywood nodded and walked out. So did Gwen. Both went to their respective vehicles, but Jordan didn't return Hollywood's gun until the man had started his engine and was ready to leave. Jenna and Cal stood inside the gatehouse and watched the duo drive away.

"Are we really leaving the estate?" Jenna asked.

"No," he whispered. "But I want to make it look as if we are. Then I can continue to beef up security here, and we can stay put until all of this is resolved."

Cal's plan seemed like their best option. She didn't like the idea of traveling anywhere while her daughter was a target.

They walked out of the gatehouse and started for the estate. After the battle they'd just had with their visitors, Jenna suddenly had a strong need to check on Sophie.

"You think Hollywood and Gwen will believe we're leaving?" She checked over her shoulder to make sure they were gone. Jordan was keeping watch to make sure they didn't double back.

"Jordan's employee will drive out of here in a couple of minutes," Cal explained. He caught her arm and picked up the pace to get them to the porch. "He'll be using a vehicle with heavily tinted windows. As an extra precaution we won't use any of the house phones. They might be tapped, and I don't want anyone to know we're here. We can use the secure cell phone that Director Kowalski gave to me."

Jenna hoped that would be enough. And that Kowalski hadn't given Cal compromised equipment. After all, someone had managed to put those tracking devices on their cars.

"Get down!" she heard Jordan yell.

Jenna started to look back at him to see what had caused him to shout that, but Cal didn't give her a chance. He hooked his arm around her waist and dragged her between the flagstone porch steps and some shrubs.

Jordan dove into the gatehouse. His eyes were darting all around, looking for something.

But what?

Jenna didn't have to wait long for an answer.

"Salazar's on the grounds," Jordan shouted.

Chapter Twelve

If Salazar was on the grounds, he had come there for one reason: to get Sophie. If the assassin had to take out Jenna and Cal, that wouldn't matter. A man like Salazar wouldn't let anything get in the way of trying to accomplish his mission.

Later, after Cal had gotten Jenna out of this mess, he'd want to know just how Salazar had managed to get through what was supposed to be the secured perimeter of the estate. But for now, he had to focus on keeping Jenna and Sophie safe.

He lifted his head a little and assessed their situation. Jordan was in the doorway of the gatehouse, but he hadn't pinpointed Salazar's position. But someone had. Probably Jordan's assistant, Cody Guillory. The man had spotted Salazar and relayed that info through the communicator Jordan was wearing. Since Cal didn't know the exact location of Jordan's assistant, that meant Salazar could be anywhere.

Cal glanced at the front door. It was a good twenty feet away. It wasn't that far, but they'd literally be out in the open if he tried to get Jenna inside. Besides, it was locked and it would take a second or two to open it. That'd be time they were in Salazar's kill zone. Not a good option. At least if they stayed put, the stone steps would give them some protection.

Unless Salazar planned to launch explosives at them.

"Call Meggie," Cal said, handing Jenna his cell phone. "Make sure she's okay. Then tell her to set the alarm and move Sophie to the gun room."

He didn't risk looking at Jenna, though he knew that particular instruction would be a brutal reminder of the danger they were in. Jenna already knew, of course, but by now she probably had nightmarish images of Salazar breaking into the house.

With her voice trembling and her hands shaking, Jenna made the call. Cal shut out what she was saying and focused on their surroundings. He tried to anticipate how and where Salazar would launch an attack. There were more than a dozen possibilities. Salazar might even try to take out Jordan first.

A shot cracked through the air and landed in one of the porch pillars.

Cal automatically shoved Jenna farther down just in time. The next shot landed even lower. It sliced through the flagstone step just above their heads. Salazar had gone right for them. Cal prayed that Meggie had managed to set that alarm and get Sophie into the gun room.

The third shot took a path identical to the second. So did the fourth. Each bullet chipped away at the flagstone and sent jagged chunks of the rock flying right at them. Hell. Maybe staying put hadn't been such a good idea after all. Now they were trapped in a storm of shrapnel.

Cal pushed aside the feeling that he'd just made a fatal mistake and concentrated on the direction of the shots. Salazar was using a long-range assault rifle from somewhere out in the formal garden amid the manicured shrubs and white marble statues. There were at least a hundred places to hide, and nearly every one of them would be out of range for Cal's handgun.

Another shot sent a slice of the flagstone ripping across Cal's shirtsleeve. Since the rock could do almost as much damage as a bullet, he crawled over Jenna, sheltering her as much as he could. She was shaking, but she also had a firm grip on the gun he'd given her earlier. Yes, she was scared, but she was also ready to fight back if she got the chance. This wasn't the same woman he'd rescued in Monte de Leon. But then, the stakes were higher for her now.

She had Sophie to protect.

His only hope was that Salazar would move closer so that Cal would have a better shot or Jordan could get to him. One of them had to stop the man before he escalated the attack.

There was another spray of bullets, and even though Cal sheltered his eyes from the flying debris, he figured Salazar had succeeded in tearing away more layers of their meager protection. Cal couldn't wait to see if Salazar was going to move. He had to do something to slow the man down.

Cal levered himself up just slightly and zoomed in on a row of hedges that stretched between two marble statues. He fired a shot in that direction.

A shot came right back at Cal, causing him to dip even lower. From the gatehouse, Jordan fired a round. He was as far out of range as Cal. But between the two of them, they might manage to throw Salazar off his own deadly aimed shots. Not likely, though. Plus, they couldn't just randomly keep firing or they'd run out of ammunition.

But there was a trump card in all of this. Jordan's assistant. Maybe Cody Guillory was working his way toward Salazar so he could take him out.

The shots continued, the sound blasting through the chilly air and tainting it with the smells of gunpowder, sulfur and smoke. The constant stream of bullets caused his ears to ring. But the ringing wasn't so loud that he didn't hear a sound that sent his stomach to his knees.

The alarm. Someone had tripped the security system.

Which meant someone had broken in. Salazar or his henchman. Salazar normally worked alone, but this time he obviously hadn't come solo. There must be two of them. One firing at them while the other broke inside. Both trained to the hilt to make sure this mission was a success.

Jenna tried to get up. Cal shoved her right back down. And not a moment too soon. A barrage of bullets came their way. Each of the shots sprayed them with bits of rock and caused their adrenaline levels to spike. As long as those shots continued, it'd be suicide to try to get to the door and into the house.

But that was exactly what Cal had to do.

Meggie and Sophie were probably locked in the gun room, but that didn't mean Salazar wouldn't try to get to them. Hell, he might even succeed. And then he could kidnap Sophie and sneak her out, all while they were trapped out front dodging bullets.

"I'm going in," Cal told her. "Stay put."

She was shaking her head before he even finished. "No. I need to get to Sophie."

"I'll get to her. You need to stay here."

It was a risk. A huge one. Salazar could have planned it this way. Divide and conquer. Still, what was left of the steps was better protection than dragging Jenna onto the porch. Cal took a deep breath and got ready to scramble up the steps.

But just like that, the shots stopped.

And that terrified him.

Had the shooter left his position so he, too, could get into the house?

"Cover me," Cal shouted to Jordan, knowing that the man couldn't do a lot in that department. Still, fired shots might cause a distraction in case the gunman was still out there and ready to strike.

Cal didn't bother with the house keys. That would take too long. He'd have to bash in the door and hope that it gave way with only one well-positioned kick.

Jordan started firing shots. Thick blasts that he aimed at the hedges and other parts of the formal garden.

"I'm going with you," Jenna insisted.

Cal wanted to throttle her. Or at least yell for her to stay put. But he couldn't take the time to do either. Jordan's firepower wouldn't last. Each shot meant he was using up precious resources.

"Now," Cal ordered since it seemed as if he would have a partner for this ordeal.

He climbed over the steps, making sure that Jenna stayed to his side so that she wouldn't be in the direct line of fire from anyone who might still be in those hedges. Cal reached the door and gave it a fierce kick. It flew open, thank God. That was a start. But it occurred to Cal that he could be taking Jenna out of the frying pan and directly into the fire.

Cal shoved her against the foyer wall and placed himself in front of her. He disarmed the security system to stop the alarm. Then he paused, listening. He tried to pick through the sounds of Jordan's shots and the house. And he heard something he didn't want to hear.

Footsteps.

Someone was running through the house. Hopefully Meggie was in the gun room. The obvious answer was Salazar.

"I have to get to Sophie," Jenna said on a rise of breath. She broke away from him and started to run right toward those footsteps.

JENNA BARELY MADE IT a step before Cal latched on to her and dragged her behind him.

Her first instinct was to fight him off. To run. So she could get to her baby to make sure she was safe. But Cal held on tight, refusing to let her go.

"Shhh," he warned, turning his head in the direction of those menacing footsteps.

Salazar had managed to break through security, and he was probably inside, going after Sophie.

Cal started moving quietly, but quickly. He kept her behind him as he made his way down the east corridor toward the gun room.

"Keep watch behind us," he whispered.

Jenna automatically gripped her gun tighter, and slid her index finger in front of the trigger. It was ironic that just an hour earlier she'd gotten her first shooting lesson, and now she might have to use the skills that Cal had taught her. She hoped she remembered everything because this wouldn't be a target with the outline of a man. It would be a professional assassin.

That was just the reminder she needed. It didn't matter if she had no experience with a firearm. She'd do whatever was necessary to protect Sophie.

Cal's footsteps hardly made a sound on the hardwood floors of the corridor. Jenna tried to keep her steps light as well, but she knew she was breathing too hard. And her heartbeat was pounding so loudly that she was worried someone might be able to hear it. Though with Cal bashing down the door, the element of surprise was gone. Still, she didn't want Salazar to be able to pinpoint their exact location.

Just in case, she lifted her gun so that she'd be ready to fire.

She and Cal moved together, but it seemed to take an eternity to reach the L-shaped turn in the corridor. Cal stopped then and peered around the corner.

"All clear," he mouthed.

No one was anywhere near the door to the gun room. Of course, that didn't mean that someone hadn't already gotten inside.

Her heart rate spiked, and she held her breath as they approached the room. The door was shut, and while keeping watch all around them, Cal reached down and tested the knob.

"It's locked," he whispered.

She released the breath she'd been holding, only to realize that Salazar could still have gotten inside and simply relocked the door.

Cal pressed the intercom positioned on the wall next

to the door. "Meggie, is everything okay?" he whispered.

"Yes," the woman immediately answered.

Relief caused Jenna's knees to become weak. She had to press her left hand against the wall to steady herself. "Sophie's okay?"

"She's fine. What's going on?"

But there was no time to answer.

Movement at one end of the hall made Cal pivot in that direction. "Get down," he ordered her.

Jenna ducked and glanced in that direction. She saw the dark sleeve of what appeared to be a man's coat. Salazar.

Cal fired, the shot blistering through the corridor.

She didn't look to see what the outcome of that shot was because she saw something at the other end of the hall.

With her heart in her throat, she took aim. Waited. Prayed. She didn't have to wait long. A man peered around the corner. He had a gun and pointed it right at her.

Jenna didn't even allow herself time to think. This man wasn't getting anywhere near her daughter.

She squeezed the trigger and fired.

Chapter Thirteen

Cal forced Jenna to sit on the leather sofa of the family room.

He didn't have to exert much force. He just gently guided her off her feet. She wasn't trembling. Wasn't crying. But her blank stare and silence let him know that she was probably in shock.

Once the director was finished with the initial investigation and reports, Cal needed to talk her into getting some medical care. She'd already refused several times, but he'd keep trying.

Two men were dead.

Cal was responsible for one of those deaths. He'd taken out Salazar with two shots to the head. Jenna had neutralized Salazar's henchman. Her single shot had entered the man's chest. Death hadn't been immediate—he'd died while being transported to the hospital. Unfortunately, the man hadn't made any deathbed confessions.

Cal got up, went to a bar that was partly concealed behind a stained-glass cabinet door and poured Jenna a shot of whiskey. "Drink this," he said, returning to the sofa to sit next to her.

As if operating on autopilot, she tasted it and grimaced, her eyes watering.

"Take another sip," he insisted.

She did and then finished off the shot. She set the glass on the coffee table and folded her hands in her lap. "Does killing someone ever get easier?" she asked.

"No."

He hated that this was a lesson she'd had to learn. What she'd done was necessary. But it would stay with her forever.

She glanced around the room as if seeing the activity for the first time. Director Kowalski was there near the doorway, talking to two FBI agents and a local sheriff. They were all lawmen with jurisdiction, but Kowalski was unofficially leading the show. This had international implications, and there were people who would want to keep that under wraps.

Jenna's eyes met his. The blankness was fading. She was slowly coming to terms with what had happened, but once the full impact hit her, she'd fall apart.

But Cal would be right there to catch her.

"Sophie," she said, sounding alarmed. She started to get up. "I need to check on her again."

Cal caught her. "I just checked on her a few minutes ago. Sophie's fine. Jordan's still with her and Meggie in the nursery. Even though there's no way she'd remember any of this, I didn't want her to be out here right now."

His attention drifted in the direction of the corridor, where federal agents were cleaning up the crime scene.

Cal didn't want Sophie anywhere around that.

Jenna nodded. "Thank you."

He saw it then. Jenna's bottom lip trembled. He slid

his arm around her and hoped this preliminary investigation would end soon so her meltdown wouldn't happen in front of the others.

"You did a good thing in that corridor," Cal reminded her. "You did what you needed to do."

The corner of her mouth lifted, but there was no humor in her smile. "You gave me a good shooting lesson."

Yeah. But he'd given her that lesson with the hopes that she'd never have to use a gun.

Kowalski stepped away from the others and walked toward them. He stopped, studied Jenna and looked at Cal. "Is she okay?"

"Yes," Jenna answered at the exact moment that Cal answered, "No."

The director just nodded. "I don't want any of this in a local report," he instructed Cal. "The sheriff has agreed to back off. No questions. He'll let us do our jobs, and the FBI will file the official paperwork after I've read through and approved it."

"I'll need to give a statement," Jenna concluded. Emotion was making her voice tremble.

"It can wait," Kowalski assured her. "But I don't want you talking to anyone about this, understand?"

"Yes." This would be sanitized and classified. No one outside this estate would learn that an international assassin had entered the country to go after a Texas heiress. The hush-up would protect Jenna and Sophie from the press, but it wouldn't help Jenna deal with the aftermath.

"Any idea how Salazar got onto the grounds?" Cal wanted to know.

"It appears he was here before your friend Jordan Taylor even put his security measures into place. There's evidence that Salazar was waiting in one of the storage buildings on the property."

Smart move. That meant Salazar had used the tracking device on Jenna's car to follow them to the estate, and he'd hidden out for a full day, waiting for the right time to strike. But why hadn't Salazar attacked earlier, when he and Jenna were outside meeting with the others? The only answer that Cal could come up with was that he had wanted as few witnesses as possible when he went after Sophie.

"Salazar and his accomplice broke in through French doors in one of the guest suites," Kowalski continued. "We believe the plan was to locate the child, kill anyone they encountered and then escape."

Jenna pressed her fingertips to her mouth, but Cal could still hear the soft sob. He tightened his grip on her, and it didn't go unnoticed. Kowalski flexed his eyebrows in a disapproving gesture.

Cal ignored him. "What about all the rest? Any idea who hired Salazar or if Hollywood had any part in this?"

The director shook his head. "There's no evidence to indicate Agent Lynch is guilty of anything. He might have been set up."

That's what Hollywood was claiming, and it might be true. Still, Cal wasn't about to declare anyone's innocence just yet. "Who was paying Salazar?"

"The money was coming from Paul's estate, but his attorney will almost certainly say that he was unaware the payment was going to a hired killer."

"He might not have known," Cal mumbled.

Kowalski shrugged. "The ISA will deal with the attorney. But the good news is that Ms. Laniere and her child seem to be out of danger."

Jenna looked at the director. Then at Cal. He saw new concern in her eyes.

"I'm not leaving," Cal assured her.

That got him another flexed-eyebrow reaction from the director. "Tie things up around here," Kowalski ordered. "I want you back at headquarters tomorrow."

Cal got to his feet. "I'd like to take some personal time off."

"I can't approve that. Tomorrow, the promotion list should be arriving in my office. You'll know then if you've gotten the deputy director job." Kowalski's announcement seemed a little like a threat.

Choose between Jenna and the job.

"I'm sorry," Jenna whispered. She stood, too, and this time moved Cal's hand away when he tried to catch her. "I'm going to check on Sophie."

No. She was going to fall apart.

"I'll be at headquarters tomorrow," Cal assured the director. "But I'm still requesting a personal leave of absence." Without waiting to see if Kowalski had anything else to mandate, Cal went after Jenna.

She was moving pretty fast down the corridor, but he easily caught up with her. She didn't say anything. Didn't have to. He figured she was already trying to figure out how she was going to cope without him there.

Cal was trying to figure out the same thing.

Jordan stood in the doorway of the nursery. His gun

wasn't drawn, but it was tucked away in a shoulder holster. "Everything okay?" he wanted to know.

Jenna maneuvered past him and went straight to her daughter. Sophie was awake and making cooing sounds as Meggie played peekaboo with her. Jenna scooped up the little girl in her arms and held on.

"The director and all the law enforcement guys will be leaving within an hour or two," Cal informed Jordan. He didn't go closer to Jenna. He stood back and watched as she held Sophie. "The threat might be over, but I'd like you to stay around for a while."

Jordan followed Cal's gaze to Jenna. "Is this job official?"

"No. Personal."

Jordan's attention snapped back to Cal. "You? Personal?"

"It happens."

Jordan didn't look as if he believed that. He shrugged. "I can give you two days. After that, it'll just be Cody. But he's good. I trained him myself."

Cal nodded his thanks. Hopefully, two days would be enough to tie up those loose ends the director had mentioned. Now if Cal could just figure out how to do that.

"Is she willing to take a sedative?" Jordan asked, tipping his head to Jenna.

Cal didn't have to guess why Jordan had asked that. He could see Jenna's hand shaking. "Probably not." Even though it would make the next few hours easier.

"My advice?" Jordan said. "Liberal shots of good scotch, a hot bath and some sleep."

All good ideas. Cal wondered if Jenna would cooperate with any of them. But when she began to shake even harder, she must have understood that merely holding her baby wasn't going to make this all go away.

Cal went to her and took Sophie. The little girl looked at him as if she didn't know if she should cry or smile. She settled for a big, toothless grin, which Cal realized made him feel a whole lot better. Maybe he'd been wrong about the effects of holding her. He kissed her cheek, got another smile and then handed her to Meggie.

"See to Jenna," Meggie whispered, obviously concerned about her employer.

Cal was concerned, too. He looped his arm around Jenna's waist and led her out of the nursery. She didn't protest, and walked side by side with him to her suite.

"It's stupid to feel like this," Jenna mumbled. "That man would have killed us if I hadn't shot him."

Her words were true. But he doubted the truth would make it easier for her to accept.

"You're so calm," she pointed out, stepping inside the room. It was the first time he'd been in her suite. Like the rest of the house, it was big and decorated in soothing shades of cream and pale blue. He wasn't counting on those colors to soothe her, though. It'd take more than interior decorating to do that.

Cal shut the door. "I'm not calm," he assured her.

"You look calm." Her voice broke on the last word. Cal waited for tears, but she didn't cry. Instead, she moved closer to him. "My baby's safe," she muttered. "We're safe. Salazar is dead. And you'll be leaving soon to go back to headquarters."

He shook his head, not knowing what to say. Yes, he probably would leave for that morning meeting with

Kowalski. He opened his mouth to answer, to try to reassure her that he'd be back. But Jenna pressed her hand over his lips.

"Don't make promises you can't keep," she said. She tilted her head to the side and stared at him. "I'm going to do something really stupid. Something we'll regret."

Jenna slid her hand away, and her mouth came to his, kissing him.

The shock of that kiss roared through Cal for just a split second. Then the shock was replaced with the jolt of something stronger—pleasure. His body automatically went from comfort and protect mode to something primal. Something that had him taking hold of her and dragging her to him.

He made that kiss his own, claiming her mouth. Taking her. Demanding all that she had to give.

His hands were on her. Her hands, on him. Their embrace was hungry, frenzied. Both of them wanted more and were taking it.

And then he got another jolt…of reality.

Sex wasn't a good idea right now. Not with Jenna on the verge of a meltdown.

He forced himself to stop.

With her breath gusting, Jenna looked at him. "No," she said. She came at him again. There was another fast and furious kiss. It was hard, brutal and in some ways punishing. It was also what she needed.

Cal felt the weariness drain from her. Or maybe she was merely channeling all her emotions into this dangerous energy. She shoved him against the door, fusing her mouth to his, her hands going after his shirt.

Part of him wanted to get naked and take her right

there. But only one of them could get crazy at the same time. Since Jenna had latched on to that role, Cal knew he had to be the voice of reason.

But then her breasts ground against his chest. And her sex pressed against his.

Oh, yeah.

That put a dent in any rational thought.

Still, somehow, he managed to catch her arms and hold her at bay so he could voice a little of the reasoning he was desperately trying to hang on to.

"You're not ready for this," he insisted.

"I'm ready." There wasn't any doubt in her tone. Her eyes. Her body.

She shook off his grip, took his hand and slid it down into the waist of her loose jeans. Into her panties. She was wet and hot.

Oh, mercy.

Then she ran her own palm over the very noticeable bulge in his pants. "You're ready."

"No condom," he ground out.

Jenna's eyes widened, and she darted away from him. She ran to a dresser on the other side of the room, and frantically began searching through the drawers. Several moments later, she produced a foil-wrapped condom.

Cal didn't give her even a second to celebrate. He locked the door and hurried to her. He grabbed the condom, and in the same motion, he grabbed her. He kissed her and backed her against the dresser.

The kiss continued as they fought with each other's clothes. He got off her top, and while he wanted to sample her breasts—man, she was beautiful—his body was urging him in a different direction.

With her butt balancing her against the edge of the dresser, he stripped off her jeans. And her white lace panties. By then, she was all over him. Her mouth, hungry on his neck. Her hands fighting with his zipper. She won that fight, and took him into her hands.

Cal didn't breathe for a couple of seconds. He didn't care if he ever breathed again. He just wanted one thing.

Jenna.

He opened the condom and put it on. "This is your last chance to say no."

She looked at him as if he were crazy. Maybe he was. Maybe they both were. Jenna hoisted herself up on the edge of the dresser.

"I'm saying yes," she assured him.

To prove it, she hooked her legs around him, thrust him forward and he slid hot and deep into her.

He stilled a moment. To give her time to adjust to the primal invasion of her tight body. He watched her face, looking for any sign that she might be in pain.

Angling her body back, she slid forward, giving him a delicious view of her breasts and their joined bodies.

She wasn't the pampered heiress now. She was his lover. Funny, he hadn't thought she would be this bold, but he appreciated it on many, many levels.

"Don't treat me like glass," she whispered.

"No intention of that," he promised.

He caught her hair and pulled her head back slightly to expose her neck. He kissed there and drove into her.

Hard.

Fast.

Deep.

Her reaction was priceless. Something he'd remember for the rest of his life. She grabbed him by his hair and jerked his head forward, forcing eye contact. And with her hand fisted in his hair, she moved, meeting him thrust for thrust.

Their mouths were so close he could almost taste her, but she was just out of reach. Instead, her breath caressed his mouth while her legs tightened around him.

Their frantic rhythm created the friction that fueled her need. It became unbearable. She closed around him, her body shuddering. The unbearable need went to a whole different level.

She sighed his name. "Cal." Jenna repeated it like some ancient plea for him to join her in that whirl of primitive pleasure.

Cal leaned in, pushing into her one last time. He kissed her and surrendered.

Even with his pulse crashing in his ears and head, he heard the one word that came from his mouth.

Jenna.

SHE WAS HALF-NAKED on a dresser. Out of breath, sweaty and exhausted. And coming down from one of the worst days of her life. Yet it'd been a long time since Jenna had felt this good. She bit back a laugh. Cal would think she was losing her mind.

And maybe she was.

This shouldn't have happened. Being with Cal like this only made her feel closer to him. It only made her want him more. But that wasn't in their future. She was well on her way to a broken heart.

"Hell," Cal mumbled. "We had sex on the dresser."

He blinked as if trying to focus and huffed out short jolts of breath. He was sweaty, too. And hot. Just looking at him made her want him all over again.

"You don't think I'm the sex-on-the-dresser type?" she asked, trying to keep things light for her own sanity. She couldn't lose it. Not now. Because soon, very soon, Cal would begin to regret this, and she didn't want her fragile mental state playing into his guilt.

With his breath still gusting, he leaned in and brushed a kiss on her mouth. It went straight through her, warm and liquid. "I thought you'd prefer sex on silk sheets," he mumbled.

Still reeling a little from that kiss, she ran her tongue over her bottom lip and tasted him there. "No silk sheets required."

Just you. Thankfully she kept that thought to herself.

He withdrew from her, gently. Unlike the firestorm that'd happened only moments earlier. Cal helped her to her feet, made sure she was steady and then he went into the adjacent bathroom.

Jenna took a moment to compose herself and remembered there were a lot of people still in her house. FBI, Kowalski, the sheriff. She started to have some doubts of her own. She should be focusing on the shootings.

But the shootings could wait. Right now she needed to put on a good front for Cal, spend some time with her daughter and try to figure out where to go from here.

Her old instincts urged her to run. To try to escape emotions she didn't want to face. But running would only be a temporary solution. She looked up and could almost hear her father saying that to her. Funny that it would sink in now when her life was at its messiest.

She needed to stay put, and concentrate on getting Helena, Holden and Gwen out of her life. While she was at it, she also needed to hold her daughter. Oh, and she had to figure out how to nurse her soon-to-be-broken heart.

With her list complete, she started to get dressed. She was still stepping into her jeans when Cal returned.

He looked at her with those scorching blue eyes and had her going all hot again. Jenna pushed aside her desire, reminding her body that it'd just gotten lucky. That wasn't going to happen again any time soon.

"You okay?" he asked.

Jenna nodded and was surprised to realize that it was true. She wasn't a basket case. She wasn't on the verge of sobbing. She felt strong because she had been able to help protect her baby.

He shoved his hands into his pockets. "When things settle down, you might want to see a therapist. There are a lot of emotions that might come up later."

She nodded again and put her own hands in her pockets. "Now that Salazar is dead, it's time to clear up Sophie's paternity with your director."

He looked down at the floor. "Best not to do that. We don't know who hired Salazar, and until we do, nothing is clear."

Confused, Jenna shook her head. "But certainly it doesn't matter if everyone knows that Sophie is Paul's biological child."

"It might matter." He paused and met her gaze. "Gwen was having an affair with Paul. Helena, too.

Either could be jealous and want to get back at you. Either could have sent Salazar to take Sophie because they feel they should be the one who's raising her."

Oh, God. She hadn't even considered that, and she couldn't dismiss it. Both Helena and Gwen hadn't been on the up-and-up about much of anything.

"Holden could be a problem, too," Cal continued. "Paul might have told him to take any child that you and he might have produced. The child would be Paul's heir, and Holden would like nothing more than to control the heir to a vast estate."

Her chest tightened. It felt as if someone had clamped a fist around her heart. "So Sophie could still be in danger?"

"It's possible." He took his hands from his pocket and brought out his phone.

Alarmed, she crossed the room to him. "What are you going to do?"

"Something I should have done already." He scrolled through the numbers stored in his phone, located one and hit the call button. "Director Kowalski," he said a moment later. "Are you still at the estate? I need to speak to you."

Jenna shook her head. "No," she mouthed.

But Cal didn't listen to her. He stepped away, turning his back to her. "I'll meet you in the living room in a few minutes." He hung up and walked out the door.

She caught his arm. "What are you going to say to him?"

"I'll tell him that I lied. That Sophie is my daughter. I want to start the paperwork to have Sophie legally declared my child. I'll do that when I get to headquarters in the morning."

Oh, mercy. He was talking about legally becoming a father. Cal would make an amazing dad. She could tell that from the way he handled her daughter. But this arrangement would cost him that promotion.

"You don't have to do this," Jenna insisted. "We'll find another way to make sure she's safe."

"There is no other way." He caught her shoulders and looked her straight in the eye. "This is your chance at having a normal life. This way you won't always be looking over your shoulder."

"But what about you? What about your career?"

A muscle flickered in his jaw, and she saw anger flare in his eyes. "Do you really think I'm the kind of man who would endanger a child for the sake of a promotion?" He sounded disappointed. "I'm going to do this, Jenna, with or without your approval."

And with that, he walked out.

Chapter Fourteen

Cal hadn't expected Kowalski's ultimatum.

But he should have. He should have known the director wasn't going to let him have a happy ending.

He stood at the door and watched Kowalski, the FBI agents and the sheriff drive away. Now that the sun had set, a chilly fog had moved in, and the cars' brakes lights flashed in the darkness like eerie warnings. Jordan was there to shut the gate behind them. He gave Cal a thumbs-up before heading in the direction of the garden. He was probably going to give his assistant some further instructions about security.

The security measures wouldn't be suspended simply because everyone else had left the estate. Jordan, or one of his employees, would stay on as long as necessary. Of course, Cal still had to get out the word, or rather the lie, that Sophie was his child. Once that was done, he would deal with the ultimatum Kowalski had delivered just minutes before he left.

Cal closed the front door, locked it and reset the security system before he went in search of Jenna. He dreaded this meeting with her almost as much as he'd dreaded the one he'd just had with Kowalski. He felt both numb and drained.

He'd killed a man today. It was never easy even when necessary as this one had been. But his difficulty dealing with the death was minor compared to Jenna's. She'd killed a man, too. Her first. In fact, the first time she'd ever fired a gun at another human being.

This would stay with her forever.

Maybe that's why sex had followed. That was a sure-fire way to burn off some of her high-anxiety adrenaline. Cal shook his head.

It had felt real. And that was a big problem.

He'd compounded it by arguing with Kowalski. The conversation had been necessary, and Cal didn't regret it. But that wouldn't make his chat with Jenna any easier. She needed to know what the director had ordered him to do. And then he somehow had to convince her, and himself, that he could follow through and do what had to be done.

Cal found her in the kitchen. Meggie was at the stove adding some seasoning to a great-smelling pot roast. Jenna was seated at the table feeding Sophie a bottle. Jenna looked as tired and troubled as he felt.

Unlike Sophie.

When the little girl spotted him, she turned her head so that the bottle came out of her mouth. And she smiled at him.

He smiled right back.

Weariness drained right out of him. He wasn't sure how someone so small could create dozens of little daily miracles.

Sophie squirmed, pushing the bottle away, and made some cooing sounds.

"I interrupted her dinner," he commented. Cal sat in the chair next to them.

"She was just about finished, anyway." Jenna's tone was tentative, and she studied him, searching his eyes for any indication of how the conversation with Kowalski had gone.

Sophie reached for him, and Cal took her into his arms. He got yet another smile. It filled him with warmth and it broke his heart.

What the devil was he going to do?

How could he give up this child who'd already grabbed hold of him?

"Something's wrong," Jenna said. She touched his arm gently, drawing his attention back to her.

"Uh, I need to check on something," Meggie suddenly announced. She adjusted the temperature on the pot roast and scooted out of the kitchen. She was a perceptive woman.

"Well?" Jenna prompted.

Best to start from the beginning. "Kowalski didn't buy my story about being Sophie's father. The ISA has retrieved one of Sophie's pacifiers from your apartment in Willow Ridge and compared the DNA to mine. Kowalski knows I'm not a match. It's just a matter of time before he learns that Paul is."

"I see." She repeated it and drew back her hand, letting it settle into her lap. "Well, that's good for you. He doesn't still think you slept with me, does he?"

"No." Cal brushed a kiss on Sophie's cheek. "And Kowalski will keep the DNA test a secret."

He hoped. Kowalski had promised that, anyway.

"But?" Jenna questioned.

"I told him I still wanted to do the paperwork to have Sophie declared my child. I want the DNA test doctored. I want anyone associated with Paul to believe she's mine so they'll back off."

Jenna fastened her attention on him. "There's more, isn't there?"

Cal cleared his throat. "In the morning you'll go into temporary protective custody. Kowalski will leak the fake DNA results through official and unofficial channels, and you and Sophie will stay in protective custody until everyone is sure the danger has passed. He thinks it shouldn't be more than a month or two before the ISA finds out who's responsible for this mess and gets that person off the streets."

"The ISA?" she repeated after a long pause. "But you said your organization doesn't normally handle domestic situations."

"Sometimes they make exceptions."

"I see." Jenna paused again, studying him. Worry lines bunched up her forehead. "And what about you? How does all of this affect you?"

Cal took a deep breath. "Kowalski will tell the chief director the truth, that this is all part of a plan to guarantee your safety." Another deep breath. "In exchange for his guarantee of your safety, Kowalski wants me to extract myself from the situation."

Her eyes widened. "Extract?" she questioned. "What does that mean exactly?"

He'd rehearsed this part. "Kowalski thinks I've lost my objectivity with you and Sophie. He thinks I'll be a danger to both of you and myself if I stay." Cal choked back a groan. "It's standard procedure to extract an agent when there's even a hint of any conflict of interest."

Though nothing about this felt standard. Of course, Cal couldn't deny that he'd stepped way over a lot of lines when it came to Jenna.

Sophie batted him on the nose and put her mouth on his cheek as if giving him a kiss.

Cal took yet more deep breaths. "By doctoring the records and the DNA, Kowalski will be protecting you. But he wants me to swear that I won't see you or Sophie until there's no longer a threat to either of you."

Jenna went still. "But the threat might always be there."

Cal nodded and watched the pain of that creep into her eyes.

She quickly looked away. "Okay. This is good. It means you'll probably get your promotion. Sophie will be safe. And I'll get on with my life." Jenna stood, walked across the room and looked out the window. "So when do you leave?"

"Kowalski wanted me to leave immediately, but I told him I'd go in the morning when the ISA agents arrive."

She stood there, silent, with her back to him.

It was because of the sudden silence in the room that Cal had no trouble hearing a loud crash that came from outside the house.

He got to his feet, and while balancing Sophie, he took out his phone to call Jordan. But his phone rang first. Jordan's name and number appeared on the caller ID screen.

"Cal, we've got a problem," Jordan informed him. "Someone just broke though the front gate."

Before Cal could question him, there was another sound. One he definitely didn't want to hear.

Someone fired a shot.

JORDAN'S VOICE WAS LOUD enough that Jenna heard what he said. If she hadn't heard the crash, she might have wondered what the heck he was talking about. But there was no mistaking the noise of something tearing through the metal gates.

And then it sounded as if someone had fired a gun. It was too much to hope that the noise was from a car backfiring.

While Cal continued to talk with Jordan, Jenna reached for Sophie, and Cal reached for his gun.

"Try to contain the situation as planned," Cal instructed Jordan. "I'll take care of things here."

He shoved his phone back into his pocket and turned to her to give her instructions. But Meggie interrupted them when she came running back into the kitchen.

The woman was as pale as a ghost. "I saw out the window," she said, her voice filled with fear. "A Hummer rammed through the gate. Some guys wearing ski masks got out, and one of them shot the man that came here with Jordan Taylor."

Jenna's gaze went to Cal's, and with one look he confirmed that was true. "How many men got out of the Hummer?" Cal asked Meggie. He sounded calm, but he gripped Jenna's arm and got them moving out of the kitchen.

"Four, I think," Meggie answered. "Maybe more. All of them had guns."

Four armed men. Jenna knew what they were after: Sophie. Salazar had failed, but someone else had been sent to do the job.

There was another shot. Then another. Thick blasts that sounded like those that had come from Salazar. Someone was shooting a rifle at Jordan. He was out there and under attack. It wouldn't be long, maybe seconds, before the gunman got past Jordan and into the house.

Cal headed for the gun room. There was no escape route there, and Jenna knew what he planned to do. Cal wanted Meggie, Sophie and her to be shut away behind bulletproof walls while he tried to protect them. But it was four against two. Not good odds especially when her daughter's safety was at stake.

"I'm going to help you," Jenna insisted. She handed Sophie to Meggie and motioned for the woman to go deep into the gun room. Jenna grabbed two of the automatic weapons from the case.

"I need to make sure you're safe," Cal countered. Though he was busy grabbing weapons and ammunition, he managed to toss her a firm scowl. "You're staying here."

Outside, there was a flurry of gunfire.

Jenna shook her head. "You need backup." She wasn't going to hide while Cal risked his life. "If they get past Jordan and you, the gunmen will figure out a way to get into that room. They might even have explosives. Sophie could be hurt."

He shoved some magazines of ammo into his pockets, then stopped and stared at her. "I can't risk you getting hurt."

She looked him straight in the eye. "I can't risk Sophie's life. I'm going, Cal. And you can't stop me."

He cursed, glanced around the room at Sophie and Meggie. If her daughter was aware of the danger, it certainly didn't show. Sophie was cooing.

"Stay behind me," Cal snarled to Jenna.

She didn't exactly celebrate the concession, though she knew for him, it was a huge one. Jenna looked at Sophie one last time.

"Lock the door from the inside and stay in the center of the room, away from the walls," Cal instructed Meggie. Then he shut it.

Jenna didn't have time to dwell on her decision because Cal started toward the end of the corridor.

"What's the plan?" she asked.

"We go to the front of the house where the intruders are, but we stay inside until we hear from Jordan. He'll try to secure the perimeter."

"Alone? Against four gunmen?" Mercy, that didn't sound like much of a plan at all. It sounded like suicide.

"Jordan knows how to handle situations like these." But Cal didn't sound nearly as convinced as his words would pretend.

Jenna didn't doubt Jordan's capabilities, either. But he was outnumbered and outgunned.

"Jordan knows I have to stay inside," Cal added. He headed straight for the front of the house, and Jenna was right behind him. "I'm the last line of defense against anyone trying to get to Sophie."

However, they only made it a few steps before there

was another crash. It sounded as if someone had bashed the front door in.

Oh, God.

Jenna's heart began to pound as alarms pierced through the house. The security system had been tripped.

Which meant someone was inside.

Chapter Fifteen

This could not be happening.

He and Jenna had already survived one attack from Salazar, and now they were facing another.

He pulled Jenna inside one of the middle rooms off the corridor and listened for any sign that it was Jordan who'd burst through that door. But he knew Jordan would have identified himself. Jordan was a pro and wouldn't have risked being shot by friendly fire.

And that meant it was the gunmen who'd bashed their way in.

So Jenna and he had moved from being backups to primary defense. He sure as hell hadn't wanted her to be in this position, but there was no other choice. They might need both of them to stop the gunmen from getting to Sophie. The gun room was much safer than the rest of the house, but it wasn't foolproof. If the gunmen eliminated them, they'd eventually find their way to Sophie.

Cal was prepared to die to make sure that didn't happen.

He heard movement coming from the foyer. He also heard Jenna's breathing and then her soft mumbling.

She was mouthing something, probably meant to keep her calm.

It wouldn't work.

Not with her child at risk. Cal was trained to deal with these types of intense scenarios, and even with all that training, he had to battle his emotions.

And that made this situation even more dangerous.

He forced himself to think like an operative. He was well equipped to deal with circumstances just like this. So what would happen next? What did he need to do to make this survivable?

At least four armed men had invaded the house. Even if they knew the layout, they wouldn't know where Sophie was. Which meant they'd have to go searching for their prize. They wouldn't do that as a group.

Too risky.

Too much noise.

They'd split up in pairs with one pair taking the west corridor. The other would take the east, which was closer to the gun room. The pairs would almost certainly search the entire place, going from room to room. That meant at least two would soon be coming their way. The other two wouldn't be that far behind.

Cal eased out of the doorway so he could see the west corridor entrance. Even though he didn't hear anything, he detected some movement and saw a man in a blue ski mask peer around the corner, so, "Blue" was already in place and ready to strike.

Cal didn't make any sudden moves. For now, he needed to stay put and stay quiet, all the while hoping the doorjamb would conceal him.

A moment later, Blue and his partner quietly stepped

into the corridor. Blue ducked into a room to search it, and the other kept watch.

Cal was going to have to do this the hard way. He didn't want to start a gun battle in the very hallway of the gun room, but he didn't have a choice. He'd have to take out the guy standing guard, and the moment he did that, it would put his partner and the other pair of gunmen on alert. Of course, they already knew he was in the house. They already knew he was trained to kill.

The question was: how good were they?

And the answer to that depended on who had hired them.

If it was Hollywood, well, Cal didn't want to think about how bad this could get. Hollywood had as much training as he did. They'd be an equal match. And God knows how this would end.

Cal didn't want to risk giving away his position, so he hoped that Jenna would stay put and not make any sounds. He got his primary gun ready, and without hesitating, he leaned out just far enough to get a clean shot.

The one standing guard saw him right away as Cal had expected. And he turned his gun on Cal. But it was a split second too late. Cal fired first. He didn't want to take any chance that this guy would survive and continue to be a threat, so he went with three shots, two to the head, one to the chest.

The gunman fell dead to the floor.

Jenna's breathing kicked up a notch, and he was sure she was shaking. He couldn't take the time to assure her that they'd get out of this alive. Because they might not. Those first shots were the only easy ones he would get. Everything else would be riskier.

Cal volleyed his attention between the room being searched and the other end of corridor. He needed help, and as much as he hated it, it would have to come from Jenna.

He angled himself in the doorway so that he was partly behind the cover of the doorframe. "Watch," he instructed Jenna in a whisper. "Let me know when the gunmen come around the corner."

It was just a matter of time.

Cal's only hope was to take care of the Blue who was still in the room, and then start making his way toward the other pair. To do that, Jenna and he would have to use the rooms as cover. And then they'd have to pray that the second pair didn't backtrack and take the same path of their comrades. Cal didn't want them to be ambushed.

And there was one more massive problem.

While he watched for Blue to make an appearance from the room, Cal thought through the simple floor plan he'd seen on the security panel door. The east and west corridors flanked the center of the house, but there was at least one point of entry that the pair in the west hall could use to get to the side of the house where he and Jenna were.

The family room.

It could be accessed from either hall.

And if the pair used it, that meant they'd be making an appearance two rooms down on the right. He hoped that was the only point where that could happen. Of course, the floor plan on the security panel could have been incomplete.

But he couldn't make a plan based on what he didn't

know. The most strategic place for Jenna and him to be
was in that family room. That way they could guard the
corridor and guard against an ambush. First, though,
he had to neutralize Blue.

There was still no movement near the dead gunman's body. No sound of communication, either. Cal
couldn't wait too long or all three would converge on
them at once. But neither could he storm the room. Too
risky. He had to stay alive and uninjured so he could
get Jenna, Meggie and Sophie out of this.

"Go back inside," he instructed Jenna in as soft a
whisper as he could manage. "Move to your right and
aim at the room where Blue is. Fire a shot through the
wall and then get down immediately."

She didn't question him. Jenna gave a shaky nod and
hurried to get into position. Cal kept watch, dividing
his attention among Blue's position, the family room
and the other end of the corridor.

Cal didn't risk looking at Jenna, but there was no
way he could miss hearing her shot. The blast ripped
through the wall and tore through the edge of the doorframe of the other room.

Perfect.

It was exactly where Cal wanted it to go. And Jenna
did exactly as he'd asked. He heard her drop to the floor.

Cal didn't have to wait long for a response. Blue returned fire almost immediately, and Cal saw a pair of
bullets slam into the wall behind them. He calculated
the angle of the shots, aimed and fired two shots of
his own.

There was a groan of pain. Followed by a thud.

Even though he knew his shots had been dead-on,

Cal didn't count it as a success. Blue could be alive, waiting to attack them. Still, there was a better than fifty-fifty chance that Cal had managed to neutralize him.

"Let's go," Cal whispered to Jenna. He had to get moving toward the family room, and he couldn't leave her alone. As dangerous as it was for her to be with him and out in the open, it would be more dangerous for her to stay put and run into the gunmen.

Jenna hurried to the doorway and stood next to him. She had her weapon ready. He only hoped her aim continued to be as good as that last shot.

"We go out back to back," he said. "You cover that end." He tipped his head toward the dead guy and the room with the bullet holes in the wall. "When we get to the family room, I want you to get down."

Judging from her questioning glance, Jenna didn't approve. Tough. He didn't want to have to worry about her being in the line of fire, and he would have three possible kill zones to cover.

Cal took out a second automatic so he'd have a full magazine, and stepped into the hall. Out in the open. Jenna quickly joined him and put her back to his. He waited just a second to see if anyone was going to dart out and fire at them. But he didn't see or hear anything.

"Let's go," he whispered.

They got moving toward the family room. Cal didn't count the steps, but each one pounded in his head and ears as if marking time. He thought of Sophie. Of Jenna. Of the high stakes that could have fatal consequences. But he pushed those thoughts aside and focused on what he had to do.

When they reached the family room, he stopped and peered around the doorway. The room was empty.

Or at least it seemed to be.

The double doors that led to the east corridor were shut. That was good. If they'd been open, the gunmen on that side of the house would have heard them. Cal was counting on those closed doors to act as a buffer. And a warning. Because when the pair opened them to search the room, Cal would hear it and would be able to shoot at least one of them.

"Check the furniture," Cal told her. "Make sure we have this room to ourselves."

She moved around him while he tried to keep watch in all directions. But Jenna had barely taken a step when there was a sound.

Cal braced himself for someone to bash through the doors. Or for one or more of the gunmen to appear in the corridor. But the sound hadn't come from those places.

It'd come from above.

He glanced up and then heard something else. Hurried footsteps. He spotted a lone gunman as he rounded the corner of the east corridor. Cal turned to take him out.

"Check the ceiling," Cal told Jenna as he fired at the man. But the man ducked into a room, evading the shot.

Cal made his own check of the ceiling then. Just a glance. The next sound was even louder. Maybe someone moving around in the attic.

He didn't have to wait long for an answer.

Two things happened simultaneously. The gunman who'd just ducked into the room across the hall darted out again. And there was a crash from above.

Cal hadn't noticed the concealed attic door on the ceiling. It'd blended in with the decorative white tin tiles. But he noticed it now.

THE ATTIC DOOR flew back, and shots rang out from above them.

Cal shouted for her to get down, but Jenna was already diving behind an oversize leather sofa. From the moment she saw that attic door open, she knew what was about to come.

An ambush.

At least one of the gunmen had accessed the attic, and now she and Cal were under attack.

She fired at the shooter in the attic and missed. He ducked back out of sight. She couldn't see even his shadow amid the pitch-darkness of the attic.

But shots continued to rain down through the ceiling. That alone would have sent her adrenaline out of control, but then she thought of Sophie.

Oh, God.

Was the ceiling in the gun room bulletproof?

She couldn't remember her father saying for certain, but she had to pray that it was. She hoped there was no attic access in there. But just in case, they needed to take care of this situation so they could make sure that Sophie and Meggie were all right.

Cal fired, causing her attention to snap his way. He wasn't aiming at the ceiling, but rather at someone in the east end of the hall. Mercy. They were under attack from two different sides.

Dividing her focus between Cal and the ceiling

shooter, Jenna saw a bullet slice through Cal's shirt-sleeve. Bits of fabric fluttered through the air.

"Get down," she yelled, knowing it was too late and that he wouldn't listen.

Cal leaned out even farther past the cover of the doorway and sent a barrage of gunfire at the shooter in the hall. If Cal was hurt, he showed no signs of it, and there wasn't any blood on his shirt. He was in control and doing what was necessary.

Jenna knew she had to do the same.

She took a deep breath, aimed her gun at the ceiling and fired. She kept firing until the magazine was empty, and then she reloaded.

There was no sign of life. No sounds coming from above. She kept her gun ready, snatched the phone from the end table and pressed the intercom function.

"They might come through the attic," she shouted into the phone. She hoped the warning wouldn't give away Sophie's location.

Jenna tossed the phone aside and aimed two more shots into the ceiling. On the other side of the room, Cal continued to return fire.

The gunman continued to shoot at him.

Bullets were literally flying everywhere, eating their way through the walls and furniture. The glass-top coffee table shattered, sending the shards spewing through the room.

Cal cursed. And for one horrifying moment, Jenna thought he might have been hit.

Then the bullets stopped.

Jenna peered over at Cal—he wasn't hurt, thank God—and he motioned for her to get up. Since he no longer had his attention fastened to the corridor, that meant another gunman must be dead.

But there was still at least one in the attic.

Except with the silenced guns, she no longer heard any movement there. Had the person backtracked?

Or worse—had he managed to get into the gun room?

"Meggie, are you okay?" Cal shouted in the direction of the phone. He was trying to use the intercom to communicate.

While Cal kept watch of their surroundings, Jenna scurried closer to the phone that she'd tossed aside on the floor. She, too, kept her gun ready, but she put her ear closer to the receiver.

And she held her breath, waiting. Praying. Her daughter had to be all right.

"I hear something," Meggie said. "Someone's moving in the attic above us."

Oh, God. Even if that ceiling was bulletproof, it didn't mean a person couldn't figure out a way to get through it. If that happened, Meggie and Sophie would be trapped.

Jenna put her hand over the phone receiver so that her voice wouldn't carry throughout the house. "Someone's trying to get into the gun room through the attic," she relayed to Cal.

He cursed again and reloaded. The empty magazine clattered onto the hardwood floor amid the glass, drywall and splinters. He motioned for her to get up, and Jenna knew where they were going.

To the gun room.

It was a risk. They could be leading the other shooter

directly to Sophie, but judging from Meggie's comments, he was already there.

"Take the phone off intercom," Cal mouthed. "Tell Meggie we're coming, but I don't want her to unlock the door until we get there."

That meant for those seconds, she and Cal would be out in the open hall. In the line of fire. But that was better than the alternative of putting her daughter at further risk.

Still keeping low, Jenna hurried back to the phone cradle and pushed the button to disconnect the intercom. She dialed in the number that would reach the line in the gun room. Thankfully, Meggie picked up on the first ring.

"Cal and I are on the way," she relayed. "Don't unlock the door until you're sure it's us."

"What's going on, Jenna?" Meggie demanded. "Where are Cal and Jordan?"

Jenna feared the worst about Jordan. They hadn't heard a peep from the man since the gun battle. Jordan must be hurt or worse.

Jenna heard a slight click on the line, and knew what it meant. Someone had picked up another extension and was listening in.

"I can't talk now," Jenna said to Meggie, hoping the woman wasn't as close to panic as she sounded. "Just stay put…in the pantry. We'll be there soon."

She hung up and snared Cal's gaze. "Someone picked up one of the other phones."

Cal nodded.

Jenna hoped the lie would buy them some time so

they could get inside the gun room. She got up so she could join Cal at the doorway.

"We do this back to back again. And hurry," he whispered. "It won't take the gunman long to figure out that they're not in the pantry."

Jenna raced toward him and got into position. She would cover the left end of the corridor. He'd cover the right just in case the gunman was still in place. They had at least thirty feet of open space between them and the gun room.

However, before either of them could move, something crashed behind them. They turned, but somehow got in each other's way.

And that mistake was a costly one.

Because the ski-mask-wearing man who broke through the doors on the other side of the family room started shooting at them.

Chapter Sixteen

Cal shoved Jenna out of the doorway and into the corridor. She'd have bruises from the fall, maybe even a broken bone, but her injuries would be far worse if he didn't get her out of there.

He dove out as well, somehow dodging the spray of bullets that the gunman was sending right at them. He barely managed to hang on to his guns.

This wasn't good. Either the guy in the attic had gotten to them ridiculously quickly, or there were more men in the house than they knew.

Cal didn't dwell on that, though. With his gun ready in his right hand, he caught Jenna with his left and dragged her to her feet. He got them moving, not a second too soon. Another round of shots fired, all aimed at them. Because he had no choice, Cal pushed Jenna into the first room they reached.

It was a guest room. Empty, he determined from his cursory glance of the darkened area. Thankfully, there was a heavy armoire against the wall between the family room and this room. That meant there was a little cushion between them and the shooter.

Cal positioned Jenna behind him and got ready to

fire. "Other than where we're standing, is there any an-other way to access this room?" he whispered.

She groaned softly, and the sound had a raw and ragged edge to it. "Yes."

Hell. He was afraid she would say that. "Where?"

"There's a small corridor off the family room," she explained, also in a whisper. "It leads to that door over there."

Cal risked glancing across the room. He figured it was too much to hope that it would be locked or, better yet, blocked in some way. But maybe that didn't mat-ter—this gunman had a penchant for knocking down doors.

He peered around the door edge, saw the shooter and pulled back just as another shot went flying past him.

Well, at least they knew the shooter's location: in-side the family room. "Make sure that door over there is locked," he instructed. "And drag something in front of it."

He'd keep the shooter occupied so that he didn't backtrack and go after them. Of course, that wouldn't do much to neutralize the one in the attic.

"Jenna?" someone called out.

It was Meggie. It took Cal a moment to realize her voice had come over the central intercom. Anyone in the house could hear her. Hopefully, they hadn't already pinpointed her location.

Cal glanced at Jenna, to warn her not to answer.

"Someone's trying to get in here," Meggie said.

Sophie was crying. She sounded scared. She prob-ably was. It broke Cal's heart to know he couldn't get to her and soothe her.

God knew what this was doing to Jenna. The sound of her baby's tears had to be agony. This was a nightmare that would stay with her.

Cal wanted to check on her, but he needed to see if anyone was in front of that gun room door. It was a risk. But it was one he had to take.

He took a deep breath and tried to keep his wrist loose so he could shift his gun in either direction. He leaned out slightly, angling his eyes in the direction of the gun room. No one was there, which probably meant someone was still trying to get through the attic. He didn't have time to dwell on that, though.

A bullet sliced across Cal's forearm. His shooting arm. Fire and pain spiked through him, but he choked it back and took cover.

But for only a split second.

With the sound of Sophie's cries echoing in the corridor and his head, Cal came right back out with both guns ready, and started shooting. He didn't stop until he heard the sound he'd been listening for.

The sound of someone dying.

Still, he didn't take any chances. While keeping watch all around them, he eased out of the room and walked closer until he could see the fallen gunman on the floor. His aim had hit its mark.

The guy was dead all right. The bullet in his head had seen to that. His eyes were fixed in a lifeless, blank stare at the ceiling.

Cal glanced up and listened, wanting to hear the position of the fifth and hopefully final gunman. He heard something. But the sound hadn't come from the attic.

It'd come from the guest room, where he'd left Jenna to block the door.

Hell.

He sprinted toward her, aimed his gun and prayed that the only thing he'd see was her trying to block that other door leading from the family room.

But that door was wide open.

Jenna was there, amid the shadows. Her face said it all. Something horrible had happened.

It took Cal a moment to pick through the shadows. Someone was standing behind Jenna.

And whoever it was had a gun pointed at her head.

JENNA REFUSED TO PANIC.

Her precious baby was crying for her. And Jenna wanted nothing more than to make sure that Sophie was okay. But she couldn't move, thanks to the ski-mask-wearing monster who'd come through the door off the family room.

It'd only taken the split-second distraction of Sophie's crying and the shots Cal had fired. Jenna had been listening to make sure he was okay. And because of that, she hadn't been watching the door. The gunman had literally walked through it and grabbed her. The gun had been put to her head before she'd even had time to react.

Now that mistake might get them both killed.

Cal stopped in the doorway, and Jenna watched him assess the situation. Either this person was going to kill them both, or he'd try to force them to give him access to the gun room.

That wasn't going to happen. Which meant they might die right here, right now.

"I'm sorry," Jenna said to Cal.

He didn't answer. He kept volleying his attention between her and the corridor, looking for the guy who'd been in the attic. Of course, that gunman could be the very person who now had a semiautomatic jammed to her head.

"I'm in here!" the guy behind Jenna suddenly yelled out. He ripped off his ski mask and shoved it into his jacket pocket. "Get down here now!"

Except it wasn't a man.

It was Helena Carr.

Jenna hadn't known whom to expect on the other end of that gun. Holden, Hollywood, Gwen and Helena had all been possibilities. All had motives, though they hadn't seemed clear. But obviously Helena's motive was powerful enough to make her want to kill.

"I'm stating the obvious here," she said, "but if either of you makes any sudden moves, I'll kill you where you stand."

"You're planning to do that anyway," Cal tossed back at her.

"Not yet. You're going to give me that screaming baby, and then you'll die very quick, painless deaths."

Oh, God. It was true. She wanted Sophie. Thankfully, her little girl's sobs were getting softer. Jenna could hear Meggie trying to soothe her, and it appeared to be working.

"Why are you doing this?" Jenna demanded.

"Lots of reasons." That was the only answer Helena

gave before she started maneuvering Jenna toward the door where Cal was standing.

"Put down your guns," Helena ordered. "All of them."

Cal dropped the one from his right hand. He studied Helena's expression as she came closer. He must have seen something he didn't like because he dropped the other one, too.

Jenna's heart dropped to the floor with those weapons.

Cal wouldn't have any trouble defeating Helena if it came down to hand-to-hand combat, but Helena wasn't going to let it get to that point. She would use Jenna as a human shield to get into that gun room. Worse, she had a henchman nearby. After all, Helena had called out to someone.

With Jenna at gunpoint and Cal unarmed, this could turn ugly fast. It was a long shot, but she had to try to reason with Helena.

"Why do you want my baby?" Jenna asked. She hated the tremble in her voice. Hated that she didn't feel as in charge and powerful as Helena. She desperately wanted the power to save Sophie.

"I don't *want* your baby." Helena shoved her even closer to Cal. "But I need to tie up some loose ends."

So this was about Paul's estate. He'd left Helena some diabolical instructions as to what to do to her in the event of his death.

"I didn't do anything to hurt Paul," Jenna pleaded. "There's no reason for you to seek revenge for him."

"I'm not doing this for Paul."

Jenna heard footsteps behind her.

Helena's associate pulled off his ski mask and crammed it into his pocket. He was a bulky-shouldered man with edgy eyes. A hired gun, waiting to do whatever Helena told him to do.

"What?" Cal questioned Helena. "You don't have the stomach to kill us yourself?"

Jenna couldn't see the woman's expression, but from the soft sound that Helena made, she probably smiled. "I've killed as many men as you have—including Paul when I learned he was sleeping with both Gwen Mitchell and Jenna. The man had the morals of an alley cat."

"He slept with me to get his hands on my business," Jenna pointed out. "And Gwen slept with him to get a story. There was no affection on his part."

"That doesn't excuse it. I'm the one who set up your meeting with Paul. I'm the one who suggested he marry you so he could inherit your estate. Sleeping with you and getting you pregnant was never part of the bargain. He was supposed to marry you, drug you and then lock you away until the time was right to eliminate you completely."

"So why kill us? Why take Sophie?" Cal demanded.

Jenna could have sworn the woman's smile widened. "Oh, I don't want to take her. With my brother out of the way, I can inherit Paul's entire estate. Once any other heirs have been eliminated."

Helena's threat pounded in Jenna's head. She wasn't going to kidnap Sophie. She was going to kill her.

That wasn't going to happen. Rage roared through her. This selfish witch wasn't going to lay one hand on her child.

"Kill Agent Rico," Helena ordered the gunman.

Jenna heard herself yell. It sounded feral, and she felt more animal than human in that moment. She didn't care about the gun to her head. She didn't care about anything other than protecting Sophie and Cal.

She rammed her elbow into Helena's stomach and turned so she could grab the woman's wrist. Jenna dug her fingernails into Helena's flesh and held on.

A bullet tore past her.

Not aimed at her, she realized. The shot had come from the gunman, and it'd been aimed at Cal.

Jenna couldn't see if Cal was all right. Helena might have had a pampered upbringing, but she fought like a wildcat, clawing and scratching at Jenna. It didn't matter. Jenna didn't feel any pain. She only felt rage, and she used it to fuel her fight all while praying that Cal had managed to survive that shot.

The gunman re-aimed.

"It's me," someone shouted. Jordan. He was alive.

That only gave Jenna more strength. She latched on to Helena with both hands and shoved the woman right at her accomplice. But the gunman got off another shot.

It seemed as if everything froze.

The bullet echoed. It was so loud that it stabbed through her head and blurred her vision. But Jenna didn't need clear vision to see the startled look on Helena's face.

The woman dropped her gun and pressed her hand to her chest. When she drew it back, her palm was soaked with her own blood. Her hired gun had accidentally shot her.

Helena smiled again as if amused at the irony. But

the smile quickly faded, and she sank in a limp heap next to her gun.

Jenna forced her attention away from the woman. But she didn't have time to stop the gunman from taking aim at Cal again.

Another shot slammed past her, so close that she could have sworn she felt the heat from the bullet. A second later, she heard the deadly thud of someone falling to the floor.

The echo in her head was already unbearable and this blast only added to it. That, and the realization that Cal could be hurt.

Or dead.

She felt tears burn her eyes and was afraid to look, terrified of what she might see.

But Cal was there, his expression mirroring hers.

"I'm alive," Jenna assured him.

So was he.

He raced to her and pulled her into his arms.

Chapter Seventeen

Cal tried not to wince as the medic put in the first stitch on his right arm.

He'd refused a painkiller. Not because he was alpha or enjoyed the stinging pain. He just wanted to speed up the process. It seemed to be taking forever. He had other things to do that didn't involve stitching a minor gunshot wound.

"Hurry," he told the bald-headed medic again.

The medic snorted and mumbled something that Cal didn't care to make out. Instead, he listened for the sound of Jenna's voice. The last he saw of her, Kowalski was leading her out of the family room so he could question her.

Cal wasn't sure Jenna was ready for that. He certainly wasn't. Cal needed to see her, to make sure she wasn't on the verge of a meltdown. But Kowalski had ordered him to get stitches first. Cal had figured that would take five minutes, tops, but it'd taken longer than that just for the medic to get set up.

He heard footsteps and spotted Jordan in the doorway. The man looked like hell. There was a cut on his jaw that would need stitches, another on his head and he probably had a concussion.

Still, Jordan was alive, and an hour ago, Cal hadn't thought that was possible.

A fall had literally saved him. Jordan had explained that he'd climbed onto the gatehouse roof to stop the attack, but one of the gunmen had shot him. A minor scrape, like Cal's. But the impact of the shot had caused Jordan to fall off the roof, and he'd lain on the ground unconscious through most of the attack.

It was a different story for Jordan's assistant. Cody had been shot in the chest and was on his way in an ambulance to the hospital.

Of course, Cody was lucky just to be alive. Their attackers had obviously thought they'd killed him or else they would have put another bullet in him.

"All the gunmen are dead and accounted for," Jordan relayed.

"What about Jenna?" Cal wanted to know.

"Still talking to Kowalski in the kitchen." Jordan looked down the hall. "But you're about to get a visitor."

Cal winced. He was going crazy here. But he changed his mind when Jordan stepped aside so that Meggie could enter. She had Sophie in her arms.

"Hurry," Cal repeated to the medic.

"I'm done," the guy snapped. He motioned for Jordan to have a seat.

Cal gladly gave up his place so he could go to Sophie. The little girl automatically reached for him, and even though he had blood splattered on his shirt, he took her and pulled her close to him. Like always, Sophie had a magical effect on him. He didn't relax exactly, but he felt some of the stress melt away.

"You've seen Jenna?" he asked Meggie.

The woman shook her head. "She's still with your boss."

Enough of that. She shouldn't have to go through an interrogation alone. Cal shifted Sophie in his arms and started for the kitchen.

"Your boss has been getting all kinds of phone calls," Meggie said, trailing along behind him. "I heard him say that the guy who works for Jordan is going to be all right."

Good. That was a start. But God knows what Jenna was going through.

Cal got to the kitchen and saw Jenna seated at the table. Kowalski was across from her, talking on the phone. Jenna had her face buried in her hands.

"Jenna?" Cal called out.

Her head snapped up, and he saw her face. No tears. Just a lot of weariness.

"You're okay," Jenna said, hurrying to him.

She gathered both Sophie and him into her arms. Her breath broke, and tears came then. Cal just held on and tried to comfort her. However, the hug was cut short—Kowalski ended his call and stared at them. God knows what the man was thinking about this intimate family embrace.

And Cal didn't care.

"Holden Carr is dead," Kowalski announced.

Cal didn't let Jenna out of his arms, but he did turn slightly so he could face the director.

"Helena murdered him before she came here with her hired guns," Kowalski continued. "It appears from some notes we found in the Hummer that she eliminated her brother so he wouldn't be competition for Paul's estate."

"That's why she wanted Sophie out of the way," Cal mumbled, though he hated to even say it aloud. He had seen the terror in Jenna's eyes when she realized what Helena wanted to do. Cal had felt the same terror in his heart.

The director nodded. "Helena was going to set up Hollywood to take the blame."

"And what about Gwen Mitchell?" Jenna asked. "Did she have anything to do with this?"

"Doesn't look that way. She just wanted a story. Helena did everything else. She planted the tracking devices on your cars. Tried to run you off the road. Faked emails from Paul and sent Salazar after you. Helena wanted to get you and your daughter out of the way."

So it'd all been for money. No hand from the grave. No rogue agent. Just a woman who wanted to inherit two estates and not have to share it with anyone.

"With Helena dead, the threat to Sophie is over?" Jenna asked. Cal reached over and wiped a tear from her cheek.

"It's over. You and your daughter are safe." Kowalski tipped his head toward Cal's stitches. "How about you? Are you okay?"

"Yeah." Cal had already decided what to say, and he didn't even hesitate. "But I'm not going to stay away from Jenna and Sophie."

Kowalski made a noncommittal sound and reached into his jacket pocket. "That's the letter from the promotion committee. Read it and get back to me with your decision."

"I don't have to read it. I'm not going to stay away from them."

"Suit yourself." Kowalski strolled closer. "There's no reason for me to continue with that order. Ms. Laniere is no longer in your protective custody. What you two do now is none of my business."

It took Cal a moment to realize the director was backing down. There was no reason Cal couldn't see Jenna. Well, no legal reason, anyway. It was entirely possible that Jenna would want him gone just so she could have a normal life.

Cal couldn't give her normal.

But maybe he could give her something else.

Kowalski walked out, and Cal realized that Jenna, Sophie and he were alone. Meggie had left, too. Good. Cal had some things to say, and he needed a little privacy.

He was prepared to beg.

Cal looked at Sophie first. "I want to be your dad. What do you say to that?"

Sophie just grinned, cooed and batted at his face.

He nodded. "I'll take that as a yes." He kissed the little girl's cheek and turned to Jenna.

"Yes," she said before he could open his mouth.

"Yes?" he questioned.

"Yes, to whatever you're asking." But then her eyes widened. "Unless you're asking if you can leave. Then the answer to that is no."

This had potential.

"Wait," Jenna interrupted before he could get out what he wanted to say. "I've just put you in an awkward position, haven't I?" She glanced at the letter. "You'll want to leave if you didn't get the promotion."

"Will I?"

She nodded. "Because it'll be my fault that you lost

it. You resent me. Maybe not now. But later. And when you look at me, you'll think of what I cost you."

Cal frowned. "In less than a minute, you've covered a couple months, maybe even years, of our future. But for now, I'd like to go back to that yes."

"What about the letter?" she insisted. "Don't you want to know if you got the promotion?"

"Not especially."

But Jenna did. She snatched the letter from the table, opened it and unfolded it so that it was in his face. Cal scanned through it.

"I got the promotion," he let her know. Then he wadded up the letter and tossed it.

Jenna's mouth opened, and she looked at him as if he'd lost his mind. "Don't you want the promotion?"

"Sure. But it's on the back burner right now. I'm going to ask you something, and I want you to say yes again."

She glanced at the letter, at Sophie and then him. "All right," Jenna said hesitantly.

"Will you make love with me?"

Jenna blinked. "Now?"

Cal smiled, leaned down and kissed her gaping mouth. "Later. I'm just making sure the path is clear."

"Yes." Jenna sealed that deal with a kiss of her own.

"Will you move to San Antonio with me so I can take this promotion?"

"Yes." There was no hesitation. He got another kiss. A long, hot one.

Hmmm. Maybe he could talk Meggie into watching Sophie while they sneaked off to the bedroom. But Cal rethought that. He intended to make love to Jenna all right, but he wasn't looking for a quickie. He wanted to take the time to do it right. To savor her. To let her know just how important she was to him.

And that led him to his next question. "Will you marry me?"

Tears watered her eyes. "Yes."

Cal knew this was exactly what he wanted. Sophie and Jenna. A ready-made family that was his.

"Now it's your turn to answer some questions," Jenna said. "Are you sure about this?"

"Yes." He didn't even have to think about it.

"Why?"

Cal blinked. "Why?" he questioned.

"Yes. Why are you sure? Because I know why I am. I'm in love with you."

Oh. He got it now. Jenna wanted to hear the words, and Cal wasn't surprised at all that he very much wanted to say them.

He eased Jenna's hand away and kissed her. "I'm sure I love you both," Cal told them. "And I'm sure I want to be with you both forever."

Jenna smiled, nodded. "Good. Because I want forever with you, too."

It was perfect. All the yeses. The moment. The love that filled his heart. The looks on Jenna's and Sophie's faces. It wasn't exactly quiet and intimate with Sophie there, batting at them and cooing, but that only made it more memorable.

Because for the first time in his life, Cal had everything he wanted, right there in his arms.

* * * * *

Read on for a sneak peek of
MOST ELIGIBLE SPY by Dana Marton,
available September 2013 from Harlequin Intrigue

Chapter One

She had that Earth Mother kind of natural feminine beauty, the type of woman who belonged at a bake sale or a PTA meeting, not in an interrogation room on the Texas border. Then again, smugglers came in all shapes and sizes.

Dressed in mom jeans and a simple T-shirt—a crew neck, so there wasn't even a hint of cleavage—she wore precious little makeup. Her chestnut hair hung in a simple ponytail, no highlights, nothing fancy. She did her best to look and sound innocent.

Moses Mann, undercover special commando, did his best not to fall for the act. "Let's try it again, and go for the truth this time."

If all her wholesome goodness swayed him, he was professional enough not to show it as he questioned her. He wasn't in the small, airless interrogation room in the back of an office trailer to appreciate Molly Rogers's curves. He was here to pry into her deepest secrets.

"When did you first suspect that your brother, Dylan Rogers, was involved in illegal activities?"

The smell of her shampoo, something old-fashioned like lemon verbena, filled the air and tickled Mo's nose.

He kept his face impassive as he leaned back in his metal folding chair and looked across the desk at her.

Anger flared in her green eyes. "My brother didn't do anything illegal," she said in a measured tone. "Someone framed him."

Mo's gaze dropped to her round breasts, which suddenly lifted toward him as she pulled her spine even straighter. He caught himself. Blinked. "Your brother was a cold-blooded killer."

He'd personally seen the carnage at the old cabin on the Texas-Mexico border not far from here, the blood-soaked floorboards and the pile of bodies. He'd been the one who'd taken to the hospital the two children Dylan had kidnapped to sell into the adoption black market. Dylan had ended up with a bullet in the head during the takedown—well-deserved, as far as Mo was concerned.

He didn't have much sympathy for the man's sister, either. "Have you ever helped him smuggle illegal immigrants into the country? Drugs? Weapons?"

Her jaw worked with restrained anger. She clutched her hands tightly in front of her. The nicks and red spots on her fingers said she saw her share of farm chores and housework on a daily basis. Her full lips narrowed, but somehow remained sensuous.

"Let me tell you something about my brother. He stood by me all my life. By me and my son. I don't know if we'd be alive at this stage without him." She stuck out her chin. "He was a good man."

Her absolute loyalty to family was commendable, even if misguided. Mo waited a beat, giving her time to calm a little before he said, "People are multidimensional. The face he showed you might not be the face he showed to others."

For the four men he'd killed at the Cordero ranch, Dylan Rogers had been the face of death, in fact. And he would have killed Grace Cordero—his neighbor— too, if not for Ryder, Mo's teammate, who'd arrived just in time to save Grace and those two kids.

Dylan Rogers had been a dark-hearted criminal. And the crimes he was publicly accused of paled in comparison to the one Mo couldn't even mention. Dylan was likely connected to people who planned on smuggling terrorists into the country—the true target of Mo's six-man undercover team.

As far as the locals were concerned, the team—all seasoned commandos—were working with CBP, Customs and Border Protection. They'd come to survey the smuggling situation and investigate recent cases so they could come up with budget recommendations for policy makers. A fairly decent cover while they did their counterterrorism work without anyone being the wiser.

Smuggling was big business in the borderlands, sometimes even with customs or police officers on the bad guys' payroll. His team gathered information from local law enforcement, but shared nothing. They trusted no one at this stage. They kept to themselves while gathering every clue, following every lead. And one of their best leads right now was Molly Rogers.

But instead of cooperating, she was looking at the time on her phone in front of her. She bit her bottom lip.

"In a hurry?"

She nodded.

Too damn bad. "If you want to leave, you need to

start talking." Mo tapped his pen on the desk between them. "Are there any illegal activities going on at your ranch at this time, Miss Rogers?"

"No. I already told you." She glanced at the phone again. "How long are you going to keep me here? If you're not charging me with anything, you have to let me go. I know my rights."

He regarded her dispassionately.

She had no idea how quickly a "terror suspect" designation could strip away all her precious rights. He'd seen people go into the system with that tag and disappear for a good long time, sometimes forever. If her brother's smuggling career included terrorist contacts... If she knew about it...

Her brother was dead, beyond questioning. Without information from her, Mo's team sat without a paddle, trapped on the proverbial creek, with the rapids quickly approaching.

She squirmed in her seat. "I have to go home to meet the school bus."

Her weak point. He was about to get to that.

He patted his shirt pocket, pretending to look for something. "I can arrange for someone to pick up your son. I have a card here somewhere for Social Services."

All the blood ran out of her face as she caught the veiled threat. She was a single mother without family. If they took her into custody, her son would go to foster care.

"I don't know anything about any illegal business," she rushed to say. "I swear. Please."

He liked her pleading tone. Progress. He'd scared her at last. He'd done far worse before to gain usable intelligence from the enemy. He'd done things that would shock her.

He pushed his chair back and stood. "I'm going to step out for a minute. Why don't you give some thought to how you really want to play this. For your son's sake."

"I'm not playing."

He didn't respond. He didn't even turn. He simply walked out and closed the door behind him.

Jamie Cassidy, the operations coordinator, sat at his computer in the main part of the office the team shared. He looked up for a second. "Singing like a bird in there?"

"I wish. She says she doesn't know anything."

"Do you believe her?"

Mo considered that for a moment, recalling every word she'd said, adding to that her body language and all the visual clues, and the depth of his experience. He didn't like what he came up with. He wanted her to be guilty. It would have made everything much easier.

He shrugged. "Bottom line is, we have nothing to hold her on." Maybe her brother did keep her in the dark about his smuggling. Either that, or she was an award-worthy actress.

"You gonna push her harder?"

He could have. "Not today."

Not because he felt that stupid attraction, but because of her son. Whatever she did or didn't know about smuggling, her son was innocent, and Mo wasn't ready to turn the kid's life upside down until he had damned good reason.

The boy had just lost his uncle. He didn't need to

come home from school and search through an empty house, wondering what happened to his mother.

"You got anything?"

Jamie shook his head. "Shep just checked in. Everything's quiet, he says."

Shep and Ray were patrolling the border—Ray's leg was still in a cast, but he felt well enough for a ride along. Ryder, the team leader, was off tying up loose ends with a human smuggling ring the team had recently busted. With what was at stake, the six-man team wasn't about to leave any stones unturned. They pushed and pushed, and then they pushed harder.

"Keith called in, too," Jamie said. "He's getting frustrated over there." Keith was across the border, doing undercover surveillance to identify the local players on that side.

"He's young. He'll learn patience." Not that Mo felt any at the moment. "Once we have our third man, we'll have our link."

From what they'd gathered so far, three men coordinated most of the smuggling activities on this side of the border. They'd gotten two. Dylan Rogers had been shot, unfortunately, before he could be questioned. Mikey Metzner, a local business owner closely tied to human smuggling, was in custody, but seemed to be the lowest ranking of the three, and without any direct knowledge of the big boss in Mexico.

"The third guy is the key." Even if he hadn't been the link to the big boss before, he was now.

"We'll get him."

Mo nodded then turned and walked back into the interrogation room.

"I can't tell you something I don't know about," Molly Rogers said immediately. "Look, I think you're wrong about my brother. This is not fair, I—"

"We're done for today. I'll take you home." He'd picked her up earlier, so she didn't have her car.

He held the door open for her, and she gave him as wide a berth as possible as she passed by him, clutching her purse to her chest. The top of her head didn't quite reach his chin. About five-four, no taller than that, and curvy in just the right places and…Mo tried not to notice her enticing figure or the way her soft chestnut ponytail swung as she hurried ahead of him.

Jamie caught him looking and raised an eyebrow.

He ignored him as he led her through the office, then scanned his ID card and pushed the entry door open. Outside, the South Texas heat hit them like a punch in the face.

His black SUV waited up front on the gravel. "Better give it a minute to let the hot air out." He opened the doors, reached in and turned the air conditioner on the highest setting.

Renting office space in Hullett's business district would have been more comfortable, would have come with climate-controlled parking. But from a tactical standpoint, the trailer office by the side of the road in the middle of nowhere made more sense for his team.

They could see for miles without obstacles, had complete control over the premises. They didn't expect an attack, but if anything did happen, the Kevlar-reinforced trailer with its bulletproof windows was a hell of a lot more defensible than a run-of-the-mill rented office. In his job, practicalities always came before niceties.

He gave the A/C another few seconds then slipped into his seat and waited until she did the same on the other side.

"Thank you for believing me," she said, her faint, citrusy scent filling his car.

He raised an eyebrow. "Don't get ahead of yourself. We're not done here. We're just taking a break."

He let her sit and stew for the first five minutes of the drive down the dusty country road before he started in on her again, gentling his voice, switching to the "good cop" part of the routine.

"Anything you tell me can only help your case. If you got dragged into something against your will… Things like that happen. The important thing now is to come clean. We need your help here."

Her posture stiffened. "Am I an official suspect?"

"A person of interest," he told her after a few seconds.

And when she paled, he found that he didn't like making her miserable. But he would, if the job called for it.

The op was too important to let something like basic attraction mess with his focus. She was the wrong woman at the wrong time to get interested in. Even beyond the op. He planned on this being his last job with the SDDU, Special Designation Defense Unit, an undercover commando team that did everything from intelligence gathering abroad to hostage rescue to counterterrorism work.

His focus was on his mission and nothing else. He could ignore the tingles he felt in the pit of his stomach every time he looked at the woman next to him. If he did well here, his CIA transfer was as good as approved. Molly Rogers wasn't going to mess that up for him.

THE CAR FLEW down the road, Molly's stomach still so clenched from the interrogation she thought she might throw up. She took in the fancy dashboard, covered with computer displays, radio units, radar and other things she'd never seen before. She so wasn't going to feel guilty if she ruined any of that.

"When do you think I can claim my brother's personal effects?"

All she wanted was to put all this behind her, for her brother's name to be cleared. And an official apology in the local paper. Dylan didn't deserve to be dragged through the mud like this.

But instead of law enforcement investigating how and why Dylan had been framed, they kept on with their idiotic suspicions about him, even dragging her into the mess.

The man next to her kept his eyes on the road. "For now your brother's personal possessions are evidence in a multiple-murder case."

"The sheriff won't let me into Dylan's apartment in Hullett, either." Everyone seemed to be against her these days.

"They need to get everything processed."

She hated Moses Mann. He had zero sympathy for her and her situation. He was twice her size and had used that in the interrogation room to intimidate her. He was missing half an eyebrow, which made him look pretty fierce. His muscles were just on this side of truly scary. She had a feeling he knew how to use his strength and use it well.

If he had a softer—reasonable—side, she sure hadn't seen it. He'd called her brother a conscienceless criminal and pretty much accused her of being the same. He threatened her with Social Services.

Her stomach clenched.

The day she saw Moses Mann for the last time would be a good day. He made her nervous and scared and so self-aware it bordered on painful. She had to watch every move, every word, lest he read something criminal into it. She looked away from him.

The land stretched flat and dry all around them as far as the eye could see. He drove the dusty country road in silence for a while before he resumed questioning her, asking her some of the same questions he'd asked before. She gave him the same answers. He was still trying to trip her when they reached her road at last.

Thank God. Another ten minutes and she would have been ready to jump from the moving car.

He parked his SUV at the end of her driveway, and she was out before he shut the engine off. Her dogs charged from behind the house, Max and Cocoa in the lead, Skipper in the back; all three of them were one-hundred-percent country mutts from the pound.

They greeted her first.

"No jumping." She pushed Max down then scratched behind his ear.

He kept jumping anyway. Skipper barked, running around her in circles. They were worked up over something.

They checked out the man by her side next, tails

wagging. They were about the three friendliest, goofi-est guard dogs in Texas, trained to be nice to everyone, since her son often had friends over.

"Be nice," she said anyway, even if she wouldn't have been too put out if one of them peed on Moses Mann's combat boots. Not that she was vengeful or anything.

But the dogs were doing their best to crowd each other out as the man gave them some ear scratching. They seemed to think they'd found a new best friend. Figured.

He looked like he enjoyed the attention. "There you go. That's a good dog."

She hoped he'd at least get fleas.

He gave a few final pats as he looked at her.

She cleared her throat. "Thanks for the ride." *Hint, hint. Go away.*

She didn't like the relaxed smile he'd gotten from playing with her traitor dogs. It made him look more human than "soldier machine." If she began to think of him as anything other than "the enemy," he'd try and trick her into a false confession or something. Since they couldn't do anything more to her brother now, he and his team would probably do anything to ruin her life instead. She couldn't afford to let her guard down for a minute.

She waited for him to get back into his car and drive away. She didn't want him following her into the house, so she went to check the mailbox, playing for time, and bit her lip as she opened the flap door, her hand hesitating.

"What's wrong?" he called over.

How on earth had he caught that half-second pause?
"Nothing."

She thrust her hand forward and grabbed the stack
of envelopes. *Everything.* Bills scared her these days.
She'd received a mortgage check the day before, for the
ranch that she'd thought had been long free and clear.
Dylan had taken out a new mortgage, apparently.

Which didn't mean he was a bad brother. Or a mur-
derer. He'd worked so hard, had so much on his mind....
He'd simply forgotten to tell her.

She kept her back to Moses Mann. "Just making
sure there aren't any wasps in there. They keep trying
to move in." Also true. She'd had a lot of trouble with
wasps this year.

She shuffled through the envelopes, then relaxed. No
unexpected bills, thank God. The new mortgage was
more than she could handle.

Her cell phone rang and she glanced at the display.
The agent from Brandsom Mining. The man had a sixth
sense for knowing when she felt desperate. But not that
desperate yet. She pushed the off button.

"Who was that?"

She wasn't going to discuss her problems with Moses
Mann. He would have no qualms about using any weak-
ness against her. "Telemarketer," she said. Sounded better than *people who are trying to take the ranch away
from me.*

The land had some collapsed mine shafts left over
from its old coal-mining days. The mine had run dry
and had been abandoned in her grandfather's time. But
Brandsom Mining wanted to buy the ranch for explora-

tion, thought that with modern methods of surface mining they might be able to get something out of the place.

And ruin the land in the process, mess up the water tables, have heavy machinery tear up the earth. No thanks. Dylan and she had always been in full agreement about that. The ranch was her son's inheritance. The Rogers Ranch would stay in Rogers hands until there was no longer a Rogers left.

She glanced at her phone. "Bus should be coming in a minute." *Feel free to leave now.*

But the guy seemed impervious to hints.

Her heart lifted at the sight of the school bus coming around the bend, its old engine laboring. She glanced at the major pain at her side, wishing he would disappear. If he stayed, Logan would be asking questions about him. But the man was looking at her pickup, his attention a hundred percent focused there, as the bus stopped and Logan ran down the steps.

For a second she forgot about Moses Mann as she caught her son up into her arms and held him tight. The dogs were jumping all over them, muscling their way in with enthusiasm.

Logan squirmed. "Mo-om, not in front of the other kids."

She let him go with a half smile. Right. He was a big kid now, supposedly—eight years old. She made sure not to take his hand, or offer to carry his bag as she turned toward the house. But she did say, "I missed you, buddy," as the school bus pulled away.

Moses Mann was walking over, his cell phone in hand. "I need you to go and sit in my car."

Her muscles clenched at the hard expression on

his face and the silent warning in his eyes. "What's going on?"

"Just for a few minutes."

If she were alone, she would have demanded an explanation. But she didn't want to get into an argument with the man in front of Logan. Because he *could* make her sit in his car. He *could* take her right back with him. She didn't want things to get worse than they were. Which meant she'd do as he asked. For the time being.

She swallowed and reached for her son's hand, big kid or not. "This nice gentleman is Mr. Mann." She did her best to sound normal. "He has a really cool car. Want to check it out?"

"Hi, Mr. Mann. Can I sit in the front?"

He nodded with an encouraging smile, the first she'd seen on him. "Just don't turn on the siren."

Logan's eyes went wide, a big smile stretching his face. "You have a siren? Is it like an undercover police car?"

"Kind of."

"Are you going to find the bad men who hurt Uncle Dylan?"

He hesitated for a second, his gaze cutting to her, before he said, "I'm working on that situation."

Logan sprinted for the car and she walked after him, the streaks of dirt on his back catching her eye.

"What happened to your shirt?"

He froze and looked at his feet. "Nothing."

"Logan?"

He turned, but wouldn't look at her. "It's no big deal, Mom."

Her heart sank. She didn't have to ask what the fight

was about. He'd been teased again with what the papers said about his uncle. "What do we always say about fighting?"

He hung his head and mumbled, "The best way to win a fight is to walk away from it."

She caught Mo watching them. He didn't look like the type who walked away from a fight. Well, that was his problem. "All right. Let's get in the car. We'll talk about this later."

When she was behind the wheel, Mo started toward her house. But then he stopped and motioned her to roll the window down, tossed her his keys. "Lock yourselves in." He fixed her with a stern look. "And if there's any trouble, you drive away."

THE DOGS STAYED by the car, whining to get in. They wanted to play with the kid. Good. Better to have them out of his way. Mo dialed his phone, keeping his focus on the house's windows as he approached.

The two-story ranch house was well-kept, had a new roof. A row of yellow roses trimmed the wraparound porch that held half a dozen rockers. He dashed across the distance to the steps just as Jamie picked up his call on the other end. "I'm at the Rogers ranch. I need a crime-scene kit."

"You better not be having fun out there while I'm filing reports at the office."

"Molly Rogers's tires were slashed. In the past three hours. Everything was fine when I picked her up earlier."

"You need backup? Ryder just came in."

Ryder had recently been appointed team leader when

the powers that be made the SDDU's Texas headquarters permanent. The top-secret commando unit mostly worked international missions, infiltration, hostage rescue, search and destroy, espionage and the like.

But when a terrorist threat had been indicated for this section of the border, the colonel sent a small team in. They'd come for this specific mission, but there was enough going on in the border region that the colonel decided to make the team here permanent.

"If you can bring the kit that should be enough." Mo pushed the screen door open as he reached for his gun, then opened the entry door with a simple twist of his wrist, and scowled. Hardly anyone kept their houses locked around here. He didn't understand that kind of blind faith in humanity, not after all he'd seen.

"I think whoever messed with the tires is gone." The dogs hadn't signaled an intruder. "But I'm going to check out the place anyway." He closed the phone and slipped it into his back pocket.

He started with the kitchen. He'd been in here before, with a search warrant and his team, after Dylan's death. They'd found nothing usable then and he didn't bother to look for any incriminating evidence now, just for possible danger. He checked the gun cabinet in the hall closet—full of hunting rifles. Locked. Nothing seemed missing.

He moved through, room by room. The bathroom at the top of the stairs still held the faint scent of Molly Rogers's shampoo, everything in its place, everything spotlessly clean.

A little more disorder in the boy's room, a dozen toy soldiers scattered on the floor. But the next room over, her bedroom, was immaculate. He scanned the old-fashioned antique four-poster bed, feminine and delicate.

Would probably break under his weight— He caught the thought. He didn't need to think about himself in Molly Rogers's bed.

But he couldn't help noticing the strappy nightgown that peeked from under the cover. He forced his gaze past the lavender silk after a long moment.

He checked the next two small rooms, including the closets, found no sign that anyone had been in the house. He put his gun away and plodded down the stairs. In the kitchen, he pulled out a business card with his cell phone number and stuck it on the fridge with a magnet decorated with elbow macaroni, probably made by Logan. Then he strode down the driveway, motioned to them to get out of the car.

He turned to the boy first. "I need to talk to your mom for a second."

Logan looked at his mother.

"Why don't you go and play some video games?" she suggested.

He grinned as wide as a grin could go, and ran up to the house, his backpack bobbing, the dogs following him. He glanced back and yelled, "Goodbye, Mr. Mann."

He lifted a hand in a wave. Seemed like a well-raised kid.

"What did he get into a fight over?" he asked when the boy had passed out of hearing distance.

"Kids have been picking on him this past couple of weeks because of what they'd heard about his uncle." She shot him a glare as if it were all his fault. "Usually he's pretty good at walking away, but he really idolized my brother."

Whatever Dylan Rogers had done, someone beating on the kid for it didn't sit well with Mo. "You can't always walk away from trouble. I could teach him how to defend himself."

"Absolutely not. I'll handle my son's problems." She crossed her arms. "What were you doing in my house?"

Mo rolled his shoulders. She was right. Her son was none of his business, had nothing whatsoever to do with his op. Getting personally involved would have been a bad idea. *Back to business.* He gestured her over to her pickup and pointed at the slashed tires, watching for her reaction.

She stared, her jaw tightening. For a second he thought he might have seen moisture in the corner of one eye as her gaze filled with misery. "I can't afford new tires."

Money was the least of her problems. "We'll be taking some fingerprints." He gave her a hard look. "I want you to keep your doors locked. Car doors, house doors, garage door, the works. Do you know how to shoot any of those guns in the gun cabinet?"

She drew her gaze from the tires at last. "I might be a pacifist, but I'm still a Texan."

He watched her, trying to puzzle her out. Back in the interrogation room, his threat of calling Social Services had scared her. The slashed tires hadn't, just annoyed her. He liked that she was brave, but he wanted her to be careful. "I left my number on your fridge. Call me if you need me for anything. Don't take this lightly."

She looked back at the tires. "Why would somebody do this to me?"

He had a fair idea. "Maybe one of your brother's friends saw me pick you up. This could be a warning to make sure you don't tell any secrets." He paused for emphasis. "We could protect you and your son. If you were to cooperate."

Instead of jumping on that offer, her muscles only tightened another notch, true anger coming into her eyes.

"Quit blackmailing me with my son. I don't know any secrets. Goodbye, Mr. Mann." Then she turned on her heels and marched up to the house, hips swinging. She let the screen door slam shut behind her.

He would have lied if he said all that fire didn't draw him in, at least a little.

To distract himself from that thought, he checked the outbuildings while he waited for Jamie. Not a single door locked—barn, stables, shed, all the outbuildings open. But he found no sign of damage inside any of them. If the tire slasher had gone through, he hadn't messed with anything else.

As he stepped back outside, he scanned the endless fields around the buildings, not another house in sight. He made a mental note to check on the status of Dylan Rogers's bachelor pad when he got back into the office. Molly and her son would be better off moving there, into town, for the time being.

Not that keeping her safe was his job. For all he knew, she was guilty as sin. But her kid didn't deserve to be in the middle of all this bad business.

There was an amazing connection between mother

and son, love and affection, obvious from even their brief encounter. Had he ever had that? Not with his birth mother, for sure. And as his foster mother had died so early, he remembered very little of her.

"How is it that you get both the girl and the action, while I'm stuck in the office?" Jamie's arrival ended the trip down memory lane.

"You're here now."

He looked around. "Sounded more exciting over the phone. Didn't find anyone here?" He sounded disappointed at the missed opportunity for a scuffle.

His steps were sure as he brought the crime-scene kit over to the pickup, but he had a slightly uneven gait. Both of his legs were missing, courtesy of a rough overseas mission that had ended badly. He walked with the aid of two space-age technology prostheses, well hidden under his black cargo pants, originally developed for Olympic athletes.

He looked over the damage carefully. "Find anything else beyond the slashed tires?"

"Nothing."

While Jamie lifted prints, Mo dabbed the tires around the slashes with oversized cotton swabs and sealed those into evidence bags.

Jamie put away the prints he'd collected. "Could be a warning for her to keep quiet about her brother's dealings."

"That was my first thought."

She had no idea how out of her depth she was in all this. He looked toward the house, not liking that he was beginning to feel protective toward Molly Rogers and her son. That could become a problem.

"She's a person of interest in the investigation," he said out loud to remind himself of the exact nature of their relationship.

Maybe if he kept telling himself that was why he was so interested in her, eventually he'd believe it.

His phone rang at the same time as Jamie's. They clicked into a conference call with Ryder.

"Hey, Shep just called. He found some chopped-off fingers. No body to go with them," their team leader said on the other end.

"Where?" Mo tensed, pretty much expecting that he wasn't going to like the answer. He was right about that.

"Rogers land," Ryder said.

Catch a thrill with
MOST ELIGIBLE SPY
by Dana Marton
Available September 2013 from Harlequin Intrigue

INTRIGUE®

Edge-of-your-seat intrigue, fearless romance.

Use this coupon to
SAVE $2.00
on the purchase of
ANY 2
Harlequin Intrigue books!

Available wherever books are sold, including most
bookstores, supermarkets, drugstores and discount stores.

SAVE $2.00 ON THE PURCHASE OF **ANY TWO** HARLEQUIN® INTRIGUE® BOOKS.

Coupon expires November 5, 2013. Redeemable at participating retail
outlets in the U.S. and Canada only. Limit one coupon per customer.

52611096

5 65373 00082 3

(8100)0 11877

HICOUPWBLDF

WIN *Vegas*
A **TRIP** TO

& **TICKETS**
TO CHAMPIONSHIP
RODEO EVENTS!

Who can resist a cowboy? We sure can't!

You and a friend can win a 3-night,
4-day trip to Vegas to see some real
cowboys in action.

Visit
www.Harlequin.com/VegasSweepstakes
to enter!

See reverse for details.

Sweepstakes closes October 18, 2013.

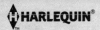

INTRIGUE®

USA TODAY BESTSELLING AUTHOR
JULIE MILLER'S
THE PRECINCT: TASK FORCE SERIES HEATS UP WHEN A PLAIN JANE AND AN EXPERIENCED COP POSE AS AN ENGAGED COUPLE.

Something about Hope Lockhart fascinated Officer Pike Taylor. The cop and his canine companion had been patrolling the neighborhood around Hope's bridal shop for months, trying to capture the criminal who targeted her. Hope bore the scars of a troubling past but when Pike is assigned to protect her by posing as her live-in fiancé, his tenderness may give Hope the courage to open her heart for the very first time.

DON'T MISS
TASK FORCE BRIDE

Available August 20, only from Harlequin® Intrigue®.

HI69711

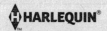

INTRIGUE®

Edge-of-your-seat intrigue, fearless romance.

Use this coupon to

SAVE $2.00

on the purchase of
ANY
Harlequin Intrigue book!

Available wherever books are sold, including most
bookstores, supermarkets, drugstores and discount stores.

- ✂

SAVE $2.00
ON THE PURCHASE OF **ANY** HARLEQUIN® INTRIGUE® BOOK!

Coupon expires January 31, 2014. Redeemable at participating retail
outlets in the U.S. and Canada only. Limit one coupon per customer.

52611100

5 65373 00082 3   (8100)0 11878

HICOUPWBLDF